JADE AND FIRE

JADE
AND
FIRE

Raymond Barnett

Random House
New York

Library of Congress Cataloging-in-Publication Data

Barnett, Raymond James.
Jade and fire.

1. China—History—Civil War, 1945–1949—
Fiction. 2. Peking (China)—History—Fiction.
I. Title.
PS3552.A6988J3   1987   813'.54   86-29777
ISBN 0-394-55859-6

Manufactured in the United States of America

98765432

FIRST EDITION

Book design by Carole Lowenstein

For D. Day and H^2

Historical Characters

An Shihlin—Prior of White Cloud Temple in Peking until his murder by fire there in 1948

Fu Tsoyi—Powerful North China warlord, ruler of Peking

Zhou Peifeng—Fu's aide

Chang Tungsun—Yenching University Professor of Philosophy

Ho Szuyuan—Former Mayor of Peking

Lin Piao—Communist Field Commander

Nieh Jungchen—Communist Field Commander

Yeh Chienying—Chief of Staff of Communist Army

Mao Tsetung—Most powerful of the Communist leaders

Chou Enlai—Second most powerful of the Communist leaders

Fictional Characters

Bei Menjin—Chief Inspector of Peking Municipal Police Force

Yuan—Bei's assistant

Lufei—Yuan's orphaned niece

Meilu—Fu Tsoyi's concubine

Meiling—An Shihlin's lover

Yu Chenling—Head of right-wing Te Wu agency

Chan—Yu's aide

Master T'ang—Abbot of the Purple Mountain

Dufeng—T'ang's aide

Captain Wang—Head of Fu's guards

Captain Li—Lin Piao's aide

A NOTE TO THE READER

The public, historical events related herein are factual, as are the public actions of the historical characters listed on the preceding page. The private actions and thoughts of these historical characters are entirely my own invention, however, and should not be construed as mirroring their actual private lives.

The romanization of Chinese words has long been a source of vexation and confusion to scholar and layman alike. I have chosen to use the traditional Wade-Giles system for most of the historical people and actual places mentioned, but have felt free to deviate from this rule upon occasion, for the sake of keeping characters with similar names from being confused with each other, and for other reasons. I also omit Wade-Giles's cumbersome hyphen between given names, as does the modern Pinyin system.

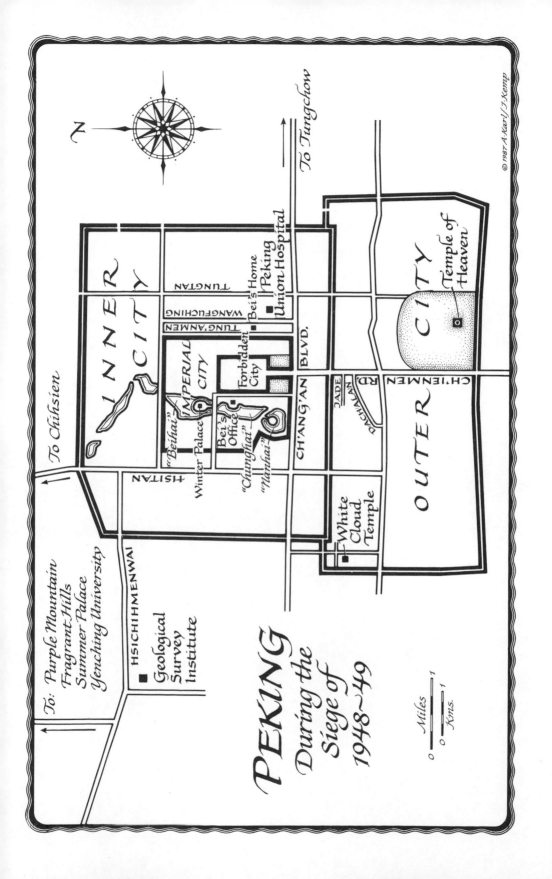

PEKING
During the
Siege of
1948~49

Miles
0   1
Kms.
0   1

© 1987 A. Karl / J. Kemp

To Chihsien

To: Purple Mountain
Fragrant Hills
Summer Palace
Yenching University

HSICHIHMENWAI

Geological
Survey
Institute

INNER CITY

HSITAN

"Beihai"
Winter Palace

IMPERIAL CITY

Bei's
Office

"Chunghai"
"Nanhai"

Forbidden City

TUNG'ANMEN

WANGFUCHING

TUNGTAN

Bei's Home

Peking
Union Hospital

CH'ANG'AN BLVD.

JADE

TACHALAN

CH'IENMEN RD.

To Tungchow

White
Cloud
Temple

OUTER CITY

Temple of
Heaven

JADE AND FIRE

Prologue: December 25, 1948

It had snowed that morning in Peking, and the young woman walking away from the White Cloud Temple that evening smiled at the memory of it, mistaking the snow for a portent of good. Her fluid, languid movement through the darkness suggested the strength in her well-trained body and the lovemaking she had recently enjoyed. The city seemed quiet, but she realized that currents of birth and death surged beneath its calm evening surface. After all, outside Peking's massive walls lay a besieging Communist army led by Lin Piao, fresh from its recent conquest of Manchuria. The city was an old island in a new sea of red. But within those towering city walls were massed two hundred thousand Nationalist troops, led by the redoubtable Fu Tsoyi.

She adjusted her collar tighter against the wind at her back and smiled again, this time at the irony of it. The city's defender at this key point in the civil war engulfing China happened to be one of the few competent and uncorrupted warlords on the Nationalist side. Fu

Tsoyi, who had actually fought and defeated the hated Japanese in battle. It all made her mission more delicate, prolonged the time she played her dangerous role. But in the end the inevitable would happen. The flow of the Tao could not be stopped, not even by Fu Tsoyi.

She glanced around her at light glowing through windows and smelled the odor of coal fires. The people of Peking, tired but patient, awaited the outcome of yet one more siege, devoting themselves in the meantime to their ancient pursuits: buying and selling, copulating, eating, dying. The old pattern, repeated how many times, she wondered, in the thousand years this city had been the capital of Chinese kingdoms and empires.

A different smell intruded upon her reverie, not from coal but from wood burning. Strange. Then she heard angry voices in the distance— back toward the Taoist temple she had left not five minutes ago. When the bell began tolling irregularly she turned and began to run back to the temple. In a minute she reached the secret opening into the Hall of the Eight Immortals and soon dashed out of the hall, past the Temple of the Western Mother and through the doorway of the high wall paralleling the main axis of Shrine Halls. She was at the edge of the courtyard fronting the Shrine Hall of Founder Ch'iu, blinking her eyes in the sudden firelight.

Nearly fifty men were in the courtyard, some frantically trying to rescue what the others were denying access to: a figure bound by ropes to a massive chair sitting halfway up the steps leading to the Shrine Hall. The figure was surrounded by large bundles of burning stalks and wood. At the moment she recognized the face of the prior of the temple, it was engulfed in a rapidly rising tide of flame and smoke. She screamed. His nightclothes burst into flame, and his eyes glazed over as the inhaled smoke seared his lungs and denied oxygen to his body. His black hair flared up in another, smaller burst of flame, and then his face melted. As the skin began to darken and char, the sweetish smell of burned flesh filled the courtyard. She desperately joined the men shrieking and pushing their way toward the figure, but the equally determined men ringing it pushed out with renewed vigor as the flames heated their backs. In a matter of seconds it was over; the figure sagged lifelessly in the chair, charred and shapeless.

She felt her arm grabbed. "Run, you fool!" the man beside her whispered fiercely. She recognized the overseer of the temple complex. "It's over for him, and they may well come for you next. Run!" She looked at him, dazed. Two others came up to her and hurried her out of the courtyard, past the three front Shrine Halls and into the alley at the temple entrance. "Go!" they commanded her, and she stumbled away, weeping.

December 26, 1948

He threw another piece of wood into the fire, and watched until it flamed up. Then he closed the fuel door on the small tin stove and settled back comfortably into his chair, waiting for the kettle of water on the stove to reach a full boil.

"Bizarre. I think I actually believe you, Yuan." A pause, as he assayed the strength of the boil. "Although it does stretch credulity: The monks at Peking's largest Taoist monastery, having for centuries gone about their superstitious nonsense in obscure peacefulness, suddenly burn their leader, the prior—alive, yet—in front of the Shrine Hall of the founder of the temple."

He leaned forward, took the kettle from the stove, and poured the water quickly into a plain ceramic teapot sitting on a small stand beside his desk. He watched with a critical eye as the green leaves slowly uncurled and swelled, and took two deep, searching sniffs of the aroma before placing the lid on the pot. "Dried a bit too fast, I imagine," he murmured to himself, as he picked up the four-minute glass timer filled with sand, turned it over, and placed it beside the pot of steeping green tea.

Bei Menjin, chief inspector of the Peking Municipal Police Force, sank back into his wicker chair again. The rhythm of preparing tea suited him, the moments of decisive action punctuated by spells of forced contemplation. The rhythm was similar to that of detective work, actually, which also suited him, much to the puzzlement of his friends in the elite class into which he had been born.

"The siege is wearing us all down, turning everyone spiteful beyond even our normal state, Yuan." As he said this, he thought not

5

of the Taoist monks but of his wife. With an annoyed shake of his head he brought his mind back to the Taoist temple and his pot of tea. "What more do you know?" he asked his assistant, Yuan Jinli, whose several decades of police work had honed his commonsense approach to a fine edge which complemented his spare old frame.

"Beyond that, only rumors, Chief. The street sweeper on White Cloud Road thinks—"

"Now, Yuan, you know I relish rumors around a case, but only after the bare facts have been firmly established in my mind," said Bei, glancing at the timer. "Facts are slippery enough as it is, without their being twisted and tinted to fit in with the presumptions of rumors already waiting for them as they enter the mind. I'll entertain all manner of ghost stories and tales of monkish magic after my investigation at the temple this morning."

Yuan sighed and remained silent, accustomed to these mild lectures from his chief. It reflected an ineradicable trait of the Confucian upbringing, Yuan had concluded. He was preoccupied, at any rate, with the pending arrival of his orphaned niece from Shansi province that day. Such a story.

Bei saw the last few grains of sand slip into the bottom half of the timer and, reaching over, poured the tea into two porcelain cups. Placing the top on Yuan's cup, he handed it to him. Picking up his own cup, he savored the aroma, then gingerly took a sip. No, not dried too fast after all, although it needs a bit more body. I'll try four minutes ten seconds next time. Not bad, really.

"I'm surprised you're taking this case yourself, sir," his assistant ventured, sipping the tea. "Especially since Chang is free."

"It promises to be out of the ordinary, and since it's only a Taoist temple, it will be of no concern to General Fu or the garrison commander, and I won't be hounded by constant phone calls from their personal secretaries. By the way, take Wan off the Hat'amen Road murder and put Chang on it—the foreigners are pressing Fu for some developments. Makes them nervous to have a murderer in their neighborhood. And shift Wan to the Ch'ienmen Road group—that place is threatening to get out of hand."

"Soldiers and prostitutes, a proven formula for trouble," remarked Yuan, who had put down his tea, and scribbled notes.

"And get together those homicide and assault figures the garrison commander wants today," continued Bei. "But don't send them until I've checked them over." He sipped at his tea, looking forward to the White Cloud Temple.

The body had been moved to a bell tower west of the Shrine Hall of Founder Ch'iu. It was merely a charred lump, hardly recognizable as human. The guest prefect, who was in charge of the temple now that the prior was dead, averted his gaze from the body and looked toward the light outside the open doorway, musing. How strange the flow of the Tao. An Shihlin, vibrant, confident with his mission, now scattered. Part of him gone as the flames' heat, part joined with the other gases of the air, the rest moldering here on this dirt floor.

Examining the body, usually a rich source of information for Inspector Bei, was useless in this case. He turned to the guest prefect, an old man with white beard, deeply etched face, and white hair gathered into a topknot showing above his open-center black hat. "How does it happen a newcomer to the temple such as yourself is the acting prior now?"

The old man regarded Bei curiously. "I was not aware you already knew so much about our temple's affairs."

"I don't, actually. All I know is that your hands are not those of a monk accustomed to monastery life."

The old man stared at his rough, scratched hands in the dim light of the bell tower. "I have just recently returned from a year as an itinerant monk, living in the mountains and gathering herbs much of the day. It is only because I resided here for fifteen years before that, and was in fact senior in time of residence even to Prior An, that I was asked to fill this unpleasant role at present."

"I would like to look at the prior's bedchambers and his study before I ask you some questions. Would you please lead me there?"

The old man's dark blue robe complemented the gray bricks and red-painted wood of a large passageway along one side of the Founder's Shrine Hall. He led the inspector north into a large courtyard enclosed by covered walkways fronting buildings on all four sides. At the north end of the courtyard, beyond shrubs and bare trees, was the red-columned Hall of the Four Deities. A smaller courtyard to its left led to the prior's chambers.

"We live simply," said the guest prefect. "His study and bedchamber are one room—here." They walked into a small room with whitewashed plaster walls. Bei proceeded according to the professional routine he had developed over years of investigations. He first took in the entire room by sight and smell. Simple furnishings; signs of struggle but not ransacking; incense strong, but doesn't quite mask the sweat of . . . at least several men, the attackers. He walked over to the bed, stripped the quilted comforter off it as he pulled a hand lens from his pocket, and bending low took what was for him a rather quick and cursory look at the sheet, sniffing as he went. The guest prefect shook his head at the ridiculous picture the inspector presented. Halfway down the length of the sheet, Bei quartered back and forth a few moments, then straightened up, a look of wry amusement on his face.

"I was under the impression you were celibate here, Guest Prefect."

The old man gazed steadily at him and said coldly, "Ours is a celibate order, Inspector."

"Doubtless. Nonetheless, a man and a woman shared this bed last night, or possibly the night before, and were intimate with each other. I presume the man could only have been your prior?"

"You can presume that," again coldly.

Bei next pulled a chair up to an ornate desk in a corner, sitting down before it with palpable relish.

"The most revealing aspect of a man's life," he commented to the old monk. He examined the row of books sitting atop the desk against the wall. "A few religious tracts . . . and quite a bit of history: the Later Han Dynasty, the T'aip'ing Rebellion, and . . . hmmm . . . very peculiar."

The several drawers below the desk's writing surface contained only receipts and summaries of temple business. Pulling the drawers out, Bei measured the depth of each with a pocket ruler from his jacket and compared it to the overall depth of the desk itself. Sticking his ruler into the open compartments above the writing surface, he measured the depths of all those larger in width than a person's hand. They were all the same, as deep as the drawers had been, until he came to one in the lower left-hand corner of the desk. Here the ruler protruded three inches more than on the others. Bei smiled, and began to search for the latch. Surely not simply at the back wall of the compartment. No. A pressure point at the back of the desk? No. The side? No. The floor of the compartment above? Yes. The back wall in the short compartment flipped down as he pressed a section of the compartment above it.

Putting on a flexible leather glove, Bei smiled at the now curious old monk. "I've had some unpleasant surprises from these secret compartments in the past, Guest Prefect. In fact, if this weren't the desk of a mild Taoist monk, guilty of nothing more than amorous activity and a suspiciously Confucian interest in history, I'd certainly not be putting even my gloved hand into his secret compartment. Snakes, spiders, poisoned blades—you'd be surprised at what I've found in places like this!" Gingerly he slid his gloved hand into the compartment, raised his eyebrows as he felt about, and withdrew his hand holding a small booklet. He took off his glove, leaned back in the chair, and began to leaf through the booklet.

"Names, places, and days of the week. Do any of these mean anything to you, Guest Prefect?" He read a page.

They were unknown to the old man.

"I shall give you a receipt for this, and take it with me, although at the moment I'm inclined to consider these code names for other lady friends. Your prior was a very vigorous fellow, was he not?"

"He was . . . quite energetic in the execution of his official duties, at least," allowed the guest prefect.

"Doubtless. Could you please tell me now what you know of the immediate circumstances which led to your prior's death last night."

"It is not totally clear to anyone," the old monk began. He spoke slowly, but not confusedly. "The star bell had rung, and presumably all of us were in our beds. About an hour later, when most were asleep, a group apparently rushed into the prior's bedchamber here, tied him to a chair, then carried him to the courtyard in front of Founder Ch'iu's Shrine Hall, where they—" here the old man winced— "burned him."

"Why carry him and a heavy chair all the way to that courtyard?" asked Bei. "Why not burn him in the large courtyard through which we walked to get here?" He paused, then added a further question. "And why burn him at all? Why not merely bludgeon him to death?"

The old monk looked at Bei as if the mere asking of such questions were an impropriety. "One cannot apply reason to mad acts," he finally said, severely.

"To the contrary, one must. Let me put it this way: How does the courtyard in front of the Founder's Shrine Hall differ from this one?"

"Well . . . the Founder's Shrine Hall was erected on the site where Ch'iu Changchun himself was cremated—out of respect, you understand—in the thirteenth century. His ashes are buried under the hall."

"Ah. So that place is the historic center of the temple complex and the former site of another . . . ceremonial burning, shall we say?"

"Yes."

"How many men were actually involved in his overpowering and murder?"

"As best as I can judge, ten men carried him to the courtyard."

"You can give me their names?

"Yes. They are now confined to their chambers."

"Excellent. And the other monks merely watched?"

"By no means!" the old man retorted. "It happened so quickly that it was over before half the monks were out of their beds and could find their way to the courtyard. We have no electricity in the temple, you see, even before the siege, so there was much confusion. Prior An was dead within two or three minutes of the time they set fire to the pyre."

"So how many monks other than the ten directly involved witnessed the murder?"

"Perhaps thirty or forty."

"Did they attempt to stop it?"

"Of course! Vigorously. But the dissident monks formed a ring around the steps on which Prior An had been placed, and prevented anyone from rescuing him until . . . until it was too late."

"I see. You said 'dissident monks.' Had they been opposing the prior previous to this?"

"Yes. The two leaders had in fact been expelled from the monastery eight years ago and only recently allowed to retake a number. They were spreading tales of offenses supposedly committed by Prior An."

"Did they know he slept with a woman?"

"Their most serious charge was in fact that he embezzled temple funds to support a mistress."

"Ah . . . And is this true?"

"Some of us suspected that he slept with a young woman who regularly attended devotions here."

"Do you have her, or her name?"

"Her given name, yes. Meiling. But I am not aware of any evidence that he misused temple funds on her."

"You have an accountant in charge of the temple's expenditures, I presume?"

"Our overseer."

"Good. I shall want to see him. It strikes me that we have no real motive for murder here. Violating a vow of chastity is common enough, I suppose?"

The old man mustered his dignity. "Not common, among us at least. But not . . . all that unusual, perhaps."

"So the dissident monks had no real grounds at all for calling their murder an 'execution' or whatever?"

"Unfortunately, an old rule of our Ch'uan Chen sect states that if a prior sells monastic property for his private gain, he shall be burned. But they had no evidence to my knowledge that Prior An actually did this, much less to support a mistress."

"And I presume that decision is usually made through an official inquiry, rather than a small mob during the night?"

"Of course."

Bei reflected on the story. "A most interesting tale, Guest Prefect. I fear the newspapers will make much of it, which will doubtless distress you and the temple." He looked into the old man's eyes and spoke in a less professional tone. "You must wish you had not returned from your mountains."

The old man smiled wanly. "I do enjoy the mountains. But the Tao we study and revere flows through all of existence, including this temple and the happenings of the temple, as well as life on the mountains. I am content to do what I can here to assist its flow in these difficult times."

"Some good will come out of this, you mean?" asked Bei, surprised.

"Not 'good.' You Confucians miss the point with all your talk of 'good' and 'bad.' There is no good or bad, only the flow of the Tao, which is beyond good and bad, and incorporates into itself even this mad act. Something will arise out of our prior's murder. It will mesh with other happenings to finally reinforce the inevitable."

Bei smiled indulgently. "I must courteously express disagreement and skepticism regarding your Tao and the cosmic effects of your prior's murder. If you will indulge me a little longer, I have my job to attend to. Could you please ask the overseer to come here, and to bring his books for the past four months."

Thorough questioning of the overseer, a thin, quick-eyed man surnamed Ba, convinced the inspector that the prior's expenditures were neither lavish nor misdirected, and that the overseer's system would in fact have detected any misappropriations had they occurred.

The guest prefect escorted Bei out of the temple complex. At the entrance, where his ricksha waited, Bei turned to the old man. "I will send a truck to pick up the ten men you have identified as being involved, and take them to the station for questioning by my men. By the way, if I were to want to question the young lady involved with your prior, would I be able to find her here?"

"She has very regularly attended our afternoon devotions on Monday, Wednesday, and Sunday. If she maintains this practice, you could see her tomorrow."

"Thank you," said the inspector. He pushed his way through the small crowd that was milling around the front gate, and climbed into his ricksha for the ride back.

As Bei walked into his office and headed for the teakettle, Yuan looked up from his desk in the corner.

"Don't settle yourself in, sir. Zhou Peifeng called. The warlord wants to see you."

"General Fu? About what?"

Yuan grinned, revealing his two missing lower front teeth. "Zhou said it was about the White Cloud Temple murder."

Bei stood with his hand on the teakettle, staring at Yuan incredulously. "You're surely joking."

Yuan's smile progressed to a laugh. "No kidding. Your obscure case for some reason interests the warlord himself. Want me to assign Chang to it?"

Bei stared at the window behind Yuan, not focusing on the water of Chunghai Lake beyond the bare trees outside the window. "What under heaven could be of interest to Fu in the burning of the prior of a Taoist temple?" he mused.

"The White Cloud Temple is the oldest and most important Taoist temple in Peking," Yuan offered.

"Perhaps. But even so, it's only a Taoist temple, and so of no consequence to anything. Most intriguing. I'll be off to see the general right away. 'When a dragon calls, it's not wise to dally.' Send a truck to the temple and pick up the ten monks directly involved in the murder, Yuan. The guest prefect is in charge of the temple now. Get statements from each of the ten, and hold them until I can read the statements and forward my report to the magistrate. I don't imagine he'll take long to decide what to do—the case is straightforward after all, and still of no importance. Unless . . . are you sure Zhou said Fu wanted to see me about the White Cloud Temple business?"

"Positive."

"He's only talked to me three times in a year and a half, always something fairly important . . . oh, well. Insufficient data, Yuan. Working the mind with insufficient data is like—"

"—carving jade without a water stream," completed his assistant wearily. "It will ruin the equipment and the piece." He had heard the inspector say it many times before.

Bei walked from his office in the old Imperial City to General Fu's headquarters in the Winter Palace, following the west wall of the Forbidden City north to the corner watchtower, then crossing the street and entering Beihai Park. The Winter Palace stood on Jade Flower Isle in the middle of the artificial lake which was the heart of Beihai Park, at the site where Kublai Khan had built his palace in the thirteenth century.

Bei showed his identification to the guards and walked the several hundred feet of Eternal Peace Bridge, noting with pleasure the small open pavilion to the left as he reached the Jade Flower Isle. He reluctantly walked past the elegant pavilion, one of his favorite spots in the city, and after several more security checks was admitted to a spacious room in the complex of covered corridors and pavilions at the northern tip of the island. The silk-covered chairs and red columns reflected the imperial luxury of the Ch'ing Dynasty. A door opened and Zhou Peifeng, General Fu's personal assistant, entered the room. He was middle-aged, in good physical shape, with the mixture of charm and efficiency requisite to his position.

"Inspector Bei, it is good to see you again."

"It is an honor to visit you, Colonel Zhou."

"We appreciate your coming so promptly."

Bei decided it would be too fawning to quote the "dragon calls" saying, so he stood silent instead.

"General Fu is able to see you now. If you will please follow me."

Bei followed Zhou through a labyrinth of covered corridors and gardens, arriving after several minutes at a large pavilion in the classical style, except for the many telephone and electrical lines leading to it. The beams and ceiling of the walkway fronting the pavilion were covered with faded paintings of gardens and landscapes in what was termed the "Soochow School" by its imperial admirers. On each of his four visits to the general's pavilion, he had reached it by different yet equally circuitous routes.

Zhou led the way through an anteroom and into the general's office, turning and watching Bei closely as he entered. The room was simply but richly decorated. To one side was a set of ebony chairs with inlaid panels of marble whose grain resembled paintings of mountain peaks, the chairs arranged around a low table of similar composition. The opposite side of the room was dominated by a large ebony table piled with an orderly profusion of maps and reports. The walls were hung with pictures of the general with various prominent personages of China's turbulent past three decades. At the far end of the room, in front of a large window, General Fu Tsoyi sat at his desk. He did not rise, but looked up after Bei and Zhou had stood politely for the required several seconds.

"Ah, Inspector Bei. You honor my office again. Please have a seat." His voice was deep and resonant, with a trace of an accent from his native province of Shansi. "Your wife is in good health?"

Bei took one of the two chairs facing the desk. "She is in reasonably good health, General Fu, although our northern winters are always hard on those from Chiang Nan." Chiang Nan, "south of the Yangtse River," referred to the region in central China in which Nanking, Hangchow, and Shanghai were located.

"Zhou, arrange for permission for Madame Bei to visit her home in Hangchow in case Inspector Bei deems it advisable within the next month."

"Oh, General Fu, I was not asking for space—"

"I know, Inspector, but I want you to have the permit in case it becomes necessary. You know, of course, that we've had planes departing for several days now from the new airfields by the Legation Quarter and the Temple of Heaven."

"Yes, I was aware of that." Within a week after the siege had cut off Peking's links with its airports outside the city walls, two new airfields had been constructed within the walls, although the planes functioned mainly to transport important or rich personages and their property to safety in the south, easily accomplished since the encircling Communist forces lacked combat airplanes.

"Inspector, I heard that a most peculiar event took place in the southwestern sector of the city last night," Fu said, staring intently at Bei. The fierce energy and intelligence which had carried him successfully through thirty years of shifting, internecine political and military warfare were plainly evident on his handsome face. They made Bei uneasy in his presence. Bei's mind again recorded an earlier impression. Fu had the face of a scholar who for some perverse reason had chosen soldiering instead. "Good iron is not made into nails, nor good men into soldiers." Apt, even though Mo-tzu had said it.

"What have you learned about this curious crime?" asked Fu.

"The case seems rather straightforward, General Fu. The prior of the White Cloud Temple was disliked by a small group of the monks there, who accused him of violating the accepted customs of the temple in various minor ways and by embezzling funds to support a mistress. There is evidence he indeed slept with at least one woman, but not that he lavished any temple funds on her. At any rate, the disgruntled monks, invoking an old rule of their sect, burned him for misappropriating temple property."

"Was the prior engaged in any unusual activities, Inspector?"

"Other than having a mistress, none that I discovered, General."

"Did you find any unusual items of evidence at the temple?"

"Only a booklet with some dozen code names, with dates and places. I imagine he had other lady friends."

"I see. Inspector Bei," began Fu, pausing to arrange his words into the most circumspect pattern. "We have reason to believe that these events in this Taoist temple may have connections with other, more weighty matters. I regret that we are not at liberty to reveal details to you, and indeed we ourselves have few details. Yet there are indications that the matter should be thoroughly investigated. I want you to continue looking into the case, using all the considerable skills to which your reputation attests. Spare no efforts or resources. And report regularly to Colonel Zhou on your progress."

Bei struggled to make sense of what he was attentively listening to. After a pause, he ventured, "If I knew even a little about these possible connections, General Fu, I could orient my search in that direction."

"I apologize for not being able to tell you more," Fu answered decisively. "I rely on your sagacity to guide you. I do think we might give you some help with those names in the booklet, though. Do you have it on you?"

"Why, yes. I have just returned from my visit to the temple and haven't yet logged this item in."

"Let Zhou take a look at it, please."

Bei produced the booklet from his pocket and handed it to Zhou. As Zhou received it, Fu continued. "In fact, we will be able to follow up this line of investigation using our own resources. Probably you are correct in thinking they represent only other female companions of the prior. We will let you know if anything comes of it."

Bei realized that he would not get the booklet back. He gazed levelly at the general, waiting for his anger to subside several degrees. "Sir, I must ask for at least a copy of the contents of the booklet. And for a receipt documenting your . . ." All three of them listened for what word would be used to describe the confiscation of the booklet. Bei discarded "seizure" as too provocative, "possession" as too bland to reflect his anger, and settled quickly on a compromise. ". . . your order for the transfer of the booklet."

Fu had not expected Bei to acquiesce easily: He knew the inspector's reputation for tenacity. "Zhou, kindly give Inspector Bei the receipt he requests, reflecting our possession of the booklet."

"And the copy?" pressed Bei.

"We will handle that phase of the investigation ourselves," Fu repeated. "And certainly let you know if anything develops. Inspector

Bei," continued the general, adopting what might have been mistaken for a conciliatory tone, "we will work together on this. It may be important. Please devote your best efforts to it. Thank you for coming, and I will look forward to hearing your reports through Colonel Zhou."

Realizing that he had been dismissed, Bei rose, bowed politely, accepted a receipt from Zhou, and left the room. A guard escorted him out of the complex.

"May I see the booklet, Zhou," said Fu as Bei left the room. The warlord flipped through several pages. Although the names were in code, he had no doubt as to whom they represented. Nor that his daughter's name would be among them. Such a strange and complicated world, he mused, not for the first time. He returned the booklet to Zhou.

"Burn it."

Zhou nodded, carefully maintaining a neutral expression. He placed the booklet in a bowl and touched a match to it. The pages glowed, curled, and turned black.

"Now that we have completed our phase of the investigation," commented Fu dryly, "let us hope that the inspector has better luck in his. I would very much like to know who had the prior killed. And why. And how much they know of what the prior was." He stood up and turned to gaze at the garden outside the window behind his desk. "This turn of events puzzles me, Zhou, and I dislike being puzzled. I have known many men for whom being puzzled led shortly to their being dead."

Fu stared at a T'aihu stone set halfway up a small hill, so that its irregular, eroded surface stood out in relief against an evergreen shrub behind it. The stone was old, had traveled far from its native place near Soochow in Kiangsu province, yet was still solid and strong.

"How long have I been wiggling out of puzzles, Zhou?"

"You joined General Yen Hsishan's forces straight out of Paoting Academy, sir, in 1918."

"Yes, but you don't deal with real puzzles until you're a brigade commander."

"Chochow, then, General Fu. 1927."

"Yes, I suppose so. Twenty-one years. Puzzles. It still puzzles me why anyone expects a relief column to actually link up with them. Yen Hsishan told me the Nationalist force from the south would join me, so I stuck out my neck and captured Chochow, even though the Fengtien armies were thick as locusts in that region. And I actually thought the Nationalists would fight their way up to me." He shook his head at the memory.

"Your endurance of the siege of Chochow by the Fengtien forces earned you much glory throughout China," ventured Zhou.

Fu was silent, staring at the T'aihu stone again. "At the end my men were starved, their arms and legs swollen horribly from the fermented grain refuse we were reduced to eating. I wanted to break out of the city and fight our way south, but it couldn't be done. And the cold. That siege was in December, too. Just like this one."

Fu fell silent again, his thoughts on the former siege and the relief column that never came. The shadow of a bird brushed over the T'aihu stone.

"It was self-delusion, Zhou."

"Sir?"

"I wanted the relief column so bad that I deluded myself into thinking it would happen. Just like Chiang Kaishek deluded himself this October, thinking his American-trained divisions from Burma could fight their way through Manchuria to relieve the Communist siege of Mukden. Instead, Lin Piao swallows up both Mukden and the Burma divisions. In two weeks Chiang Kaishek loses half a million men. My friend General Wei Lihuang flies here to safety in Peking as the Communists march into Mukden." He paused. "And forty-three days later Lin Piao's advance elements have *us* surrounded. How does he do it, Zhou? How does Lin Piao move an army from Manchuria to Peking in forty-three days?"

"It is a puzzle," Zhou ventured.

Fu roared with laughter. "Yes, Zhou, another puzzle." He laughed again, then became serious. "Zhou."

"Yes, General."

"Keep me from self-delusion."

"You do a good job of that yourself, General."

"But I need help. Be rude if you must, provoke my anger, but keep me from self-delusion. We may survive the next month, if we solve our puzzles, in spite of the loss of Kalgan Friday. But we are doomed if we succumb to self-delusion. Lost: us, and those who are dear to us." He thought of the burned booklet, and then of Meilu. "This was my last meeting this morning?"

"Yes."

"And when is my first appointment this afternoon?"

"Fourteen hundred, General."

"Good. Knock on my door twenty minutes before then."

"Yes, General."

He turned from the window and strode with fresh energy to the door leading to his private quarters. "Tell General Yu Chenling I want to see him tomorrow to discuss further defensive measures for the city—perhaps we can get his Te Wu agents something constructive to do. Have Mayor Liu deputize someone to coordinate the food drops into the city from Nanking. Get me a copy of Lin Piao's radio broadcast yesterday. 'War criminal' indeed! And give the inspector whatever help he wants."

"Yes, General."

"And tell Intelligence I want an update on Lin Piao's artillery strength. Numbers, if possible."

"Yes, General, although . . ."

"I know, I know. Why are men in Intelligence always so stupid? So full of self-delusion. Keep it from me, Zhou!"

"Yes, General."

As Fu shut the door behind him, the problems of a besieged city, of Lin Piao and hollow promises, were securely shunted to one side of his mind, and he slowed his walk as he approached Meilu's chambers down the hallway. He knocked.

"Yes?" came a high but firm voice from within.

"It's me," he answered.

"Come in."

He entered her sitting room, feeling the heat from the modern coal burner in one corner, and gazed on her figure at the table in front of the window looking out onto the same garden. The long, jet-black hair gathered atop her head and spilling down on all sides from the knot. The quilted blue silk robe embroidered with golden chrysanthemums enwrapping her slim body except for one long naked leg, which gracefully stretched to the side in the familiar position she assumed when writing. The smooth golden skin of her slender neck, which revealed itself through her hair as she turned her head to him.

"I'm just finishing your poem about Kalgan," she said with enthusiasm, her large black eyes sparkling.

Such a beautiful face, Fu thought, absorbing her prominent cheekbones, high forehead, and full mouth.

"Oh, come. Quit staring at me and see what I've done with your poem," she scolded, pleased.

He walked to the table, put his hands on her narrow but smoothly muscled shoulders, and looked at her calligraphy as he lightly massaged the muscles.

"For me to criticize your calligraphy is like making poems before Confucius," he said, pleased with the vigorous characters boldly brushed onto the paper.

"No empty compliments, warlord," she said severely. "What do you think, really?" She relaxed her shoulders, letting his hands have their way.

He looked at the calligraphy closely, her rendition of a poem about his capture of Kalgan from the Communists two years earlier, and its recapture by them two days ago. "I truly am unqualified to judge any calligraphy, much less yours," he began. She shook her shoulders in pretended anger. "But if I had to judge," he quickly added, resuming his massage, "I would say it has the appearance of a cultured lady striving to write like an uncultured warlord."

She considered it. "Is that a compliment or a criticism?"

"It is an observation," he said, sliding his right hand under her robe.

"I still have to stamp my seal on the poem, mighty warrior," she said, lightly mocking his advances. He rubbed the soft skin on the inner surface of his wrist against her nipple as she stamped her seal in the red ink pad and then imprinted it on the lower left corner of the paper. "Besides, I would think your Jade Stalk would be exhausted after last night's Dark Cicada Clinging to a Tree."

"Now that was a major battle," he smiled, as she leaned back in the chair and relaxed, languorously stretching her long legs. They both gazed at the poem.

. . .

Bei was still angry as he walked into his office. He stomped over to the tin stove, restarted the fire, and put the teakettle on. Yuan walked in soon, as he was pouring the boiling water into the pot to steep. He upended the timer.

"I've got the prisoners from the temple, Chief. They've just now been put into the interrogation cells."

"Good," growled Bei.

"An interesting visit with the warlord?" Yuan asked obliquely, as befitted his station.

"He wants us to dig deeper into this case. He is of the opinion there may be more to it than is apparent on the surface."

"Such as?"

"He didn't give any hints."

Bei decided not to tell Yuan about the booklet, partly because it had humiliated him, partly because Fu might retaliate if the story was spread.

"And you have no ideas?"

"Ideas. But no data. So the ideas wait until I get some data to work with. Which means me spending a long afternoon of very thorough questioning of a rabble of ignorant Taoist monks," Bei said angrily, "instead of letting my men handle it."

"You don't sound enthused, Chief."

"I am not, at the moment. But actually, it's curious. We now have two problems: Why was the prior burned, really? And why is the Nationalist warlord in charge of northern China concerned about it, when he's surrounded and besieged by several Communist armies? An interesting puzzle, actually."

Yuan was about to comment, when a soft knock sounded at the door. He opened it to reveal a small, almost frail young woman with the round face of a northerner, looking rather beautiful in a vulnerable sort of way.

"I'm looking for Yuan Jinli," she said in a timid voice with a thick Shansi accent.

"You're Yuan Lufei?" he asked eagerly.

"Yes," she gasped, nearly sobbing in relief.

"Come in. Sit down."

Bei poured a cup of tea and passed it to Yuan, who handed it to her.

"I apologize for bothering you at your place of work, but it is the only address I had."

"Of course," answered Yuan. "I thought you'd find it easier than my home. And I'm here during the day. I'm glad you've found me. You can relax now, Lufei. Everything is going to be all right for you now."

The girl sipped the tea eagerly. As they watched they could see the strain slip wearily from her, and a glazed look come to her eyes, as if only the burden had been keeping her alert, and that for far too long. As they realized she was about to fall asleep, Yuan and Bei glanced at each other in embarrassment, then Yuan put his hand on her shoulder.

"Lufei, my next-door neighbor, a widow, is expecting you. I'll send you to my home in a ricksha, and she'll get you settled in. Do you have a bag?"

The young woman looked blankly at him. "A bag?"

"Yes, any clothing you brought with you, or anything?"

She roused herself. "A bundle. In the hall there," pointing toward the door. "I am too much trouble to you."

"Not at all. What else is family for?" Yuan helped her up, set the empty teacup on a table, and walked out the door with her leaning on his arm. He reappeared some minutes later.

"That, I presume, was your orphaned niece from Shansi," Bei said.

"Yes. I apologize for receiving her here."

"It's of no importance. She seems to be under quite a strain."

"Her story is a bad one. But common, these days."

"Tell me about her while we sip our tea. I can gladly put off the Taoists for a few minutes."

Yuan shook his head sadly. "My uncle's family is in Shansi. One of his sons—my cousin—was prosperous, for a peasant. He fathered a son and two daughters. When the Japanese got there in 1938, they 'appropriated' all his belongings and animals, reducing the family back to poverty. It was hard on them, I'll say, after living well for so long. The children had received high-class private educations. The son, especially, showed promise, and my cousin had hopes of his entering government service."

"But weren't their goods returned, or reimbursed, in 1945?"

"No. It's true that the warlord Yen Hsishan tried to make right

22

what the Japanese had taken away from people in his province, but my cousin lived in a remote and poor county, and only the largest local landowner managed to get what he had lost, plus a good deal more, when the Japanese surrendered. My cousin's son was so enraged at this that he threatened the landowner, was beaten by the landowner's men, and then disappeared. Everyone assumed that he was beaten to death, or joined the Communist bandits, who were strong there."

"As they were in many counties in northern China. And now they surround us and cut us off from everything," remarked Bei.

"Yes. Well, at any rate, my cousin's wife soon became ill, and my cousin sent one of his daughters into town regularly for medicine, borrowing heavily from the landowner to pay for it. The daughter attracted the attention of the landowner's son, and he persuaded his father to pressure my cousin to sell this daughter to him. He owed the landowner a lot of money, and he needed more for his wife's medicine, so . . . he sold her. Some months later she was killed in a drunken orgy with the landlord's son. The mother soon died, as much from grief as anything. The father and his one remaining daughter scraped by as best they could for several years. It was bad for them. Real bad. Then the landowner demanded payment of my cousin's debts, and declared he would take the remaining daughter. This was too much for my cousin—he arranged for the daughter to be sent here to me by some friends, and then—then he hanged himself. And now she has arrived."

Bei finished his tea. The various elements of the tale were familiar enough to him, being common in times of war and turmoil, which meant China's last hundred years. "What will you do with her?"

"I don't know. Take care of her until she's a little older, I guess. It's a family obligation."

Bei looked at Yuan keenly. His assistant was a widower, not yet sixty years old. "In the old days, Yuan, it would have been your obligation to marry her."

Yuan looked flustered, but it seemed apparent to Bei that the idea was not entirely new to him. "What? Marry her? Why, I could be her father."

"True, but what does that matter? She is beautiful. She needs kindness. You could use some company yourself. Think about it."

He put down his cup. "But think about it later. I have a lot of questioning to do, and you a lot of note taking. And instead of routine questioning it will now have to be searching, thanks to Fu's suspicions. I already dread all the nonsense about the Tao they'll barrage us with. Let's go."

December 27

Bei spent the next morning writing his initial report of the case. He had elicited as much gibberish as he expected regarding a host of baleful spiritual powers which had directed the monks to punish the traitorous prior. Only two of the prisoners related relatively coherent and rational explanations of the prior's transgressions, and the necessity of punishing him according to the rules of the Ch'uan Chen sect. These two Bei marked as the leaders in the crime. His years in detective work had convinced him that a confusing story was often an honest one, but that a tight thread of coherence was the sure mark of premeditation and guilt. Reality unfettered was chaotic; coherence was imposed upon the world by men, either for good or for evil. Which was why he had astounded his family and friends by choosing the detective profession. His job was unraveling the rational skeins of criminal acts immersed within the chaotic matrix of passion and violence, a greater challenge to his intellect than any of the purported intellectual vocations, such as academics or writing.

Late in the morning he presented his report to the Peking High Magistrate, and obtained reluctant clearance to pursue the investigation according to the plan he had outlined in the report. Before going to his home for lunch with his wife, Bei returned to his office to instruct Yuan.

"We're going to release them, Yuan."

"Free the Tiger, is it?"

Bei resorted to this procedure only rarely. If a case was barren of clues and no line of investigation was apparent, or if evidence was too meager for a conviction, Bei would occasionally drop the case publicly, release his prime suspects, and rely on them to provide fresh clues or evidence. A risky procedure, to be sure, in that it frequently led to new crimes. But if Fu wanted to get at something deeper, there was no recourse. Actually, Bei enjoyed invoking this procedure because it raised the stakes in the game and held out the possibility of converting a failure to a victory.

"In this case, more like Free the Goblins," answered Bei. "I've never run into a more superstitious lot. Tell them and the guest prefect when you deliver them to the temple that we consider it temple business and the civil authorities will not take action at this time. Then post a plainclothesman outside the temple entrance, with orders to follow either of the two I've picked out as leaders should they leave the temple. Tell the guest prefect I'll be there shortly, after lunch, to talk to him again. I'll spend the afternoon and evening around the temple myself. A newly freed man is often least cautious."

With his plans in motion, the inspector put on his quilted coat and stepped out into the lake-shore park in which his office was located. The long artificial lake west of the Forbidden City formed the axis of the Imperial City in which high officials of the Chinese empire had worked since the time of Kublai Khan. The lake was arbitrarily demarcated here into three "seas": Beihai, or North Sea; Chunghai, or Middle Sea; and Nanhai, or South Sea. The shores around these three "sea" lakes had been turned into imperial pleasure gardens for the exalted officials who worked there. The area around the North Sea now comprised Beihai Park, with the Winter Palace on the lake's Jade Flower Isle reserved for the current ruler of the city. But the park area around the lower two connected portions of the lake continued to be the site where prominent members of the city's administration worked, including Bei, whose office fronted the shore of Chunghai Lake.

As Bei walked through the Chunghai Lake compound, his eye was caught by the old, decaying pavilion rising above the water some six meters into the lake from its shore. Wasn't there a Taoist inscription in that pavilion? No way to tell, though. The bridge connecting it to the shore had long since been obliterated by the ravages of time. He shivered. Too many Taoists, too much of their superstition, had intruded recently into his ordered Confucian world. He stared past the old, isolated pavilion at the water of Chunghai Lake, now mostly frozen, and the stiff wind whipping along its surface. For that matter, disorder and chaos were pushing in from everywhere, threatening to engulf even this ancient capital of reason, order, and empire. What was happening? Why was it all converging in his lifetime?

He shrugged his shoulders, turned from the lake and walked through the cold to his waiting ricksha at the little-used eastern gate of the Chunghai Lake compound, only a hundred meters or so from the Forbidden City's West Flower Gate. As the ricksha turned south, Bei took comfort in the sight of the moat and high purple walls around the Forbidden City. But as they came abreast of the imposing West Flower Gate, he saw the soldiers inside the Forbidden City, and remembered that even it was occupied by the armies massed into Peking as a result of the siege. Turning onto Ch'ang'an Boulevard and traveling towards T'ian'anmen Gate in front of the Forbidden City, more reminders of the siege thrust themselves at him. The absence of streetcars due to the Communist capture of the electricity-generating plant at Shihchingshan south of the city. The lines of horse-drawn carts filled with military necessities: weapons, ammunition, bales of wire, food stuffs, hay for the horses. Several of the carts had wounded men in them, the dull red blood of their bandages standing out amidst the drabness of Peking in the winter, with its bare trees and gray bricks and tiles covered with a generous layer of the yellow dust blown by the north wind from the Mongolian steppes. And the frequent military trucks careening through the streets at ridiculous speeds, scattering frightened pedestrians before them. Bei huddled deeper in the ricksha, hoping he would not be added to the list of casualties of the trucks.

As they passed T'ian'anmen Gate and the maze of buildings and shops to the south of it, more peddlers and goods began to appear on the sidewalks. They had left the wall of the Forbidden City and were approaching Tung'anmen and Wangfuching streets, one of the commercial and market centers of Peking. Bei saw the street corners piled high with olive-drab American surplus foodstuffs, people gathered around them haggling over prices. Whole families stood behind stacks of furniture and goods representing their entire life's holdings, anxious to exchange them for food. Luckily only the very poorest are running out of food after only two weeks of the siege, thought Bei. Most of the city has food for another month or two. Those who live in Peking have learned through the ages the virtue of stocking up on food and fuel, he reflected bitterly. It's mainly the refugees from Kalgan and Mukden and the rest of Manchuria who are so badly off.

He pulled his coat tighter about his neck as the driver turned north up Tung'anmen Street and exposed the open front of his ricksha to the northern wind. He was now riding along the eastern wall of the old Imperial City, the huge domain of the imperial court which had the Forbidden City in its center and stretched from the three "seas" in the west here to Tung'anmen Street in the eastern part of the city. He rode over the bridge spanning Reed River, which once drained the moat surrounding the Imperial City, and turned east onto a small side street shortly after passing Peking Union Church. The ricksha took him east almost to Wangfuching Street, which the foreigners had the effrontery to call Morrison Street. This area, between Tung'anmen and Wangfuching just east of the old wall of the Imperial City, had been the neighborhood of the Manchu aristocracy in the last century. Indeed, Wangfuching meant "Well of the Princes' Palaces," referring to the sweet-water well located in the prestigious area. Even though the prices were beyond his means, he and his wife had used his modest inherited wealth to purchase a beautiful small villa in the neighborhood. He had in fact cached a good deal of the pure water from the well in his storeroom, meaning to use it for tea. But with water flowing at only a trickle in the two weeks since the siege began, they were putting it to everyday uses, managing to avoid sending their one servant girl to stand in the long line at the well.

He instructed the ricksha driver to wait for him as they came to a stop, and unlocked the crimson, brass-fitted door which was the only entrance into his high-walled compound. Inside, a covered corridor ran south along the east wall of the compound, with various rooms and courtyards opening off to the west. He walked past the kitchen and servant's quarters and the first courtyard and entered the dining hall. His wife was sitting on a sofa at the far end of the hall. She presented a formal appearance, even when casually leafing through a magazine, with her carefully coiffured hair and perfect clothes. He had fallen in love with her elegance and culture, her fine features, and slim figure when they had met in Hangchow ten years earlier.

"Hello, Jinglo," he said cordially.

She did not look up from the magazine. "Hello. Are you ready for lunch?"

"I suppose so."

"All right." She pulled a cord which rang a small bell in the courtyard.

They seated themselves at opposite sides of the heavy, highly polished round table.

"Has everyone accepted our invitation to dinner tomorrow night?" he asked, bringing up a subject he hoped would cheer her up.

"Yes. Madame Chang called this morning. It will be good to see them again. And the Hos."

"Yes, it promises to be a splendid time. What teas should we serve?"

She did not respond to the forced happiness in his voice. "Menjin, I've been thinking more about the situation here. According to Madame Ho, it's quite hopeless, and bound to get worse."

Bei sighed. They both remained silent as the servant girl placed three dishes on the table, steam rising from them in the cold room. He savored the principal aromas: onions, white cabbage, oyster sauce, garlic. Then he returned to the business at hand, concentrating to keep his tone light and free from reproach.

"Well, 'hopeless' depends on what it is you hope for, does it not? Here we have warm food, plenty of water in the storeroom, friends arriving tomorrow night, and—"

"Menjin, I 'hope' for more than that," she interrupted, and the frustration rushed forth in a familiar torrent of words. "By all that's under heaven I hope for a place to live that's not surrounded by bloodthirsty bandits who parcel out the wives of officials to their soldiers. For a place where winter doesn't last seven months of the year. A place where you can get away from the smell of onions and garlic. A place—"

"Jinglo," he said firmly. A suggestion of hysteria had crept into her voice again, and he had no wish to replay the ugly scenes that had become so common between them. Even before the siege, her elegance had long since turned into stiff formality, and her composure was now simply gone.

"Jinglo," this time more softly, "it has been very hard on you. I realize that." She began to bite her lower lip and tears welled in her eyes. "Peking is a beautiful city, but this winter started early and the siege has made everything worse. And you are afraid of the Communists and the rumors. I have been thinking, too. It is indeed too much to expect of you to stay here in these conditions. I think you should return to Hangchow, at least for the foreseeable future."

A frantic eagerness lit up her features as she looked at him. Then her sense of propriety reasserted itself. "But you can't go with me, and a wife's place is beside her husband."

"Normally, yes. But these are extraordinary times."

"Please don't tease me with it. The travel passes are impossible to get if you are not military or—" she glanced at him bitterly—"higher in the government." His choice of a police inspector's profession rather than the more prestigious posts offered to him in government and academics had long been a source of friction between them. He would not reopen that subject today.

"I have a surprise for you. In my talk with General Fu yesterday, I obtained permission for you to fly to Hangchow. The permit arrived today." He handed her the document, with a certain feeling that it would signify the end of their marriage, but that it was unavoidable.

She clutched it to her breast, then read it with unbelieving eyes. "Oh, you do look after me!" she cried, her eyes more alive than they had been for years as she beamed at him. Bei reached across and took her hand warmly. "Of course I look after you. I'm sorry about . . . all this. Things will be better for you, and us, when you get to Hangchow."

"Hangchow." She repeated the name eagerly, and visions of warmth and lush green scenery and family and friends and safety rushed over her. She trembled the tremble of salvation perceived. "Hangchow." She placed her hand atop his. "You must come with me," she said intensely. "I need you there. I want you to come!"

He smiled at her intensity and her sudden happiness. "I would like to, Jinglo, but it is impossible. You know that. No one rules his own life these days."

She acknowledged it but persevered. "Then just for the trip. Take me down to Chiang Nan. You can say I need to be escorted there."

Bei shook his head. "If I could, I would. But . . . it wouldn't look right, and at any rate I certainly couldn't get permission. Sorry."

She was genuinely sorry, but only for an instant. "Hangchow," she whispered again, savoring the sound of the word as he had savored the aroma of the food. Suddenly she jumped up. "I've got to tell Madame Ho and Madame Chang. The dinner will be a farewell dinner now! And I've got to pack." She rushed to her room.

Bei sat there, glad to see her happy, realizing too that once she left, he might not see her again for a long time, if ever. The war was not going well for the Nationalists, and no one had any sure idea of what the Communists, if they were finally victorious, would do to officials in the Nationalist government. A bloodbath was certainly talked of, and was not impossible. The Communists were so unknown, so unpredictable. Chaos. He wondered how many other marriages were breaking up under the strain of the siege. No, that wasn't fair. It wasn't just the siege. He had known a Hangchow woman would find it difficult to live in Peking. Food, climate, language, customs—so much was different here. And his profession . . . she had not expected to be married to a policeman, even a high-ranking one with some independent wealth. But not having children. That was the hardest of all. And then the war, and the siege to top it all. The smell of the food intruded into his reverie. Oh, well. Perhaps it will all work out. And at any rate one must appreciate what culture is left to one. He ate with what pleasure he could muster, and tried to think of the teas to serve tomorrow night.

Bei arrived at the White Cloud Temple early in the afternoon. The place seemed to have returned to an atmosphere of normalcy very quickly: No crowds jammed the entrance, a few monks walked briskly along the pebbled pathways, and Bei saw rooms filled with monks participating in what looked to be study sessions as he was led to the guest prefect by the gateman. They walked north along the main axis of Shrine Halls and finally passed into the large courtyard in front of the Hall of the Four Deities.

The guest prefect looked up from a desk in a room on the east side of the courtyard. On his open, craggy face was a hint of annoyance. Bei decided to open on a courteous note. "Have you eaten, Guest Prefect?" he said, the customary greeting between acquaintances.

"Not since breakfast," the old man returned coldly. "We only have two meals a day in the winter here."

"Oh," said Bei. "What are the groups of monks doing in the rooms I observed on my walk here?"

"They are participating in one of Prior An's innovations: education classes."

"You attach great importance to these classes?"

"They permit us to study and better understand the flow of the Tao through the world. No task is more important," returned the guest prefect. "Or more delightful," he added as an afterthought.

"Really? I was not under the impression that the Taoist religion was confined to the study of books."

"In a temple complex we study the Tao through the sacred writings and devotional practices. Our religion also recognizes that you can study the Tao in the mountains or on a lake shore. Even," he smiled, "in a police station."

"Your Tao is not so pure if it can be studied in the cases that flow across my desk."

"The Tao is not pure. It is not above life or apart from life. It *is* life, human and nonhuman."

"Doubtless," said Bei.

"Inspector, why did you return the ten men to us?" asked the guest prefect suddenly.

"My visit today is partly to explain that to you. The magistrate concluded that this affair is primarily a temple matter," lied Bei. "We leave it to you to first punish them as your monastic rules dictate. We may or may not subject them to civil punishment, depending on the results of a few more inquiries we will make."

The old man stared at Bei, the annoyance unmistakably plain now. He thought of his mountains, then spoke wearily. "Inspector, the most severe punishment the temple can levy is expulsion from our order. Does this seem an adequate punishment for murder?"

Bei shrugged his shoulders. "To protect the public from these men until monastic discipline has run its course, and until we decide whether to subject them to civil punishment, I will post a plainclothesman around the temple, to keep an eye on any of them who leave the compound."

The guest prefect sat looking at Bei, refusing him even the courtesy of inviting him to sit down. "I have heard that many prisoners have been released from the city's jails, that food and personnel for the jails are so scarce because of the siege that the authorities are retaining only the most vicious criminals. Is this true?"

"More or less."

"Then perhaps I understand. You simply don't want the trouble of holding men whose only crime is the murder of a Taoist."

"Authorities above me have decided that these men should be subject to monastic discipline first; perhaps the situation in our overcrowded jails was a factor," said Bei. "But do not think that we consider your prior's murder unimportant. I want to pursue my investigation. In fact, I am here today to do that. I want to speak with the woman who was involved with Prior An, if she comes to the devotional service. And I am interested in hearing if you have uncovered any more information that may be pertinent to the case."

The guest prefect cast a puzzled look at Bei. "I still don't understand all this. The crime is not important enough to jail the murderers, yet you wish to continue your investigation." He sighed. "But I do have more information. Our overseer, Ba, is particularly devoted to Chungli Ch'uan, the chief of our Eight Immortals. He has told me that one evening over a month ago, while he was motionless in the shadow before the statue, the young lady who was friendly with Prior An entered the hall and placed a packet against the opening of the gourd slung on the back of Li T'iehkuai, another of our Eight Immortals. She quickly left. Nearly an hour later, Prior An appeared and collected the packet from the gourd."

"What was in the packet?"

"The overseer observed that also. Prior An, believing that he was alone in the hall, stepped into a shaft of moonlight from a window and opened the packet. The overseer saw him quickly glance at a sheet of paper which appeared to him to have a list of names on it, then quickly count out the bulk of the packet, which consisted of"—here the old man paused for dramatic effect—"some five hundred silver dollars!"

Bei raised his eyebrows, and felt the delicious tingle when a case takes an unexpected turn. "Some five hundred silver dollars," he grinned. "That is truly bizarre." Then it hit him. "Now just a minute. The silver went from the woman to the prior?"

"Yes."

"Even more strange. So money *did* exchange hands between the prior and his mistress, but it was in the opposite direction that you might expect. And it evidently had nothing to do with their sexual relations, because—well, your prior may have been a vigorous fellow, but it's most unlikely any woman would pay that much money for any man's sexual favors." A shadow of a doubt flickered over his face. "Unless . . . is the woman very rich and very ugly?"

The guest prefect, enjoying the effect his news had wrought in the inspector, smiled. "She is most decidedly not ugly, nor is she rich, so far as anyone knows."

"Can you take me to this hall and have Overseer Ba meet us there?"

"Certainly. The evening devotionals begin in fifteen minutes, so we cannot stay there long if you wish to see whether the woman Meiling is in attendance."

The Hall of the Eight Immortals was west of the main axis of Shrine Halls, reached through a door in the wall running beside the Shrine Hall of Founder Ch'iu, and beyond the Hall of the Western Mother. It was small, consisting only of four statues against each of the west and east walls, with a red-lacquered table fronting each row of statues. The overseer joined them in front of the second statue from the south end of the west wall.

"Good afternoon, Overseer Ba. This is the statue where the packet was deposited by the woman Meiling and picked up by Prior An?"

"It is."

The three of them gazed at the statue. Before them was depicted in life-size Li T'iehkuai, a lame beggar with dark skin, curly beard, and powerful arms. His outstretched right hand held a large peach, symbol of immortality and sexual potency. His other hand rested on a rough wooden crutch propped under the arm and supporting his left leg, which ended at the knee in a wreath of clouds. A large golden gourd was strapped across his back.

"Tell me where the packet was hidden."

"It was wedged between the mouth of the gourd and Li's back," answered the overseer.

"The guest prefect tells me you spend some time in here."

"I do."

"How many evenings a week are you practicing your devotions here?"

"It varies, but usually only one evening. My duties as overseer are so pressing, I have difficulty in even freeing one evening."

"I see. So you actually have no idea how frequently these exchanges of money and lists between the prior and the woman—I believe her name is Meiling—may have occurred."

"Not really. At least once, that is all I know."

"And you were where during this one time?"

"Over here," answered the overseer, pointing to the last statue on the opposite wall. "I am on my kneeling cloth, in the corner, so it is easy to overlook me in the dark."

"And whose statue is that before whom you kneel?"

"Chungli Ch'uan."

The stout green-robed figure, also life-sized, had a flowing black beard and held a red-tasseled fan in his left hand, his right hand thrust forward in salutation, or perhaps admonition.

"What is the significance of the fan?"

"It is a rather long story, Inspector."

"Then by all means let me hear it. I am becoming quite fond of Taoist stories."

The overseer glanced at the guest prefect, who nodded his permission.

"Ch'uan, a distinguished statesman in the Chou Dynasty, retired to his native place and married a beautiful young wife. On one of his long walks he passed a young woman in mourning attire, fanning the soil of a freshly dug grave with that red-tasseled fan. When Ch'uan inquired, she explained that her late husband had asked her to wait at least until the earth around his grave was entirely dry before she married another man; she was now fanning the earth around the grave to help it dry more quickly.

"Deciding to help her, Ch'uan invoked the aid of the spirits and struck the ground with her fan, at which the earth dried completely. The woman gave him the fan as a token of her gratitude, then rushed off to marry her new lover. When Ch'uan told his own wife what had happened, she declared that the young widow was devoid of all decency. Ch'uan, deciding to test his wife, feigned death in his own body and took on the form of a handsome young man who promptly wooed his newly widowed wife and requested the brain of her recently departed husband to concoct a powerful magic potion. His wife quickly agreed, and opened his coffin without hesitation, whereupon Ch'uan came back to life and sat up in the coffin, while the handsome suitor at the same time vanished into air. In her humiliation, the young wife hanged herself from a beam of their house. Ch'uan set fire to the house, with his wife's body still in it, and walked off, never to return, taking with him only the fan and his copy of the *Tao Teh Ching.*"

It had grown dimmer in the Hall of the Eight Immortals. The three of them stood in silence. Finally Bei spoke.

"So you come here to meditate on the fickleness of women."

The overseer was startled. "No. Not at all. I meditate upon the futility of suspicion and testing, and on the need to accept things as they are in this world, to be grateful for them, weak and flawed though they may be. And I meditate upon the wonder inherent in the world, how an ordinary object such as a fan can be a symbol and instrument of grace."

"Doubtless," said Bei. "Tell me, Guest Prefect, do all your Taoist stories involve the burning of bodies?"

"No, Inspector. You have merely heard one that does."

"Two, counting the cremation of your founder. Three, counting the murder of your prior. Are there others I should be aware of?"

"None come to mind, Inspector. May I remind you that our evening devotions begin quite soon?"

"Oh, yes. I am more eager than ever to meet with this mysterious young woman who carries bags of silver coins into Taoist temples."

The devotional ceremony had already begun when the guest prefect and Bei slipped past the red wooden doors of the Jade Emperor's Hall. A large, highly burnished statue of the Jade Emperor gazed coolly at them from the back of the hall, a large black beard flowing over his chest and a tapered kuei tablet held by both hands before his mouth to signify his authority. From the ceiling numerous silk hangings and banners decorated the hall and partitioned it, their red and gold colors emblazoned with embroidered red-crowned cranes, phoenixes, dragons, and ancient ideographs. A row of monks immediately in front of the Jade Emperor led the crowd of laymen packing the hall in a series of chants and prostrations, accompanied by the beating

of wooden and leather drums and ringing of bronze bells. Bei caught
the fragrance of several types of flowers intermixed with the vapors
of burning incense and scented waxes as his eyes traveled over the
crowd. It was a varied group: old and young; rich and poor; ignorant,
simple faces and learned, complex faces; those accomplishing the
prostrations with great difficulty, and those who seemed to glide from
one posture to the next. One cloaked figure, especially, seemed to
defy gravity and the mechanics of exertion as it flowed among standing, kneeling, and prostration. It was to this figure that the guest
prefect led Bei upon the conclusion of the service.

"Meiling."

The cloaked figure turned and regarded them through wide, alert
eyes whose black center seemed to glow out of the lustrous white
perimeter. She was startlingly beautiful, and Bei suppressed a desire
to sigh in admiration and surprise. There was no shyness in her gaze:
She seemed accustomed to men staring at her, and received Bei's look
with an indifference that seemed to him more neutral than cool. She
was tall for a woman, her high cheekbones and rich mouth at a level
with Bei's face. Her age was impossible to guess. Bei thought she
would be between twenty and thirty, having the fresh body of the
former and the demeanor of the latter.

"Yes, Guest Prefect?" she said, her voice full and resonant though
high-pitched, her tone respectful. Something in her tone reminded
Bei of her face; then he recognized the neutral quality again.

"I regret to disturb you after your devotions, daughter. But this
gentleman wishes to speak with you. I further regret that it is of Prior
An's death that he wishes to speak. This is Chief Inspector Bei of the
Municipal Police."

Bei had been studying her face as the old man spoke. He often read
guilt or fear in a person's eyes as he was officially introduced to them
during the course of an investigation. He detected no change in her
eyes, only a fleeting alteration of depth, as when a thin cloud floats
across the moon, a change which suggested not fear but grief.

She turned to him. "Yes?" Neutral again.

Somewhat flustered, Bei asked the old man, "Is there a more private
place where we might talk?"

"Of course. There is a room nearby." He led them to a small room
with several chairs around a plain wooden table.

"Please be seated," said Bei.

"I am comfortable standing."

A pause. "Very well. I am investigating the murder of Prior An. This necessitates learning everything about his activities that I can, in order to judge what motives might have prompted his murderers."

He paused again, then silently berated himself for his reluctance to treat this woman with the direct and clinical approach he adopted when questioning other witnesses.

"I understand your given name is Meiling. What is your surname?"

"T'ang."

"Where do you work?"

"The Shop of Ten Thousand Gems."

"On Jade Street?"

"Yes."

"Now, Miss T'ang, I must be blunt. Is it true that you and Prior An were lovers?"

She did not respond for several seconds. "I do not see that this is any of your business," she finally said.

Her answer irritated him, which made Bei feel more comfortable. He had managed to slip into the inspector-witness role with her.

"Miss T'ang—I assume it is 'Miss'?"

"Of course," icily now, with dislike coloring the former neutrality. Bei noted it with satisfaction. She was human, after all, responding as all witnesses did.

"Miss T'ang, the men responsible for the prior's murder state that they were following an old rule which prescribes death to a prior who misuses temple funds to support a mistress. You are named as that person. Please answer the question."

"If I do not?"

"Then I can take you to jail and let the magistrate put the question to you."

Her dislike was plainly evident now. "We were," she said, without a trace of emotion.

"How long had you been lovers?"

She gazed at him, calculating the consequences of refusing to answer this question. "A little over a month."

"Did the prior ever give you any money or gifts?"

Anger plainly flared in her eyes, but her voice was perfectly controlled. "No."

"You are sure of that?"

"I have no need of money or gifts."

"And did you ever give the prior money or gifts?"

"None at all," she answered, without hesitation or change in her expression.

"Really?"

"Really."

Bei decided to play Free the Tiger with her, and not to put her on her guard by revealing what the overseer had witnessed.

"How is it that you and the prior met each other?"

"I worship the Jade Emperor regularly here."

"But I saw perhaps a hundred other worshipers tonight. Surely not all of them are so . . . intimate with the prior?"

No anger revealed itself on her face. "The prior was very learned in our religion. I desired further instruction. He was a generous man and gave it to me, as he gave such further instruction to others."

"And in the course of these further instructions you fell in love?"

"Whether we loved each other is truly none of your business. In your profession, you need know nothing more than that we copulated."

It was an effective insult, stinging Bei both as a person and as a policeman. He hastily put on a cool face, and waited for his anger to subside.

"Why did you pick the White Cloud Temple for your devotions, and Prior An for your instruction?"

"This temple is near my place of employment. Just down Chu-shihk'ou Street, Inspector, onto Tsaishihk'ou, and then out Kuan'anmen'nei until I turn onto Lishilu." A trace of a smile suggested itself on her lips as she imparted the geography lesson of the city to Bei. He returned in kind.

"Correct me if I am wrong, Miss T'ang, but is not the Tung Yueh Miao Temple closer to you than this temple?"

She smiled perceptibly now, not the reaction Bei had expected. "You are correct, although it is not much closer. The White Cloud Temple has the Shrine Hall dedicated to the Jade Emperor, though, and I am particularly devoted to jade and hence the Jade Emperor."

"I see. Let me now become more specific. Were you with the prior on the night he was murdered?"

She paused. "I was."

"At what time?"

"I was in his room from dusk until nearly an hour later."

"Did you make love?"

"You may go copulate with your turtle, Inspector." She said it casually, even though it was one of the coarsest sexual insults.

Bei let his anger show. "You can let the magistrate ask you, if you wish!"

"Fine," she replied without hesitation, but with complete composure. "I promise you I will give him the same answer."

Bei sighed. He had lost his temper with witnesses before, but it had usually frightened the answer he wanted out of them, and he had never felt inferior because of his show of anger, as he did now. Damn this woman.

"Had you left his room and the temple when the monks broke into his room?"

"Yes."

"How long had you been gone?"

"Only several minutes."

"Oh, really? So you evidently knew exactly when that occurred. How did you know that?"

She stared at him levelly for several seconds. "I heard the bell and the uproar from the street, returned, and saw him die." There was no denying the grief in her eyes now, and Bei felt almost sorry for her, in spite of his former anger.

"And then?"

"Then I left."

"And returned directly to your home?"

"Yes."

"Where is that?"

"I live above the Shop of Ten Thousand Gems."

Bei could think of no more questions. "Do you know of anything else which might help us in our investigation of the prior's murder?"

"No," she answered, with a hint of a sob.

"You may go now. Thank you for your help."

She swiftly turned and vanished out the door.

Bei stood silently for a moment, savoring the conflicting moods and information the questioning had imparted to him. Then he remembered the guest prefect standing across the room. "An interesting woman," he said, feeling that something should be said.

"Doubtless," returned the guest prefect dryly, with a smile, mocking Bei. "Tell me, Inspector, why did you not press her regarding the exchange of money?"

"Because I didn't think I could unnerve or frighten her sufficiently to force her to tell the truth. I would only have let her know what we know with nothing from her in return. So instead we keep her ignorant of what we know, let her go her way freely, and observe her until she provides us with more clues."

The old man narrowed his eyes. "I see. And I believe I understand why you have returned my ten monks to me."

Bei winced, realizing he had revealed too much. Not a good afternoon, all in all, for a chief inspector. He still had absolutely no idea of why the mysterious lady who likes jade was giving the prior of a Taoist temple five hundred silver dollars, or indeed whether that had anything whatever to do with the prior's murder by the group of monks. The monks, surely, were the key here.

"When are your monks finished with their daily routine and free to wander about?"

"In the winter months, they have about half an hour free after dinner, which will be served very soon."

"And the two leaders of the group that murdered the prior are still in the temple?"

"They are."

"Then I shall shortly join my plainclothesman outside the temple." Bei was developing a liking for the intricacies of this case. "Before I do that, though, may I ask you to tell me a few things about the temple?"

"You may. Would you care to eat dinner with me?"

"Oh, no. That would be intruding too much."

"Not at all."

"But I'm sure your food is limited."

"We have enough of our plain food for one more of our modest servings."

"If you insist, then, I shall be glad to join you."

After telling a novice monk to have an extra serving provided, the guest prefect led Bei to his private rooms off the large courtyard in front of the Hall of the Four Deities, on the other side of the hall from the prior's rooms. His outer room was spartan, a large landscape painting on one wall being the only decorative touch.

"A lovely painting," remarked Bei.

"It is a scene from the Huang Shan mountains in Anhwei province, in which I have spent much time."

"Who painted it?"

"My son."

"Indeed! So you have not been a monk all your life."

"Some Taoist orders are celibate; others are not. But yes, I was fortunate enough to father him before I joined the Ch'uan Chen sect, which is a celibate one."

"The quality of the painting is quite good. Is he a professional artist now?"

"He was killed by the Japanese in 1937."

"Oh. I'm sorry."

"He lived a full and rich life, although short."

A monk brought in dinner. It consisted of a bowl of white rice for each of them, and three modest dishes from which they ate communally, bringing the contents to their rice bowl and mixing it with rice before eating it. One dish was a spicy tofu with peanuts, another was asparagus in a creamy sauce, and the third was silver fungus mixed with bamboo shoots. They were among the best dishes Bei had ever tasted.

"Your high cook is indeed accomplished."

"His skill is much overrated. I apologize for these plain dishes."

"Not at all. Do you always eat in your rooms alone?"

"All the high officials of the temple do. Our official duties take up so much time that the community gives us meal times alone."

"Tell me about the temple's history, if you would."

The old man glanced at Bei in surprise, took several large bites, and laid down his nearly empty bowl of rice.

"How long would you guess a Taoist temple has stood on this site?"

"Well, I know your temple is indeed old. Perhaps even older than the Ch'ing Dynasty. I would guess Ming Dynasty. Late Ming Dynasty, which would make you over three hundred years old."

The old man smiled. "Our actual age is four times that."

"Twelve hundred years?" Bei was incredulous. "But that would put you at the middle of the eighth century—in the T'ang Dynasty."

"Yes. The glorious Hsuan Tsung himself had a stone statue carved of the seated Lao-tzu and built a Taoist temple here around it. We were called the T'ian Chang Temple then, and were an important center of Taoism in North China for over four hundred years, through the T'ang, Sung, Liao, and Chin dynasties."

"But your buildings here are not twelve hundred years old, surely."

"No. In the early thirteenth century, in the troubled times when Genghis Khan's armies were sweeping over northern China, our T'ian Chang Temple suffered a great fire."

"So the temple was rebuilt by Kublai Khan in the 1260's as part of his construction of the Mongol capital here, I would guess," said Bei.

"Actually not. Genghis Khan was interested in creating goodwill for himself among the Taoist people and rulers of North China, so he rebuilt the temple in 1224, renamed it the T'ai Chi Palace, and persuaded the famed Master Ch'iu Changchun to move here from the Great Snow Mountains. After Ch'iu's death in 1227 and the burial of his ashes here, the temple complex was renamed the Changchun Palace.

"We then experienced two hundred years of relative quiet. When the Yungle Emperor rebuilt the city during the early Ming Dynasty in the 1420's, the temple complex was enlarged and the name was changed to the White Cloud Temple. We have again served as the center of Taoism in North China for the five hundred years since then, with relatively few major disasters."

Bei had listened closely, with growing interest. "I am impressed, Guest Prefect. And perhaps I understand better why you are able to place the murder of Prior An in a larger perspective. Tell me about Prior An."

The old man sighed as he realized that the inspector's interest in the temple was strictly professional, as was his interest in the prior. "What do you wish to know?"

"Where he was born. Where he lived before he came to White Cloud Temple. Who his friends were outside the temple. What he was interested in, other than his religion."

"I don't know a great deal about him. Our past lives are not important here. I do know he was a Chekiang person, had evidently received a very solid education in the classics, and came here in 1937 from the Yellow Dragon Temple in Hangchow, where he had been the prior for some years."

"Hangchow? Really? Was he born in Hangchow?"

"He was a Chekiang person. I don't know which city in that province. But he must have been at the temple in Hangchow a number of years to have risen to prior."

"Interesting." Perhaps he would accompany his wife to Hangchow after all.

"And what of his interests and friends outside his religion?"

The old man laughed softly. "He considered nothing outside the Tao. Everything was part of the Tao's flow. He knew quite a bit of history and literature. I remember his quoting from the *Dream of the Red Chambers,* the *Outlaws of the Marsh,* even *Gold Lotus,* which, as you know, is not polite reading for educated men and women. There was nothing he was not interested in. For such a man to be murdered by those ignorant fools who know nothing of themselves or the Tao . . ." He sat glaring into space, his old frame shaking with anger suffused with sadness.

Embarrassed by the old man's emotion, Bei averted his eyes. But his mind was racing. Prior An, a Chekiang person, perhaps from Hangchow itself. There until 1937.

They resumed eating in silence. "You know nothing of any friends he had outside the temple?" Bei asked after a minute.

The guest prefect was tiring of Bei's questions. "As prior, he met many people in the community, arranging funeral services, conducting temple business, and many other duties. It is impossible to list these people."

Bei pursed his lips. There had to be a better way than tracking down every person the prior had talked to in the past six months.

They finished the meal. "Tell me, Guest Prefect: What happened to Hsuan Tsung's statue of Lao-tzu?"

"It is here still. After twelve hundred years it is still here."

"Sometime I would like to see it. But now I must rush off and take my post outside, in case any of our dissident monks take a stroll after dinner. Do not bother to show me out. By now I can find my way perfectly well."

Even though it was barely four o'clock, the late-December sky was beginning to grow dimmer as Bei took a seat on a bench some thirty meters from the temple's entrance and pulled a newspaper out of his coat pocket. The cold intensified as dusk waxed, and just as he was about to stand up and walk around to warm himself, he saw the dissident monk emerge whose tight story had marked him in Bei's mind as one of the leaders. The man, a corpulent figure whose long hair was sloppily pinned in his topknot, walked rapidly by Bei without a glance at the figure obscured by the newspaper in the gathering gloom. As Bei followed at a distance, the blue-robed figure walked east in the alley fronting the entrance to the temple complex, away from White Cloud Road, and turned south on the first major street in this direction, Lishilu. Some four blocks down Lishilu was a small park wedged between the street and the sidewalk, with several rows of benches and bare areas where grass and flowers grew in the summer.

Bei saw the monk sit down on one of the benches next to a slim figure who appeared to be in uniform, although their backs were to him and in the gloom he could not see the second figure as well as he wished. They appeared to talk for a few seconds. Just as Bei was about to approach them to get a better look at the second figure, they rose and the other strode rapidly away into the dark as the monk retraced his steps toward Bei, stuffing something into his robe. Silently Bei cursed his luck that in order to quickly follow the stranger he would have to reveal himself to the approaching monk, who would without doubt warn his confederate and give him ample time to make his escape in the dark. Bei let the monk pass him, reluctantly noted the complete blackness into which the confederate had long since disappeared, then followed the monk back to the temple. He signaled his plainclothesman who had stayed behind, and the two of them converged upon the stout figure as he approached the temple entrance. The temple gateman joined them at another signal from Bei.

44

"What is this?" demanded the monk nervously as he saw himself surrounded.

"Who was that you talked to on Lishilu just now?" Bei demanded.

"I didn't talk to anyone."

"Don't lie to me. You know me, don't you? You know what happens to people who lie to a chief inspector? I just saw you with my own eyes talking to that man. What did you talk about?"

"The weather. It's cold."

"You're lying again. You went there to meet him. He was waiting for you. In fact, he gave you a package. Let's see it."

Now thoroughly alarmed, the monk looked around and calculated his chances of escape. He was immediately grabbed firmly by the gateman and the plainclothesman.

Bei reached into the struggling monk's robe, found an inside pocket, and pulled out a small cloth sack. The sound of metal came from the sack. Nearly two dozen silver coins fell out as the sack was opened.

"Weather? It looks more like payment for a service. Now what service could you have performed for that man? Not perhaps the murder of Prior An? Admit it—this is payment for the prior's murder!" Bei slapped the man's face soundly as he shouted the charge. The blow had the intended effect. Securely held by the other two, the monk was plainly frightened of receiving a beating, as well as unnerved by the revelation of his crime.

Speaking in a menacing tone, Bei pushed his advantage. "The magistrate's men are expert torturers. You know that, don't you? You go to them next, and they'll get it out of you. But it will hurt, you know how it will hurt, don't you?"

Bei's tone changed to solicitude. "Save yourself all that pain. Just let me know who that man is. I'll put in a good word for you. We remember our friends. You help me and I'll help you."

A menacing edge came back as he curtly said to the monk, "Well? What about it?"

"You'll help me? You'll not let the magistrate's men get to me?" the monk blurted, his voice breaking with fear.

"Of course. Of course."

"It'll go easier for me? I'll probably get out quick?"

"It will go easier for you. The more you tell me the easier it will be for you."

"Good, good. I'll talk."

Bei motioned the gatekeeper to leave them.

"Who was that man?"

"I don't know his name. He just asked me to do a job."

"When?"

"Nearly six months ago. He came to me, said he understood I'd been unfairly treated by the prior. Said he'd pay me good money, silver, to get the prior into trouble." The monk gazed forlornly at the bag of silver in Bei's hand. "Can I have some of the silver back?"

"Maybe. Why did he want trouble for the prior?"

"I don't know. I don't know anything about the man, really. He's spooky, he scares me, really. But he gave me some silver at the first, and promised a lot more."

"Did he tell you to kill the prior?"

"Not at first. Just trouble. But it was difficult to cause much trouble. I'd already been expelled from the temple once, years ago, and they watched me close, and would expel me again. And the prior had brainwashed nearly all the monks. It was only a couple of weeks ago that he showed up again and suggested the burning idea. I didn't want to do it, I swear."

"But you did."

"He made me. Said he'd tell on me and get me expelled again if I didn't do it. I can't be expelled again. I had spent all the silver he'd given me at first. I can't do anything for a living. I'd starve outside the monastery."

"What was the man's name?"

"I don't know. Really, I don't. He's strange. I didn't want to get to know anything about him. He just gave me silver. We met on that bench every couple of months, and he'd ask me what trouble I'd caused, and he'd suggest things to me, and then he told me to murder the prior, to burn him. I didn't want to."

"What about the other monk. He was in on this too?"

"Yes, yes, Fenji. He was actually in charge of all this. I just followed his orders."

Bei laughed at the man's pathetic eagerness to lessen his role in whatever way he could. Then he pressed on, taking advantage of the monk's present state.

"Where does this fellow live?"

46

"I don't know. I only saw him at the bench."

"Is he a soldier?"

"Sometimes he wears soldiers' clothes, sometimes he doesn't. He doesn't talk like a soldier. He talks smart. He talks like you, Inspector."

"Why did he want you to kill the prior?"

"I don't know. He never said why. First it was causing trouble, then later he said we should kill him. Actually he told Fenji. I just helped. Fenji was in charge."

"What else about the man? Any scars, anything to identify him?"

"No, nothing. He . . . he was strange. Talked smart. But . . . like he was never where his body was, like his eyes were far away somewhere else, looking through his body at you." The monk shuddered. "I hated to look at his eyes. I avoided them." Another shudder. "You know what I think, Inspector?" Acute embarrassment joined abject fear in the monk, and he seemed reluctant to say it. Finally he whispered in an intense voice. "He is a baleful star, Inspector. A baleful star, come to cause us harm. I couldn't help but obey him, Inspector. Against my will, he forced me to help Fenji kill the prior. A baleful star!"

The man was shivering so badly he could hardly stand, and began to sob. Bei called the gateman back and instructed him to get the monk Fenji, and told his plainclothesman to tie both monks up, and get them to jail. Then Bei wearily climbed into his waiting ricksha and instructed the man to take him back to his Chunghai Lake office. It would be a long report to the magistrate. And he was not any nearer to knowing the why of it all.

The town was dark, dark as his village. But so different. So many women, although none as lovely as her. Her legs, her shoulders. And her neck. Especially her neck, so slender, so high. White, curved, slender, high. Don't think of her. You have a job, you are important. He needs you. He will punish this city and all its deceitful women. So many, everywhere, leading you to wantonness, with their slim necks. No—don't think of that. There's some, there. Oh, they are lovely. But deceitful. Not so lovely as her, but like her. Wanton. No, she wasn't wanton. Not her. So high, so white . . . You must do it, after all. You must. She requires it, to end her restlessness.

December 28

He saw her framed in the ginkgo trees surrounding the small meditation grove. It was his favorite spot in the entire Purple Mountain complex, of which he was abbot. Meiling sat as straight as ever in the traditional posture in the grove, but tears were streaming from her closed eyes, and her breathing was deep. She appeared small, wrapped in her yellow quilted robe under the ancient trees, like a precious fruit that had dropped from one of the branches sharply angling off the trunk. He stood watching her, and knew again the pain of a father for a wounded offspring.

Soon she was finished. When he saw her eyes open, he walked quietly into the grove and dried her damp face with the sleeve of his dark blue robe. He stroked her hair, which streamed black over the gold collar of the robe.

"Still the pain, eh?"

"Yes, Father." She breathed deeply again.

"It will ease, child. Considerably. And soon."

"It has only been three days since he died."

"A pity you had to witness it."

"No. It was right. Else it would have seemed unreal, and I would not have truly believed it, him not bursting with life still."

He continued stroking her hair as the morning sunlight streamed feebly through the ginkgo's bare branches.

"When your mother died, also in violence, I did not eat for two days, could not sleep for four. But after seven days I could meditate without weeping."

A thrush flew from the tree to the ground at the edge of the clearing and began energetically poking its bill in the underbrush.

"He told me once that a part of him still mourned for his wife and son after twenty-one years, that he would never regain that part of him."

"Yes. But, of course, new life arises. Sometimes from the death itself."

She sat, staring at the thrush, then looked up into his face. "He died in violence, Father. His wife and son died in violence. My mother died in violence. When will it stop?"

He stood silent, looking at the clean angles of the branches coming off the trunk. Somehow their crispness comforted him, and he loved winter because then he could see the ginkgo branches clearly.

"I don't know. It is our fate to live in a violent period, my child. Chinese against Japanese—that took your mother. Chinese against Chinese—that took his wife and son. And now it has taken him."

"But why, Father? It could not have been just the jealousy of ignorant monks. But what?"

"I don't know, child. I would indeed like to find out. His death has hurt our work, just as the critical days approach. As well as hurting you. But it is very difficult for us. I do not know that we shall ever get to the root of it."

"I will get to the root of it. I will avenge his death."

"No, child!" He spoke fiercely. "Don't let the desire for revenge lodge in you. It kills the capacity for new life, and takes you as surely as if you had also died. Banish it!"

She lowered her head, but proudly. "I . . . do not know that I want to banish it."

"Child! It is—"

"And I am no longer a child," she interrupted with feeling.

He sighed. "That is true enough." He moved away from her slightly. "And it is true also that the desire for revenge cannot be banished. It must seep out, of its own. It must be crowded out by health and new life. Come. Will you at least do the Dance of the Water's Surface with this old busybody?"

She arose in a graceful motion, and walked with him silently through the trees to the T'ai Chi Ch'uan courtyard. They positioned themselves facing each other, raised their arms until their fingers touched, then brought them back to their bodies in a slow circular motion across the face and chest. Her left hand sailed back to the front as did his right, nearly touching, while her right hand executed a circular

49

block to the right, as did his left. Her body shifted and she unfurled a sweeping arc with her right hand as she turned to face that direction, her left hand "grabbing air" to anchor the movement. He simultaneously executed the mirror image of her movements.

It was one of the most difficult and absorbing of the T'ai Chi Ch'uan rituals, two partners performing the stylized movements in the mirror image of the other, beginning together, sweeping apart, then coming together throughout the entire sequence of over a hundred moves. It added a fifth dimension to the three spatial and one temporal in which T'ai Chi usually occurred: the reflected dimension of perfectly mirrored distance and timing between two moving bodies. The smoothly gliding blue and yellow robes in the courtyard incarnated the interplay of yin and yang, a working out of the constantly shifting balances of strength and yielding, movement and stillness, hope and despair, pleasure and pain. As she turned and advanced, whirled and retreated, struck and parried, joining every neuron, bone, and muscle into a finely integrated whole, she knew the desire to avenge her lover's death was being crowded out. She watched it diminish, but knew it would not extinguish, knew it would grow again, knew that violence was not merely of this time but of all times, and that she could wield it as well as any.

Bei sat at his desk, finishing up the report he had started the previous night. He sipped his midmorning tea. Yuan had been sent early that morning to look into the murder of a courtesan in the Flower House section off Ch'ienmen Street last night. The murder of a common prostitute was usually noted and then dropped, but a courtesan—a woman trained in the arts of poetry and music as well as love, and housed in an exclusive brothel—was a different matter altogether. It should have been Chang's case but Chang was busy with three other cases. The whole city was unraveling, and he had fewer men than normal. He shook his head as he wrote. A sound across the room caught his attention.

"Oh. Good morning."

"Most sorry to bother you, Chief Inspector. My uncle forgot his lunch, so I am bringing it to him. This is his desk, I believe?"

Yuan's niece looked considerably fresher than she had yesterday. Her hair was neatly arranged in bangs and reached her shoulder in back. There was no weariness in her movements today; indeed, her figure seemed more trim than frail, and a certain strength suggested itself in her body. The young recuperate quickly, Bei reflected. The hint of vulnerability remained in her face, though. A pretty face, thought Bei.

"You are a devoted—" he almost said "wife," but caught himself. "A devoted niece to come here with your uncle's lunch."

"He is being most kind to me. I would not be filial if I did not serve him. He is the only family I have."

Bei approved the Confucian sentiment, and admired the courage suggested in her voice and words.

"Yuan has told me that you have had a most unfortunate family history. I admire your courage in surviving it so well."

"I have an obligation to my ancestors to carry my name proudly. And when I marry, to honor my husband's ancestors as well."

"With so clear an understanding of your duties, you will have no difficulty securing a husband," said Bei, noting the polished tone of her words and remembering that she had received a good education before the Japanese came.

"I am indeed a woman, with a woman's needs. It is best to marry."

Bei raised his eyebrows. She sounded more like a coarse peasant now; educated ladies never referred to their physical needs. He politely said, "Yes, it is best to marry," as he looked at her again. There was an interesting mixture of peasant and patrician in her air as well as her words. With her family's history, she would have needed the peasant's sturdy strength to survive.

"But marrying the right person is crucial, is it not?" she said.

Bei put down his pen, glad to exchange the report for a conversation with this strangely forward yet vulnerable girl from Shansi.

"Of course. I understand that your sister married poorly."

Her eyes glowed. "She did not marry at all. She was sold to a worthless son of a worthless landlord. She was his property, not his wife."

Bei berated himself for not remembering Yuan's story correctly.

"His property, and his friends' property. Her death released her from an intolerable situation." She turned away from him to hide her emotion. "But then, in peasant society a wife is her husband's property. So does it matter?"

Bei was uncomfortable at blundering into this conversation. But the girl's distress and spirit touched him.

"It must be difficult to have received an education in the classics, then to be reduced to a peasant's poverty again."

"It does strange things to you. It made my sister eager to be sold to a landlord's son." Her back was still to Bei. "And it made me entirely too forward, especially with strangers," she said with a smile as she turned around. She bowed in the old manner of a courtesan bowing to her master, clearly acting out a role. "You will pardon my impropriety, honored sir. It has been my pleasure to speak with you. Good day." With a final flourish she glided out of the room.

Bei sat, not knowing what to make of her. But he had enjoyed the episode, somehow. He turned back to the report, worked on it for another hour, then sent it by messenger to the magistrate. He then made a phone call to General Fu's office, talked with Zhou Peifeng for several minutes, and hung up the phone as Yuan walked into the office.

"Any problems with the courtesan murder?" asked Bei.

"Well, some things are clear. She's dead. She's a courtesan, and a relatively high-class one, too. But there are some strange things. In fact, several strange things. I think it's over my head, Inspector. You'd better take a look. I've left everything as it was."

There were several areas of "Flower Houses" in Peking. The oldest ones were in the Chinese "Outer City" south of the old wall separating it from the "Inner City" where the Manchu overlords had resided for the last three centuries. Ch'ienmen Street was the main thoroughfare in this part of the city. Shops lined its length, as well as the side alleys branching off it, of which the first three leading to the west were most renowned: Lantern Street, Jade Street, and Silk Street. The high-class Flower Houses were clustered close to Ch'ienmen Street, the low-class ones farther away from the thoroughfare.

Yuan led Bei down Lantern Street and through an alley, arriving soon at the "Lao Soochow," a two-story house surrounded by a high wall of red bricks. The "Mother" of the house met them at the door, a plump figure in traditional Chinese dress, wringing her hands in agitation.

"This is the chief inspector himself? We are honored, sir. This is dreadful, dreadful. But please do not make too much of it, sir. It might hurt business."

"Many courtesans are killed every year, Mother."

"But only in the low-class houses, Chief Inspector. Rarely in a true Flower House in the old tradition. Ours is an exclusive House, Inspector. Only the best girls here, although thank goodness Plum Blossom was only from Shansi and not one of our Hangchow or Soochow flowers. But, of course, it is dreadful still."

"Where is the body, Yuan?"

"Still in her room, exactly as I found it."

"Let's go there, please. I will talk to you later, Mother."

They walked past a series of small private dining rooms and ascended the stairs to the second floor. The room was around a turn in the hall, toward the back of the house. Yuan opened the door for Bei.

A bed occupied the middle of the room, which was barely three meters square. A washstand stood against one wall, a stringed instrument against another. The body on the bed was completely covered with a red silk comforter, which was tucked under the body.

"You arranged the comforter this way?" Bei asked Yuan.

"No. It was like this when I arrived. I pulled the top down to verify that she was dead, then replaced it as I found it. The mother swears that this was the way they found her early this morning."

Bei stared at the figure. "It looks like . . . like a burial shroud, does it not?" Yuan didn't answer. "Or at least a ceremony of some sort." He breathed deeply as he walked around the bed. Blood, of course. Perfume. Sweat. Semen. And something else very faint. Flowers. Gardenias, probably. He looked around for a vase. None. But what would flowers be doing here in December, anyway? "Did the Mother remove anything at all from the room?"

"No."

"Go ask her if there were flowers in here. Gardenias. Or a chest with dried flowers in it."

As Yuan left, Bei looked slowly about the room once more, and smelled deeply. Yes. Gardenias.

He next studied the wooden floor, especially on either side of the bed. No dirt or dust. The place was kept too clean. As he stepped to the bed, Yuan came back. "Nothing has been touched, much less removed."

Bei nodded, and gingerly lifted the comforter away from the head. As he did so, the head rolled suddenly to its right side at a grotesque angle. It was attached to the trunk only by the vertebral column, nearly all the soft tissue having been severed. Bei pushed the dangling head back to the correct position.

"Throat slit. Nearly completely."

"Yes. Not the usual way to kill a girl, is it?" said Yuan.

Bei slowly removed the rest of the comforter. The girl was naked except for a bracelet and several rings. Her arms were folded onto her chest. There were no bruises on her body. Bei returned his attention to her throat. "Take notes please, Yuan." Yuan pulled a pad and pen from his coat pocket.

"Young female of medium height and weight. Body lying on its back. Deep slash wound on throat. Completely severed on right side, victim's left, down to vertebrae, wound more shallow on victim's right side, only ventral skin and muscles cut there. Hair shows evidence of being gathered together on victim's right side. No bruises or marks on head." As Yuan scribbled, Bei moved down the body.

"No bruises or marks on shoulders or torso. Arms folded up on chest, in burial position." He lifted the arms. "Rigor mortis advanced in arms."

He pulled out his magnifying glass. "Evidence of semen on thighs and sheet. No bruises or marks on legs." He lifted her right leg. "Rigor mortis also advanced in legs."

He stepped back. As Yuan finished writing, Bei gestured for him to come around to the side of the bed he was on. "Let's lift the body off the bed onto the floor and see if anything is under it." They did so, Bei cradling the head in the crook of his left arm.

"Take this down, Yuan. Large blood stain covers most of bed. Smaller stain on victim's right side of bed, thigh region. This stain thicker on peripheral margin, thinner and tapering towards center of bed."

He turned to the adjacent wall. "Blood splattered also on wall beyond victim's head, and floor in between." He shook his head. "Lots of blood."

They lifted the body back up to the bed, Bei again reinforcing the head, and replaced the comforter.

"What do you make of it, Inspector?"

"It's unusual, to be sure. A left-handed man, with powerful arms, cuts the throat of a courtesan shortly after having sex with her, perhaps during the climax itself. He wipes the knife clean while still atop the victim. He then arranges her body carefully, almost courteously, in a ceremonial position and covers it up with a comforter, again carefully and courteously. He leaves, taking with him a bunch of fresh or, more likely, dried gardenias."

Bei turned around and looked at the water basin. "After washing the blood off his hands."

He took one last look and smell around the room. "I'll talk to Mother now, downstairs."

The Mother was still wringing her hands.

"Oh, Chief Inspector, I—"

"A few answers is all we require from you, Mother," Bei interrupted her curtly. "Who greeted this man as he came in last night?"

"I did. I make it a firm habit to—"

"Describe him, please."

"Oh, well. He was . . . just normal, really. Normal hair, normal soldier's uniform—"

"So he was a soldier, then."

"Oh, yes. Most of our visitors are soldiers, what with the siege and all. Officers, mind you, not common soldiers."

"Was he tall, short? Fat, thin?"

"No, normal, not fat, certainly. Handsome, in an unsettling sort of way."

"How so, 'unsettling'?"

"Oh, I don't know. Handsome, but unsettling."

"Did he speak like a Hopei person?"

"Oh, no. A Shansi accent, or maybe Honan. That's probably why he asked for a Shansi girl. I told him we had plenty of Hangchow and Soochow girls who were very talented, but he would have none of it. Wanted a Shansi girl. Luckily for me I had one, one we give out when the Hangchow and Soochow girls are all taken, and we tell her not to talk much."

"What else did he say?"

"Nothing, really. If the men don't want to talk, I know enough to—"

"Yes. Anything else about him?"

"No. He looked very fine, really. Not by any means the roughest we've had. But at least it was only the Shansi girl. You have no idea how expensive the Hangchow and Soochow girls are, and the airs they put on. But I expect this'll quiet them down some."

"Yes. Lucky for you. Allow no one in the room, Mother. The morgue will pick the body up soon."

"I hope so. What with the scarcity of meat these days, I wouldn't be surprised to see someone steal her body. I had a cousin arrive from Manchuria just last week; it is so bad up there that a person isn't safe alone at night. Why, she knew a person who found a fingernail in her meat dumpling. And—"

"Thank you, Mother. Let us know if you remember anything more about the man."

"I will, Chief Inspector. Come again, by yourself, in more pleasant circumstances. We would be honored to have you."

Bei sat with his two dinner guests in the formal garden which filled the courtyard at the south end of his small villa, glad for their diverting company after his afternoon's activities. Ho Szuyuan, former mayor of Peking and before that governor of Shandong province, had been Bei's constant boyhood companion before going to France for much of his education. A handsome, urbane man in his mid-forties, Ho was the opposite in some respects of the other guest, Professor Chang Tungsun, a short, peppery old man who had also been born into the elite ruling class, but in central China—Chiang Nan—rather than the north. Chang had been one of the country's most prominent intellectuals and political independents—more of a gadfly, in truth—for most of the last three decades, and had many contacts among the Communist intellectuals. Bei and Ho had taken philosophy classes from Professor Chang at Yenching University, where their intelligence and culture had caught the old man's attention and, soon, his friendship.

The three sat in wicker chairs facing the rock "mountain" and its surrounding pool in the corner of the courtyard, helping themselves to watermelon seeds.

"So how are your classes coming now that you are part of the new liberated China, Professor?" asked Bei. Yenching University was located some ten kilometers northwest of Peking's city walls, and had been "liberated" by the Communists when the siege was imposed.

"The university resembles a propaganda factory more than a place of learning, I'm afraid. I'm teaching mainly Marxism, which the students are very eager to learn." He paused. "It is rather strange, I will admit, to be able to come into the city here from a Communist area. Life is surprisingly normal outside the city, with no real checkpoints set up by the Communists. Getting in and out of the city is infinitely more difficult than moving about outside the city."

"I assume Fu has given you some sort of official pass to get in and out through the city gates," commented Bei.

Chang nodded.

"He will expect something of you for that, Professor," pointed out Ho.

"Of course. He will ask me to contact the Communists for him when he is ready to negotiate, and I will be happy to oblige him. The civil war has bled our country long enough."

"I've heard," interjected Bei, "that Fu has already contacted Lin Piao once, that they arrived at an understanding, but that the agreement was somehow aborted, leaving Fu and Lin Piao suspicious of each other and reluctant to explore any further negotiations."

"I know nothing of that. Mayor Ho?"

Ho shrugged. "I've heard rumors of it. That some such agreement was reached, and that Lin Piao betrayed it by annihilating Fu's brigade guarding the Nank'ou Pass route to Kalgan."

"Which hurt Fu far more than just the loss of a brigade," observed Bei, "since that cut off the only link between his new base here and his old base in Inner Mongolia, where the bulk of his troops are still located."

Ho stared into the sky. "I believe I also remember some peculiar tales from back before Lin Piao's troops got here from Manchuria and imposed the siege. Something about Fu waiting outside the city in the Fengtai railyards for a huge shipment of American arms and ammunition being shipped up from Tientsin, when one of Lin Piao's advance elements swooped in and captured the arms and nearly captured Fu as well."

"Quite a story," admitted Chang. "But I've heard dozens, some even as outlandish as this one. Who knows what to believe?"

"Indeed," admitted Ho. "All we know is that Fu dislikes and distrusts Lin Piao intensely, that he has for two weeks refused to even open negotiations with him." He cocked an eye at Chang. "It is true that no negotiations have occurred, is it not, my 'politically independent friend with connections to the Communists'?"

Chang laughed. "Not through me, at any rate." He became serious. "Nor through anyone I know of. And that is serious. If Fu refuses to talk, for whatever reason, then that means only two outcomes are possible: a long siege, with mass starvation in this city; or Lin Piao storms the city before it starves, and destroys it in the process."

They glumly contemplated the alternatives. "No chance of the Nationalists mounting a counteroffensive?" ventured Bei.

Chang and Ho sighed. Ho spoke. "Chiang Kaishek did his best with the American-trained Burma divisions in October. Landed them on the Manchurian coast, and sent them toward Mukden. Lin Piao surrounded them, and they promptly surrendered, with all their armor. Then Mukden fell. And last week Kalgan fell, and Fu's army there was mauled. No, friend. Here in North China, Peking is a Nationalist island in an advancing red sea. We, and Tientsin."

The darkness had overwhelmed the garden as they spoke. Bei picked up a pebble and tossed it into the frozen pool. They all watched it skid across the ice.

"Of course you're right," Bei finally said. "I find it so hard to face because . . . because it seems to me that more is retreating than the Kuomintang party and their Nationalist government. That something much more important is being swept aside by the Communists. I feel somehow that our whole Chinese culture is being threatened, that everything of value our people have managed to build and develop and refine in four thousand years is about to be broken apart and disappear."

A sadness enveloped all of them as they sat in the garden. The bare limbs of the large pear tree to their right clattered in a sudden cold wind from the north. A few last withered leaves floated down onto the pool's ice.

"You may be right, Bei," Chang spoke softly. "I really don't know. But my friends among the Communists are still Chinese. They know about the old culture, they—"

"They are Communists!" shouted Bei, embarrassing them all by his vehemence. "I'm sorry. But Chang, they base their entire belief structure on a Western philosophy. They ridicule Confucius. They consciously wish to sweep away every vestige of the traditional social order. What's left that's Chinese? What's left?"

Another silence. "I don't know, Bei." He shrugged.

"Nor do I, my honored Inspector," said Ho gently. "But all is not gone yet. Chiang Nan is still held. We sit in a lovely garden here, lovely even in the winter. And usually our host serves one of his excellent green teas before dinner."

Bei laughed sadly. "Of course. I have neglected my duties as host, even while waxing dramatic over the imminent demise of our glorious culture. You are right. Let us enjoy what culture we have, while we have it." He walked over to the study behind them and pulled a bell rope. Shortly the servant girl brought a tray and set it down on a bench fronting the frozen pool.

"What do we have tonight?" inquired Ho, a trifle more heartily than any of them felt.

"In honor of my worthy wife's upcoming departure for Hangchow, Dragon Well tea from the hills west of that city."

As he spoke, he took the kettle of boiling water and poured it into the teapot containing the tea leaves. "We must get the water onto the leaves while it's still hot, my old friends."

Ho reached down and upended the glass timer. "This is your four-minute timer, I presume?"

"You're becoming a regular connoisseur, Mayor. Four for green, three for red."

Chang and Ho helped themselves to more watermelon seeds. When the four minutes were up, Bei poured the tea into a second, insulated pot, thus removing the leaves and terminating the infusion process. Then he poured from the second pot into delicate white cups, which he handed his guests.

"That is a lovely gold," admitted Ho.

"Lustrous," said Chang.

"I have only seen this golden luster once before," Ho murmured. "In France, many years ago. We had motored to Germany and purchased a fine white wine there, a Beerenauslese. It shone in the glass just as this shines."

"But you were younger then, my friend, and perceived such qualities more readily," added Chang.

"We have all been younger, and more full of hope," admitted Bei.

"My only source of youth and hope now is my children," sighed Ho, settling back and cupping his hands around the tea to warm them. "But I do feel young around them. Especially my youngest, Mingyu. Bright Jade. She is truly named."

"I know what you mean," said Chang. "Except I get it from my students. They are a constant source of energy, enthusiasm, and freshness."

"Even when they are studying Marxism?" remarked Bei somewhat dourly, leaning forward to pour more tea for them all.

"Especially when they are studying Marxism. I tell you, Inspector, they are positively bursting with hope and confidence for the New China."

"I'm afraid I prefer the Old China," Bei declared.

"For that matter, I prefer it too," said Ho.

The friends' imminent descent into a glum reverie was mercifully interrupted by the servant girl's announcement that dinner was being served. The three gratefully rose and walked past the study and a smaller courtyard to the dining room, where they joined their wives.

They sat down with the ladies to several plates of cold dishes, took up the chopsticks provided, and all began to help themselves to sliced fermented eggs, roasted peanuts, pickled vegetables, pigs'-feet jelly, and thin-sliced jellyfish skin in vinegar and soy sauce. As they ate, the conversation drifted along pleasantly, with Madame Ho mentioning her children.

60

"Mayor Ho has admitted to us that Bright Jade is a rich source of youth to him, Madame Ho," said Bei.

"What he means is that his youngest daughter gives him ample excuse to vent his youthful caprices," she rejoined, setting the table to laughter. "You should see them playing 'guessing fingers' and making faces at each other."

"There are some aspects of having a young daughter, though, that are not so merry," interjected Ho. "The siege has unsettled her—I do think young children are most sensitive to the social atmosphere around them—so she regularly joins Madame Ho and me in our bed at some point during the night. Which makes things very crowded, what with all her kicking and tossing and turning."

"So my honorable husband usually retreats to the study and sleeps on the sofa, leaving me to receive the bruises," added Madame Ho.

"Inspector, I want to congratulate you for obtaining a permit from the general for Madame Bei to return to her home city of Hangchow in these difficult times," said Madame Chang, a self-composed lady of considerable learning herself.

"He volunteered the permit, actually. But I am nevertheless delighted that my worthy wife is able to return home for a visit. I fear I have not made her as happy as I had wished to be able to." He turned his gaze to Jinglo. "I want nothing so much as her happiness."

Amid murmurs of "Well said" from around the table, she reached out and touched his hand. "You are a most excellent husband," she said, and meant it at that moment.

"We have been expressing our envy of her," said Madame Ho, "going south to Chiang Nan and wearing silk and satin again, eating rice and delicacies every meal."

"She will doubtless miss the north wind and the loess dust after a day or two of the warm breezes off West Lake," Mayor Ho said with a straight face, which set everyone laughing again.

"Truly," declared Madame Bei, "I will miss all of you, and my husband."

"Then don't go!" Chang suggested. "Stay with us, our dust, our cold, our millet soup, our bandits on every side. Did not Confucius say that adversity builds strength?"

All except Madame Bei laughed loudly, the laugh of northerners glorifying in their hardships.

"We have only one trait that you Chiang Nan people truly might envy," said Ho, looking at Chang and Madame Bei. "We have history. The history of China is the story of the north. This very city, Peking, the capital of all of China the last seven hundred years under the Yuan, Ming, and Ch'ing; of half of China for three hundred years before that under the Liao and Chin. One thousand years of glory and glorious deeds, of wealth and beautiful arts and crafts."

"One thousand years," Madame Bei interrupted, "of blood. And death. Of burning cities. Of betrayals. Of sieges." The table grew quiet. "You can have it all, Mayor Ho. I will take the silks and satins and delicacies of Chiang Nan, the gardens of Soochow, the breeze off West Lake, and let you have all the rest."

Chang smoothed over the embarrassment. "True enough, Madame Bei. History comes with a price. I am a Chiang Nan person myself, as you know, and there is much to be said for the south as well as the north. We can all agree that China benefits from both. United."

"Which is hard to conceive of at the present," Bei said laconically, "so let us instead concentrate on our rough and uncultured northern dishes." He had signaled the servant, and she wheeled in a tray laden with hot dishes and placed them in the center of the round table to the accompaniment of exclamations of pleasure from all. Shrimp sautéed in their shells, pork with bamboo shoots, tofu with peas, broiled chicken with peanuts, fried chicken carved into bite-sized pieces, scallops with scallions, large "lion's-head" meatballs, and pork shreds with cabbage, all suffused with the pungent odors of ginger and garlic.

"Eight Big Bowls!" exclaimed Chang. "We have an early New Year's dinner here!"

Bei beamed. "I could not bear to celebrate the lunar New Year without my wife, so we celebrate it tonight, a month early." He picked up the glass of wine beside his plate. "A toast: to a New Year, and better times for us all—" he looked at Mayor Ho—"and our families, especially young daughters."

The rest of the party emptied their glasses as he did his.

"I wonder what the new year will see here," mused Chang. "Much can happen in a month."

"I just hope it is over, regardless what it is," said Madame Ho.

"Unless it is the destruction of the city," said Ho quietly.

"You surely don't think that could happen?" cried Madame Chang.

Ho raised his eyebrows, wrinkling his brow. "At this point, anything could happen. We simply can't tell. It all depends on two men: Fu Tsoyi and Lin Piao."

An awkward silence ensued, during which they all devoted themselves to the food.

"Well, regardless of what happens, I am going to start chopping pork, cabbage, ginger, and scallions tomorrow for my *chiaotse*," said Madame Ho. "It is certainly cold enough to keep them frozen in our storeroom until the New Year."

"There is the spirit of northerners, Madame Bei," said Chang. "Her city under siege, no electricity, little water, the coldest weather in memory, and the mayor's wife is preparing her New Year's *chiaotse* as she has for decades!" Madame Ho reddened as everyone else laughed. The remainder of the evening passed in pleasant conversation and dedicated eating.

After his guests had departed and his wife had retired, Bei sat alone in the garden. The new moon cast no light on the ancient city, and the pear tree and rock "mountain" in Bei's garden loomed darkly in the starlight. He savored the tea from a fresh pot—black tea now, to aid the digestion. The hollow bursts of faraway artillery shells and the staccato rattle of machine guns occasionally broke the silence enveloping the city.

His garden served as retreat and source of renewal for Bei—the closest thing he had to Ho's young daughter and Chang's students, although he had been embarrassed to mention it earlier. The elements of his garden made concrete for him the civilizing imposition of coherence by humans upon the naturally chaotic world. The high red walls which defined the garden. The covered corridor leading to it and around it. The carefully crafted artificial piling of stones to form a "mountain." The small pond surrounded by a rock border. The tall T'aihu stone carefully selected for its ruggedness and its pitch when struck, and positioned in the perfect open spot. Humans crafting nature, imposing their own order and artistry upon nature's raw material, to produce a place of beauty and repose. A miniature microcosm of what the world could be. If wars and bandits didn't interrupt the civilizing activity of the Chinese culture.

He shook his head and let his eyes wander over the dark lines of the T'aihu stone, examining the new contours created by the faint starlight. He would miss Jinglo. Tonight had been pleasant. He loved her and knew she loved him. But they had ceased to be able to give each other joy. Or even comfort. So sad. So many sad things in the world.

He refilled his teacup, and noted the dark, bloodred color of the tea. Like the trouser of the soldier he had seen on his way home this afternoon. A young man, on a cart pulled by two other young men, with a bloody shred of trouser where his left leg had been. War is physically hardest on the young. And mentally hardest on the old. Hard for everyone.

He thought of his brother, also young, also a soldier, now in Nanking. He had courted Jinglo also, and was her age. But she had chosen Bei, for his culture and his promise. Perhaps that had been a mistake. But at least he had not chosen to be a soldier. Good iron is not made into nails.

He swirled his cup, enjoying the luster of the liquid in the white cup. It reminded him of the luster of the Taoist girl Meiling's eyes. She had been bothering him all day. He had lost his composure while questioning her yesterday. He had lost his composure before with other people, but somehow it hadn't mattered then. She was a strange one. The whole case was strange. But somehow it intrigued him, and it provided him a source of energy, of hope almost. He had phoned Zhou Peifeng that morning and obtained permission to accompany Jinglo to Hangchow, in order to delve into Prior An's background there. Why did someone want the fat monk to kill the prior? What did the names in the prior's booklet signify? Why had Fu taken the booklet? And why did the girl give the prior five hundred silver dollars? Where could she get that much silver? Did she have anything to do with whoever hired the monk?

He took a sip of the warm liquid, savoring the body of it, the essential oils of the fermentation. He swirled it in the cup again. Such luster. Such eyes. Neutral, yet attentive. Such a flow, from kneeling to standing to prostration, like water. He dozed off, as random images surfaced in his receding consciousness. *She swiftly turned. As he sat up in his coffin, the suitor vanished. In the old days, it would have been your obligation to marry her. A vulnerable face. And then he hanged himself. Taking with him only the fan. But marrying the right person is crucial, is it not? She kicks and tosses and turns so. Like his eyes were far away, looking through his body at you.*

Fu woke with a yell, sitting up bathed in sweat as the cry echoed through his room in the Winter Palace. Immediately he felt to his left. Yes. Slender arms. Muscled. But soft. He felt her thighs. Yes. Full of life, giving life. His breathing came more slowly.

"Chochow again?" asked Meilu sleepily.

"Yes," answered Fu after a pause. He took several deep breaths.

She moved against his body, hugging his hips, pressing her naked breasts against his thighs. He lay back down.

"The whole dream?"

"Yes. All of it. The swollen arms. The shrunken thighs. Hollow eyes. The dead ones."

She rubbed his smooth chest. "It won you the praise of China."

He laughed bitterly. "Praise. For persuading men to starve, some to death." His breathing was normal now.

"You are a mighty warlord. Where you lead, men follow."

He pulled her on top of him and held her, letting her warmth envelop his body.

"Yes. But even mighty warriors have bad dreams. And now there are two million in my hands."

She kissed his neck and chin.

"My mother wanted me to become a merchant, my precious jade. To become rich and fat."

She pushed her hips against his stomach. "You are not fat. But you are rich."

"Yes. And I have you." He cupped his hands around her buttocks. "I had no one there. No one at all. Only starving men. And the cold." He stroked her smoothly with his middle fingers, from the front to the back, feeling the dampness grow, pausing at the anus before moving to the front again. "But now there are two million."

She whimpered softly, and snuggled onto his body. "It is as you have written, my lord."

> *"They go gladly and gaily into battle,*
> *Thinking only of honor and glory.*
> *The General sits alone in his tent,*
> *Thinking of provisions, terrain, and death.*
> *Who must answer to Heaven?*
> *Who creates the orphans?"*

She whimpered again, and found his lips with her mouth.

December 29

Jinglo was genuinely delighted when Bei told her the next morning that he would be escorting her to Hangchow. Partly, she was fearful of the trip, and welcomed the security his presence would add. But she also had an unspoken hope that once they were in Hangchow he would remain there with her, where their marriage and their lives would brighten.

Their luggage was light, since ostensibly even Jinglo was not permanently relocating to Hangchow. A short ricksha ride east from their home took them across Wangfuching Street, through alleyways and past Peking Union Medical College, and finally to Tungtan Street, east of which was located one of the airfields hastily constructed during the early days of the siege.

A battered C-46 Commando sat heavily on the rough runway, the plane a veteran of many crossings of the China-Burma "Hump" during the war against the Japanese. Several high military personnel and their families were gathered around the old plane, waiting for the loading to be completed. Stacks of crates were being carried into the hold of the plane by workers, and it was obvious that these contained expensive tables, chairs, paintings, and statues. One general was noisily supervising the loading of a grand piano, berating the porters for not treating the heavy instrument more gently. Bei recognized him as a Te Wu official, the extreme right wing of the Kuomintang party. His wife, a large woman wearing several layers of expensive fur coats, loudly bemoaned the discomfort of moving and the certainty that the piano would be out of tune when they reached Nanking.

"Nanking?" Jinglo whispered to Bei nervously. "Aren't we going to Hangchow?"

"Yes, of course we are. We'll catch another plane in Nanking. There's only a short wait there, enough for my brother to see us for a few minutes."

"Menjung will be there? How delightful!"

"Yes, it will be good to see him." Bei was not on the best of terms with his brother. Their breach had begun when Jinglo chose Bei over him, and widened when Menjung had chosen the military as a career.

Finally the loading was completed, the passengers aboard, and the plane lumbered down the runway picking up speed. It barely cleared the buildings at the end of the runway, and began a slow arc towards the south. Since they were seated at one of the four windows in the fuselage, Bei and Jinglo could see the golden roof tiles of the Forbidden City below them, surrounded by the Imperial City with the "Three Seas" on the west and Coal Hill on the north. The square "Inner City" filled in the space to the walls around the Imperial City, and the rectangular "Outer City" stretched to the south of it. The massive walls were clearly visible around all of Peking, dwarfing it in their stone embrace. Seen from above, the city was indeed a fort, with the enclosing walls the dominant feature. Rising nearly twenty meters high, and wider than a street on their top, the walls seemed convincingly impregnable, and the city appeared to be safe. So long as food held out.

As the plane gained altitude and the city receded, Bei realized with a chill that outside the walls the land stretched bare and brown as far as one could see, and it was all Communist territory. Seen from above, Peking was after all a small island in a vast sea of countryside, and it now appeared fragile and vulnerable.

Jinglo hid her face in her hands and began to weep softly. Bei put his arm around her, and she whispered to him, "Menjin, I'm so glad to be leaving it."

Craning his neck, Bei caught a glimpse out the window of the city far in the distance, the eastern wall gleaming in the sunlight. They were flying over the barren winter landscape of Hopei province now. Men and donkeys and trucks were clearly visible among houses and fields and irrigation ditches. It seemed strange to Bei to see what appeared to be relatively normal activity in what he knew was Communist territory. For so long he had regarded the coming of the Communists as the end of the world. But don't be a fool, he told himself. From several thousand feet, of course physical appearances haven't changed much. But down in the villages, you may be sure that the social structure is utterly different. And that after all is China: the people, the culture, the human structure of reality so painfully and laboriously crafted over four thousand years of history.

The plane droned on. The great flat expanse of the North China Plain stretched in all directions. A rich, fertile layer of loess, blown south and east from central Asia for millennia, out of which the Chinese civilization had grown four thousand years ago, and which had nurtured that civilization and defined its central locus ever since. Ho had been right: The history of China was the history of its north, of the peoples who settled on the loess land along the Wei River and the Yellow River. Hopei province passed from them and they entered Shantung. Soon Bei could make out a gleaming yellow ribbon snaking through the brown landscape. He shook Jinglo awake. "The Yellow River!" Even from their height, it was immense. Its width dwarfed the roads and houses alongside it, and it stretched to the horizon in both directions. Bei searched but could not find the old course. Ten years earlier, as the Japanese army approached the crossing of the great river, Chiang Kaishek had ordered the dikes dynamited, and the entire river from there to the sea had shifted course, reverting to an ancient path which emptied into the Bohai Gulf of Shantung, rather than its previous path to the Yellow Sea. The advance of the Japanese had been substantially delayed—but at a devastating cost. Millions of acres of land flooded, hundreds of thousands of people drowned as the yellow, muddy waters swirled over their homes and fields. Our people have suffered so long, thought Bei. Perhaps peace is what we need most, after all, at any price, regardless of who wins it.

As the river faded to the north, Bei knew that Tai'erhchuang was located somewhere to the east now, the scene of China's greatest victory against the Japanese—indeed, its only major victory other than General Fu's in Inner Mongolia. Li Tsungjen was the hero there, the man who now was said to have plotted with Fu to replace Chiang Kaishek in a coalition government with the Communists, the man who recently ran against President Chiang's hand-picked nominee for vice-president of the Nationalist government and actually won the post, to everyone's astonishment. Perhaps Li Tsungjen would do better than Chiang as president. The country was suffering so. Yet how to oust Chiang? That was the problem. And would the entire country swiftly fall to the Communists if Chiang was gone? A coalition government was one thing; certain checks on the Communists' extremism would still exist. But what if the Communists took over the coalition and won complete control?

Bei shook his head. It was all so complicated, so difficult to judge. And he was glad again that he had chosen not to follow his family and friends' expectations and enter the political arena.

The sound of battle loomed up vaguely from the ground. That must be the vicinity of Hsuchow, thought Bei, which means we must be in northern Kiangsu province now. He had heard of the Communist Huai-Hai offensive, aimed at capturing the important railroad center of Hsuchow, which they had launched in early November. If Hsuchow fell, the way to Nanking would be clear for them. Peering out the window, all he could see were clouds of smoke to the west, accompanied by the rumble of artillery. But at least they were finally over Nationalist-held territory now. From now on they would be flying into the heart of the Nationalist domain, to land in the Nationalist capital of Nanking.

The terrain, which had been becoming more hilly as they flew south, was now definitely mountainous as they entered the eastern margin of Anhwei province. Good, high country for growing tea, thought Bei. The best black teas came from the mountains of Anhwei above 1,000 meters, in the Keemun and Kintuk regions. They would pass east of there. The green of the mountain pines seemed unnaturally luxuriant after the hours flying over the barren North China Plain. Jinglo awoke, and looking out the window sat up in excitement. "Mountains! And greenness! We must be close!"

"Yes, we are. This must be Anhwei. Soon we'll pass into Kiangsu again, and reach Nanking."

"Will Menjung really be there to meet us?"

Bei shrugged. "I telegraphed him that we would be there. I suspect he will." He smiled wanly. "He still likes you, after all, even if he dislikes me."

"Oh, Menjin. Don't be silly," said Jinglo, but her eyes were shining.

It was now well past noon, and they opened the box lunch they had packed and ate the *chiaotse* and bits of chicken. An hour later they began their descent into Nanking, passing over the Yangtse River only minutes before landing.

As they stepped down onto the ground, Jinglo stopped and looked around, looking more beautiful and animated than Bei had seen her for years. "Oh, feel it, Bei! It's almost warm here! Look! No dust. All the planes. All the cars. And people in bright clothes. There's Menjung!" She waved to a tall figure resplendent in an officer's blue uniform with gold braid and white gloves. It waved back and Bei halfheartedly raised his hand. Bei and Jinglo walked across the runway to the gate.

"Elder Brother. Jinglo. Good to see you safely here in the south." Bei and his brother shook hands in the Western style, and Menjung bowed politely to Jinglo.

"Oh, you cannot know how good it is to be here!" blurted Jinglo.

"I can guess. Come inside the VIP lounge and we'll have some tea."

Bei and his brother had little to say to each other, and Jinglo was trying to hold her happiness within the bounds of decorum. They sat in silence as a waiter poured tea. Bei tasted it: horribly astringent, as he expected, since commercial establishments left the leaves in the pot.

"So how is the city holding out?" asked Bei's brother.

Bei shrugged. "All right, I suppose. Most people have plenty of food."

"There's no electricity, and hardly any water," added Jinglo.

"We're waiting for help from the south," said Bei pointedly, staring at his brother.

Menjung put down his tea and straightened the crease in his trousers.

"We have our hands full at Hsuchow, at the moment. Once we've beaten them back there—who knows."

"There must be a hundred planes on the field here. We have two airstrips inside the walls of Peking now. Why doesn't the Air Force send a dozen planes to us? They could wreak havoc on the Communist armies encamped around the city."

It was a hostile question, and Menjung initially tried to deflect it. "I don't know. We have other priorities here at the moment."

Bei pressed. "Other priorities? I thought you were fighting Communists? There's lots of them around Peking."

"There's lots of them closer by, in northern Kiangsu, north of Hsuchow."

"A dozen planes, Menjung. Why, no one would even notice the loss of a dozen planes off this field here. Do you know what damage a dozen planes could do to the Communists around Peking? The Nationalists *own* the skies, Menjung. The Communists don't have a single fighter plane. What in the name of heaven are all these damn planes doing on the *ground* here?"

Menjung's anger flared. "All right, Menjin, if you insist, I'll tell you. We're saving these planes for the battle that matters. Yes, we could send a few to Peking. And some of them would get shot down, and some would run out of parts. For what? To save a warlord who's scheming to betray us all down here? A warlord who won't obey the orders we send him? Why should we do that?"

"Fu Tsoyi is the most competent general the Nationalists have, and you know that," retorted Bei. "And he's not thinking any thoughts that Li Tsungjen and a dozen other Kuomintang generals aren't thinking either, right down here in your southern paradise. You know why you can sit comfortably down here and drink your bitter tea in an immaculate uniform? Because Fu Tsoyi and Yen Hsishan are doing the dirty work of holding out against massive Communist armies in the north, that's why!"

The brothers glared at each other. Menjung spoke slowly, controlling his anger. "You're tired from a long plane ride. I will ignore your words, Elder Brother. The military situation is very complicated. Our first thought must be to save the country's heartland from the Communist bandits. Nanking. Shanghai." He turned to Jinglo. "And Hangchow, Younger Sister. You have my personal assurances that Hangchow and the rest of the heartland will remain in legitimate hands." He turned back to Bei. "Whatever the cost to other areas, the heartland will be defended. Successfully. Of that you may be absolutely sure."

They heard the Hangchow flight being announced. As they all stood, Bei addressed his brother. "Younger Brother: I was wrong to vent my anger on you personally. It has been good to see you. Please look after Jinglo while she is down here."

"I accept that as a filial obligation, Elder Brother." He lowered his eyes and spoke more softly. "I realize it must be hard up north, Elder Brother. A pause. "Must you return? I have made inquiries. We can find a position for you here."

Jinglo looked up sharply, and hope flared in her eyes. Bei stood silently for several seconds.

"Thank you, Younger Brother. You are most filial to think of me. But you must understand. You left Peking when just a boy, and grew up in Chiang Nan. You have no ties there." He was now speaking to Jinglo, even though he faced his brother. "But I am a northerner. My friends and my official responsibilities are all in Peking, bound there with unbreakable bonds. It is my city. Peking's fate is my fate. To desert it would be to betray myself."

Menjung sighed. "I suppose I understand."

"I don't," declared Jinglo. "I don't understand at all. But then, I am a Chiang Nan person."

"Yes," said Bei. "You are."

"You'd better board your plane," urged Menjung.

They walked to the runway.

"Be careful, Elder Brother."

"Thank you. Good luck yourself, Younger Brother. And look after Jinglo."

"I promise."

"Good-bye, Menjung," added Jinglo.

"I may occasionally visit you in Hangchow, Younger Sister."

"I look forward to that."

They boarded the plane. Bei glumly stared at the rows of fighter planes on the runway as their C-46 ascended. They followed the Yangtse River for a ways, then cut south and were soon flying over T'ai Hu, the huge lake from which the original T'ihu stones were dredged. They saw Wuhsi on its northeast shore, then the lights of Soochow farther south in the gathering twilight. The land was criss-crossed by numberless small canals, each packed with small craft. The setting sun reflecting off the many canals created the illusion that the area was a sea dotted with many islands of land, an illusion not far from true. Every time Bei traveled to Chiang Nan, he was struck by the profusion of water. Water literally everywhere. Unfrozen, even here in late December. Greenness here and there, even in late December. Truly Chiang Nan was different.

The lights of Hangchow came into view in the dusk. The city was located between West Lake and the Ch'ient'ang River, just before the river flowed into Hangchow Bay off the East China Sea. The plane landed and taxied to a stop. As they stepped out of the plane, Jinglo immediately spotted her brothers beside a large shiny car, and waved gaily to them. Bei waved also, halfheartedly again. He knew it was stupid, yet he felt as though he had somehow failed by taking her up north ten years ago, and was now admitting that by returning her to her family. The family had certainly been aghast at the prospect of her moving to Peking, but had acquiesced as gracefully as possible due to the prospect of Bei's eminent position there. His final choice of the profession of police inspector had horrified them and certified all their suppressed misgivings. Not to enter the lucrative fields of business or politics was bad enough. Even to become an academic was preferable, for though penurious, it was still respectable. But police inspector! Bei knew that her family was receiving her with all intentions of never allowing her to return to Peking. He knew that Jinglo knew this also, and would not fight it. This was the reason he had been so reluctant to have her leave Peking, at a time when so many others had already left. He braced himself for a difficult two days as they stepped out onto the runway.

It was late. After the joyous reunion of Jinglo and her family, and their strained but courteous greeting of Bei, they had mercifully been allowed to retire early to the guest room in the family mansion in the suburbs west of West Lake. Jinglo and Bei were exhausted from the trip, and both had fallen asleep quickly. But Bei now arose, being careful not to waken Jinglo, and walked to the window. Opening it, he gazed on the dim but magnificent starlit view of West Lake to the east, and the town beyond it. It was cold, but not the numbing cold of the north, not remotely close to that. The contrast between the opulent Shen family mansion and their Peking villa was painful. He nodded his head, in love and sympathy and understanding of Jinglo. She had, after all, sacrificed much to come north with him. It was a measure of her love of him, and her belief in his promise, that she had defied her family's misgivings and done so. In retrospect, he understood better how difficult it must have been for her, and he loved her for it. At the same time, though, he understood and sympathized with how she must feel now, returning to Chiang Nan. Childless. Her husband a police inspector. Perhaps it had been a mistake to spurn all the offers and join the police force instead. No, Bei, let's not go through that again, he thought. Jinglo was unaware of how many times he had replayed that decision in his mind. He loathed the grasping, self-serving worlds of business and of politics, the constant concern over being bested or betrayed by opponents. And the penury of academics ruled that profession out. Crime detection suited him in so many ways. The opportunity to serve his beloved Peking, to make it a better city, a safer city. It paid, not well, but not too badly, either, as chief inspector. He was at the top of his field, respected by colleagues. And best of all, it gave his mind the constant intellectual challenge it demanded. He loved the puzzles, the search for clues, the delicate balancing of motive, opportunity, and fact. No, he had not gone wrong.

What then? The lack of children? That was a pity. Certainly Jinglo and he had performed their marital duties conscientiously, well aware of their duty to their ancestors to produce male children. The children had simply not come. Would it have made a difference if they had? Perhaps. Perhaps not. He gazed at the sleeping city beyond the lake. Perhaps the marriage was doomed from the start, by a variety of factors, not the least of which was the hold of Chiang Nan upon its children who moved north. He could understand the hold, and didn't resent it, didn't think Jinglo was weak to feel it. He shrugged his shoulders in resignation, shut the window, and turned back to bed.

Perhaps it would all work out. Perhaps it wouldn't. Either way he would accept it. Anyway, he had a job to do. Tomorrow he would visit the Yellow Dragon Monastery. And then renew his depleted stock of Jade Valley tea, he thought with a smile.

December 30

After a family breakfast brimming with courtesy, Bei obtained directions to the Yellow Dragon Monastery and set off in one of the family's several cars, embarrassing himself by his jerky start out of the Shen compound. He had driven in his younger years, but rarely did so after marriage.

The monastery was not far. He drove north along narrow Huanhu Hsi Road on the west side of the lake, then onto Shukuang Road, which led behind the hills on the lake's northern shore. A right turn after several miles took him into the hills, past small fields where rice and rape were grown in season, with tea bushes dotting the hillsides around the fields.

This road soon ended in front of the monastery. Bei parked in front of a gate topped by two black-tiled roofs, with saffron-colored walls stretching to either side. Blue panels on each side of the opening were inscribed with gold characters which proclaimed "As a stream flows murmuring, so flows the mighty Tao." Getting out of the car, Bei contemplated the inscription. He never could understand Taoist sayings. He walked through the doorway into a bamboo grove, the early morning sunlight filtering through the leaves. A flagstone pathway, bordered by old cypresses and hardwoods, led gently uphill past a small pool on his left and into the grove. As he walked up the path another saffron wall came into view through the bamboo, and hills loomed up ahead of him and on either side. Nearing the inner wall he noted that the monastery was surrounded on three sides by steep, heavily wooded hillsides, and could only be easily reached through this bamboo grove. The pathway turned to the left, paralleling now the inner wall, which was decorated with openings in which dragon figures sported in various poses. A turn to the right brought Bei to the gate of the inner wall, which he could now see surrounded the monastery proper. He informed the gateman of his identity and asked to be shown to the prior or abbot. The gateman excused himself, then returned shortly and asked Bei to follow him.

They walked through an entrance hall containing statues on either side, and out to a large central courtyard with four ancient cypresses in the corners. The main Shrine Hall was ahead, at the far side of the courtyard, fronting a steep hillside. Bei followed the gateman to the right through the courtyard, and walked along a covered corridor which skirted a large pool at the base of a cliff. A small open-sided pavilion with a lifelike statue of a red-crowned crane atop it overlooked the pool at the end of the corridor. The gateman indicated for Bei to sit on the balustrade seat running around the pavilion. As he did so, Bei noticed a large stone dragon's head carved in the cliff side, out of whose mouth flowed a steady stream of water which cascaded down thirty feet of rock formations into a small pool, which in turn fed the larger pool. Bei was reminded of the inscription on the front gate, and looking around reflected that this Taoist monastery certainly conveyed a different atmosphere than the White Cloud Temple in Peking.

Several blue-clad monks emerged from a large hall behind the pavilion where he sat, and walked along the corridor toward the main Shrine Hall, eyeing him suspiciously. Another figure emerged and brought two cups of tea to Bei on a tray, set them down on the ledge of the balustrade seat, and silently withdrew. Finally an old figure in a flowing blue robe with black felt trim tottered down stairs alongside the hall behind the pavilion and shuffled along the corridor to Bei. He rose.

"Reverend Prior?"

"Yes. We are honored by your visit."

"Thank you. I regret that the visit is professional."

"The Tao flows through all of life, including all professions."

Bei smiled despite himself. "So I have already been told, by your counterpart in Peking's White Cloud Temple."

The old man started. "You spoke with An Shihlin before his unfortunate death?"

"No. I was speaking of his replacement, the guest prefect."

"Ah. Old Shang. We roamed the Huang Shan mountains together. Many years ago. Please be seated."

They sat in silence a few seconds. The old man seemed perfectly happy to sit listening to the water cascading to the pool.

"Reverend Prior," Bei began, "I am investigating Prior An's death."

"Indeed?"

"Yes. Although we have the monks who were the immediate cause of his death, we have reason to believe that the crime may be more complicated than appears on the surface."

"Things usually are."

"Uh, yes. I understand that An Shihlin was previously prior here. What can you tell me about his early life, and his activities here?"

The old man sat still, staring at Bei vacantly. Slowly Bei realized he was listening to the falling water. "Prior?"

"I heard your question. We will not be able to help you. Our past lives are unimportant when we enter the monastery. While here, our lives are totally taken up by our monastic duties, which have little connection with the human world outside." He paused. "An Shihlin was with us from 1927 to 1937. He was conscientious and competent. We elected him our prior in 1936. He left us one year later to assume the post at the White Cloud Temple." Another pause, which lengthened. Bei realized that the old man had finished and was listening to the water again.

"Uh, Prior. Did he have any friends here or in Hangchow who might tell me more about him?"

The old man smiled. "He was surrounded by friends here. The very rocks and water were his friends. None of his friends pried into his past life. There is nothing more to be known. The Tao is all."

In his firmest official voice, Bei addressed the old man. "Prior, I am Chief Inspector of the Peking Municipal Police. We are trying to bring to justice the murderers of An Shihlin. To do so, we need to know about him, his past. By refusing to provide me with any information, you are interfering with my investigation and protecting An Shihlin's murderers. I can have you questioned by the local authorities if you refuse to answer my questions."

The old man stared vacantly at Bei again. Then his mouth opened, and he laughed. He laughed softly at first, then more audibly. The laughter soon echoed off the cliff face. Still chuckling, he slowly stood up, bowed to Bei, then turned and shuffled off, motioning to the monk in the hall behind to collect the tea, and to the gateman waiting at the end of the corridor to escort Bei out. Bei sat, smarting from the old man's response. Taoists didn't react like normal people, of that he had ample evidence. The monk came up beside him with his tray, put the two cups on it, and then swiftly traced two complicated characters with his index finger on the surface of the tray before Bei's eyes: crane flies. Bei stared stupidly at the tray for a moment, then glanced up at the monk, a question on his lips. The question abruptly died as he saw the slight warning shake of the monk's head, and the fright in his eyes. As the gateman arrived, Bei stood and was escorted out of the monastery, wondering what crane was flying where, and who the monk with the tea tray was. As he walked through the central courtyard he slowed, and half-turning, cast a quick glance back toward the pavilion where he had talked with the prior. Yes. There was a life-sized statue of a red-crowned crane atop the pavilion.

On the strength of his reputation, Bei was given an officer from the Hangchow Municipal Police to help him comb the city's records for any mention of An Shihlin. Nothing. The newspaper files were searched next, especially the 1936 editions for an announcement of An's election to prior. Again nothing. Bei had lunch with the Hangchow Chief Inspector, who confirmed what Bei already knew: The Yellow Dragon Monastery was a hidden world. The chief inspector doubted seriously whether coercive interrogation would have any results at all. And he had only a vague notion of the significance of the crane atop the pavilion in the monastery. Something having to do with some poet in ancient times. Bei realized he had run into a blank wall. At the end of lunch he thanked the Hangchow inspector, excused himself, and wearily climbed into the car.

Bei brightened as he thought of his last task in Hangchow: securing more Jade Valley tea. He drove north out of town, turned west on Hanghui Road, and followed it for nearly half an hour. A left took him through a small village, with geese and ducks scouring the streets for food, and then the road began to climb. He was now driving into the back side of the hills west of Hangchow. The road deteriorated as he traveled into the hills. Finally he stopped the car in the middle of what had now turned into a path, and walked. After another fifteen minutes the path narrowed, and wound through a narrow gorge along a stream. Emerging from the gorge, Bei saw his destination: a small valley, protected on all sides by hills, with tea plants lining the hillsides, and a cluster of three buildings beside the stream in the middle of the valley. He walked up to the largest building and through the open door.

Inside were four large iron bowls a half meter in diameter and depth, with fireboxes connecting them in pairs. Between the fireboxes a short man of perhaps sixty years hunkered on the wooden floor with his back to the door. He tossed a chunk of wood into one of the fireboxes and closed the grating. His arms were muscular. At the iron bowls to the left of the fireboxes sat two slender young women, quite beautiful. One man, somewhat older than the man hunkered on the floor, sat at the nearest of the bowls on the right.

"Does anyone here know how to make tea?" asked Bei.

The man on the floor looked up, still facing away from Bei. "Only a northerner would ask such an impudent question! I believe we are visited from Peking by Judge Dee's current incarnation!" So saying, he turned around with a grin and bowed politely to Bei. Bei returned both the smile and the bow.

"Old Liao. It brings health to my eyes to look at you."

"Only green tea brings health to your eyes, Dee."

"By now, you are green tea yourself, old friend, after fifty years of making it."

Liao laughed, loudly. "You are right. Do you know that Hsiao'jie and Hsiao'mei here swear that my old skin smells exactly like our Jade Valley tea, even in the middle of the night?"

"It does not surprise me," said Bei. "But do not interrupt the processing on my account."

The girls, who had paused, now resumed the first drying of the tea leaves. Each of their iron bowls contained three handfuls of large tea leaves, which they would crush gently against the bottom of the hot bowl, scoop up the side of the bowl with one hand to the rim, catch and turn the mass of leaves with the other hand, then gently lower them to the bottom again and swirl them around the bowl several times before repeating the whole process.

"Can you believe late December, Dee? Even in our sheltered Jade

Valley, this is the very latest we have cured the fourth picking. It was cold and rained all of April and half of May, you see, and the bushes didn't even yield their first pick until late May, so what do you expect."

The girl nearest Bei looked up at Liao with a radiant smile. "He is not truly a reincarnation of Judge Dee, is he, Liao?"

The other girl and the other man laughed easily.

"What is a reincarnation, Hsiao'mei? He has the intelligence of our famous T'ang Dynasty magistrate. He has Dee's sharp eye for finding significant clues where others see only debris. He has the bearded judge's uncanny ability to fashion disparate bits of information into a clear chain of events. And he works as hard as did Dee."

The girls looked at Bei with respect.

"But no, he is not Dee's reincarnation," continued Liao. "He lacks Dee's ambition, which is serious. And he lives in Peking, which means he is surrounded by uncouth persons incapable of a crime sufficiently ingenious to truly test his abilities."

"Liao, more fire," murmured the other girl, Hsiao'jie, somewhat sadly.

Liao tossed another chunk of wood into the firebox connected to her bowl. "Do you see how conscientious they are? The last of the last picking today, tea fit only for uncultured northerners," this with a twinkle in his eye, "and yet they monitor the warmth of the bowls as carefully as in late May with the first pluck."

Bei understood the sad note in the girl's voice. Every other year in February, at the peak of Chekiang's relatively mild winter, Liao traveled to the province's poorest counties. This was the season when many poor families simply ran out of food, and sold their daughters to buy food for the rest of the family. This common practice was the source of the "Hangchow" prostitutes in brothels throughout China, in which the girls could look forward to perhaps ten years of virtual slavery, after which they were put out on the streets, penniless and far from home. Only a few were purchased as concubines by rich men, if they were particularly beautiful and showed signs of remaining so.

Every other year Liao spared no expense to search the province and purchase the two most beautiful girls being sold by their families.

He then brought them to his secluded valley and taught them what he knew best: the art of producing superior tea. How to prune the bushes. How to fertilize them. When to carefully pick the leaves. How to crush and dry them in the iron bowls, and what temperature to maintain the bowls at. How to tell by hefting the leaves when they had the proper amount of moisture driven out of them. And how to extract the best price for your precious tea without being cheated. Which meant he taught them to read and write also.

At the end of two years, the girls were free. He required them only to leave his valley and never return. Still young and beautiful, now healthy and educated and in possession of a skill highly valued in this part of China, the girls invariably secured either a good husband, a good job, or both.

Of course, they were sad to leave, after the last picking of their second year there. Partly because the secluded valley was so dear to them. Partly because they were unsure of their life in the world outside. But mainly because they knew they would never again find a lover like Liao. A lover so strong, yet solicitous of their feelings. A lover so full of zest for life. A lover so kind to them, or important in their lives.

Liao ignored the sad note in Hsiao'jie's voice, as he had ignored the same note in young girls' voices at this time for forty years. "How's your heat, old Wan?" he asked, addressing the old man on the other bowl. His bowl, and the one beside it at which Liao sat, was used for the second drying of the leaves. The second drying bowls were kept somewhat less hot than the first drying bowls.

"Good."

Liao nodded. "And what of interest from the north, Dee?" Liao knew Bei's name well enough, but preferred to address him by the name of the most famous detective in China's history.

"Lots of Communists there, in regular armies, now, not just bandit bands."

"Pshew! I don't mean surface news, Dee! News of things that change from day to day or year to year is of no consequence to me here. I asked for things of interest, Dee, something that will be as good and interesting to know a decade or century from now as it is now."

Bei smiled. "I'd forgotten your ideas on news. No, nothing that satisfies your strictures, Liao. The world outside is—well, it is as if a new age is dawning, like it or not."

"You hear, Hsiao'mei and Hsiao'jie," Liao said, turning to the girls. "An exciting time for you, with many opportunities for persons with skills and intelligence. Apply yourselves and you will prosper."

Hsiao'mei rolled her eyes upward, as if she were full to overflowing of advice from Liao. Hsiao'jie burst into tears and rushed from the building.

Liao watched after her. "She is too attached. She will learn that you must not become too attached in this world. But I cannot teach her that." He turned to the other girl. "Hsiao'mei. Could you get some hot water for us?"

"Certainly, Liao." She walked to a side room.

"It is hard for them. They leave tomorrow. It is hard on all of us." Liao stared at the floor. "Except old Wan here. He has seen most of them go."

"None lovelier than these," declared Wan.

Liao roared with laughter. "He says that every time! I was wondering when he would sally forth with it this time."

"But old Liao, I sincerely mean it every time."

Liao was still laughing. "I believe it. As a matter of fact, I agree with you every time."

Hsiao'mei returned shortly with a tray and set it down on her bowl. She quickly showed the amount of tea leaves in one pot to Liao, who nodded his approval, then she poured steaming water into the pot and sat back down.

"So what brings you to Hangchow, Dee? We haven't seen you here in several years."

"I've run out of Jade Valley green," said Bei innocently.

Everyone laughed again. "It's a long way to come, through Communist bandits, even for my tea."

"Well, there are several other minor reasons. I escorted my wife here; she is staying with her parents until things . . . clear up in the north."

"The lady is one of Shen's daughters, Wan."

"You married well, my lord Judge Dee."

"Thank you. And also I have a case involving the former prior of the Yellow Dragon Monastery here. I don't suppose you know anything of a monk named An Shihlin?"

Liao glanced at Wan. "Old Wan here is a devout Taoist."

Wan nodded. "I knew who Prior An was when he was here, but nothing more. Although I have been to the Yellow Dragon Monastery for many of their Renewal Rites, I am not a frequent participant in their devotionals."

"I was there this morning. They have a pavilion there, in front of the pool fed by the spring emerging from a carved dragon's head. On top of this pavilion is a life-sized statue of a crane."

Wan nodded. "I remember that."

Bei attempted to frame his next comment casually. "A most realistic statue. It appears ready to fly, at any instant."

Liao leaned over and poured the tea from the first pot into a second. The old man had the ability to judge time up to five minutes absolutely accurately. He then poured four cups and handed them around.

Bei's comment hung in the air. Then Wan spoke.

"They say it does fly, Judge Dee. According to legend, it was formerly fed by the poet Lin Heching in the Sung Dynasty, shortly after the monastery was built. He would feed it on Solitary Hill in the morning, then it would fly to the monastery and perch atop that pavilion during the day, and fly back to Solitary Hill to view the sunset every evening."

Liao had watched Bei intently during Wan's recital, and noted the carotid artery in Bei's neck beat more quickly at the end of the story, as Bei guessed what the tea server in the Yellow Dragon Monastery meant by tracing "crane flies" on the tray: Solitary Hill, at sunset. With sudden excitement Bei glanced at the window behind Hsiao'mei, gauging how much light was left in the day.

"I wasn't aware you were so interested in Taoist stories, Dee," commented Liao.

"Oh, uh, yes," stammered Bei, attempting to quell his excitement. "Actually, I've been hearing quite a few of them recently. An Shihlin was burned to death in Peking several days ago."

"That indeed is shocking," said Wan.

They all sipped the tea.

"Ah," said Bei courteously. "It has been too long without Jade Valley green." He swirled the tea in his cup and studied it. "And its lustrous golden color."

Liao smiled. "It gives me great pleasure to share my tea with a connoisseur." Then he looked shrewdly at Bei. "Hsiao'mei. Please get four packages of this year's first pick for Dee. He will have to leave soon to get to Solitary Hill by sunset." She left the room.

Bei glanced up in surprise. "I think you would have made a good detective yourself, old friend."

"Not at all. I know only tea. And old Wan here knows more of that than me."

Wan merely shook his head and chuckled.

Bei stood up. "But you are right. I must be going. And Wan is right about the girls: They are lovelier than ever."

"Thank you." He stared at the floor. "It is becoming harder to see them go, each time." A silence. Bei touched his shoulder warmly, just as Hsiao'mei returned.

"Ah. Your Jade Valley tea," Liao said with forced heartiness.

"My most precious cargo," said Bei, discreetly slipping a wad of money onto the tea tray. "Good-bye, old friend."

"Good-bye, Dee. Take care."

Bei walked out of the small valley, noticing Hsiao'jie sitting on a rock beside the stream. He passed through the gorge and reached his car with mounting excitement. Looking to the west, he judged the time until sunset. Nearly two hours, or so. That should suffice, barring a flat tire. He started the motor, backed up to where a side path took off, turned the car around, and rattled down the rough road back toward Hangchow.

Solitary Hill is the largest island in West Lake. It is reached by a causeway originally built by the T'ang Dynasty poet Po Chuyi when he was governor of Hangchow. West Lake and its islands and views had been celebrated in verse by a thousand years of poets—including Lin Heching in the Sung Dynasty, who often inserted into his poems allusions to the red-crowned crane, the Taoist symbol of immortality. Bei parked the car in front of Chung Shan Park on Solitary Hill and walked between the two marble lions on pedestals at the entrance. A man was lifting his young daughter to kiss one of the lions as Bei passed, and it reminded him of Ho and his daughter. At the enormous wall on the hillside inscribed with the characters Chung Shan, Bei took the right-hand stairs up the hill, came quickly to the level of a first pavilion, then climbed again, to the left of it, through pines and hardwoods, reaching the top in five minutes. He proceeded east along the ridge line of the hill, past a rock garden dominated by two large T'aihus inscribed with poems.

Soon he reached the large, open pavilion at the very summit, just as the setting sun reddened the entire lake stretched to the south before him. The pavilion, set among hardwoods and shrubs, had four pillars on each side, whose western edges gleamed dark red in the sunlight. A figure moved in a corner of the pavilion. Blue robe. The monk who had served him tea, and secretly conveyed the encoded request to meet him here at this time. Bei sat down in the shadows of the northeastern corner, tingling with excitement that he had correctly deciphered the "crane flies" message. The monk approached. He was in his late forties, with a calm demeanor despite the clandestine nature of the meeting.

"You wish to know about An Shihlin?" he asked, in a Hangchow accent.

"I do," Bei answered. "To help find his murderers."

"I had heard he was burned by several monks."

"He was. But they were hired to do it, and I need to know more about An to find out who hired them, and why."

The monk weighed his words. "I will tell you what I know."

"Thank you. Tell me everything you know about An: his family, his friends, his background."

"We joined the monastery in the same month, May, of 1927. So we were friends. He had suffered a deep tragedy and needed to confide in someone, to get it out of him."

The monk turned toward the lake, which was changing from blood red to a dull orange as the sun sank behind the hills to the west. "He was born into a wealthy family in Ningpo, east of here. He had every advantage, including a thorough education in the classics. He could quote from all the old stories. He had more life in him then, even with his grief, than any of us." The sun sank out of sight and the air above the lake seemed to sparkle with clarity.

"In spite of being rich, he was sensitive to the misery around him, and especially to the way the foreign devils treated us Chinese, and to the fact they had taken over our country. China, ruled by barbarians. He became obsessed with driving the foreigners out of our country, of standing up and regaining our independence. He went to Shanghai and became involved in organizing workers in the trade unions to assert their rights against the foreigners. And against the Chinese who had grown rich by aiding the foreigners. He met many people there, impelled by the same ideals. He married one of them, a lovely girl, and they had a son."

"What year was this that he was in Shanghai organizing workers? Not—"

"Yes. Late 1926, early 1927. Not a good time to be a Communist in Shanghai."

"Communist?"

"Another one of the persons he met in Shanghai was Chou Enlai, who directed the March twenty-first insurrection in which the workers took control of the city. He also met Nieh Jungchen there, who was working with Chou. He didn't begin as a Communist. But when he discovered that they were the hardest workers and the most intelligent in his cause, it was natural for him to join them."

"Then came April. April twelfth. Chiang Kaishek had been approached by a group of wealthy Shanghai businessmen who offered to finance his political future if he would swing to the right, betray the Communists who had worked in the Kuomintang party with him so long and so diligently.

"He readily agreed. So Yu Hsiach'ing, the businessman who headed the Shanghai Chamber of Commerce, hired the services of Tu Yuehsheng. You know of Tu?" Bei nodded. Tu Yuehsheng, the ruler of the Greens, Shanghai's powerful underworld of opium and crime.

The monk continued. "Stirling Fessenden, the American who headed the foreigners, gave Tu's gangsters permission to pass, armed, through the foreign concession area. So it was, that early in the morning of April twelfth the Greens snuck up on the Union headquarters. Chou Enlai and An Shihlin had just left. Chou often worked through the night. An's wife and son were there, however. They were killed outright by the Greens, with the others. Shot in the head by pistols. Throughout the morning, Union leaders and those suspected of being such were executed by the Greens. Bodies piled up in the streets. It was . . . a horrible slaughter. Chou was actually captured and questioned, but they didn't realize who he was, and a guard sympathetic to the workers' cause let him escape. Chou went up the river to Wuhan. An Shihlin also escaped, heading south, and ended up here in Hangchow. He arrived in early May, crushed in every way. His wife and son were dead, his work destroyed in one day of betrayal. He gladly turned his back on everything, and entered the monastery, to try and rebuild something in himself."

The sliver-thin crescent moon had risen in the east while the monk spoke. Its feeble light shone upon his face, revealing tears.

"I believe you were in Shanghai with An, weren't you?" asked Bei.

The monk nodded, not taking his eyes from the lake below them, now shimmering dully in the faint moonlight. "An's wife—she was my sister. A lovely girl." Tears streamed down his face now, but he made no sound.

Bei looked away. After a while he asked, "Did An continue to be a Communist, as he rose to responsibility in the monastery?"

The monk breathed deeply several times. Finally he was able to continue. "I don't know. We never spoke of it. I know he did not lose his concern for the common people. Nor his conviction that the foreigners had no right to own Chinese land and control Chinese lives. That made him a Communist in his heart, whether he called himself one or belonged to their party. But no, he had no contact with Chou Enlai or the Communists while he was here. He was too busy with monastery business. He lived his Taoism very deeply, you understand. If he believed in communism too, it was secondary to his life in the Tao and its flow through the world."

Bei thought back to the books on An's desk. The histories of the later Han rebellions, the T'aip'ing revolt—all uprisings of the Taoist peasants against the wealthy ruling class. The Taoist commoners against the Confucian rulers.

"Why did An leave the Yellow Dragon Monastery and go to Peking? He was a Chekiang man, after all."

"That puzzled me also. It's true that the White Cloud Temple is a prominent one, the head of the Longmen sect of the Ch'uan Chen school. And it is located in Peking. It gave more opportunity for him

87

to exercise his considerable talent. But something else was going on. His old grief was with him always, but he knew that the Tao continued to flow past grief, and he was full of its flow. He was happy to be prior of the Yellow Dragon, to live in such a beautiful place.

"Then one day, it changed. He received a letter—an unusual event. And it changed everything. We were close, then—we always were. All he said to me was that he had been called by the Purple Mountain. I asked him what that was. He smiled—I can see it now, as vivid as then; he smiled a lot—and said it was in the hills outside of Peking, and when the Purple Mountain called, you had to go. I think . . . he felt he owed me an explanation as to why he was leaving. We had been together so long, since Shanghai, and our lives intertwined so. He told no one else anything, and enjoined me to secrecy." The monk turned to Bei. "I am telling you this only because you are trying to avenge his murder."

"Not avenge. I am merely trying to find out who had him murdered, and bring them before the magistrate with the evidence."

"That is close enough."

"You know nothing more of this Purple Mountain outside of Peking?"

"Nothing. It is a Taoist place, or organization, I suppose. But I had never heard of it, before or since. Which is strange, actually."

"Nor have I heard of it, and I am a Peking person. But then, I am certainly not a Taoist."

"Perhaps you are and know it not. Perhaps you will become one," said the monk.

"Not likely. But thank you for meeting me and telling me An's story. It may help me."

"I hope so." He hesitated. "You realize—my talking to you would mean my expulsion from the monastery if our prior came to know."

"He will not. I promise you."

"Thank you. Good-bye." The monk stepped off the pavilion and walked away.

Bei remained seated, gazing at the lake, trying to absorb what he had heard. An Shihlin, whom he had supposed to be an obscure Taoist monk, working with Chou Enlai and the Communists in Shanghai in 1927. Chou Enlai, the man who now was second only to Mao Tsetung in the Communist command. A secret organization, the Purple Mountain, summoning An Shihlin to Peking. Why? What all this had to do with An's death by fire a week ago, and how the fat monk fit in, was still a mystery to Bei. But now he knew where the answers lay: the Purple Mountain. Somewhere in the hills outside of Peking. In Communist territory, therefore. But he would get there. Somehow he would get to the Purple Mountain.

December 31

B ei and Jinglo arose early and walked down Huanhu Hsi Road. Bei would leave that morning to return to Peking. A mist hovered over the lake, and its fingers reached up the streams flowing into the lake. They paused to watch the fishermen at one such stream, the long bamboo poles mirrored clearly in the water below the mist, the fishermen squatting at the concrete embankment in their thick coats, cigarettes glowing in the mist. Upstream a young man dipped a triangular net into the water, with cypresses and bare hardwoods behind him mirrored on the stream. They walked across a small bridge and followed a path to the edge of the lake. A cluster of shallow fishing boats was anchored offshore, and beyond them they could see the bare trees of Su Dongpo Causeway, which ran along the western margin of the lake and divided the Inner Lake before them from the main Outer Lake east of the causeway. Silently they stared at the humped bridges of the causeway emerging out of the mist, and Bei could barely make out the pavilion containing the stele inscribed "Spring Dawn on Su Causeway," a famous spot for viewing the lake for centuries.

There was too much to say, so they said nothing. But questions lay clouded in their minds. Whether she would ever return to Peking. Whether he could live in Hangchow any happier than she had been in Peking. What would happen to him if the Communists took Peking. And underneath these, deeper questions. Whether their marriage could possibly survive the obstacles. Whether they would ever see each other again.

Bei turned her to him, looked into her sad eyes, and embraced her softly. "I love you, Jinglo."

"And I love you, Menjin. Be very careful."

"I will."

They turned and walked back to her family's mansion. He courteously bade her family good-bye, then her oldest brother drove him to the airport.

The plane approached Peking. It was past sunset, and stars and the crescent moon shone in the clear black sky. Bei could identify Peking's location by the lack of lights, the city having been deprived of electricity since the Communist capture of the power plant south of the city. So Peking sat dark and brooding, surrounded by well-lit smaller cities in Communist hands. Fengtai to the south, where Lin Piao had seized the trainloads of arms. Mentouk'ou to the west, at the foot of the Western Hills. The universities Yenching and Tsinghua to the north, and beyond them, on the horizon, Chihsien, where Lin Piao was said to have his headquarters. Tungchow to the east completed the circle of light, in the midst of which squatted Peking, a black hole. From the airplane it almost looked as if nothing existed inside the city's immense walls, as if the surface gave way inside the walls and plunged deep into the earth. Only the world outside the walls looked real and normal, and the city seemed insubstantial, hollow. "No," murmured Bei. That was an illusion. The Communists were outside, in the lights. Bei's world was inside, the old China. It was a trick of the night.

The plane approached an airfield and passed over it, alerting personnel to light fires along the loading strip. Seen from close up, the city swelled into life in the dim moonlight. The golden tiles on the roofs of the Forbidden City gleamed dully. Sparkles of light flickered on the ice covering the surfaces of Nanhai, Chunghai, and Beihai lakes. The three "seas" of the Imperial City. Yes, this is my city after all, thought Bei. The illusion is dispelled. The city which has ruled China for a thousand years. Destroyed often, always rebuilt, arising larger and more glorious than before from its own ashes. The Liao, the Chin, the Yuan, Ming, Ch'ing. A thousand years of splendor and creativity. And blood and fire and betrayals, yes. But history, the history of the Middle Kingdom devolving in upon the precious city within these towering walls. His home. He was glad to return.

The plane circled to the north, and began its descent traveling south over the heart of the city. Soon the wall stretching to either side of Ch'ienmen Gate passed beneath them, and Bei realized they would be landing on the temporary airfield at the Temple of Heaven in the southern sector of the city. Fires gleamed to either side of the runway to assist the pilot, and the plane bounced to a halt.

Bei had been indignant when he had heard of the four hundred ancient cypresses, with trunks up to three meters wide, which had been cut down to make room for the airfield at the Temple of Heaven. And the twenty thousand smaller trees and shrubs also removed. But he was unprepared for the site which greeted him as he stepped off the plane. The ugly bare spaces where stately groves of trees had stood. The debris which littered the grounds, throwing odd shadows. The thousands of refugees crammed into the sacred halls and squalid shelters dotting the terraces and paths. The refugees peeked out of their makeshift shelters as the aircraft's passengers walked by, their faces sullen and dirty. Debris themselves, the debris of war swept into the last stronghold of old China in the north. Students from Shansi and Manchuria, landowners from the countryside around Peking. Piles of human excrement were scattered haphazardly over the marble terraces and walkways. Bei trudged out of the temple grounds and looked for a ricksha.

January 1, 1949

Yu Chenling, Peking head of the right-wing Kuomintang secret police known as the Te Wu, flicked off his battery-powered radio angrily.

"Chan!" he bellowed, his old man's thin voice cutting into the small side room.

His aide entered the larger room, an intense man in his late twenties, whose remarkable physical strength had always struck Yu as incongruous, given Chan's upbringing in one of the richest landowning families in Honan province. But then, much about Chan was curious.

"Sit," Yu ordered peremptorily. "Chiang Kaishek just issued a snivelling little call for peace from Nanking."

"Will anyone heed it, sir?" asked Chan calmly.

"Who knows?" Yu snapped, the veins in his thin neck bulging as he attempted to control his anger. "How could Chiang even consider dealing with the Communists?" he yelled, slamming shut a file cabinet in anger. "Fools. And cowards. He's surrounded by fools and cowards who don't realize that it's us or it's them, and there's no in-between. Not for them and not for us." He stood up and began to pace in his jerky, old-man gait. "And Peking. This cowardly city is losing more of its nerve every day. We'll have to counter Chiang's proposals. Sabotage them."

Chan smiled. When Yu said sabotage, it usually meant killing, either Communists or Communist sympathizers. "One of the so-called independents? Perhaps that Yenching University professor who's always coming into the city?" When Yu didn't answer, he ventured another guess. "Or Fu himself?"

Yu sat again, fidgeting, casting angry glances at the portrait of Chiang Kaishek on the opposite wall surrounded by Nationalist flags. "I don't know," he blurted out. "I can't figure Fu out. Sometimes I think he realizes what devils the Communists are. Sometimes I'm not so sure. And he's strong. No. Let me sound him out on it, first."

Chan pursed his lips.

"Get me the file on the Communist underground here," Yu commanded, even though he sat directly beside the file cabinet.

Chan crossed to the cabinet, located the file, and laid it on the desk in front of Yu. Yu opened it and concentrated on its contents.

"Let's pick the most important Communist agent we can get. Our object is to anger the devils, to see if we can get them to reject Chiang's proposal. 'Peace,' indeed," he snorted. He contemplated the file. "Who is this jade dealer?"

Chan smiled, broadly now. A distinct image of Meiling came to him, and the thought of killing such a beautiful one pleased him.

"She is one of their most valuable agents. Probably their chief contact with the forces outside the city."

92

Yu looked up from the file. "It will anger them when she is eliminated?" he asked, satisfaction lighting up his face.

Chan nodded, then added, "She is a lovely woman, General Yu. Young, tall, with long legs."

Yu's eyes glazed, and a hoarse chuckle bubbled up from his throat. "Ah. I can picture her. Taller than me, no doubt? Long legs?"

Chan nodded.

Yu savored it.

"Kill her," he whispered.

Chan grinned. "I'll be at the wheel myself."

"It must be done soon," the old man said.

"I believe she comes regularly to the Taoist temple in the southwest sector. Does the file note it?"

Yu glanced down. "Yes. Monday, Wednesday, Sunday." He looked up eagerly. "Tomorrow, then?"

"No problem," Chan replied. "I'll get Yang and Ziwu."

Yu settled his bony frame back into the chair and began to imagine the killing. A Communist. And female. Tall. Bigger than him. It aroused him. Then he remembered, and sat bolt upright with a little cry of anticipation.

"You have her? From the P'ing K'angli brothel?"

"In the villa, General. Awaiting you."

Yu jumped up and eagerly shuffled for the door leading to the courtyard and his villa beyond, but stopped halfway out the door.

"She's already strapped down?"

"Yes, General."

"Tall?"

Chan nodded. "And beautiful."

Still Yu hesitated.

"Any trouble getting her?"

Chan felt the anger rise in him. "These turtle-spawned whores. They want to be treated like royal concubines." He sat there glowering.

"But she's here? And strapped?" Yu asked anxiously. "I can do whatever I want?"

"Yes, sir. She is yours."

Yu hurried out of the room. Chan sat there a moment, got up and put the file away, then resumed his seat, still angry. Like they were royal concubines. Procuring girls for Yu was not the hardest part of putting up with the man, but it took considerable charm to accomplish it, particularly after one of the girls at the house had already been through it.

The Communist girl came to his mind. It would be messy, he would see to that. Another messy death. His anger turned cold as he remembered, farther back. His father and two younger brothers. A brightly lit afternoon in late fall, at their mansion in northern Honan. The produce taxes had just been collected from the peasants leasing their land. Their land. The vast loess fields, painstakingly assembled by hundreds of years of his Chan ancestors' work and intelligence. Raising themselves from the lowest of peasants to a great landowning family by sheer dint of generation after generation of Chan sweat and Chan brains. He swelled with pride when he thought of his ancestors and all they had accomplished. All snuffed out in one afternoon, when a ragged patrol came to the mansion in the bright autumn sunlight. His father and he, as soon as they saw the bandits round the corner of the granary, knew who they were and why they had come. The Communists. He had grabbed a rifle, but his father had ordered him to drop it and hide in the secret cellar. He, of course, had refused, the first time he had ever disobeyed his father. An unexpected blow from his hefty father had knocked him out, and when the gunfire woke him he was in the hidden cellar with his mother. The shooting was over quickly, and he and his mother sat stunned in the dark as coarse bootsteps thundered above them, then left.

The sun was setting when they ventured out. They found the bodies in the courtyard. His father, tied to the pear tree, his face blown away. His two brothers, too far away to make it to the cellar, lying in a heap at his father's feet. The russet of nearly ripe pears glinting in the last rays of the sun. But it was the sign which stood out most clearly over the years. The crude sign in badly formed characters above where his father's face had been. "Death to all corrupt and idle rich, who live off the work and sweat of the peasants." His father, who worked harder with his hands as well as his brains than any of the ignorant peasants who leased his land. His father, staunch embodiment of the Confucian virtues handed down by his ancestors through the millennia. Father. With a preposterous sign where his head had been. Father.

The predictable stack of paperwork had greeted Bei upon his return to the office. He had instructed Yuan to handle everything that came in that morning, while he attempted to catch up with the important matters. It was after lunch before he looked up, the most pressing items dealt with.

"I'm going to the White Cloud Temple, Yuan."

"Yes, sir. One message you should know about this morning."

"What is it."

"Zhou Peifeng called. General Fu is wondering how you are coming along in the White Cloud Temple case."

"I'll talk to Zhou after I've checked out a few more things here."

Yuan raised his eyebrows. "What happened to 'When a dragon calls'?"

Bei ignored him. "I may or may not be back later."

The afternoon streets were packed with more soldiers than ever, although Bei saw no wounded ones; piles of garbage and debris were beginning to appear even on the main streets. Arriving at the White Cloud Temple, he insisted on walking to the guest prefect's quarters without assistance from the gateman. He walked up the main axis of halls, past Founder Ch'iu's Shrine Hall, and crossed the courtyard in front of the Hall of the Four Deities. The guest prefect was as he had seen him the last time, hunched over papers on a desk.

"We both seem to be struggling with mounds of paperwork, Guest Prefect."

The old man looked up, and tried to focus on Bei. "Oh, it's you, Inspector. Yes. I never knew so much paperwork was involved in running a temple," he said wearily. "I wish I had An's energy."

"I appreciate how you feel. Has any more information regarding the murder come to light while I have been gone the last few days?"

The old man moved to a more comfortable chair in the small room, and invited Bei to be seated also. "Things keep coming up. Yesterday the overseer, Ba, remarked that he had seen a new woman at the last two evening devotions. That is not unusual, of course. We get many visitors and curious people. But Ba remembered having seen her once before, several months ago—going into An's quarters with him after one of the evening devotions."

"Interesting," remarked Bei. "Another one of An's lady friends, then?"

"Possibly. But that was the only time Ba could remember seeing her before."

"What does she look like?"

"Ba described her as rather tall for a woman, with plain features."

"That's not much help."

"She may come to tomorrow night's devotions. You could see her yourself."

"I may do that. But now I have a question for you, if I may."

"Certainly. Every minute away from that paperwork is its own reward."

Bei laughed, then stared closely at the old man. "What do you know about a 'Purple Mountain' outside of the city?"

The old man's eyes narrowed perceptibly, and an air of caution settled over him. He returned Bei's stare in silence for several seconds.

"Where in the world did you hear of the Purple Mountain?"

"That is not important. You know of it, don't you."

The old man weighed his words. "Yes, I know of it. But very little. No one knows very much of it."

"I presume it is a Taoist temple, or monastery."

Another weighing of words. "I suppose you could call it that."

"What do you mean?"

"Well . . . it is a highly heterodox . . . group. Some do not consider it Taoist at all."

"Is it Buddhist, then?"

"Oh, no. It is Taoist. Or at least they consider themselves Taoists."

"Then why do others not consider them Taoists, or at least not orthodox Taoists?"

A pause. "They do not share our scriptures. All orthodox Taoists, whatever school they subscribe to, at least recognize the contents of the *Tao tsang,* the Taoist canon. The Purple Mountain masters don't."

"Then what do they subscribe to?"

"Only the *Tao Teh Ching* and *Chuang-Tse,* and several old and highly heterodox writings. They consider themselves to be purists, the elite."

"What do they base their devotions on?"

"They have no devotions. They . . . I cannot say."

"What cannot you say?"

"Nothing," the old man said with determination.

"What is the chief point of their doctrine?"

"I cannot say," the old man repeated.

"Why not?"

"It is heterodox. Highly heterodox. They are elitist. You should stay away from them." The guest prefect was nearly trembling.

Puzzled, Bei was at a loss how to proceed. Clearly, the guest prefect was not going to talk anymore about it.

"May I speak to the overseer regarding the woman he saw?"

The guest prefect regained his composure. "Of course." He rose.

"Please don't bother to show me there. I remember where he is."

"Very well."

"Good luck with your paperwork. And thank you."

The old man bowed formally as Bei left the room. Bei hurried to the overseer's office in the row of buildings east of the Jade Emperor's Shrine Hall.

"Overseer Ba. The guest prefect said I might see you," said Bei as he entered.

"Certainly. Please be seated."

"I won't be long, thank you. I just talked to the guest prefect. I wonder if you could be so kind as to provide me with a description of the woman you saw attending devotions again recently."

"I'm afraid I can't be exact, because I've never had a good look at her. She is somewhat above average height for a woman, with ordinary features. But you will be interested in this: One of our younger monks has a sister who works at the foreigners' Peking Union Medical College Hospital. His sister was also at the service last night and saw her, and recognized her as a fellow worker at the hospital. Her name is Fu Hsiawen."

"Ah, thank you for that information," said Bei, jotting down the most likely characters for the name. "By the way, your tales of the Eight Immortals have gotten me interested in Taoist folklore, so I've been reading up on it. One old book mentioned several temples and monasteries in the Peking region. I knew all of them except one. Do you have any idea where something called the Purple Mountain is located?"

The overseer laughed. "I'm not even sure it does exist. Or does anymore, if it ever did. It has a peculiar reputation. Bizarre sexual rites."

"Bizarre sexual practices?" That certainly fit in with the popular notion of Taoists. "I suppose Purple Mountain refers to a peak in the Yanshan mountains north of the city?"

"Not at all. This place is supposed to be in the Western Hills. In fact, there's an old legend, strictly among us Taoists, of course, that the only way to find it is to follow a line from the Summer Palace's Spring Heralding Pavilion through the pagoda atop Jade Spring Hill."

"Really? Well, that's an interesting story, but since that's all in Communist hands now, it will remain just an interesting story. Is the woman Meiling still coming to evening devotions?"

"She was at Wednesday's."

"And this woman who works in the hospital, how long has she been coming to the devotions?"

"Only the last two, I believe."

"In other words, she began attending the devotions just after the prior's death."

"Why, yes, I suppose you could say that."

"Thank you very much for the information, Overseer Ba."

"Good day, Inspector."

As his ricksha neared Ch'ang'an Boulevard, Bei leaned out to the driver and on an impulse directed him to go to Peking Union Medical College. He had gotten nothing out of the woman Meiling in his questioning of her several days earlier. Perhaps this female friend of An's would prove more helpful, this Fu Hsiawen. The hospital was east of Wangfuching Street, and several blocks north of Ch'ang'an Boulevard. Bei inquired at the hospital desk and was told that the woman worked in the surgical section, employed as a dresser of incisions. In the surgical section, her supervisor was a foreign nurse, probably American since the American Rockefeller Foundation operated the hospital. But then, Bei had trouble telling one foreigner from the other. She spoke atrocious Chinese, but managed to convey to Bei her irritation that yet another man was looking for her only dresser, with a patient due out of surgery any minute. She had evidently left only seconds before with the other person. "In fact, there she is," said the nurse, more or less, pointing out a window.

Outside stood a woman in hospital uniform, talking to a tall man in a heavy coat with the collar turned up and a Western-style hat pulled low over his forehead. Bei thanked the foreign nurse, and quickly headed to an exit at the other end of the room. He came out into the hospital grounds some twenty meters from the couple, and melted into some shrubbery beside the building. A curious old foreign gentleman, wearing a Chinese gown, wandered past. The man and the woman were engaged in intense conversation. Despite the man's back being toward him, something about his posture seemed familiar to Bei. They seemed to come to some sort of conclusion, and began to walk back to the door. Bei sank further behind the shrubbery, well concealed now. They stopped not five meters directly in front of Bei's hiding spot, and the man lifted his hat brim as the woman kissed his cheek. Bei stifled a gasp. The man was General Fu.

"You won't fail me, little one? You'll have no trouble getting my offer to negotiate to Lin Piao?"

"No, Father. But you must be careful."

"Of course. And write your mother."

"Yes, Father."

He squeezed her arm affectionately, and strode off in the opposite direction. The young woman sighed, shook her head, and reentered the hospital.

Bei sank back against the wall, his mind too dazed to think. After a minute he emerged from the bushes, startling the old foreign gentleman in the Chinese gown, walked dizzily to his ricksha, and instructed the man to take him home.

Bei unlocked the door to his compound, walked down the corridor to the study, and from habit flicked on the electric light beside his desk. To his surprise, it came on. The electricity was running again! But the Communists controlled the power plant at Shihchingshan.

Puzzled, he went over to the radio beside his soft chair and flicked it on. It spluttered to life also. He settled into the chair and pulled the newspaper that he had purchased on the way home out of his coat pocket. As he opened it, a loose slip of paper fluttered out. "Citizens of Peking!" was emblazoned on the right margin. Bei read on. "The Peoples' Liberation Army is patiently waiting for General Fu to bow to the peoples' demand to surrender this city. But its patience is not unlimited. The determined voice of the people must make itself heard. You know the exalted status the workers have in the New China. You know the old injustices will finally be stamped out, and the common people will rule their own lives. Unite behind the glorious workers of the Communist Party!"

Bei whistled softly. So it has come to this. Mimeographed Communist propaganda inserted into the newspapers. He had assumed there must be a Communist underground in the city, but it had never shown itself before, especially during the siege with all the soldiers packed into the city. He heard a loud knocking at the gate, and leaning over pulled the bell rope to signal the servant girl to answer it. He listened for the sound of the door being opened, not being sure the girl was in. He soon heard her answering the door, then the shuffle of her footsteps.

"Master Bei?"

"Yes, Hsiaoyu."

"The *Chia* head is at the door. He says he must talk to you about an important matter."

Bei wrinkled his face in dislike. The *Chia* was a neighborhood organization of ten households, by which the central authorities kept tabs on the local population. Ten *Chias* together comprised a *Pao*. Taxes were collected through the *Pao-Chia* system. The military had in addition levied demands for supplies and labor through the system during the siege. Thanks to the high ranks of the inhabitants of this neighborhood, Bei had received few serious demands from his *Chia* chief.

"Very well. I suppose I'll receive him."

She left and escorted him back. He was a thin, grasping man who had been given the *Chia* post because of his politics rather than his abilities—which was common.

"Ah, Inspector. So sorry to disturb you. We have received an urgent request straight from General Fu's command. Funds are desperately needed to fortify and defend the city." The words were almost exactly the same as the last several times he had called. Always urgent. Always straight from General Fu, or the mayor, or the garrison commander.

"How much this time?" Bei asked wearily, getting straight to the point.

"Five hundred gold yuan, Inspector."

"Five hundred yuan?" Bei yelled, acting properly amazed. "I would have to save for months to pay that, fire my servant girl. It is impossible. I, in fact, have only fifty yuan I might pay you."

"I'm sorry, sir. Our orders are very strict. We are required to receive five hundred."

"It can't be done."

"Sir, you are a valuable neighbor. I might persuade my *Pao* chief to allow you to give only three hundred. He may do it as a special favor to me. I could try."

"Try. Try all day. But I simply don't have the money. I could borrow up to seventy-five yuan, perhaps, but no more."

The *Chia* chief was enjoying the bargaining. It pleased him to gain access to these compounds of the rich, to haggle with them in their studies as if an equal with them, to observe the opulence of their surroundings.

"Sir, I do not see how I could reduce the amount lower than I have. These are desperate times for our city, sir. We are all sacrificing mightily. I myself am working without rest. Perhaps if you pawned some of your possessions, sir, just temporarily. You have those two lovely landscape paintings, sir, they would fetch many gold yuan. And those three very impressive Mongol axes, sir, that have doubtless beheaded many a soldier—"

"Out!" Bei shrieked, jumping up from the chair. "Out of my house, immediately!" The easy familiarity with which the man spoke of Bei's paintings had angered Bei, but his unfortunate mention of the Mongol axes had touched a raw nerve. The axes, heavy long-handled war axes sharpened to a razor's edge, were valuable antiques which had been given to Bei by Jinglo's father upon their wedding.

Bei despised them from the start, for they were military pieces; and now they had the further unpleasant trait of reminding Bei of his faltering marriage.

The *Chia* chief was bewildered by this unexpected turn in what he thought was just another enjoyable bargaining session. "But, sir, I have my job, my collections."

"You shall have one hundred yuan and not a fen more. Call for it tomorrow. The girl will give it to you. Now leave, before I take one of these war axes to your despicable scrawny neck!"

Bei made a move to snatch an axe from the wall. The *Chia* chief's eyes bulged and he scuttled from the study with surprising alacrity. Bei collapsed back to his chair, and did not allow his anger to subside until he heard the servant girl bolt the door behind the man. He was just ready to pick up the paper when she reappeared.

"Sir?"

He looked up. "Yes, what is it, Hsiaoyu?" he snapped.

She cringed, but spoke. "We are nearly out of cooking oil, sir. I need to buy some more."

Bei looked at her in angry wonderment. "So buy some more. That's what we give you the household allowance for."

"Sir, begging your pardon, but the household allowance is gone."

"Gone! Why, we gave you two months' worth at the start of December! How could it be gone already?"

"Sir!" she burst into tears. "You don't know how prices have risen, sir. I looked all day for cooking oil, and the small jars cost thirty yuan, the small jars! We are already out of rice, and the bags we normally buy are one hundred and fifty yuan, sir. And my *Chia* chief is demanding two hundred yuan from my family for defense of the city, and we've already given them my younger brother to be conscripted into the army." At this point she was overcome with great sobs, and stood there weeping loudly into her hands.

Bei sighed deeply. He missed Jinglo already. She was the one to deal with this. He worked hard all day long, and now had to work doubly hard at home in addition.

"I understand, Hsiaoyu. I know prices have risen." Her sobs became less convulsive. "I should have increased the household allowance long ago. You will have more money for food. I will give it to you in the morning, when I give you the money for the *Chia* chief.

But buy only the essentials, nothing other than food and cooking oil, and only small quantities of those. And I will put an extra twenty-five yuan into your pay tomorrow as well."

She sniffled. "Today is the first of the month, sir."

"Yes, I know that!" he said angrily. "But I've just returned from Hangchow and I won't be able to get you all this until tomorrow morning. Now serve dinner in fifteen minutes."

She withdrew, sniffling.

Bei sat there, still fuming. He became aware of the radio, which had been on through all these scenes. The voice was describing "today's momentous political events from Nanking." Bei leaned over and turned the volume up.

"President of the Republic of China, Chiang Kaishek, this morning made a bold move and advanced the cause of peace dramatically by declaring a 'New Year's peace offensive.' Addressing himself to the leaders of the Communist forces, he declared that Chinese had fought Chinese for too long. 'If the Communists are sincerely desirous of peace,' he declared, 'let them meet us at the negotiating table.' He stated that he was ready to meet them at any place to negotiate an end to the civil war. He urged the peoples' representatives of China to bombard the Communists with exhortations to join the generalissimo at the peace table.

"While expressing his bold new move for peace this morning, President Chiang warned the Communists that if they spurn his offer, 'the government, with no other alternative, will fight to the finish.' He resolutely stated that 'the Shanghai-Nanking area, as the political nerve center of the country, will be defended at all costs.' The entire nation is awaiting the Communists' reply to the generalissimo's conciliatory peace overture."

Bei was relieved, for Jinglo's sake, to hear that the Nationalists would defend Chiang Nan at all costs. Then it struck him that Peking had not been mentioned in the defense statement. The Shanghai-Nanking area was identified as the political nerve center to be defended at all costs. Where did that leave Peking? Where it had been for the past year, really: an island in a hostile sea, connected only tenuously with the Nationalist south, by railroads before, now only by airplanes. Really, how could it be defended "at all costs"? Except by Fu fighting to the end.

The servant girl brought in dinner on a tray. She set it on a small side table, and Bei moved there.

"Tea water in ten minutes, sir?"

"Yes, Hsiaoyu. Thank you."

He ate the simple meal of a bowl of rice and a sautéed vegetable dish with no pleasure, still angry over the scene with the *Chia* head. Only when he walked over to his tea cabinet did he begin to feel himself again. Opening the cabinet door, he viewed the two dozen airtight tin containers, each meticulously labeled. He looked them over, smiled, and withdrew the one with the Jade Valley green he had recently refilled. Popping the lid off, he smelled deeply of the contents, then put an exact amount of leaves in the pot below the cabinet, replaced the lid carefully, and put the tin back in its place. He put the four-minute timer and an insulated pot on a tray beside the pot containing the leaves, selected a light green cup, and met the servant girl in the corridor.

"Your water, sir."

"Thank you, Hsiaoyu. Until the morning."

"Until the morning, sir."

He walked softly to the garden, placed the tray on the bench in front of the frozen pool, and immediately poured the steaming water onto the leaves. Upending the timer, he watched with satisfaction as the tightly curled leaves straightened out slowly and the golden color spread through the infusion.

With a glance at the timer he sat back in the chair. It was cold, but like all northerners he wore several layers of bulky undergarments and did his best to ignore the cold during the winter. Space heating was absent in most Peking homes, even the rich ones, so one became accustomed to the cold. He glanced at the stars, and consciously let the waiting for the tea calm him and empty his mind. When he estimated twenty seconds remained on the timer, he poured the tea into the insulated pot, and poured his first cup out of it. He smelled the aroma deeply. Yes. Jade Valley. The fragrance was unmatched. Not fruity, but brisk and clean. He took a sip. The full body, nearly that of a red tea. Yet the taste was light, nearly sparkling, with but a hint of pungency. He soon emptied the first cup and poured himself a second, which he would linger over.

A "peace offensive." Bei chuckled, despite himself. The Communists and Nationalists had been launching peace offensives at each other for nearly four years now, ever since the Japanese surrender. All it meant was that the offering party now felt it had more to gain at the table than on the battlefield. Or wanted some time to consolidate its position. In this case it was probably the latter. As his brother had hinted, the Nationalists were digging in for the defense of Chiang Nan. And Peking was still on its own, isolated except for a few airplane flights a week. Chiang's words had not changed anything, but they had underlined Peking's isolation, its position away from the Nationalist "nerve center." Surely Fu would have realized that when he heard the original broadcast this morning. What would he think of it? Bei's mind, relaxed by the tea, wandered back over the day. Fu's disguised meeting with his daughter. The Communist sheet swirling out of the newspaper.

Of course. Bei sat up with a start. Of course. And that was what An was also. It doesn't explain why he was murdered, and by whom, but it explains what he was doing. But the daughter of Fu Tsoyi? And how far was Fu himself in it?

He would see Fu tomorrow morning, and have something to report.

January 2

General Fu had risen before dawn, as always, and spent the first hour in his calligraphy instructions from Meilu. She was an exacting teacher, and he delighted in submitting himself to her discipline. To a man who made decisions and issued orders all day, an hour of quietly accepting instructions—especially from a beautiful woman on the art of calligraphy—was a perfect way to begin a day.

But now his real work began. He strode into his office from the side door to find Zhou setting the newest revised appointment list on his desk.

"Who first, Zhou?"

"General Yu Chenling still, sir. He wanted to see you immediately after the news of Chiang's speech yesterday morning, but I was able to put him off until today."

"Any reason you can think of not to play his game?"

"I've thought of it, sir. No. He'll know it is for his consumption only. But he won't know how much is just facade and how much sincere. Which is how we must play him, since he is the Chen brother's man, and they are dangerous."

"I'm afraid you're right, although I would like nothing more than a good pretext to force him back to Nanking where he belongs. But while he's here, you're right. We must keep him off balance, and certainly ignorant of the steps we set in motion yesterday."

"After General Yu, sir, I've inserted a short meeting with Inspector Bei, to report what he's learned on the White Cloud Temple business."

"Our wild card. It's been what, a week? Do you think he's gone beyond what we already know?"

"He's good. But this is complicated."

"It is all so complicated." The general stared out his windows.

"Shall I bring in General Yu?"

"Oh. Yes." With an effort, he concentrated his mind and mentally reviewed the role he had to play. The Chen brothers, Chen Lifu and Chen Kuofu, headed the radical right wing of the Kuomintang party, the "CC Clique." Unalterably opposed to the Communists, they controlled the Security Bureau of the Kuomintang and wielded the dreaded Te Wu secret police with deadly efficiency. Even in Peking, Fu's own domain, the Te Wu were nearly autonomous and their leader, Yu Chenling, a force to be reckoned with in any important decision.

Zhou escorted Yu into the room. Fu arose and advanced beside the desk. "General Yu. So glad to see you again," he said, bowing courteously.

"I am honored you could find time to see me, General Fu," returned the thin old man, bowing also.

"We have a common mission, my colleague. We must stay in close contact," said Fu earnestly. He used his reputation for honesty to mask the lies that were necessary. They both sat down.

"It is about that mission that I wish to speak, my friend. Did you hear the generalissimo's speech yesterday morning?"

"Of course. Could I neglect my commander's words?"

"Of course not. What did you think of it?"

A dangerous question. But he was prepared. The delusions of the CC Clique could be relied upon. "The Communists, of course, are badly overextended. Lin Piao failed to consolidate his Manchurian victories before rushing here. In the Huai-Hai campaign towards Hsuchow they are pushing far south beyond their base. They are exhausted, and beginning to despair of ever conquering us. The generalissimo knows all this. So he is tempting them with the peace offensive. It is another brilliant stroke. If they accept it, we swallow them up in a coalition government. If they reject it, they are exposed as the war-mongering bandits they in truth are. And meanwhile we have won time to improve our already excellent position both here and in the south."

Yu Chenling was impressed. "My analysis exactly. So there is no need to take all this talk of 'peace' too seriously. Oh, we should use it for what it's worth. But our real goal is as it has always been: to destroy the Communists. To uproot their evil influence. To punish the weaklings who have yielded to their impure allure, to their . . ."

Fu allowed him to rattle on. He was always fascinated with the intensity of Yu's hatred of the Communists, and his apparently sincere blindness to the true root of his hatred. Yu, in association with the Chen brothers, had grown rich. Not so fabulously rich as the Four Families of course, the Chens themselves, the Chiangs, the Kungs, and the Soongs. But quite rich nonetheless. And the Communists wanted to strip him and his kind of their wealth and give it back to the peasants. It was so transparent. Yet Yu insisted in clothing his fear and hatred in such high-sounding principles. That was the problem with hatred and fear: They usually blinded you. A dangerous state to be in. More dangerous even than the Chen brothers.

". . . and their filthy parceling of women to their lecherous soldiers—how can anyone even seriously suggest coalition with people like that?"

Fu shrugged, and quelled the contempt which rose at Yu's mention of lechery. Yu was inviting him to criticize Chiang Kaishek and his recent small moves to appease the left wing of the Kuomintang, but Fu would have none of that. It would contrast too strongly with Fu's own reputation as a moderate or even a left-winger himself, and throw everything he said into question. Better to maintain his moderate image with Yu. Even the deluded have moments of clarity.

"I don't know what to say to all that, General Yu. I am a plain soldier. I have a city to defend. I'll defend it."

"That is spoken like the heroes of old, General Fu. I have heard conflicting stories about you, but there I am positive: You are a true soldier and know a soldier's duty. I share that trait with you. We both understand duty. Duty to a principle. Duty to our superiors."

Fu glanced at the door. Zhou, taking his cue through the peephole, opened it and announced that Fu's next appointment was waiting.

"General Yu, you will excuse me. I have so many things to do, although none, of course, as important as conferring with you. Will you please keep in touch, and let me know if you think of anything else we can do to improve the city's defenses."

"Of course. I have enjoyed our conference immensely." He rose. "Good-bye, General." As he left the room, he noticed Bei sitting on the bench outside the door. "Inspector," he said curtly as he passed.

"General," Bei said in return. They had experienced jurisdictional difficulties in the past, and the Te Wu security forces had impressed Bei with their arrogance.

Zhou showed Bei into General Fu's office.

"Please be seated, Inspector," said Fu from his chair. "Have you made any progress on the White Cloud Temple case?"

"Some, sir. I traced the murdered man's background in Hangchow. He worked with Chou Enlai and Nieh Jungchen in Shanghai in 1927 before becoming a monk—"

"Chou and Nieh?" Fu asked in genuine surprise.

"Yes, sir. And he had been receiving cash—silver coins—from his concubine for the last several months. This all suggests strongly to me that he was centrally involved with the Communist underground here in the city, General. His concubine relayed money to him to fund their activities. The names in the booklet you . . . now have are probably a list of important Communist agents in the city." He paused, wondering whether to say it. "Have you made progress in tracing those names, General?"

"Zhou has energetically followed it up. Unfortunately, he reports to me that all the names and places are coded. We have our top experts at work on the code, Inspector."

"I see. We can conclude, of course, that his concubine, who works on Jade Street, is a Communist agent also. And I have strong evidence of another underground agent, General. A wound-dresser at the Peking Union Medical College Hospital."

General Fu betrayed not a sign of emotion. "Really? How did you discover her?"

"She had been observed meeting with the prior before, and recently began meeting with his concubine at temple services."

Fu stared at Bei, wondering if Bei knew this second agent's relationship to him. Bei dropped his eyes, and covered it by asking a question.

"Do you want me to arrest these agents, General?"

Fu thoughtfully gazed at the ceiling. It was bright gold, with red dragons sporting amongst clouds. "Since they are evidently Communist, the matter is out of your hands, Inspector, and comes into my jurisdiction, or perhaps the Te Wu. I shall handle the matter entirely. My present inclination is to have them watched carefully rather than arrested, however. They may lead us to others." So far the general had not learned anything from Bei about Prior An's recent role in Peking that he did not already know. But this was all he knew.

"Anything else, Inspector?"

"Yes. Two things. The dissident monk who masterminded the murder was hired by an outsider. He doesn't know the man's identity, though, and only met him several times."

"Do you have a description of the man?"

"Yes, although it is vague. I got a glimpse of him myself, when I followed the monk. But it was nearly dark."

"So what does he look like?"

"Rather tall. Slender. Sometimes in uniform. With eyes that had the monk babbling about 'baleful stars'."

Fu laughed. "Not much to go on. But most interesting. What ideas do you have as to the identity of this Baleful Star?"

"None whatever, actually. But I have a man in the evenings watching the place where he and the monk met, in case he returns. The man also watches the temple itself, during the day."

"Spare no effort to get this mysterious man. He is the key."

"Yes, sir."

"You said two things. The second?"

"Oh. It seems tangent to the problem of who murdered the prior, but it may shed a light on 'why.' When the prior came to the White Cloud Temple from his monastery in Hangchow—the Yellow Dragon—he apparently was ordered to do so by a mysterious Taoist organization called the Purple Mountain. The mere mention of it provokes strange reactions among the Taoists at the White Cloud Temple. It seems to be located in the Western Hills west of Jade Spring Hill."

Fu looked skeptical. "The Taoists are known for their superstitions. Their Baleful Stars."

"Of course. Yet I have a feeling that this may lead to something."

"Need I remind you, Inspector, that the Western Hills are now in Communist hands?"

"Of course. But if you could give me a pass, to Yenching University, for example, I could take off from there."

"Inspector. It is extremely risky. The Communists would love to capture a ranking member of our police force. And for what? To look into a Taoist superstition that may not exist, and that has no promise of telling us who had the prior murdered even if it does exist? Concentrate on the Baleful Star, Inspector."

"You will not give me a pass through the gates, then?"

"No," said Fu with exasperation. "In fact, I forbid you to waste time and risk your personal safety by looking for this place. Concentrate on your promising leads, Inspector. Is that clear?"

Bei dared not contradict him. "You are the commander of the city, General."

"Good. Anything else?"

"No, General."

"Then I commend you. You have made progress in a week's time. Find the Baleful Star."

"I shall do my best."

"Thank you for coming."

Bei fumed as he walked to the south end of Jade Flower Isle, past the general's guards. "I forbid you," indeed. He stomped across Eternal Peace Bridge, turned right off the bridge, and sat down heavily at a bench in Beihai Park on the south shore of Beihai Lake. The south part of Beihai Park had been reopened to the public the day before, and skaters thronged the ice of the lake, being careful to skirt Jade Flower Isle where the guards around General Fu's Winter Palace were conspicuously abundant. Bei glanced across the ice at the small open-sided pavilion on the island, just left of the large Double Rainbow pavilion. He had never studied the small pavilion from this side before. He smiled despite his anger. It was precious: the curved lines of the roof, the delicate red columns, the willow to the side. He had given it his own name, Imperial View Pavilion, because from it you could see the watchtower at the northwest corner of the Forbidden City, its three roofs covered with gleaming golden tiles. He had drunk many cups of tea sitting in the pavilion with his wife and friends, enjoying the scene.

His eyes wandered over the skaters next to the shore. One girl caught his attention, skating rather poorly on primitive skates. It was Yuan's niece. What was her name? Lufei. He watched her awkward attempts to glide, and admired her spirit, if not her skill. Her face was flushed and smiling and she seemed to be having a good time despite her lack of skill. After several minutes she climbed onto the bank and sat down to remove the skates. Bei walked up to her.

"A lovely place to skate, Miss Yuan."

She looked up in surprise. "Inspector! What are you doing here?"

"I have just been to see the mighty general," answered Bei, nodding toward the Winter Palace.

Her eyes grew wide. "So important! He is from my Shansi province, you know."

"Yes. His accent is still that of Shansi."

She finished unstrapping her skates. "I am a very poor skater."

"You appear to be enjoying yourself, though," said Bei diplomatically.

"I skated often in Shansi, but was never as good as my sister or brother," she said, then frowned.

Bei groped for something to say. "Was your childhood happy, then, before the Japanese came?"

"Oh, yes." She turned shining eyes on him, her face open and eager. Not beautiful, Bei thought, but full of life. And young. "My sister was always so cheerful. And my brother—he is good at everything he does, a truly talented person." She looked toward the lake.

"He was an excellent skater. I sometimes wonder where he is, whether he is skating this winter, doing his turns or racing down the ice."

"I was under the impression that your brother was dead."

"Beaten to death by the landlord's men? That is possible. But I don't think so. No body was ever found. And there were stories." She paused, clearing a catch in her voice. "Stories that a young man would often come at night to look at my sister in the landlord's compound. They say he was there the night she died." She smiled wanly. "I like to think that was my brother. He was very fond of my sister."

"Your story is very sad. You are brave to retain your good cheer."

"China is full of sad stories, especially a poor province like Shansi. And we all have to live for the present, don't we?"

She stretched a hand out, and he took it and helped her to her feet. She stumbled a little, and he put his arm around her waist. She laughed and gently leaned against him. "Walking is different than skating!"

He disengaged himself from her when she got her balance. "Yes." He was embarrassed at how much he had enjoyed touching her.

"You are returning to your office at Chunghai Lake?"

"Yes."

"May I walk with you? My uncle forgot his lunch again."

"I'd be delighted."

They chatted pleasantly along the way, Bei telling her of his boyhood in Peking, she responding gaily with stories of her quite different childhood in Shansi. The sun flickering through the bare sycamores on either side of the road and the crisp air gave the day more an aura of autumn than winter. They passed a street vendor with a portable oven at one end of his wooden pole and a basket of raw sweet potatoes at the other. Baked sweet potatoes hung from hooks at the side of the oven, which had a small charcoal fire burning in it. Seeing her eye the potatoes, he stopped and bought her one, over her laughing protestations. She munched happily on it as they continued down the stone sidewalk. When they came to a vendor selling the famous roasted chestnuts from Hopei province's Liang-hsing district, she insisted on buying one for him, amidst peals of laughter. They contentedly exchanged bites of the snacks, and breathed deeply the crisp cold air. Both were flushed and laughing when they arrived at his office.

Considering that he was the Communist's most successful troop commander and the recent conqueror of Manchuria, Lin Piao was surprisingly unimposing physically. Short and thin, his spare frame suggested frailty to those who saw him sitting or standing still. But when he was in motion, as now, the frailty was overshadowed by the tense nervous energy that coursed through his body. He restlessly paced back and forth in the study at his Chihsien headquarters north of Peking, popping roasted beans in his mouth for energy. So Fu Tsoyi wanted to negotiate the fate of Peking. That Kuomintang turtle, wallowing in bed with his Taoist nun. Lying to me about truces while he waits for trainloads of American arms. We will see. Whether the turtle learned the lesson at Nank'ou Pass. We will teach him another pleasure, the exquisite joy of bowing meekly to a superior force.

He snatched the latest telegram from Mao Tsetung off his desk and reread it.

HAVING ENCIRCLED PEKING, RESPOND POSITIVELY TO ANY OVERTURES FOR NEGOTIATIONS. GRANT PARDON TO FU TSOYI AND MAKE OTHER REASONABLE CONCESSIONS TO SECURE CITY INTACT. AVOID ARTILLERY BOMBARDMENT IF POSSIBLE.

Mao. Always right. Right as far back as 1928, mobilizing the peasants while the fools Li Lisan and Chou Enlai led the comrades to death in the cities. Right on the Long March, leading our band northward while I feinted and parried and struck to all sides. Right about the Japanese, using our peoples' hatred of them to build our own strength in the north. Uncanny. The man was always right. All he did was read books and think, but he was always right.

I'll let Fu have his pardon, if Mao says so. But the turtle will get little else. He and his city will learn about justice. Learn to regret their suave manners and luxurious living squeezed from the countryside. A long siege will do Peking good. They will learn their lesson well. It will be like Leningrad again, starvation and despair and desperation. Except this time I'll be on the outside, not on the inside. The inside. Eating leather without being filled. Copulating without being satisfied. Nothing but an endless striving for some pleasure, some security, that is receding further and further in the distance. Striving, striving.

A knock on the door interrupted his restless pacing.

"Yes?" he said impatiently in his high, thin voice.

"Captain Li, comrade."

"Come in, Li."

He smiled as Li Sungji entered. He liked Li's intensity, his single-minded devotion, the strength in his eyes. He understood Li, and Li understood him.

"Sit down, Li. I've heard from Fu Tsoyi. He wants to talk."

"Oh, really?" the aide said, pausing a second as he lowered himself to the seat. The little pause was a touch theatrical, and showed the physical strength and mental control that Lin Piao liked about his aide. Every movement was controlled, every thought tightly bound by mental energy. His whole personality was concentrated and poised, a bundle of intelligence and energy sharply focused on the job at hand: obliterating the Kuomintang reactionaries. Yet he was, at the same time, the most imaginative man Lin Piao had ever known, except for Mao himself. Li could be relied upon to come up with the most unexpected strategies, and much of Lin Piao's success was due to the bewildering flow of ideas from his young aide. What must his dreams be like, Lin Piao mused.

"He sent word through his daughter in our underground," Lin Piao continued.

They both laughed derisively.

"What are your ideas on it, Captain?"

Li narrowed his eyes and considered it. "To begin, I suggest putting them off balance in every way. Insist their envoys meet with you here, on your territory, far from Peking. Treat them with contempt while they're here."

Lin Piao considered it. "But what about the negotiations themselves?"

Li's eyes lit up with hatred. "I have seen Kuomintang being harsh, demanding everything, then carelessly exacting the ultimate punishment from their hapless victim—why should they not experience it themselves?"

"Why not, indeed?" answered Lin Piao after a pause, noting the vehemence of his aide's words, and wondering again what wound lent the young man his tightly controlled fury. "Except, of course, there is Mao, and his concern that we gain control of the city without damaging it, and quickly." He glanced at the telegram. Grant reasonable concessions, it said.

Li reined in his emotions. "Yes. Mao. Always it is Mao, the first among us." His dark eyes went empty as he thought. "Yet he is not near, and only a telegraph connects us with his Hsipaipo headquarters. He has always given you considerable leeway in the field, comrade. You should trust your judgment. It is in no way inferior to his. I anticipate the day when your star will outshine his."

Lin Piao smiled, despite himself. Had he not been in the inner circle of power from the Long March on? Was he not the brilliant conquerer of Manchuria? And did he not now encircle Peking? No other field commander could equal his success.

"We will see, Captain Li. I appreciate your suggestions. Go to Peking tomorrow. Fu's aide, Colonel Zhou Peifeng, will meet you at 0900 hours, at the northwest corner of the Forbidden City, facing the old watchtower across the moat. Tell him we agree, and will meet two envoys of his choosing—when? Day after tomorrow?"

"Make them wait. Let them consume a few days more of their food and fuel reserves."

"Good. Three days from tomorrow, then. The sixth. And while you're in the city tomorrow, look around. Spend the day there, and keep your eyes open. You'll have no trouble getting in and out of the city?"

"No, sir. I never have." He smiled.

Bei drew a line from the Summer Palace's Spring Heralding Pavilion to the peak of Jade Spring Hill, where the pagoda was situated, and continued it into the Western Hills. He stepped back and surveyed the wall map in his office. The line ran several degrees below due west, straight for the northern entrance of Fragrant Hills Park, one of several old imperial pleasure gardens in the Western Hills. This park, like the Summer Palace and the others, had been pillaged and burned by English and French troops in 1860 and again in 1900, so that only ruins now remained.

Between the Summer Palace and Fragrant Hills Park were several other parks and Buddhist temples, including the Temple of the Recumbent Buddha and the Temple of Azure Clouds. Bei judged that the Purple Mountain—whatever it was—would not be located in this region, because it would be better known if it were. He gazed at the line running west of Fragrant Hills Park. Deeper into the Western Hills. Nothing was marked on the map there. That would be where the Purple Mountain was. Whatever it was. If it existed at all. Fragrant Hills was about twenty-one kilometers from the city's center. Yenching University was about twelve kilometers. He would somehow get past Fu's guards at the city gates and out to Yenching, perhaps on the pretext of visiting Chang, then the remaining nine kilometers to Fragrant Hills and however many beyond that—for those he would be on his own.

He called Chang at Yenching University. Strange, picking up the phone and talking to someone in Communist territory.

"Yes?"

"Professor Chang. It's Bei. I'm glad I caught you at home."

"Even in the New China we take our after-lunch relaxation time."

"How about lunch tomorrow? You and I and Ho."

"Sounds delightful. I haven't been to the city since your dinner party. Madame Bei had a safe journey to Chiang Nan?"

"Yes, thank you. Shall we meet at the Ch'uanchuteh?"

"Excellent! Eleven-thirty?"

"Fine. You'll have no trouble getting into the city?"

"Not with my magical pass from General Fu."

"See you then."

"Until then."

He next called Ho, and then made the reservations at the restaurant, Peking's oldest "Peking Duck" establishment. He reluctantly sat at his desk to eliminate the last vestiges of the pile of paperwork that had greeted him on his return from Hangchow. He had until late afternoon to work on it. He would be at the White Cloud Temple for the evening devotions.

Bei settled onto the bench in front of the White Cloud Temple and pulled the Western-style hat over his forehead. The hot biscuits and bowl of noodles he had purchased from a stand on Lishilu Street coagulated in his stomach. He unfolded the thin newspaper and desultorily began skimming it, wondering why he had eaten the biscuits. From within the temple he could hear the sound of bells and drums from the Hall of the Jade Emperor, and the muffled low rumble of the chants. He put down the newspaper and listened. In the cold twilight the sounds somehow seemed familiar and comforting, seemed a bulwark against the chill and the gathering dark. He scoffed at himself and shook his head. Their superstition is infecting you, he thought accusingly, and returned to the ideographs of his newspaper. Some people soon began drifting out of the temple. He lowered his newspaper so he could see over the top of it. Other idlers sat on nearby benches, so he felt inconspicuous, especially with the hat pulled down.

The two tall female figures were not difficult to spot. Meiling and Fu's daughter were engaged in earnest conversation as they emerged from the temple, their heads bowed close together. They walked past Bei towards Lishilu Street, absorbed in their conversation. When they were some ten meters past him, Bei got set to rise, but froze as he noticed two other men get up from an adjacent bench and hurry off, their eyes intent on the two women. Bei delayed his departure to put four meters between him and the men. His first inclination was to regard them as merely amorously interested in eyeing two attractive women, but they seemed too well-dressed and serious of mien for that. They were all moving in the crowd of people who had left the temple, so Bei knew he could stay close to the two women and the two men without being noticed by them. When the women emerged out of the alleyway onto Lishilu Street, they stopped next to the road and finished their conversation, then split up with a curt nod to each other. Fu's daughter took off south, towards Kuan'anmen'nei Street, while Meiling strode to the north, towards the Hsipienmen Gate. The men followed the figure north, as did Bei. Soon the crowd thinned somewhat, until the two men were walking directly behind Meiling on the edge of the road, some two meters from her. They glanced back, down the road, and one of them nodded. A military truck twenty meters away accelerated, and soon was rushing past Bei at a high speed, hugging the side of the road. Bei saw the two men glance at each other as the heavy truck hurtled towards the girl, then move to her left to block her escape.

"Meiling!" Bei yelled. She looked around to her left just in time to see the two men rush at her, their arms extended to push her into the truck's path. In a blur she instantly pivoted on the ball of her left foot and swung her body down and to the right as she kicked her right foot high in a clockwise 180-degree arc. The outside edge of her right foot slammed into the temple of the man nearest Bei, who staggered back, stunned. As she continued her clockwise turn she glimpsed the truck nearly upon her, and flexing the right leg she set it down directly in front of the other man. She crouched and caught his oncoming right elbow in her right hand. Taking advantage of her clockwise momentum as well as his forward motion, she threw him easily over her body into the path of the truck, using his weight and her planted right foot to then check her clockwise momentum and permit her to roll to her left, away from the street. The man's body exploded with a dull splatter as it hit the speeding truck's grill, spraying blood and chunks of flesh over the truck and street.

Bei blinked. Meiling was gone. His mind struggled to comprehend what had happened. Upon hearing his call, she had simply crouched and turned a high-kicking circle, injuring one man and killing another. And now she was nowhere to be seen. Bei walked to the man who had been kicked, now slumped with his back against a building, vainly trying to focus his eyes. A huge bruise throbbed on the side of his head, and he vomited as Bei approached. Bei grabbed his hair and jerked his head up. Yes. It was one of Yu Chenling's Te Wu. He released his hair and walked away, knowing there was no need to check on the other man. And he knew to whom the truck belonged.

January 3

General Fu looked up as the guard showed Bei in. "Inspector. I am surprised to see you back so soon."

And irritated, thought Bei. But this early morning meeting had to be. He steeled himself. "My investigation is at a critical point, General, and I need your help."

"What is this 'critical point'?"

"Yesterday evening I was following Prior An's concubine after the evening devotional at the White Cloud Temple. She was in the company of the hospital dresser."

No reaction from the general.

"After they parted company, a murder attempt was made on the concubine by two men."

"Attempt?"

"Yes. She killed one of them and badly injured the other."

Fu laughed. These Communists. They were tough, whatever else you might say about them.

"So?"

"I recognized one of the men."

The General leaned forward. "Ah. And whoever wanted to kill her probably wanted the prior killed also. Well, who was it?"

"The injured man was one of the thugs employed by General Yu Chenling. Te Wu, in other words."

Fu masked his emotions. Te Wu! The Kuomintang's secret police—brutal, and thus dangerous. Certainly motivated and capable of murdering the prior if they had discovered he was the head of the Communist underground in the city. And of attempting to murder Meiling, the prior's agent and mistress. He felt a rush of alarm as he thought of his daughter, another agent of the dead prior, and was thankful he had promptly burned the prior's booklet that Bei had found.

"You're quite sure that it was the Te Wu that killed the prior, then?"

"Oh, no, General. Granted, that is the logical conclusion, based on their attempt on the prior's accomplice. But several things about it are not quite right, in minor ways. One: Why hire a monk to direct the killing of the prior? Why not simply do it themselves? Two: Having a group of monks burn the prior for embezzlement of funds to support a concubine is very imaginative, a quite clever way to hide another motive for the murder. Such imagination and boldness is beyond the Te Wu. Pardon me if I offend you, General, but the Te Wu's characteristic operation is usually considerably more . . . coarse than that. Like throwing a woman into the path of a truck—that's their style. There may be witnesses who will swear two thugs threw her, but the Te Wu can insist that it was merely another of many traffic fatalities that are now plaguing the city, what with so many military vehicles speeding through overly crowded streets."

Fu leaned back in his chair and cupped his hands under his chin. "Go on."

"There is another point to consider. The monk says that his contact man—the Baleful Star—only met him several times, with several months between meetings. Why so long between meetings? That suggests that it might have been directed by someone outside of the city, who only came in periodically."

Fu pondered Bei's points. They had merit. It was a puzzle. Although the Te Wu were behind the attempted murder of Meiling, the prior's agent, it was not at all clear that it was they who had ordered the murder of the prior.

"So who then, if not the Te Wu?"

"I have no firm ideas. But we can't dismiss the Te Wu. They after all have a motive—their hatred of the Communists—and we know they did try to kill the prior's agent. Which means we have to investigate them, even if it is to satisfy ourselves that it wasn't them."

Fu smiled grimly. The man is methodical. And tenacious. And a fool. "Inspector, one does not investigate the Te Wu."

"I realize that, General. I'm not suggesting you call Yu Chenling in and grill him. But you have your own intelligence unit. I'm betting you have a list of Yu Chenling's Te Wu agents, along with descriptions and home addresses. There can't be too many. A dozen, perhaps. Give me that list. If the Baleful Star who hired the monk is among them, we can identify him. I've caught a glimpse of him, and might recognize him. But the monk knows him well by sight, and is eager to help us."

"I can't have Yu Chenling gather his agents for a viewing by your monk, Inspector."

"Of course not. I'm not stupid, General."

Fu raised his eyebrows, but let the indirect reprimand pass.

"We can begin by hiding the monk where he can see who comes and goes from Yu's compound. He may spot the Baleful Star there."

"The Baleful Star," murmured Fu. "It comes again to the Baleful

Star." He pondered the proposal. "If Yu's Te Wu men number fourteen, how long would it take?"

"Assume half of them come and go regularly from Yu's compound. One day for the monk to view them. Assume the descriptions are sufficiently detailed for us to know whom we missed. We let the monk view them at their homes. Two a day there, morning and evening. So four more days for them. Less than a week."

"It would be risky. Yu is not a man to be trifled with. Nor his men, in spite of their lack of imagination."

"I understand that."

"And what do we have at the end of five days?"

"We either have the identity of the Baleful Star and know who had the prior killed and why. Or—and I think this is more likely—we know it wasn't the Te Wu, know we have to look elsewhere."

"And if it is the latter? I think I know who you're thinking of. 'An organization outside the city,' you said. You still have this mysterious Purple Mountain on your mind, don't you, Inspector?"

Bei shrugged his shoulders. "It's a lead, General."

"A lead that takes us into Communist territory is no lead at all, Inspector."

"Perhaps. But will you give me that list of Te Wu agents, with their descriptions? And their home residences?"

Fu thought. It was more than risky, it was dangerous. But if Yu discovered his men were being watched, Fu could simply disavow any knowledge of it. Bei would be killed by the Te Wu, of course, and Fu would not be able to stop it. But it would not touch Fu, whatever. And it might work.

"All right. Call here after the midday relaxation. Fourteen hundred. Zhou will have the list for you. But he and I will swear you did not get it from us."

"I understand." Indeed he did. He was in this on his own. If the Te Wu find out, it would be him they'd come after. "By the way, where is Zhou? This is my first visit to you that he has not shown me in."

"Zhou is . . . attending a meeting elsewhere in the city. He will return shortly. The list will be ready for you at fourteen hundred, at Zhou's office. Thank you for calling."

Bei rose.

"Unless there is anything else we need to discuss," added Fu, thinking suddenly that Bei was no longer a man to be dismissed so curtly as he had previously thought.

"No, General. Good-bye."

As Bei left, Fu turned in his chair and stared out the window at the garden. Perhaps his wild card had not evaporated, after all. And perhaps his wild card would come to nothing. That was the nature of wild cards. You never knew. But thirty years of struggle had convinced him that you never ignored the possibility of obtaining a wild card. That wild card often popped up in places where reality was too complex to be readily comprehended. And this burning of a Taoist prior was becoming complex. The Baleful Star. A Te Wu agent? A Purple Mountain man, whatever that was? Or someone altogether different? Someone from a gray area of some incomprehensibly complex patch of reality. A puzzle. His eye rested on the T'aihu stone. Yes. That was what it was like. Full of unexpected angles and unlikely surfaces. Pitted, pounded by the waters of experience until the soft material was destroyed and only the hard remained, running in surprising veins. Unbelievably complex. The ultimate puzzle. A soft knock from the door to his private quarters interrupted his reverie. Meilu? Then he remembered that Zhou would be returning covertly.

"Come in, Zhou." His aide entered and softly shut the door behind him. A Shansi man like Fu. Captured by the Communists in 1947 and released. His aide from as far back as Suiyuan. Could he trust even him? One had to trust at least a few. And keep your guard up.

"So?"

"It is arranged. For the sixth."

"You and Chang were acceptable?"

"Yes."

"Call Chang immediately. Set up several hours for us all together on the afternoon of the fourth—no, make it the fifth. This can't leak out."

"Yes, sir."

"Any preconditions on the agenda?"

"None."

"And where?"

"Chihsien."

"That's nearly a hundred kilometers. Why so far?"

"The aide said it was Lin Piao's headquarters. That we'd have to go there if we wanted to talk with him."

"It was Colonel Tao?"

"No. A young aide. I haven't seen him before."

"Probably Wufen. Decisive, short, stocky, powerful?"

"No. Decisive, yes. Intense. Well-muscled, too, but thin. Introduced himself as Captain Li Sungji. He seemed very competent, and spoke with Lin Piao's full authority."

"Good. How long will it last?"

"Two days, with a third possible if we need it."

"Good." Fu leaned back in his chair, motioning for Zhou to take a seat. "What will they want, old friend?"

Zhou sat, and leaned back also. "Surrender. Unconditional surrender."

"Yes. As a first position. We will reject that and offer a coalition government, six of ours to four of theirs. When they reject that, we will put on the table what issues?"

Zhou ticked the most important issues off on his fingers. "Pardons. Who and what nature. Evacuations before the turnover. Who and how many. Disposition of the troops, and timing. Your own troops and the other troops. Respect for personal property. Yours and that of others."

"Yes. When all these are added to the pot, we stir well, exact concessions, and reluctantly concede for our part a coalition of five to five. If we have to, we will go four to six, assuming we have done well on the other concessions."

"I am looking forward to the bargaining, General," said Zhou, with grim relish.

"So am I. You will do well, my friend. You have bargained with Communists before. We will go over our positions on the issues in detail this afternoon. For now, another pressing matter has arisen."

Briefly Fu told Zhou of his discussion with Bei, and the need to share their list and descriptions of the Te Wu agents.

"You don't think that Yu might have used one of his officers in the Ninety-fourth Division?"

"You may have a point there. Some of the young officers are quite capable of this. Include on the list any officers of the Ninety-fourth who regularly visit Yu at his compound—say no less frequently than once every three days, over the past month."

"That may bring the list up to sixteen or eighteen."

"It can't be helped. Can you have it for the inspector by fourteen hundred?"

Zhou thought. "Probably. Of course I'll have it on a paper and in a style that can't be traced to us."

"Good."

"I'll go call Chang and then get on this immediately, if you'll excuse me."

"Of course. Any more appointments this morning?"

"None, sir."

"Good. I've got a lot of correspondence with Nanking. Report back to me after fourteen hundred when you've given the list to the inspector."

"Yes, sir," said Zhou, and left the room.

Fu attempted to concentrate on the paperwork, but failed. He abruptly stood and began pacing before the window, his mind brimming with thoughts and emotions. It was at hand. Soon he would join with Lin Piao to decide the fate of Peking. And perhaps the fate of the country. The impending confrontation sent a steady pulse of energy through his sturdy body, and a keen sense of anticipation mixed with fear. In his hands. Two million people, in the ancient capital. He had fought and plotted and survived for thirty years for this moment. How many others in history had held the fate of Peking in their hands? Three? Four? No one since Wu Sankuei in the middle of the seventeenth century. Wu, commanding the best army in China at the Mountain-Sea Pass at the eastern end of the Great Wall. The only entrance into China proper from Manchuria, where Dorgon's powerful Manchu armies were gathering to launch an assault on the tottering Ming Dynasty, ruled now by the court eunuchs. The last Ming Emperor had hanged himself on Coal Hill as the powerful bandit hordes of Li Tsucheng swarmed toward Peking from the other direction, from their mountain stronghold in Shansi. The same mountains in which the Communists holed up after their Long March, ironically enough. Wu, trying to decide whether to rush his armies to Peking's defense against the bandit rebels, or stay at the Mountain-Sea Pass and deny the restless Manchu armies of Dorgon access to

China. Was he pacing like this? Did he feel this mixture of anticipation and fear? He had chosen to guard the pass, and it meant the fall of Peking and the Ming empire to Li's rebels.

But then in taking the city the bandit Li unwisely permitted the death of Wu's father and, worse yet, Li appropriated Wu's favorite concubine, the ravishing Cheng Yuanyuan. That was too much for Wu, the thought of that Shansi bandit sleeping with his Cheng Yuanyuan. Wu promptly met with Dorgon at the Mountain-Sea Pass and joined forces with the Manchus, let them through the pass, and in one staggering onslaught their combined armies destroyed Li's rebel forces and much of Peking. Which allowed Dorgon to set up the Ch'ing Dynasty, and put Manchu emperors over the Middle Kingdom for nearly three hundred years.

Wu Sankuei: The fate of Peking and China decided by a beautiful woman, Cheng Yuanyuan. Could it happen to him? Fu smiled. Meilu was beautiful enough. And accomplished. And if his guess was correct, she had come into his life because of this century's bandit army. But no. This time the fate of Peking would not be controlled by the square inch that drives men mad, now as well as then.

Because this time the forces were more evenly balanced in a more classic confrontation. Fu realized he held Peking as a connoisseur holds a precious vase in his hands. He smiled at the image. The vase could survive only if he voluntarily gave it up. He knew the Communists intended to legitimize themselves and their conquests by establishing their capital at Peking. They needed an intact Peking, a capital where the continuity of China's history and their role in that history was plain for all to see. If they destroyed the city, they destroyed their carefully wrought image of themselves as constructive builders of civilization. A Peking in rubble would certify Chiang's charge that they were nothing more than brutal bandits, and might well be the event that finally united the quarreling warlords and factions of the Nationalist cause into a successful military and political force.

They needed Peking. Intact, not in rubble. And with two hundred thousand troops under his command, and ample artillery, they couldn't have it intact without Fu's permission. The precious vase was in his hands, and he could name his price.

But the bargaining would be fierce. He was surrounded, after all. Cut off from the Nationalists in the south. Fu grinned as he paced.

Yes, the confrontation would be fierce. Historic. And he had a few surprises for them. And perhaps a wild card or two. He laughed aloud, a laugh of relish and eagerness for the battle. A laugh which savored high stakes and the interplay of chance, toughness, and intelligence. Still laughing, he strode out of the room to his private chambers.

Meilu was sitting before her calligraphy table when he burst into the room, eyes ablaze. She recognized part of what was in those eyes.

"My lord General Fu," she said in surprise and mock reproach.

"No," said Fu. "I am Wu Sankuei, and I have fought from the Mountain-Sea Pass to Peking and deposed the upstart Li Tsucheng to claim my concubine, Cheng Yuanyuan."

Meilu rose and stood there regally, her tightly sashed robe revealing her body's contours. "You have saved me from that filthy bandit chieftain, my lord Wu."

"Did he touch you?" he demanded angrily.

"He meant to, but I would not allow it, and put him off until my lover could rescue me."

"He is now here," Fu said, striding up to her and unbuckling an imaginary sword which they both could plainly hear clatter heavily onto the floor as he reached for her sash.

"Finally I can love as a true lady loves a true man, with wit as well as passion," she said teasingly as she intercepted his eager hand and brought it to her cheek.

He smiled ruefully. "Ah, yes, the clouds must gather before the rain will fall."

"But the rain will be fierce and torrential when it comes," she said with allure, kissing his palms. She began to unbutton his quilted coat and the shirt underneath as he ran his hands over her shoulders.

"All alone in the bedroom, it seems unbearably lonely,"

she began, chanting a poem from the two-thousand-year-old essay "On a Beautiful Woman."

"Thinking of a handsome man, my emotions hurt me.
Why did this charming person tarry in coming?

126

Time runs out fast, the Flower will wither—
I entrust my body to you, for eternal love."

She slipped his coat and shirt off, and leaned her head on his chest as he held her close. It was now his turn. He began the strong cadences of a poem eighteen hundred years old.

"There is a girl, worthy companion to Hsishih,
Tall and of handsome appearance,
With a soft and finely chiseled face,
Full of languorous charm."

She turned her face up to his and interrupted him with a kiss, full and sweet, as she unfastened his belt and let his trousers drop. His hands followed his words as he continued.

"Her figure as faultless as a sculpted statue,
Waist as thin as a roll of silk.
With a neck long and white as ivory,
Of extreme elegance and wholly fascinating.
Of gentle nature and modest behavior,
Yet of luxurious and alluring beauty."

Knowing the lines to come, she withdrew from him and backed slowly to the bed with wide eyes, as if frightened of his inflamed manhood.

He advanced, chanting the lines with a soft yet deep and full voice.

"With jet black hair done up in a chignon
So shining it could serve as a mirror,
With a mouche that stresses her conquering smile,
With clear eyes, their moist gaze limpid,
With white teeth and red lips,
And her body a dazzling white color—"

Here she undid her sash and let the robe fall to either side of her breasts and hips as she leaned back on the bed.

He whispered the last lines reverently.

"When the Red Flower shows its beauty
And exhales its heady perfume."

She spread her thighs and arched her back, letting him feast on the sight and smell of her sex.

"While she is staying with you in the night
And you feast and sport with her,
Such are the delights of carnal love."

As he finished, he slowly ran his hands along her thighs and bent down to kiss her sex and inhale her aroma, letting his tongue caress and massage her warmth and moistness, gently licking her liquid up and savoring it as he swallowed.

Moaning softly, she arched to the side so she could reach his manhood and began the lines of a one-thousand-year-old poem by Emperor Li Yu of the T'ang Dynasty.

"The copper tongues in the Sheng mouth organ
Resound in the cool bamboo tubes,
As slowly she plays new tunes
With her jade-like fingers."

So saying, her fingers fluttered up and down his Jade Stalk, smooth strokes on the top surface, rougher pinches on the bottom surface.

He took up and finished the poem.

"Her eyes look at me invitingly—
As autumn waves, swiftly changing.
We knew the rain and the clouds
In the intimacy of the curtained chamber,
Where our deep passion united us."

He swung onto the bed atop her and they were joined in the classic Turning Dragons position, their bodies undulating like autumn waves, her fragrant Red Flower blooming robustly in response to the tunes his Jade Stalk was playing in her. Two slow, resonant strokes; eight quick, light ones; then the resonant ones again. She quivered as her gathering clouds sent ripples through her Cinnabar Cleft. As he kissed her neck, she arched it back to expose it the better. He squeezed and caressed her neck with his lips up and down its length, even as the two petals of her Red Flower squeezed and caressed the length of his Jade Stalk.

She pushed him gently to one side and he rolled over onto his back as she came atop him. She placed her hands on his chest as she positioned her feet beside his thighs and squatted above him, then pushed her left leg out in front, assuming the Overlapping Fish Scales position. She began to rock up and down on her flexed legs, feeling his manhood plunge deep into her Cinnabar Cleft, then slowly raising herself until the lips of her sex were nibbling at his expanded tip, caressing it as surely and warmly as he had caressed her Red Flower with his tongue. After a minute he moaned loudly, feeling the rain about to descend. She leaned forward so that his Jade Stalk lashed her Jeweled Terrace fully, and in a steady rocking motion she plunged him deeply into her again and again, raising herself as he arched his back higher and higher. Her clouds gathered again as his rain came in great long waves and they cried aloud together. She fell onto his chest and they lay still, his arms around her, his hands gently moving up and down her back.

In a whisper, he slowly began another poem by Li Yu. She drowsily joined, and they said it in unison, softly and contentedly.

"The moon of dawn is waning;
The overnight mists dissolve.
Speechless I seek the rest of my pillow,
Thinking with fond longing
Of our fragrant dream.
I faintly hear the sparse cries
Of geese flying in the sky."

He reached down and pulled the heavy quilt up over them, and closed his eyes. A final couplet drifted across his mind as the warmth enveloped them.

"Who must answer to heaven?
Who creates the orphans?"

The Ch'uanchuteh was Peking's most famous roast-duck restaurant, which had opened in 1864 south of Ch'ienmen Gate. As Bei, Chang, and Ho entered the restaurant the chefs in the kitchen next to the entrance called out their names with boisterous pride in their distinguished clientele. The three friends were shown to their customary private room upstairs.

"An excellent idea, Inspector," said Chang. "How long has it been since we've been here?"

"At least three weeks," said Ho. "Far too long. This siege has worn us all down into a siege mentality, making us forget the better things of life."

"That's what is so valuable about the inspector," said Chang, as they took their seats. "He is constantly reminding us of the finer things in life."

"Actually, with Madame Bei gone, I find myself spending very little time in cultured pursuits and must rely on you friends to get me away from my work."

"How is your work going? I presume the business at White Cloud Temple is all cleared up?" asked Ho.

"Not at all. We know the monks responsible for the murder, but the case has taken on a twist with the discovery that the prior was probably a member of the Communist underground here, and that a mysterious man hired the monks to have him killed."

Ho and Chang glanced up in surprise. "Underground agent? In a Taoist temple? Those places are not so otherworldly after all," said Ho.

"You are treading on dangerous ground, Inspector. Be careful," added Chang.

"I thought you might help me. Who would want a Communist agent killed?"

"That's relatively easy," said Ho. "The Nationalists. Of which there are two principal factions in Peking, either one of which could have done it. The ultra-right wing, which means the Te Wu. Or the middle-to-left wing, which means Fu Tsoyi."

It was Bei's turn to be surprised. "General Fu? I hadn't thought of that."

"Why not?" asked Ho. "He is an obvious choice."

"Well, I suppose mainly because it was Fu himself who called me into the case and ordered me to go deeper into it, and who has been very interested in my investigation all along."

"And Mayor," interrupted Chang. "Why would Fu need to conceal it if he had killed a Communist agent? Or why have the renowned inspector investigate it, if he wanted it to remain concealed?"

"Good questions, Professor." They stopped talking while the waiter brought in the first course, sautéed ducks' kidneys and deep-fried duck's tongue.

"While I have no answers, I do know that when you deal in covert intelligence operations, different rules apply and common sense is no longer adequate," continued Ho. "For example, if Fu were contemplating negotiating with the Communists at some point, he would not want them to know that he had been responsible for killing one of their agents. As to why have the inspector investigate a case for which he might already know the solution, perhaps Fu knows only part of the solution. Perhaps Fu might have had the prior murdered because the prior was blocking Fu's access to some critical information, and the inspector's real function is to get that information, rather than track down the murderer."

Bei's head began to swim.

"In any case, old friend, the professor is right: You are treading on dangerous ground, and must be careful. New rules apply, whether it is the Te Wu or General Fu. Or rather, I should say there are no longer any rules at all. Everything is permitted. Which is why it is so dangerous."

Bei barely noticed the dishes. He had never even considered Fu. What game might he be playing?

"Have either of you ever heard of an organization called the Purple Mountain?"

Chang shook his head, but Ho stopped with his chopsticks halfway up to his mouth. "That's very strange you should mention that name."

"Why?"

"Because I haven't heard it for years. Decades, actually."

"What is it?"

"I don't know." Ho lowered his chopsticks and tried to remember. "When we were boys, Inspector, I heard tales. That the parents of one of our peers were approached by the Purple Mountain with the offer to take the boy in and educate him."

"And?"

"Again, I don't know. I don't really remember anything other than the tale. I don't know if he stayed here, or disappeared. Perhaps it has nothing to do after all with your Purple Mountain."

"It sounds like it might. It was an organization called the Purple Mountain that ordered the prior to come to Peking from Hangchow."

"Some Taoist secret society?"

"Perhaps. I know little more about it than you do. Except they are rumored to practice strange sexual rites. And I have a good idea where it's located: in the Western Hills, west of Fragrant Hill Park's northern gate."

Ho and Chang looked at each other. "Uh, Inspector," began Ho. "The Western Hills are thick with Communist troops, you know."

"Nonetheless," said Bei with determination, "I am going there."

The other two put down their chopsticks and stared at Bei incredulously.

"And in fact you are going to help me, Professor," added Bei.

"This is madness, old friend," began Ho.

"To begin with, you can't get outside the city gates," said Chang.

"I will get myself outside the city gates," said Bei. "And to your house in Yenching, Professor. Don't ask me how; I will. All I need from you, Professor, is a good bicycle to get from Yenching out to the Purple Mountain."

"The bicycle, of course, is very easily arranged," said Chang. "But do you really intend to ride straight into the Western Hills?"

"I do."

"We both wish you wouldn't," said Ho.

"Sorry. It's my only good lead currently to solve the case."

"Is the case so important?" asked Chang.

Bei paused and groped for words. "In itself, it may be of some real importance for our city. And beyond that . . . it has assumed importance for me. With my wife gone, and the city straining to survive the siege and our very civilization threatening to unravel before my eyes . . . it has become important to me to solve the case. It is all I have to live for now."

Ho and Chang shook their heads in the silence. "My friend," began Ho, "you have a good deal more to live for than this case. You have us, your old friends. You have your lovely wife, waiting to return from Hangchow. And you have many more teas to drink and roast ducks to consume, such as this magnificent specimen here."

As he spoke, the waiter brought in a platter heaped with thin slices of duck meat and skin, along with a plate of thin pancakes and a bowl of shredded green onions and garlic in a sweet bean sauce.

They all savored the fragrance and sight of the dishes.

"You're right," said Bei. "This is worth concentrating on." They all three put slices of meat and skin into a rolled pancake, added the sauce, and took large bites of the mixture, contemplating the taste at length. Bei then picked up the duck separately and tasted it. He glanced at his friends. "On second thought, perhaps you're wrong."

All three laughed.

"But it's not so bad, Inspector," protested Ho. "Really, granted it is somehow different, what is the problem?"

"There is indeed much to be said in its favor," answered Bei. "The meat is tender and well cooked, indicating the duck hung for a sufficiently long time, and that the steaming water pumped into its digestive tract cooked it sufficiently from the inside. The skin is crisp and well separated from the meat, testifying to adequate pumping of compressed air between the skin and meat before it was hung up. So far so good. And the sauce is really quite good."

"Yes. But somehow the flavor of the meat is not quite right, is it?" ventured Chang.

"Excellent, my learned Professor. For two reasons. First, it has not been cooked in a fire of peach or pear wood. This almost tastes like a coal fire, which it may well have been. And, more fundamental, the duck has been improperly fed during the last three weeks of its life. Somehow the proper mixture of millet, mung beans, sorghum and wheat chaff has not been achieved. Or perhaps it was allowed to move around those weeks, and added all manner of coarse greens to its diet. Whatever. It tastes . . . coarse. Wild. And the delicate peach wood or pear wood flavor is missing also."

"You're right, of course, Inspector," said Ho, fixing himself another pancake. "But it's still good and I'm glad to be here."

"So am I. But I do wish the Duck King at Pachiatsun was still sending his ducks to the Ch'uanchuteh. He would not send improper ducks," said Bei.

"Which is why he is no longer sending ducks at all," declared Chang.

Bei abruptly turned to Chang and spoke. "Professor, can you get me a bicycle?"

Chang paused. "Yes. Of course. But I would prefer you would not do it."

"I appreciate your advice. I will need a day or two to make my arrangements. And I am counting on your silence, my friends. How about the sixth, Professor?"

Chang looked up sharply, then lowered his eyes. "I . . . I shall be occupied all of the sixth as well as the seventh. Sorry."

Ho and Bei knew from his manner that something was amiss.

"No problem with Madame Chang, I take it?" asked Ho.

"No, no."

"Nor at the university, I hope?" asked Bei.

"No, all is fine. It is merely that I am . . . occupied those days."

Ho and Bei glanced at each other. "So, he has made his move," said Ho in a low voice. "The sixth. How long have you known?"

Chang knew it was no use to deny it. His friends knew him, and the role he would play, far too well to fool.

"Only an hour. Zhou Peifeng called just before I left to come here. I know nothing yet, really, nor could I tell you if I did."

"Of course," said Ho. "Good luck, friend."

Chang nodded his head.

"Which means I will have to make my trip the fifth," said Bei. "And start and finish my preparations tomorrow. May I call on you at Yenching late in the morning the day after tomorrow, Professor?"

"In the morning, yes. And be careful."

"We must all be careful," responded Bei.

"Except me," said Ho expansively, patting his belly. "No one cares about a retired mayor. Except my youngest daughter, whom I must pick up from her violin lesson on the north side of town in thirty minutes. She can coax some surprisingly decent sounds out of the instrument, my friends. So let us finish this lunch with what pleasure we can muster, eh?"

How they all hurry from place to place, selling, buying, searching. She will come back, if she comes, to a place like this. A fox vixen becomes restless in a grave. She gathers vital essence from the earth around her until she cannot be resisted, then on a dark night she emerges—to seduce us and derange our minds. She must be killed, each time, to protect us.

But how can you resist her? Her slender white throat gleaming in the moonlight, blood pulsing through the veins as her Shady Valley receives the strokes of your Positive Peak, absorbing all your yang into herself. She exhausts you, robs you of your own vital essence for herself. But I know how to trick her, how to retrieve what is mine, and more. How to send her back to her grave, blood pulsing in her neck, slender, gleaming, a film of moisture on it from her lewd exertions.

Yes, I send the vixen back, just as he sends the males. They are all fox incubi, why else hoard all that land, fields full of fox holes. They have to die, for hoarding, for being incubi, just as she has to die, be sent back to her grave. She likes it that way, I have seen how she squirms, she enjoys it so.

She's in there. I can feel her essence calling me. She always wanted me, needed me, even before the son turned her into a fox like himself and killed her. She's in there, in a back room, thirsting for my Positive Peak, her neck long and white, pulsing. I must. He will understand. He kills the fox males, I the vixens. I must.

January 4

It was past his usual hour when Bei arrived at the office. He had waited at the gate to his villa that morning for the old man with the green cart who collected night soil in his neighborhood. The man had trouble comprehending what Bei wanted, but finally a large gold yuan note had persuaded him to cooperate, although it didn't help his understanding. Shaking his head, he had resumed his morning's emptying of the wooden buckets in front of each door into his barrel, promising to meet Bei early the next morning.

"Good morning, Yuan," said Bei upon entering the office. "Anything pressing?" he asked as he headed for the teakettle.

"I'm afraid so, sir," responded his assistant. "Another courtesan murdered. Late yesterday afternoon. I got the notice just after office hours, and instructed the ward officer to seal the room and post a guard."

Bei put down the teakettle. "I presume from your precautions it was not the normal stabbing or bludgeoning by a drunk soldier at a low-class brothel."

"No, sir. It was the P'ing K'angli brothel. And they said she was nearly beheaded."

He sighed. "Let's go, then."

Half an hour later they were at the gates of the P'ing K'angli, just a block off Ch'ienmen Street. The name of the house referred to the famous area of high-class brothels in Hangchow during the last century of the Sung Dynasty, seven hundred years earlier. This house, which patterned itself on the elegant tradition of those times, was located in a neighborhood of costly villas with high surrounding walls. At the entrance hung a bamboo lampion with red silk sides, identifying the house's nature in the old tradition. The husky gateman showed Bei and Yuan to the house itself, a large mansion with kitchen quarters occupying most of the ground floor. As in the Hangchow brothels, the clients were led first to a ground-floor room richly appointed with fine ebony and rosewood furniture and costly antiques, where they were served tea at an exorbitant price by the hostess. Only after paying this preliminary entrance fee, termed the *Tianhua Cha,* "Teacup for Checking Flowers," was the guest led upstairs to another luxuriously decorated room where wine was served and the available girls mingled with the guests. Boys with trays containing various dishes and delicacies also circulated around the room, and after choosing a girl the guests would place their orders with the waiters and retire to their private rooms for elegant eating, carousing, and sex. The girls in this house, who were trained in song, dance, and poetry, made quite interesting and agreeable companions to the rich merchants and high officials who frequented the place.

As before, Bei chose to examine the body first, walking through the tea room and upstairs to where the body lay. The room was large, some five meters square, with its center taken up by a bed in the Ming style: a large raised platform, with mats, sheets, and covers, surrounded on three sides by a low partition with landscape scenes. On one wall two expensive chairs flanked a table on which empty plates and wine glasses sat. A marble bowl filled with water occupied the back of the table, and a pair of fine linen towels hung on the wall above the basin. A wooden clothes closet occupied another wall. The room was wallpapered and had a thick rug in front of the bed, with a coal-burning brazier in the far corner. Curtains blocked the window on the outside wall.

On the bed lay the body, again wrapped, this time in a red silk sheet. Bei unwrapped the sheet, carefully. Even so, the head rolled to one side, assuming the same peculiar angle he had seen before. The face was heavily rouged, with darkened eyebrows and a black mouche on the cheek. She had been very pretty before last night.

"Notes, Yuan."

Yuan got out his notebook and pen.

"Body lying on back. Arms folded on chest. Throat severely lacerated. Cut is clean on the right side, victim's left, becomes ragged on victim's right, in fact, muscles are grossly ripped there in places. Hair is gathered, as if pulled, to victim's left. No bruises on trunk. Or legs. Rigor mortis quite advanced, arms and legs."

He produced a magnifying glass from his coat. "Open those curtains please, Yuan." He bent over her thighs in the extra light. "Semen present."

He looked at the sheets to the left of the thighs. "Blood stains on sheets left of body just above knee, broader at periphery, narrower towards body. No wound that region on body."

He stepped back and gazed at the body. Slowly he walked around the bed, occasionally sniffing deeply, gazing over the low partitions at the covers, lifting them and shaking them as he went. The covers in her head region were soaked with blood, and made a slushing noise as Bei lifted them. The painted partition beyond her head was heavily splattered. It was a winter scene, but changed now. The gleaming white snow covering the mountain slopes was streaked with long russet flows, and the pine trees and bamboo were festooned with myriad splotches of russet, like ripe pears lodged inexplicably on the wrong plants. Only a plum tree flowering in the corner of the scene had escaped the pulse of doomed life spurting out of her severed arteries.

Bei walked to the clothes closet and peered in closely. At the table he looked closely at the water in the basin, and sniffed to either side of the bowl.

"No items on bed or in clothes closet," he dictated to Yuan. "Faint signs and odor of blood in basin. Faint odor of flowers alongside basin. Possibly gardenias." He got down on his knees and peered under the bed. "No items on floor."

He got up and stepped back, looking again at the body.

"There's something wrong with the body, Yuan. Do you see it?"

"Well . . . it's mutilated, of course, sir."

"Yes, of course. Although actually only the throat is mutilated. The rest of the body is perfect. No, I mean the position of the body."

"Well, I see nothing wrong with the position."

"I see two things that strike me as curious. First, where are the pillows on the bed?"

"Along the right-hand partition."

"And where is her head?"

"Along the left-hand partition."

"And the covers and top sheet also open up on the right-hand side, by the pillows, do they not?"

"Yes."

"So why were they lying with their heads at the foot of the bed?"

"Well, the room was heated with the brazier. What if they weren't going to get under the covers?"

"Yes. But still it would be normal to have your heads on the pillow side of the bed. Perhaps it is stretching the point. But it becomes significant in conjunction with the second point. Notice how close to the open edge of the bed the body is lying. Why not in the middle of the bed?"

"The body could have been moved."

"No, Yuan, look at the blood stains. Why, the body is so close to the edge that some blood has dripped down the frame of the bed there."

With a soft exclamation he suddenly whipped his lens from his pocket and stretched out on the floor upon his stomach, examining the bare wooden area below the bloodstained frame. "Ah. Yes. Of course. It is all clear now." He got up with an eager look on his face.

"Notes, Yuan. Distinct blood stain on floor, beside and below victim's neck. Stain in an oval outline, indicating presence on floor of a boot, down and around which blood flowed."

He looked around once more. "Well, I don't think there is anything else to be gained here. It is obviously our same left-handed killer of courtesans. Except now we know why there's been no sign of a struggle, other than that of sexual passion, from the victims. He mounts them, and at the height of sexual passion simply reaches for his knife which is hidden in his boots to the left of the bed. Hence the curious location of the body at the very edge of this bed, oriented in such a way that the man's left hand is at the bed's edge, even though that requires their heads to be at the foot of the bed. He secures the knife, brings it backhanded to the right edge of the victim's neck, on the victim's left, while holding her head steady by her hair with his right hand. Then, in a extraordinarily powerful sweeping motion, he rips the razor-sharp knife backhanded across and through the victim's throat, right to left, cutting cleanly and deeply at first, less so by the time he gets to the left side, her right. She dies instantly. He wipes the knife on the sheet at thigh level, forehanded now, climbs off the victim, then washes his bloody hands in the basin of water, provided to allow the partners to wash their sexual organs in more normal circumstances."

Bei paused, checking if he had left anything out. He exhaled with a shrug. "Then he ritually wraps his partner in a sheet, puts his clothes and boots on, returns his knife to the boot, and walks away, taking his bag of dried gardenias with him."

Yuan shivered. "A strange one, Inspector."

Bei nodded. "Yes. A most peculiar person, Yuan. On the inside. Let's see what the madam can add to our description of the outside of him."

They encountered the madam waiting in the hall outside the room. She was an attractive, composed lady, middle-aged, and had a refined air about her that reminded Bei of his wife, though he suppressed the thought immediately. She escorted them down the carpeted hall, past the luxurious wine room, down the stairs and into her private office.

"We are all most shocked, Inspector," she said as soon as the door had shut. "Nothing like this has ever happened in our establishment, in two hundred years of 'The Wind and the Flowers.' "

"Doubtless," responded Bei. "It is distressing, I realize. I may assure you that we shall not publicize it, ourselves, if you cooperate in answering questions."

"Of course."

"Did you see the man?"

"Yes. I served him his initial tea."

"What did he look like?"

"Quite charming. He was well built, although not large, and gave the impression of being quite strong."

"Tall? Short?"

"More tall than short, although not unusually so."

"What accent?"

"Northern. Shensi, Honan, Shansi."

"Was he wearing a uniform?"

"No. He was dressed simply, but well. Not extravagantly, certainly. Not even particularly fashionably. But you could tell he was a gentleman."

"How so?"

"Oh, I don't know. The way he looked at you when he talked. Very penetrating. Direct, and yet polite. Like a true gentleman." She caught herself. "Well, that is, he had the appearance of a gentleman. Obviously he was not."

"Obviously. Did he talk to anyone in the upstairs wine room?"

"Yes. To everyone, or at least all the girls. Just brief conversations. He picked one of our most accomplished girls, really our best dancer." She shook her head. "It will be quite a loss for us."

"Yes," said Bei dryly. "Did he pick her because of her dancing abilities?"

"There's no way he would know that, unless he had attended one of the larger banquets at which she danced. According to the other girls who were in the room—I've questioned them all, quite thoroughly, Inspector—he only asked superficial questions."

"Was your best dancer by any chance from Shansi?"

The woman was surprised. "Why, yes, she was. Just on the border between Shansi and Honan. How did you know that?"

"Just a guess. He was talking with them to hear their accents." He paused. "Anything else about him, his appearance or behavior, that you or any of your girls noted?"

"Well, one other thing, although it's probably silly."

"What?"

"The girl in the room next to her had just completed The Clouds and the Rain, and was resting with her gentleman. She heard the man speaking, in a somewhat loud voice, the way . . ." She pretended to blush. "The way one will in passion. She was not sure of the words, but to her it sounded like he was saying, 'Younger sister, younger sister.' " She paused. "Of course, it probably means nothing. Men say . . . many things in their passion."

"Doubtless. When did the murder occur?"

"Probably around dusk. He came in around two o'clock or so, then spent time in the tea room and the wine room, talking to the girls. Then they had a light meal and wine in her room."

"What did he order?"

She smiled, pleased with herself. "I asked that. I thought you might be interested. You have a reputation for thoroughness, Inspector Bei."

Bei liked her smile. He fleetingly wondered if she still, or ever . . . then pushed it out of his mind.

"What was it that he ate, then?"

"Actually, nothing special. *Chiaotse,* and pork with peppers."

"You have access to pork, still?" Bei knew that most of the city had run out of pork last week. The farmers in the outlying villages preferred to barter their pigs with the Communists.

She laughed, showing perfect white teeth. "Many of the gentlemen that visit our house regularly have . . . shall we say, a good deal of influence, Inspector."

"I understand."

"If you wish some pork, we would be glad to serve you," she said softly.

Yuan was seized with a coughing spell, and Bei was becoming rather uncomfortable himself. He had just remembered how much he had heard the Teacup for Checking Flowers cost, and realized that most months he would barely be able to get past that preliminary stage.

"Uh, well, thank you, Madam, for your very able assistance. Rely on us to be circumspect in our investigation of this unfortunate matter. Good day."

She rose with them, and courteously escorted them to the door, bidding them an elegant "Good day" herself.

The news was broken to Yuan after lunch. "Congratulations, old friend. I have just located your long-lost younger brother." Yuan narrowed his eyes and looked at his chief askance. "Unfortunately, your natural joy will be somewhat abated when you learn that you both are destitute and must sell all you own."

Yuan masked his bewilderment by shuffling the papers on his desk. Bei smiled at his discomfort. "Come, my worthy assistant. You must do better than that if you are going to fool the Te Wu. They are not incompetent, after all."

Mention of the Te Wu made Yuan even more ill at ease. He finally said something. "I'd rather not deal with the Te Wu, sir, with or without a mysterious brother."

Bei became more or less serious. "You'll not be dealing with them at all, Yuan. My plan is this: The fat monk knows the Baleful Star by sight. Every afternoon, beginning tomorrow, you'll memorize the names and addresses of two Te Wu agents from a list I'll keep in our safe here. Never mind how I came by the list. You will reconnoiter the neighborhoods and find their homes. The following day, before dawn, you and the monk will spread your worldly possessions for sale on the sidewalk near the first agent's home. Heaven knows there are enough people doing just that throughout the city. You will observe the agent leaving the home. Assuming he is not the Baleful Star, after an hour or so you will dejectedly pick up your possessions and move to a more likely site—at the next agent's home. If you're lucky, you will catch him coming to or leaving from the midday relaxation. If not, you're stuck there until he returns home in the evening. Or night. Dress warmly, my friend."

"It doesn't sound like particularly strenuous work," commented Yuan.

"No. In fact, feel free to take stools for yourself and the fat one. You can purchase them today when you go shopping for the possessions you will be spreading before you. Observe closely these poor refugees who line the streets, Yuan. See how they look, how they stand or sit, how they act. Most of them have a dazed, hopeless look about them. Their eyes are often glazed over—perhaps from hunger. They're quite stationary, hardly ever moving about or even talking. Act like them, and instruct the monk to do the same. Here's some money from our petty cash. Keep a record of your purchases, of course."

"Will the monk go along with it?"

"He will be glad to get out of our overcrowded jails, especially when you tell him his cooperation will be noted by the magistrate. But tell him that just looking for the Baleful Star is his job, and he will be rewarded for it. We don't want to make him think his reward is for finding the man, or he's liable to make up an identification. Keep him liberally fed with noodles and biscuits between stakeouts, and keep receipts, again."

"I'm nearly beginning to like this assignment, Chief. No paperwork involved?"

"No, although you'll have to find time each day to reconnoiter two more homes for the next day's stakeouts. By all means memorize the addresses; do not jot them down. You must not have a Te Wu name or address on you if anyone questions you. Do you understand?"

"I'm good at remembering things that, forgotten, can cost me my life."

"Don't tell the fat one that you're watching Te Wu agents. He is to think that these are merely ordinary underworld thugs that we suspect may be the Baleful Star."

"All right."

"The first day, tomorrow, I want you two to stake out Yu Chenling's compound, and observe his agents entering and leaving. We'll get as many as we can of the agents observed there by the monk, before we resort to staking out the individual homes of those we miss at Yu's villa. Jot down complete descriptions to check against the descriptions on the list. I'll go reconnoiter Yu's villa this afternoon. I would prefer to be able to get a room somewhere within view of the gate, so the monk can observe it surreptitiously. Any questions about the plan?"

"Not at the moment. I'll be off now to study the refugees and buy some of their goods."

"Fine. I'll visit Yu Chenling's neighborhood, and meet you back here, at say, four o'clock."

"See you then," said Yuan, as he left the room.

Bei started a fire for a cup of tea before setting out. He was excited. Today he began his stalk of the Te Wu. Tomorrow he would stalk the Purple Mountain. Worthy game, each. He savored the anticipation and dread that tingled through him. As he was pouring the boiling water onto the leaves, Lufei walked in.

"Hello!"

"Miss Yuan. You just missed your uncle." He upended the timer.

"Oh. Too bad. But I was just out looking for cooking oil, and thought I'd drop in. No special reason."

"Oh. Glad to see you again. Tea?"

"That would be good."

He was surprised at how glad he was to see her. She took off her quilted coat, and looked very nice, even in her everyday trousers and blouse. There is no substitute for youth, he thought.

She broke the silence as he waited for the tea to infuse.

"You must be visiting many restaurants while your wife is gone, and eating fine food."

"Not really. In fact, the meals at home are hardly worth the effort of the servant to prepare, for only one person."

"Are you fond of Shansi cooking?"

"As a matter of fact, I'm rather ignorant of it."

"I should save you from your boring meals. Why don't you give your servant the day off tomorrow, and I'll come over and cook you some typical and delicious Shansi dishes for lunch."

The proposal was made in tones of utmost innocence, but the significance of it was not lost on Bei. It was shocking, of course. But tantalizing. He wrestled with it. It would be indecorous, in his home. But how pleasant it would be. A lunch filled with gaiety. Then afterward . . .

"Oh." He remembered, with some relief. "Oh. It sounds . . .

144

delightful, Miss Yuan. I'd love to taste Shansi cooking. But I have some very important business planned for tomorrow, all day."

She was crestfallen, and embarrassed.

"Really, it is already planned, and I'll be gone from early until quite late."

"All right," she said in a small voice.

"But, uh, the prospect of having a meal with you is really . . . delightful. When I return, perhaps . . . perhaps we can arrange it."

"Fine," she said with a show of gaiety. "Well, I must be going." She rose.

"Please don't. Sit down. The tea is ready. Sit. Tell me about how you like Peking while we sip our tea."

Soon they were engaged in a pleasant conversation, Dei reflecting on how full of life she was, and beginning to genuinely regret that he had business all day tomorrow, at the same time he was genuinely relieved that he did. Heaven knows that casual liaisons are common enough, he thought, as she chatted brightly. And most wives accept them, some even welcoming them as a source of entertainment that put their husbands in a better mood at home. Certainly there were no explicit or implicit vows of chastity made in marriage, as the Western barbarians did. Incredible notion. Might as well make water promise to flow uphill.

They finished their tea.

"Well, I really must go. It will take time for me to find some cooking oil at a decent price."

"Yes, I understand from my servant that prices are continuing to skyrocket. May I have the pleasure of a Shansi-style lunch some time later?"

"Any time. Let me know."

"Fine. Have a good day, Miss Yuan."

"Inspector." She turned, picked up her coat, and jauntily strode out.

He sat, pondering. Then he drove it all from his mind. He was about to commence on risky business. He couldn't afford to be distracted. Now, at least. He took a quick look at Yu's address, checked his memorization of it, and put the list back in the safe. He turned the tumblers, and was off.

.   .   .

Chan sat in his cubicle next to Yu Chenling's office. Being the top aide of the man who headed the Te Wu in Peking kept him very busy. But even his heavy workload could not distract him, or blunt the anger that rose in him in wave after wave. So hard. He worked so hard, fighting the Communist bandits. He poured himself out in the fight, in prodigal expense of his considerable strength and intelligence. Yet still they prospered. Why? He hit the desk hard, in exasperation. All his Chan sweat and brains seemed to stop the tide no better than had his father's. Would he end up like his father, his head blown off by Communists, a crude sign proclaiming nonsense above him?

He glanced at the worn photo of his father on the desk. There was one key difference between them. If he died at the hands of the Communists, he would have no son to carry on the battle. He ground his teeth and closed his eyes to fight back the tears that threatened to well up. A cold sweat broke out on him as the thought of breaking the Chan family line lodged again in his brain. It frightened him. Fifteen named generations of male ancestors, and all those before even them. Their honor and well-being entrusted to him. Why hadn't he married and fathered a son already? The land could be regained after the Communists had all been killed. But the family line—once the chain was broken, it was gone. Lost irrevocably, for all eternity. His own father, dishonored, uncared for. He breathed hard, in long, deep gasps, to calm himself. I will live, he vowed. I will live, and marry, and produce sons. I promise it, Father. I am young and strong and intelligent. I will not let you down, or your father, or all those Chans stretching down the ages. I vow it.

Still he was frightened, although he was calm now. The anger returned. Anger that the war with the Communists had thrust itself upon him before he had married. Anger that the girl his family had betrothed to him had disappeared as the Communists swept over their district. Anger that the Communists had killed his two brothers that awful day, leaving only him to carry on the line. And finally, anger that he had ended up with Yu Chenling, and been forced to frequent brothels to satisfy Yu's cravings. Anger that he had developed a craving himself for the pleasures of the brothels, a craving that shamed him and imprisoned him and kept him, *oh father help me,* kept him from finding a decent woman and marrying her and fathering a son, *oh help me, father, I'm trying so hard.*

January 5

He woke long before dawn. The night was bitterly cold. He lay under the thick quilt, staring at the ceiling. Joints and pipes groaned in the cold. Today Yuan and the fat monk would observe the comings and goings at Yu's compound. When they had met later yesterday afternoon, Bei had told Yuan of the gatehouse across the street from Yu's entrance, with the grated window looking directly out at his door. How the gatekeeper had been easily convinced by Bei's story that the wealthy homeowners in the neighborhood had requested police protection in keeping the undesirable refugee beggars off their street. How two police agents would therefore be occupying the gatehouse with him for a day or two, by order of the chief inspector, to scan the street for beggars. It was so plausible that even if the gatekeeper spread the story, it would not be questioned by anyone. Yuan and the fat monk would be in the gatehouse before dawn.

His body was tight, his mind racing. He would soon be off, in disguise, for the Purple Mountain. What would the day bring? He had absolutely no idea. He had been to Yenching University and to Fragrant Hills Park often enough. But never when they were in Communist territory. Never when he could be arrested, perhaps executed, by any number of people whom he would pass that day. The fear overrode the excitement now, lying in the frigid dark room. All sorts of nameless horrors swarmed up and overwhelmed him. The night. It is no time to plan anything, or make any decisions. Always make decisions during the day. And stick with them, regardless. It had to be done. No matter how the night and the cold quailed, the dictates of the day were absolute. He shut his eyes and willed himself to doze off until dawn.

· · ·

It was early morning. In rags, Bei trudged up the street pulling the green cart with the flag bearing the characters "Peking Municipal Manure Cart." The odoriferous contents sloshed inside the barrel as he pulled. Fear and discomfort prevented him from appreciating the humor of the situation. He was sweating in his layers of undergarments, despite the still bitter cold which had frozen water pipes all over the city that morning. Glancing up, he saw the Hsichihmen Gate close ahead. With luck, no one would even notice him. The manure carts were the only traffic permitted in or out of the city without special permits. The ancient return of these waste materials to fertilize the fields surrounding the city was a rhythm beyond wars or other such minor affairs. The countryside, Communist or not, was as eager to obtain the rich fertilizer as the city was to get rid of it.

Bei did not even glance up as he trudged to the gate. The heavily armed guards unthinkingly opened the massive doors as they had for a dozen carts that morning, and Bei pulled the cart out of the city without breaking stride.

Outside the huge walls, the density of buildings dropped dramatically. This area had once been a thriving part of the city, but for the past several years had been neglected as no man's land. Now it was practically deserted. He trudged up Hsichihmenwai Street past the zoo, and stopped to rest beside the entrance to the massive Geological Survey building on his left. Like the Peking Union Medical College, it too was assisted by the American Rockefeller Foundation. Except it dealt with the dead rather than the living, for it had unearthed the famous "Peking Man" skulls several decades ago. Bei looked around for a spot to dump the contents of the barrel. The smell had bothered him most at first, but now the effort to pull the wooden-wheeled cart was draining him. Labor was so unpleasant and undignified. It was rightfully despised by a gentleman.

Deciding that to empty the barrel here might arouse suspicion among the few people on the street, he put the strap around his shoulder once more, gripped the handles in front of the cart, and set out with a grunt. Shortly he turned right up Paishihch'iao Road, and soon the first fields appeared on his left. He spotted a concrete pit alongside one of the fields, and clumsily but eagerly dumped the barrel's contents into it. Without waiting for a receipt from the field worker, he resumed his place in the harness and continued moving north up the road. The relative lightness of the cart now permitted him to move much faster. He ignored the ache in his arms and legs. It was already late morning, and he still had four or five kilometers ahead of him to reach Yenching University and Chang's bicycle. Although he was in Communist-controlled territory, he felt reasonably secure in his anonymity, since the Communists had no formal checkpoints or boundaries demarcating their territory.

Lin Piao was pacing in his study at Chihsien, north of the city, periodically tossing roasted beans in his mouth for energy. Tomorrow. Tomorrow he would grapple with Fu Tsoyi for Peking. How would Fu's envoys, this Zhou Peifeng and the professor, respond to the tactics he had decided upon? A knock on the door interrupted his reverie.

"Come in, Li."

Captain Li entered. Strong, confident, controlled.

"You'll go now?"

"Yes, comrade. Since I meet Colonel Zhou and the fool professor at dawn, I'll spend the night in the city."

"Keep your eyes open, as always. I'll be interested to hear if the mood has changed in the city—be particularly alert to antagonism toward the soldiers. And it's possible the food reserves may be running low. Check how many hawkers are on the streets."

"You may expect a detailed report as usual, Commander."

"Good. Here is your authorization to draw whatever funds you need for bribes or expenses from the purser, as always."

A pause. Lin Piao looked up at him shrewdly. "How do you think it will go tomorrow?"

His eyes went vacant as he considered it. "They will be surprised. They won't expect this game from us."

"Will they play it?"

Li raised his eyebrows in mock surprise. "But, Commander, they'll have to. It is our game, and we control them, and their city." He became serious. "It will be good for them. For too long, our people have been forced to play the Kuomintang's coarse games, and taste Kuomintang steel if they faltered. Finally they will learn what it's like to play another's game—and to taste another's steel."

Lin Piao smiled. "I believe you hate them as much as I do."

Li stared at him, but again declined to reveal the source of his hatred. Lin Piao wondered what it could be. Li had joined them on the Shensi-Shansi border, shortly after the Japanese surrender. Badly bruised, nearly dead actually, but no less full of hatred than he was now. But his past remained blank to all. In truth, it was irrelevant. All that mattered was the brilliance, the driving energy, the imagination he had shown as he rose quickly in their ranks. And the hatred. Yes, that was important, too.

"You have the pass Fu sent?"

"Yes. Although I've gotten in without it before."

"Use it this time. There'll be no risk with it. Be careful."

"I will, comrade. Until tomorrow."

"Until tomorrow."

Lin Piao sat down at his desk as Li departed, and ate another handful of the roasted beans. Two city maps were on top of the pile of papers: Peking and Tientsin. Tientsin would be no problem, since the foreign devils had destroyed its wall when they stole the city from us in the nineteenth century. We can come in either from the north or the west of the city. Probably feint from the west, then shortly afterward drive in force from the north. The hills there will conceal our initial buildup. But Peking. A different story. He traced the wall's position on his map, noting the gates and the possible weak points marked. Enough troops inside to defend nearly the entire periphery. And enough artillery to return our fire, once they get our positions. Yes, Mao, we'll avoid bombardment, for a few days, but it will come to that. But morale—what is their morale? How hungry are they? How hard will they fight? Does Fu have their allegiance like he did thirty years ago at Chochow? Or is his time taken up with reconciling the Kuomintang factions inside the city, and satisfying his Taoist nun?

It could be done. It could be taken. But it would be costly. And it might take time. Changchun had taken ten months. And Mukden had held out long also. But like them, Peking was encircled, completely cut off. With two million people to feed. It would do them good to feel what starvation is like.

. . .

After the manure cart, the bicycle from Chang seemed effortless. Until he hit the first hills, west of the Summer Palace on Fragrant Hill Road. He had shed most of his undergarments into the bicycle's basket, leaving the cart and his manure-splattered outer trousers at Chang's. It was already past noon, and he soon pedaled past the villages of Fenghuying and Chenglanch'i, marveling at how normal and prosperous everything looked. Ducks and chickens thronged the dirt streets, donkeys stood patiently before carts overloaded with twigs and millet stalks, and old women sat on the steps to their homes eyeing the passersby while their grandchildren toddled around. Indeed, life here in the Communist-held territories seemed little different on the surface, at least, from what it had always been. The atmosphere contrasted strongly with Peking's fortress, besieged atmosphere of tension and shortages. Every time he began to feel he was on a holiday, though, a column of Communist troops would pass him or he would note a Communist guard watching him suspiciously, and the dread would quickly return.

He passed the road to the Temple of the Recumbent Buddha without incident, though, and soon pedaled past the northern entrance to Fragrant Hills Park itself. From this point onward the road became much more rough, uphill climbs longer, and villages less frequent. Most of the time he was passing through rocky, uncultivated hills, littered with gaping pits where trees had been felled for fuel. His legs were beginning to tremble now, from the unusual exertions he had subjected them to that day, and he resorted to walking the bicycle up most of the hills, then coasting down. Half an hour beyond Fragrant Hills Park he came to a small village. Leaning his bicycle against a building, he collapsed against a wall and sat there staring dully at the sparse traffic on the road. What to do now? It was midafternoon, and he had made it here. Now how did he find the Purple Mountain? He leaned his head back against the wall and closed his eyes, too exhausted to formulate any course of action. After several minutes he began to feel the cold, for the first time that day. He reached up to the bicycle's basket and put a sweater on. What to do? A flock of ducks waddled in front of him, driven leisurely by a boy with a stick.

He was wondering whether to bluntly ask the boy where the Purple Mountain was when he noticed a familiar figure out of the corner of his eye, coasting down the hill into town on a bicycle. Meiling.

Quickly he shaded his face with his hand and pretended to be dozing. She did not notice him, and coasted by. Oblivious to his still-trembling legs he leaped up, grabbed the bicycle and hopped onto it, scattering the ducks as he did so. She was some thirty meters ahead of him, and soon disappeared around a corner to the right. Frantic lest he lose her, he pedaled furiously to the intersection and rounded it, to see her leisurely proceeding up a slight hill. With a groan he followed, wondering whether he could make the hill. They were on a pathway now, which followed a creek's winding path on a slight uphill, upstream grade between steeper hills on either side. Bei's legs would hardly obey his commands after fifteen minutes, and the girl's lead grew steadily wider until he only occasionally glimpsed her at the end of a straight portion he had just begun. In another ten minutes he had to dismount, nearly falling in the process, and walked pushing the bicycle as fast as his legs could manage. By now the path was quite rough, and soon he left the bicycle behind some shrubs beside the road, knowing he was physically unable to ride anymore that day. The path still followed the stream, and as he rounded a curve he saw the path abruptly end at a massive wooden gate. He looked around. No sign of Meiling. She must have gone inside the gate. She, like An, was connected with the Purple Mountain. And he now stood before the Purple Mountain himself.

"May I assist you, sir?"

Bei jumped in surprise and whirled around, his legs finally giving out as he did so. He crashed to the ground heavily. Feeling stupid and undignified, he struggled awkwardly to his knees and found himself gazing at the white leggings and blue trousers of a Taoist monk. Raising his eyes, he saw the rest of a young man who was trying very hard not to burst out in laughter, and only partly succeeding. The youth reached down and assisted Bei up.

"So sorry to have frightened you, sir, but I was wondering whether I could assist you?"

The words were courteous, but the tone was now serious, with a tough edge to them.

Bei gazed vacantly at the youth, not fully recovered from the fright and the fall. He was Bei's height, slender, with shining eyes which struck Bei as either laughing or threatening. Or perhaps both. Bei shook his head to clear it, and with a great effort managed to say hoarsely, "I am looking for the Purple Mountain."

The youth's expression did not change. "You have found it, sir."

A silence. Neither moved.

"I want to talk to the woman Meiling."

The youth appraised him. Certainly not local. Out of the ordinary.

"We can arrange that. In fact, I think we shall insist on it. Will you follow me?"

Bei nodded, and followed the youth up the path to the massive gate. Large oaks framed the gate, and extremely thick shrubs three meters high fanned out to either side of the oaks, curving out of sight. The gate opened noiselessly from the middle as they approached it, and Bei stared at the incredible depth of the doors—easily a hand's width deep. As he stepped through the doors Bei was greeted by a park-like scene, with trees and shrubs everywhere. More trees, whole and uncut at least, than Bei had seen all day in the countryside. The youth ahead looked back questioningly, and Bei hurriedly caught up with him. They walked along a broad, pebbled pathway which curved to the right, the stones arranged in neat geometric designs. Soon they crossed over a wooden bridge spanning the stream, after which the path began a long slight curve to the left. On his right Bei heard the twang of bow strings being released and the thunk of arrows hitting targets, along with various loud yells and softer thuds. He could see little through the bushes beside the pathway, however. In another several minutes he saw a large two-story building of finely mortared stone to his right amongst trees, and smelled the odor of vegetables being stir-fried. He nearly stumbled at the rush of hunger which gripped his body. He had eaten only a light snack at Chang's, and his extreme exercise had left him suddenly ravenous. With difficulty he restrained a wild impulse to crash through the bushes and claw his way to the source of the smell.

The Purple Mountain compound was huge. They had been walking for nearly ten minutes. Finally the youth slowed, and stepped through an opening in the bushes to the right. Bei followed him along a side path toward an imposing building, again two-story and of finely mortared stones. Above the heavy oak door was a stone lintel bearing the inscription *Wan Wu Chih Mu,* "Nature, the Mother of All Things."

They passed under the inscription into a long hallway, lighted from the right by a peculiar green glow. Meiling had just hung up her traveling cape and was removing her cap when she turned and saw Bei and the youth enter. She stopped in astonishment, which changed to wonder after a moment. She removed her cap finally and shook out her long black hair which had been gathered under the cap. She was as beautiful as ever.

"Inspector Bei. What are you doing here?" she asked with a puzzled smile.

Bei attempted to pull himself together, and answered as casually as possible, "Oh, still working on the White Cloud Temple case. I thought I'd like to see the Purple Mountain."

She remained staring at him in puzzlement, to which was soon added a look of respect.

"Many people would like to see the Purple Mountain. Few actually do."

She hung her cap atop her cape, and turned to face him fully. "How did you get here? By following me?"

"No. I followed the line from the Spring Heralding Pavilion through Jade Spring Hill."

The youth turned an impressed gaze on Bei, and Meiling raised her eyebrows.

"They said you had formidable talents. Now I believe it." She looked him up and down. "Although it appears your journey has left you somewhat worse for wear."

Bei realized how ridiculous he must look after the day's exertions and the fall.

"Dufeng. Please allow the inspector to freshen up a bit in the meditation room. My father and I will receive him in the Great Hall afterward."

The youth bowed, and opened the door to a room on their left. Mustering what dignity he could, Bei nodded to the woman, and walked into the room.

"Oh, Inspector Bei."

He stopped at the doorway. "Yes?"

"Thank you. For saving my life several days ago."

He felt a flush of pride. "You're welcome. It was my pleasure."

She turned and left, and he entered the room.

A wooden stool in one corner was the only object in the room other than a straw mat covering the stone floor. Light streamed in feebly through a window in one of the stone walls. After several minutes the young man returned with a bowl of warm water and a cotton towel, then left again, closing the door behind him. Bei took off his coat, dipped the towel in the water, and gratefully rubbed his face and neck with it, then wiped his hands on it. He brushed the dirt off his trousers as best he could, straightened his shirt and sweater, and again wiped his hands on the towel. Finally he ran his fingers threw his hair several times, and sat down on the stool.

You are the chief inspector of the Peking Municipal Police, he reminded himself. You may appear disheveled, but you nonetheless are the inspector. Act it. He felt more or less composed by the time the young man Dufeng reappeared and motioned for him to follow. They walked down the hall to a large opening on the right and turned. Despite his intentions of remaining composed, Bei jerked to a stop and gazed open-mouthed at the huge room. Its ceiling was the full two stories high, with a deep row of windows ringing the room just below the ceiling, through which light poured into the room. The walls and floor were of light-colored stone, and the only decorations in the room were three of the largest pieces of jade Bei had ever seen. Above a large fireplace in the wall facing Bei as he entered the room was a circular jade disk some two meters in diameter. Two veins of jade swirled within the disk, a creamy white one and a dark green one. The green vein was fullest to the upper left, and tapered off towards the right; the white vein was fullest to the lower right, and tapered off towards the left. Together they formed a surprisingly close approximation of the classic yin-yang symbol.

On the floor against the wall to Bei's left a dark green T'aihu stone towered some three meters tall. It was slender at its base and thicker toward the top, with the irregular shape and array of swirling hollows characteristic of the best stones—except this was solid jade, not limestone.

The last piece was mounted on an ebony pedestal against the wall to the right. It was a statue of an old man atop a buffalo—Lao-tzu, riding to the Western Lands. The piece was a meter square, the buffalo mainly of a light green hue, the bearded man mainly white, flecked evenly with light green speckles.

All three pieces seemed to gather the light pouring in through the high bank of windows and transmute it into a thicker medium imbued with the cream and green hues of the jade, which then emanated from the pieces to fill the entire hall with a distinct glow. The room seemed to be under water, in a way, and Bei found himself taking a tentative breath to insure that it was indeed air in the room.

Other than the three giant pieces of jade, the only other objects in the hall were ten high-backed wooden chairs with small tables between them, arranged in a semicircle in the center of the hall facing the fireplace and the jade disk. Meiling and a man were sitting in the center portion of the ring of chairs, their backs to Dufeng and Bei as they entered the hall. Meiling rose and turned to them, a look of suppressed humor on her proud face.

"Come in, Inspector, and please have a chair here."

Bei walked to the chair that she indicated, trying hard not to show the stiffness which wracked his legs.

"Permit me to introduce you to the abbot of the Purple Mountain: Inspector Bei, this is Master T'ang."

The man inclined his head in an abbreviated bow. As Bei bowed, he noted the abbot's appearance with surprise. Rather than the robed, white-bearded Taoist he had expected, the man was clean-shaven and wore a blue jacket in the modern cut above his leggings and trousers. His close-cropped hair was jet black, and the lined face had an energetic, zestful look to it. His age was impossible to guess: somewhere between fifty and eighty, Bei judged.

He spoke in crisp tones, with an only half-suppressed grin. "Few people see us uninvited, Inspector. I congratulate you on finding us, and on the strength of your reputation which has persuaded us to have you meet with us here in the Great Hall."

Bei acknowledged the compliment with a slight nod of his head.

"I am here on business, Master T'ang. You may be able to help me solve a murder."

"Why should we be able to help you with a murder that presumably occurred many kilometers away in Peking?"

Bei decided to plunge in. "I have reason to believe that the murdered man, An Shihlin, was an agent of yours. I believe that he, and you, are connected with the Communists, and are working to infiltrate Peking."

An amused look came over the abbot's face. "And are you here now to arrest us for being Communists?"

Bei's face reddened at the reminder that he was, after all, in Communist territory.

"Master T'ang, in Peking we still view murder as a crime. It is the murder that I am concerned with, not your political inclinations."

The abbot's face became serious. "You are right. I was wrong to joke of it. What do you want of us?"

"I want to know who had An Shihlin killed."

The abbot stared levelly at Bei, and spoke in a distinct voice. "I may assure you, Inspector, that if we knew who had killed Shihlin, we would already have seen to it that justice was done."

"You do not know, then?"

"No. We do not. But we are as desirous as you to discover his murderer. We do not have your resources, nor your talent in detection, nor your access to the scene of the crime. But if we can help you to find the murderer, we will."

"Thank you. You can help me by telling me whether my assessment of An's role—and yours—is correct."

The abbot swiftly calculated the consequences of giving Bei the information. "I can see no harm in revealing his role to you. Others are aware of it already, others potentially more dangerous to us than you. And if we work together, you and I, perhaps we can together trace An's murderer. I presume you would be willing to reveal what you know to us if we reveal what we know to you?"

"I agree," said Bei after a pause, already calculating how much he would withhold from them.

"Then yes. You are correct regarding An Shihlin's role."

"You are directing the Communist underground in Peking?"

"Not directing. We offered our services to Mao Tsetung and Chou Enlai late in 1935, shortly after their arrival in Yenan from the Long March. They have used our . . . peculiar skills for over thirteen years now. Most recently, we have helped them place agents in Peking and coordinate the activities of those agents."

"You are now working specifically for Lin Piao, then."

"No. Not at all. When the Chungking negotiations between the Communists and the Nationalists broke off finally in the spring of 1947, Chou Enlai returned to Yenan and was given the task by Mao to begin infiltrating key northern cities. We have worked on that mission under Chou's supervision, with Mao always having the final word. Lin Piao has only recently arrived here from Manchuria, as you know, although it is true he commands the majority of the troops in this area now."

"There is no point in quibbling whether your contact is Chou Enlai or Lin Piao, surely—"

"They are quite different men, actually."

"Doubtless. But they are Communists, and you are 'coordinating' their activities in Peking, is that correct?"

"Yes."

"Insofar as An Shihlin was acting as a Communist agent, then, I can see two parties that might wish to see him eliminated: Fu Tsoyi, as the top Nationalist general in northern China; and Yu Chenling, as the head of the Kuomintang's right-wing Te Wu."

"And what evidence do you have for either of these possibilities?" asked the abbot.

"I am presently investigating the Te Wu; in five days I should know whether they are involved."

"And Fu?"

Bei paused. "To be frank, I do not know how to go about investigating his role. Nor do I feel he was involved, actually."

"We may be able to help you there," said the abbot. "We have a . . . contact who is close to General Fu. We will learn what we can from this person. If Fu is involved, we will know."

"You seem very sure of this contact's knowledge of General Fu's affairs."

"With reason, I assure you."

Bei knew it was useless to ask the contact's identity. Zhou Peifeng? He certainly was privy to everything the general did. How much did Fu's daughter know of his day-to-day activities?

"Can you think of any other parties that might have wished An Shihlin out of the way, Master T'ang?"

The abbot stared pensively at the huge jade disk on the wall. "Only one. In addition to being a friend of the Communist cause, he was also—indeed primarily—a Taoist. We have enemies, ourselves. He may have been killed because he was a prominent Taoist, not because he was a Communist."

"What sort of enemies?"

The abbot smiled wryly. "We are . . . misunderstood, and thus hated, by many. And understood and still hated by others. I am thinking of other religious groups now. Certain Taoist sects. And the Buddhists. Although violence among religious groups is practically unknown in our civilization—in contrast to Western cultures, where it is the rule—we cannot rule it out, I suppose, especially in these violent times."

He turned to Meiling. "Daughter, what do you know of the Tibetan Buddhists and Mongolian Buddhists in Peking?"

"Their monasteries are rich and influential. The monks there hate us. And if adherence to their vow of nonviolence is on a level with adherence to their vow of chastity—then their hands could be bloody indeed."

Bei and the abbot both wondered where she had gained her familiarity with Buddhist monks' lack of chastity.

"Can you look into the possibility?"

"Easily, Father."

"Safely?"

"I believe so." She glanced at Bei. "Actually, Buddhist monks are rather easily handled. Only eunuchs are dangerous. Plus the Te Wu, of course."

"Then please look into the Buddhists. But take every precaution."

"Yes, Father."

"So you will complete your investigation of the Te Wu, Inspector, while we are using our contacts to investigate General Fu and the Buddhists. I believe we can rule out other Taoist sects, but I myself will check that out. We can probably have some initial conclusions for you in, say, a week, Meiling?"

"I should think so."

"Good. I am happy to be working with a man of your talents, Inspector, rather than against you." He glanced up at the windows. "It will be time for our evening meal soon. Will you join us for dinner?"

His body clammered for an affirmative reply, but Bei felt constrained to say, "Thank you, Master T'ang, but unless I leave soon I will not make it back to Yenching University by dark."

The abbot looked at him humorously. "Inspector, had you left an hour ago you would not make it to Yenching before dark. No. I must insist that you take dinner with us, and that you spend the night with us here."

Bei began to protest, but the abbot cut him off in a firm voice.

"Inspector. If you attempt to reach Yenching tonight, you will very likely be shot in the dark by Communist troops somewhere between here and there. You will stay with us, for dinner and for the night. We insist."

Bei realized the abbot was right, and moreover that he was a virtual prisoner, regardless. He acquiesced, with a slight bow.

"Good. Dufeng. Escort Inspector Bei to the guest house. Prepare a warm bath for him, and lay out fresh clothes and a robe. Then escort him to the study. We will take our dinner there, in thirty minutes."

Feeling immensely refreshed after the bath, Bei was led from the small cottage behind the stone building back to the hallway and into a room next to the meditation room he had occupied earlier. The abbot and Meiling were deep in conversation at a round table when he and Dufeng entered. A pot of tea and three cups were on the table.

"Ah, Inspector. Please join us. I rather imagine you must be famished." He glanced at Dufeng and made a series of subtle movements with his left hand. The young man nodded and left the room.

Bei took the proffered seat, noting the books lining the walls, and the desk with writing brushes and ink tablets on it.

"Let me give you a cup of tea. Are you an expert cyclist, Inspector?" asked the abbot.

"Why, no," answered Bei, accepting the tea.

"Then your journey today is all the more remarkable. We have recovered your bicycle from the bushes where you left it, along with the rest of your clothes in its basket. They, plus what you have left in the guest room, will be cleaned and ready for your departure tomorrow morning."

Meiling looked at him with a humorous glint in her large, expressive eyes. "The ride back to Peking is mainly downhill." She was wearing a red robe embroidered with blue peonies and white cranes, her lustrous black hair gathered up by jade pins which matched her jade and ivory necklace. Bei knew the appreciation of her beauty was writ large on his face, but he could not erase it.

"You . . . you are both too kind to me," he managed to stammer. He drank the tea somewhat too greedily, barely noticing its odor or color.

"Nonsense," declared the abbot, amused as always at his daughter's effect on men. "We are partners in a mystery. We must help each other."

"Of course. How did you find my bicycle?"

"By inquiries in the village. We have a close symbiotic relationship with the village."

Bei recognized the word, but could not remember its meaning, since it was one of the scientific terms recently introduced into the language from the West. He made a note to look it up, and thought it quite strange that a Taoist should be familiar with it.

As she refilled his teacup, Meiling added, again with a gleam in her eye, "You seem to be rough on duck flocks, Inspector."

He glanced at the table in embarrassment, just as Dufeng brought in a large tray laden with food and drink. The young man deftly set the heavy tray on the table without a sound and distributed the bowls, his dark eyes glowing. Individual bowls of coarse millet grain were placed before the abbot, Meiling, and Bei, then four communal vegetarian dishes in the middle of the table. Dufeng made a soft click with his fingers and fluttered his hand. The abbot answered with some quick movements of his fingers, and Dufeng noiselessly left the room as the three of them picked up the ivory chopsticks provided. Bei restrained himself and ate decorously, although the delicious dishes would have urged him to gluttony even had he not been famished.

"If anything, your food here is even more delicious than at the White Cloud Temple," he said after a minute.

"Thank you. It is very plain, of course. Have you ever had millet grain before?"

"As a matter of fact, I have not."

"Yes, only the poor eat millet. We are not particularly poor, but we eat nothing that we do not grow ourselves, and rice growing is not practicable for us here."

"The servant, Dufeng," began Bei. "He seems familiar to me. Is he ever in Peking?"

"Occasionally. He is our contact with Meiling when she is in Peking."

"I couldn't place his accent when he spoke to me on the road. Is he a Hopei person?"

The abbot and Meiling glanced at each other. He spoke. "Dufeng is originally from northern Honan, close to southern Shansi."

"He has strange eyes."

The abbot sighed. "Well he should. He was in Nanking as a boy in December of 1937."

"Oh," Bei said softly. The Japanese had taken Nanking that month and allowed their soldiers to run amok in the city. Over forty thousand civilians had been killed, most of them women and children. Few women between the ages of ten and sixty had escaped being brutally raped, usually in public. Groups of men were tied together for casual bayonet practice by the Japanese soldiers. Others were buried alive in mass graves. When they tired of this sport, the soldiers doused people with kerosene and set them aflame. For nearly a month the horror continued, despite the protests of Japanese diplomatic officials in the city.

"I trust he was spared the worst of the horror," said Bei.

The abbot shook his head. "Unfortunately not. As an eight-year-old he observed his mother raped repeatedly. One day his younger brother wept loudly while a pair of soldiers took turns with his mother, so the annoyed soldiers crushed his brother's skull with their rifle butts, then resumed with his mother. She became hysterical upon seeing her youngest son killed, and they soon shot her, inserting their rifle barrels between her legs. Dufeng sat beside her and comforted her the four hours until she died. He then began to wander north, in search of more intense cold, evidently. We found him in the village below us, emaciated but alive, in the spring, asking everyone where the cold was going, and where he could find more cold."

No one was eating now. Meiling spoke softly. "I have never heard his story before now, Father."

"I know. It is time you did. You should know that others have wounds just as you do. You should know what life is capable of, even the horror of it."

Bei spoke after a short pause. "I understand why his eyes are so strange."

162

"Yes."

"He is very . . . tentative in the Nourishing Essence Hall, Father."

"I am not surprised. It is a testament to the power of the Tao that he attends the hall at all." A pause. "But the Tao flows on. It subsumes even horrors into itself, and uses them to create life and health. To which ends even lowly millet and peppers and peanuts are utilized—so let us eat heartily."

They resumed the meal and soon the impression of Dufeng's story began to fade.

"Master T'ang, I was surprised to learn that the White Cloud Temple was twelve hundred years old. May I inquire about the history of the Purple Mountain?"

"You may," responded the abbot, bringing his millet bowl to his lips and finishing the last grains before setting the bowl down. "Ordinarily, we guard the secrecy of the Purple Mountain zealously, but the practice does us little good these days, with more people in the Western Hills and our once again assuming a visible role in the course of China's history. Our story is intertwined with that of the White Cloud Temple. How much do you know of theirs?"

"A little," Bei responded. "That it was founded twelve hundred years ago, in the T'ang Dynasty. That it was destroyed when the Mongols overran us, then rebuilt by Genghis Khan in 1224, who persuaded the Taoist Master Ch'iu Changchun to make it the center of his Ch'uan Chen reform sect."

The abbot and Meiling laughed. "Your 'little' is quite a lot," the abbot observed. "And it is the part that is pertinent to us. Our history begins with Master Ch'iu's move of his Ch'uan Chen reform sect to the Khan's rebuilt Taoist temple. Because one of Ch'iu's foremost disciples refused to accompany him in that move—a man named T'ang Weilong."

Bei smiled. "That would be your ancestor, then, and Meiling's. Why didn't he follow Ch'iu Changchun to the Khan's newly rebuilt temple?"

"Just exactly because it was 'the Khan's' temple," interjected Meiling with intensity, her eyes burning bright as she jabbed her chopsticks in the air to make the point.

The abbot laughed. "We T'ang folk have always found rule by foreigners particularly abhorrent. So while Master Ch'iu accepted the

Mongol Khan's lavish hospitality, T'ang Weilong broke with his master and came here, to this very spot, seven hundred years ago and began a reform sect."

Bei chuckled and shook his head as he pushed his empty millet bowl aside on the table. "Now just a moment, Abbot T'ang. Ch'iu's Ch'uan Chen sect already was a reform sect. Was your ancestor T'ang reforming a reform sect?"

All three of them laughed now. The abbot leaned over to refill Bei's teacup. "I suppose we T'ang folk have also always been a bit contentious. The problem was this. Ch'iu Changchun founded the Ch'uan Chen sect in reaction against the Taoism which had developed during the twelfth and thirteenth centuries, a religion consisting largely of colorful, dramatic liturgies of exorcism and cosmic renewal, emphasizing control of hordes of demons and baleful stars."

Bei's head jerked up at the abbot's last two words and he fixed an intense stare on the old man.

"Anything wrong, Inspector?" asked Meiling, noting his sudden intensity.

"No, uh, it's nothing," muttered Bei. He willed himself back to the abbot's story. "So Ch'iu was reacting against this, uh, overly dramatic form of Taoism."

"Exactly," continued the abbot. "He saw it as good theater but poor religion. It thrives even today, though mainly in the south of China, where it has come to be called the Chen Yi school of the Heavenly Masters. Ch'iu wanted a simpler, more intellectually rigorous Taoism, emphasizing the perfection of the individual through meditation and other arts, rather than focusing on control of demons and colorful exorcisms."

"But your ancestor T'ang Weilong must have largely agreed with him, if he was initially a disciple of Ch'iu's," said Bei, taking a sip of the tea.

"Oh, he did. But Ch'iu in addition adopted many practices from the then powerful school of Chan Buddhism into his reformed Ch'uan Chen sect—celibacy, for one. And many Buddhist sacred texts, for another."

"So T'ang was already dissatisfied with Ch'iu's leadership," observed Bei. "Even before Ch'iu accepted the Khan's hospitality."

"Precisely," nodded T'ang. "Ch'iu's collaboration with the Mongols was simply the final straw. While Ch'iu went to Peking and lived off the Khan's funds, T'ang Weilong came here and founded the Purple Mountain. Ch'iu created a monastery of celibate monks. We view celibacy as a perversion of nature. In that respect we are actually similar to the Chen Yi school of the south, which permits its priests and priestesses to marry and have children. Ch'iu incorporated Buddhist and Confucianist texts into his canon. We find our Taoist texts sufficient. And while Ch'iu accommodated himself to the foreign invaders, we have devoted ourselves to driving the foreigners out of China, whether they be Mongols, Manchus, Japanese, or Westerners."

"That may be an admirable goal, Master T'ang, but really, what can your community do about that?" Bei said skeptically.

"You'd be surprised," rejoined the abbot, raising an eyebrow. "First, we train ourselves in the martial arts and fortify our community's boundaries so that we can defend ourselves. When the English and French troops were pillaging in the Western Hills in 1860 and again in 1900, they left much of their blood around our walls. They soon returned to easier sport, such as burning undefended imperial summer palaces.

"But secondly, and more importantly, we have been deeply involved in the political and military movements to drive out first the Mongols, then the Manchus, and most recently the Japanese and Westerners. We do this by training leaders in the broad range of martial and tactical arts, based mainly on Sun-tzu's *Art of War*."

"Including a language of hand signals?" Bei interrupted, thinking of the young man Dufeng.

The abbot smiled. "Of course. Noiseless communication is crucial in many situations. As I mentioned, our training is quite broad. When it is completed, we send these leaders into society to use their skills against the foreigners. We work with whatever groups share our goals."

"All very admirable," commented Bei courteously, swirling the tea in his cup and wondering if it was from Szechuan province, since it had the typical smoothness and color of Mount Emei teas. "But may I inquire, Abbot, whether your people have made any discernible impact after they've been returned to society?"

"Sometimes they have, sometimes they have not. Our most notable involvement was against the Mongols, when T'ang Weilong himself launched the plan. As soon as he saw Kublai Khan found the Yuan Dynasty in 1271 with an elite ruling class of Mongols and Turks, he began to devise and coordinate measures of resistance. He died soon afterward, but his son assumed the mantle. By 1307 open armed revolts were occurring. In 1341 we had several armies in the field, most of them commanded by men trained by us. Twenty-seven years later, years of unrelenting warfare, Peking was taken and the Mongol Dynasty destroyed."

Bei inclined his head toward the abbot to acknowledge that he was impressed.

"We had less luck against the Manchus and their Ch'ing Dynasty. Our people were heavily involved in the T'aip'ing Rebellion, though. For over a decade we ruled much of central China, in the 1850's and 1860's. But when the Manchu troops combined with the Western troops, we could not withstand them.

"Against the Japanese recently, we were more successful," continued the abbot. "As soon as the Communists arrived in Yenan from the Long March, we recognized that they alone had the will and the discipline to resist the Japanese. We worked closely with them in the 1930's and 1940's, supplying leaders and tactical skills for their guerrilla units. And now, we are again supplying skills to them, to defeat the foreign-dominated Nationalists."

"Yet the Communists themselves are dominated by foreigners—the Russians," snapped Bei angrily.

The abbot carefully placed his teacup on the table, allowing time for Bei's anger to diffuse. "Meiling works more closely with them than I do," he commented, looking at her.

She shrugged her shoulders, and spoke matter-of-factly. "They probably were dominated by the Russians in their early years—the twenties. But the Russian segment of the party was discredited when the Russian advisers' insistence on focusing on cities failed disastrously—Shanghai in 1927, and in Nanchang later that year." She stared straight at Bei. "I can assure you, Inspector, the Communists now spurn the Russian line, and are concentrating on the Chinese brand of communism, with their strength in the peasantry of the countryside. Mao Tsetung had the vision—or perhaps the luck—to see where the true strength of China was located, so he is their leader today. The Communists will soon rule all of China, a China that has stood up, rediscovered its strength, and no longer bows to foreign powers." Her eyes glowed as she finished.

"But the Communists are atheists," pressed Bei. "How do you work with them?"

"We do not seek a Taoist state, nor even Taoist favor from rulers," the abbot said courteously. "We seek a China that is ruled by Chinese. We can and will happily pursue our private religious exercises under any ruler."

"And if the Communists abolish all religious expression?"

"Then at that point we will oppose them on that issue," continued the abbot. "We will diligently work to change their minds. We will become secret and invisible again, if we must. We have survived seven hundred years, through several dynasties that did us no favors. We are tough and self-sufficient. We will survive, no matter who rules China, as we always have. But at least the rulers now will be Chinese."

Bei sat back, silent, still angry over the abbot's support of the Communists and dismissal of the Nationalists as foreign-dominated.

As Dufeng entered the room, Abbot T'ang discreetly cleared his throat and broke the awkward silence. "Is the after-dinner red tea ready in the Great Hall, Dufeng?"

Bei's ears perked up as Dufeng nodded. "An after-dinner red, Abbot?"

The abbot smiled and rose. "Shall we adjourn to the Great Hall?"

As the three of them entered the large room across from the study, Bei noted that a fire had been set in the fireplace and three of the chairs and side tables pulled up close to it. On one of the side tables sat a cream-colored porcelain teapot with a cobalt blue dragon curled around it, the eyes and scales of the dragon highlighted in crimson. As Bei took one of the seats, he noted the cups were also cream-colored, with the character for "dragon" inscribed in cobalt blue inside the cup at the bottom.

Meiling poured the tea and offered a cup to Bei, which he gratefully accepted. He first sniffed the tea, noting with pleasure the aroma of the several volatile oils produced by the oxidative processes that distinguish red from green teas. Then he swirled the tea about as he stared into the cup, enjoying the way in which the cobalt dragon character twisted and dipped and disappeared and reemerged with the flow of the reddish liquid within the cup. Even the feel and heft and warmth of the cup in his hand were a source of pleasure to him. He smiled broadly, contemplating the many joys of tea, and only then actually sipped the liquid. Yes. A definite tartness, but not the over-powering dominance of tannins which ruins a red too-long-brewed. And the mixture of the volatile oils, complementing each other rather nicely, lending an aura of complexity and richness to the drink. And beneath it all, balancing everything out, the subtle, yielding fragrance of the original tea leaf itself. He took a longer sip, and idly glancing above the fire saw the huge jade yin-yang disk, and thought that somehow the disk mirrored his understanding and enjoyment of tea.

The popping of a log in the fireplace broke his reverie, and reminded Bei of the company he was in. He turned to Meiling. "A very lovely tea, Meiling. From Kiangsi, I believe?"

She nodded. "Wuyuan, in Kiangsi. Father's favorite red."

"With good reason," Bei said to the abbot. He paused, wondering whether it would be impertinent to ask the question in his mind, then decided to plunge ahead. "I was just thinking, Abbot T'ang, relating to what you've been kind enough to tell me of the Purple Mountain's history, how . . . how strange it seems to me that anti-foreign military activity should be the focus of a Taoist community."

"Oh, that is by no means our focus," said the abbot, settling back into his chair. "We've merely been speaking of that. Even now, when we're heavily involved in anti-foreign activity, the life of our community goes on. As when T'ang Weilong founded us, our fundamental pursuit is the perfection of our selves. We seek to allow the Tao to fill us. We align our inner and outer lives with the flow of Tao."

"By meditation, you said."

"Meditation is very important. But also by T'ai Chi Ch'uan, by martial arts, by growing and preparing our food, by the yin-yang arts. All permit the Tao to flow more fully in us."

Bei again gazed at the huge jade disk above the fireplace. "You obviously put a good deal of emphasis on yin and yang, as do Taoists in general. Yet the prior at White Cloud Temple labeled you 'heterodox' when I mentioned the Purple Mountain to him. Is it in your interpretation of yin and yang that you differ from other schools of Taoism?"

Bei glanced over at the abbot, who was in the midst of a long sip of tea, and thus gave a quick hand signal to Meiling to answer. After an initial moment that hinted of embarrassment, Meiling responded.

"Well, it is not so much our interpretation but the manner in which we put that interpretation into practice that so disturbs the celibate monks at the White Cloud Temple. Like all Taoists, we envision the Tao as taking the form of *Ch'i* in living creatures, which has two aspects, the yin and the yang. The yin, of course, comprises traits such as gentleness, receptivity, softness, and humility. And yang includes vigor, assertiveness, hardness, and pride.

"There are two central truths in us humans regarding yin and yang," she continued, the glow from the fire accenting the contours of her face as she stared into the fire. "The first is that all of us possess both yin and yang traits, in varying balances. Females tend to have more yin than yang, males more yang than yin. The White Cloud monks would agree with us there, but perhaps not in the second truth which we hold, that to remain healthy in spirit and body we must continually nourish our *Ch'i,* which is our essence, by intimate contact with the *Ch'i* of members of the opposite sex. And by far the most potent source of this contact is sexual union."

"I see nothing so shocking in all that," commented Bei. "After all, an active sex life is normal in many solidly Confucian marriages."

Meiling stretched her long legs toward the fire. "True enough, and that brings us to the aspect of our practice most disturbing to others. We view the restriction of sexual activity to only one partner as seriously diminishing the benefit of the activity, because your *Ch'i* is being nourished only by the particular balance or blend of yin and yang that the one partner possesses. That particular blend is not of itself unhealthy, but you require nourishment from a variety of blends, just as any one food is not unhealthy, but a varied diet is essential to receiving all the nutrients you need to maintain health.

"In short," she concluded, reaching for the pot of tea to refill her cup, "and I suspect this is the reason we're viewed as 'heterodox,' we practice frequent random sexual union between males and females in the Nourishing Essence Hall."

Bei leaned over to permit her to refill his cup as well. "The idea behind all that is not impossible to tolerate, if I may say so. But really, Meiling and Abbot T'ang, does not the practice engender all sorts of jealousies, some participants feeling overexploited and others feeling neglected?"

The abbot laughed. "As for some of us feeling neglected, our method of arranging sexual union prevents that. When I wish to Nourish the Essence, as we term it, I go to the hall and seat myself in meditation at the yang side of the hall. If other males are there, I seat myself beside them to the right. When a woman enters the hall, after a few minutes of meditation she retires to one of the Union Chambers with the left-most male in the yang half of the hall. Thus over a period of weeks we usually have Nourished the Essence with most members of the community of the opposite sex, by mere random chance."

"I cannot imagine that some males do not covet certain females," said Bei.

"We do not pretend that preferences do not exist," said the abbot with a wry smile. "Nor that some of the younger members of the community do not contrive to visit the hall together at odd hours to insure that they are the only available partners. But there is less of that than you might think. For example, we all keep ourselves rather strong and pleasing of body through our vigorous schedule of martial arts and T'ai Chi Ch'uan. Our meditation maintains our mental dispositions at a healthy, alert, inquisitive level. And we are all trained in the yin-yang arts, so that we know many techniques of bringing pleasure to our partners. Finally, we find that Nourishing one's Essence with a variety of partners is itself so desirable and stimulating, both spiritually and physically, that the wish to concentrate one's attention on any single partner does not usually last long."

"For some reason it strikes me as both coarse and idealistic at the same time."

The abbot shrugged. "Consider it how you wish."

"If I may say so," offered Bei, "my main problem with your system is not so much what goes on in the Nourishing Essence Hall, but rather that you seem to have eliminated what to me, Confucian that I am, is the most important institution of life—the family. And come to think of it, how do you even establish paternity in your system?"

Meiling spoke up. "We have something that perhaps corresponds to marriage and the family. If a man and a woman desire a child, they are granted permission to withdraw from the activities of the Nourishing Essence Hall and live together in our family quarters. They may have one child and live together as a family until the child is eight years old. Then the child and its parents move back into our communal living quarters, and the parents resume the activity of the Nourishing Essence Hall."

"But what about the couple then?"

"Sometimes they remain close, sometimes they do not. But at any rate they resume their normal participation in the Nourishing Essence Hall."

"But what about pregnancies resulting from all this 'normal participation in the Nourishing Essence Hall'?" pressed Bei.

Meiling shook her head. "No pregnancies result from unions in the Nourishing Essence Hall. We are taught a series of massage techniques which prevent implantation of a fertilized egg in the uterus. We also drink a special tea which has the same effect. And, of course, the males do not emit their sperm every time."

"What was that?" asked Bei.

"The males do not emit sperm with every sexual encounter," repeated Meiling.

"Another practice of ours difficult for others to understand," said the abbot. "Females, being in constant contact with the earth, have a virtually inexhaustible supply of yin. Males, on the other hand, only contact heaven sporadically, so their supply of yang is limited. Thus when a woman emits her liquid secretions during sexual activity it is of no consequence to her—she readily recoups her loss.

"But for a male, even though he emits his liquids only at the very peak of The Clouds and the Rain, the loss of his liquid may be harder to remedy, in spite of his being nourished by his partner's yin essence. If a male engaged in sexual activity every day and sometimes several times a day, as many of our younger males do, then the loss of that much yang sexual essence might be serious. So we male Taoists have for several thousand years practiced the art of Returning the Semen to the Source. We arouse our female partners to the peak of The

Clouds and the Rain, and thus absorb their yin essence and nourish ourselves. But we retain our yang essence, and thus are doubly invigorated."

Bei tried to show neither the amusement nor the disgust he felt. "That is indeed peculiar, Abbot. It strikes me as being a deliberate hindrance to the natural flow of the Tao you hold so dear, for the males; and for the females it seems to constitute a rather cynical theft of their essence without their receiving anything from the male in return."

The abbot nodded his head. "Yes, it is difficult for others to understand. I will only say this. As regards the male's experience, when we have sexual activity several times a day, regularly, it is not so difficult or unnatural to withhold our semen as you might think. And of course we do not deny ourselves the peak of The Clouds and the Rain every time. For us, reaching the peak once every three or four encounters is adequate. I should also say that as a result of our study of the yin-yang arts, and our partners' expertise in these arts, we receive a good deal of pleasure from sexual activity independent of the peak."

Meiling spoke up, staring into the fire as she talked. "When I first studied the yin-yang arts, before being admitted to the Nourishing Essence Hall myself, I shared your suspicion that the female was being unjustly used, Inspector. It seemed that she was nothing but a source of nourishing yin essence for the male, that the male was a sort of sexual vampire, preying upon the female." Her face was serious, and frowning as she spoke this, the firelight playing on her forehead and cheekbones.

"Then I actually began Nourishing the Essence in the hall." A bemused look replaced the frown, and she turned away from the fire to face Bei. "And it soon became apparent to me that regardless of how it may have sounded in theory, we females were being robbed of nothing. We reach the peak of The Clouds and the Rain at each encounter, usually several times, due to the expertise of our partners. In fact, since they often deny themselves the peak, our joined dance is usually much longer in duration, and my own time on the peak quite long and leisurely.

"As for being robbed of our yin essence with nothing being given in return, I can testify that I receive a very adequate yang essence regardless of whether my partner withholds his semen or not, and we females in no way suffer from the arrangement. Our yin is indeed copious, and we never feel any lack of it."

Now she turned a mischievous look upon the abbot. "Shall I tell you what I truly think, Father? After only ten years of Nourishing the Essence, I have become convinced that the whole outlook was devised by females. Yes! Consider. The males are convinced they must arouse us to the peak each time, to stimulate the flow of our yin essence so they can absorb it. And they must practice control over their peak, and postpone it indefinitely in many encounters, thus lengthening the time we females spend on the peak." She spread her hands. "It may perhaps sound like exploitation in theory, but in practice it works entirely to our benefit. We are essential to male happiness and well-being, and our pleasure is their greatest concern. We must have devised it!"

Bei was delighted with the reasoning, and laughed aloud. The abbot assumed a look of pretended shock, which soon was replaced by an animated thoughtful look. "Meiling, in addition to being most shocking, your thoughts are interesting. Many of us have long known that the *Tao Teh Ching* and *Chuang Tse* of the third century B.C. were not the first appearance of our Taoist philosophy. Those works instead must have represented the expression and fruition of thousands of years of observing nature and pondering over our own role in the natural system. Which puts our origins back into the neolithic era. And would you believe"—here his eyes shined on his daughter— "would you believe that the neolithic society of China, the Yang Shao and Lung Shan cultures, are thought to have been *matriarchal* in organization? In other words, the cultures from whence Taoism sprang were indeed dominated by females!"

Meiling clapped her hands. "I told you so!"

The abbot laughed and shook his head. Then he addressed Bei, as he extended his hands toward the fire to capture its warmth. "At any rate, there you have it, Inspector. The Purple Mountain. Only seven hundred years old. Convinced that Chinese should rule China. Devoted to developing our *Ch'i* through Nourishing the Essence, T'ai Chi, and meditation. All for the purpose of letting the Tao flow through us and our society more fully and freely."

"All very interesting," admitted Bei. "But you haven't told me the one thing I want to know."

"Oh? And what is that?"

"Who had An Shihlin burned? And why?"

The abbot frowned again. "Ah, yes. The question that has brought you to us. Perhaps, working together, we can find out. I will check on the other Taoist sects, Meiling will check on the Buddhists—carefully—and our contact will check on Fu Tsoyi. You will check on the Te Wu. Surely one of us will either discover who ordered it, or discover some new facts."

"Surely," echoed Bei, not entirely believing it.

"If you two will excuse me, then, I must retire," said the abbot, rising. "Until the morning, Inspector."

"Master T'ang," said Bei, rising also, and bowing to the man. "Good night, Father."

"Good night, Daughter."

Bei and Meiling stood in silence, awkwardly, after the abbot left the room. They both gazed into the fire to mask the awkwardness.

"You must be tired from your journey, Inspector," Meiling finally offered.

Bei became aware of his aching body and sluggish mind.

"I suppose so."

"I will escort you to the guest house," she said, leading the way out of the Great Hall. Bei followed her, keenly aware of her graceful movements, the sheen of her hair piled atop her head, the womanly fragrance about her. As they stepped outside behind the Great Hall, the soft glow of the skin on the nape of her neck aroused in him an impulse to plant a tender kiss there. She walked on, though, and turned at the door to the guest house. Her eyes had the amused, knowing look of a woman who realizes she has aroused a man's ardor.

"I hope you have a restful night, Inspector."

Bei could not bring himself to merely say good night and let her walk away. He obliquely raised the subject which filled his mind. "You must still be . . . sorrowful at the death of Prior An."

"I am."

"You have not . . . visited the Nourishing Essence Hall since his . . . passing?"

She paused and smiled wanly. "No. But I am a woman, still." She reached her hand to his cheek, and brushed it gently. As he flushed at her touch, she leaned forward and lightly brushed his lips with a kiss, and was gone.

He put a hand to the door to steady himself. His cheek and lips burned, even though the touch and kiss had been fleeting. He nearly called out her name, so strong was his desire for her. But she had quite disappeared, again. After several minutes of hoping she would return, he reluctantly turned, opened the door and entered the room. He was asleep the instant he pulled the quilt over himself.

January 6

Zhou Peifeng and Chang Tungsun sat silently in the back seat of the car, a shiny black Citroën limousine. In the dim light of the early dawn a few old men were doing T'ai Chi Ch'uan on the south shore of Beihai Park, apparently oblivious to the nearby automobile surrounded by guards. Chang and Zhou sank deeper into their heavy quilted overcoats inside the dark interior of the car, the curtained windows isolating them.

A slender figure in a uniform appeared before one of the guards and said a few words. The guard knocked on Zhou's window and Zhou parted the curtain. He took a look at the man and nodded his head. The guard opened the front door and the man climbed in, as the driver started the engine.

"Captain Li, may I present Professor Chang Tungsun. Professor, this is Captain Li Sungji, aide-de-camp of General Lin Piao." The young figure half-turned in the front seat and acknowledged Chang. He was as Zhou had described him: the round full face of a northerner, but intense and hard, with a proud air of cold, penetrating competence about him. The eyes of a man fully committed to a cause, shining with suppressed excitement and eagerness. He struck Chang as very young and naive. But then Chang remembered the many other times he had been the go-between for warlords and the Communists. Perhaps he struck the young aide as cynical and old. Perhaps he was.

They were silent as the car glided through the nearly deserted streets towards the Teshengmen Gate at the northwest corner of the city. At the gate Zhou rolled down his window and showed the guard a slip of paper. The guard jumped back and executed a salute, then opened the gates. Quietly the car slipped through the gates and headed north towards Chihsien, where Lin Piao waited.

It was fortunate that the bicycle ride to Yenching University from the Purple Mountain consisted mainly of downhill coasting, given the ache in Bei's arms and legs. At Yenching he reclaimed the green manure cart from Madame Chang, donned the rags again, with disgust, and set out for Peking harnessed to the empty cart. He hated every step, but accomplished the trip in a little over two hours. It was only late morning as he limped through the Hsichihmen Gate and headed for his own neighborhood across town. The traffic on the streets was heavy by this time. On one street to the east of the Forbidden City a small crowd blocked his passage. In the middle of the crowd a foreign lady was attempting to help a young man lying limply on the sidewalk. The man appeared to be in the last stages of starvation, his eyes glazed over, his replies to the questions of bystanders incoherent. The foreigner looked around desperately, but nobody made any move to help the man. Finally she stuffed some money in the man's jacket pocket and left, explaining something in English, Bei judged, to the bystanders. Bei maneuvered the cart around the crowd and pressed on. Foreigners were so strange. Better to let the man die with some dignity. Soon he would suffer the added shame of being robbed of the money.

As he neared his home Bei noted the still-full chamber pots along the street. The real owner of the cart would be overwrought at his returning it so late. He was right. It took an extra ten yuan note to cool the man's anger, but Bei gladly paid it and slunk into his own compound, managing to get to his private quarters adjacent to the study without the servant girl seeing him in the rags. He quickly washed, put on fresh clothes, and discarded his disguise in the refuse bin on the street. After telling Hsiaoyu to fix a light lunch in twenty minutes, he retired to his study for a cup of tea and pondered the results of his foray into Communist territory.

He had learned a lot about the Purple Mountain, but precious little that bore on his murder case. Could he believe what the abbot had told him? He thought so—An Shihlin had been one of their men, and you could usually rely on the desire for revenge. Who was their contact with Fu? He didn't know enough about the warlord to guess who that would be—unless they meant his daughter, but she hardly seemed close enough to his everyday political activities. He was on unknown ground when it came to judging whether Buddhist or other Taoist organizations might have arranged the prior's murder. But at least he would soon know whether it was the Te Wu.

He sorted the possibilities in his mind. Fu. Te Wu. Buddhist. Taoist. Somehow none of them seemed to fit. Something was missing, some piece of information that would make everything come together. There was nothing to do, though, except keep plodding along on the leads you had until you stumbled on that key ingredient that put everything into focus. He had the feeling that it wasn't far away, somehow.

The Purple Mountain. A peculiar place, to be sure. Sitting in his familiar study sipping tea, the Purple Mountain seemed unreal, unlikely. Had it truly existed? His eyes fell upon the trio of war axes mounted on the wall. Yes. Much existed outside his study that seemed unreal from here. War. Butchery. The rape of Nanking. He shook his head. What would it do to a boy to see what Dufeng had seen? How many others had seen things like that, or worse? He was glad to end his reverie as Hsiaoyu brought in his lunch. He would eat quickly, then see what Yuan had to report at the office. Perhaps the Baleful Star was already identified. Nothing would surprise him.

It took nearly three hours for Chang, Zhou, and Lin Piao's aide, Li, to be driven the one hundred kilometers north to Chihsien. Troop movements, peasant carts loaded with twigs, flocks of ducks—everything conspired to slow their progress. Chihsien finally came into view. Captain Li directed the Citroën into an elegant compound on the edge of town. It had evidently belonged to a prosperous merchant or landlord previously, and been commandeered by Lin Piao as his headquarters. Soldiers opened the doors as the car came to a halt. Zhou wondered if Lin Piao himself would greet them; probably not, as it would indicate too great a concern for pleasing them. He was right. Captain Li curtly asked them to follow him, and they strode up the steps and into the large house.

"You may have a few moments to freshen up and unpack your bags," he announced crisply. "Your room is to the left here, Colonel Zhou. Mr. Chang, yours is to the right." Since the negotiations might take two or three days, they had each brought a small suitcase. Chang noted with relief that his room had a basin with running water. He lay down on his bed nervously and shut his eyes. In the room across the hall, Zhou sat erect in a chair before a desk, mentally reviewing the positions he had been instructed to take, and the circumstances in which he could change the initial positions. He felt neither fear nor anxiety, only anticipation for the talks.

In five minutes Captain Li returned and knocked loudly on Chang's door. Chang jumped up as Li entered the room.

"Mr. Chang," Li said, speaking with precision in a Shansi accent with not a trace of warmth, "I regret that Commander Lin Piao will not require your presence in the initial talks this afternoon. We hope you will find your quarters here comfortable. Lunch will be served to you soon." Without waiting for Chang's reply, he turned and strode out of the room, the thud of his heavy boots echoing in the hall.

Chang stood, puzzled, then heard the key lock the door shut from the outside. As he stared at the door, it dawned on him. He was present merely for show, as an official mediator who legitimized the meeting. He was superfluous to the actual negotiating. This was the first time he had been shut completely out of a meeting he had been involved in arranging between the two sides. But then, this was the first time the two sides had consisted of Lin Piao and Fu Tsoyi. He stood staring at the door, angry and humiliated. Then he shrugged, and walked over to his suitcase. He picked up a book on the philosophy of Hegel he had brought to read at night. He would now have considerably more time for it than he had anticipated. And after all, one couldn't understand Marx if one didn't know Hegel.

Zhou had heard the exchange and the locking of Chang's door.

He had quickly decided that to protest it would merely add to Chang's humiliation. As a matter of fact, it made his job easier. Now he wouldn't have to go through the show of consulting with Chang or making gestures to include him in the negotiations.

"Colonel Zhou?"

"Yes, Captain Li."

"Commander Lin is awaiting you. Would you follow me?"

"Certainly."

They walked down the hall, through a large reception room with guards at each end, and into what had formerly been a study. A table had been placed in the middle of the room, with two chairs on one side and one on the other. Lin Piao rose as Zhou entered.

"Commander, this is Colonel Zhou Peifeng," announced Li. "Colonel, Commander Lin Piao."

Each of them stood at attention and nodded slightly to the other.

"Thank you for coming, Colonel Zhou."

Zhou nodded again.

"Please be seated. Li, may we have some tea."

Zhou took the single seat, as Lin sat down across the table from him. Zhou noted how different he was from Fu. The long, prominent nose. The thin face, and small, nearly frail body. Only in his eyes was there any similarity: Both men had the alert, inquisitive eyes which bespoke an active intelligence engaged in compelling tasks.

They sat silently as Li served the tea, and drank the first cup with no words as well.

"So, Colonel Zhou," began Lin Piao at last in a high, reedy voice. "Having missed his six trainloads of foreign arms at Fengtai, General Fu is ready to ratify his surrender at last."

Zhou stared at Lin Piao's thin face, haughtiness and dislike plainly stamped on it. It could be a long, unpleasant day.

Yuan was not in when Bei arrived at the office, but a note on his desk reported that the Peking High Magistrate was wondering how the White Cloud Temple case was progressing. Bei reluctantly sat down to write another report, this one the most delicate of all, since his unauthorized trip to Purple Mountain and his possession of the list of Te Wu agents could not be directly mentioned. It was late afternoon by the time the report was finished and sent to the magistrate, along with other routine reports. Yuan dragged into the office looking bedraggled, and flopped down in his chair.

"You missed me today, it appears," commented Bei.

"Today and yesterday," responded Yuan. Bei had not told him where he was going, only that it was covert and involved the White Cloud Temple case. Yuan had adopted the attitude that his chief had been on some sort of holiday.

"So—what's happened?"

Yuan shook his head. "Plenty. Yesterday we spent twelve freezing hours in that cursed guardhouse. Do you realize how cold it got night before last, and how cold it remained all day?"

Bei smiled, and nodded. "Did you find the Baleful Star?"

Yuan laughed, with a trace of bitterness. "Baleful Star. I'm beginning to think that fat turtle made it up. No. We didn't find the damned Baleful Star. But the monk managed to consume six bowls of noodles and more biscuits than I care to think of."

"How many men on the list do you think you saw?"

"There's a bright spot. The place was a beehive. Something's up there, I tell you, Chief. We saw probably twelve of the Te Wu men, as best as we can tell from the descriptions and the few I know from our previous run-ins with them, like Yu's top man, Chan. We may have seen more, but we couldn't be sure. Plain views of them all. The fat turtle said none was the Baleful Star, in between mouthfuls of noodles."

"Twelve, eh? That would leave five out of the list of seventeen you still have to go. Did you get your two done today?"

"Only one. Something came up this morning that I thought I'd better handle myself. Another one of those courtesan murders."

"Oh? The same man?"

"Yes. Nearly beheaded, wrapped in a sheet, high-class Flower House, the Huamei."

"Was she from Shansi?"

"Close to it. Northern Honan."

"Northern Honan, you say?"

"Yes. What's wrong?"

"Nothing. So you investigated it?"

"I did, Chief. Had no idea when or if you'd be back."

"You were right. Anything unusual?"

"Plenty unusual, but nothing beyond what we already know. It occurred very late last night or possibly early this morning. No new clues beyond what we already have. Same description. Slender, gentleman, unsettling eyes, northern accent, Shansi or Honan."

Bei was irritated. One more problem. He wanted to ignore it, but three identical murders in a little over a week. And at high-class places, frequented by the city's rulers and their friends. No, he'd have to pay attention to it.

"Go to the twenty most prestigious Flower Houses, Yuan. Give them the description we've got, including the preference for Shansi girls, and warn them to be on their guard."

"Now do you want me to work on Te Wu or Flower Houses?"

Bei sighed. "That's right. I forgot. Do we have anyone else free?"

"Is that a joke, sir? Everyone has got more than full caseloads."

"Great." He knew his men were working beyond their limits. "All right. I'll do it myself. Starting now. Do you have your stakeouts for tomorrow reconnoitered?"

"Not yet. I was going to do that now."

"Then do it. Try to get three in tomorrow if you possibly can."

"We'll try." He breathed heavily and pushed himself out of the chair with a grunt.

"And Yuan."

"Yes, Chief."

"I don't want any jokes about my visiting every Flower House in Peking as soon as my wife is gone."

Yuan laughed. "I'll try. But, of course, there's nothing wrong with visiting Flower Houses, Chief, married or not. You're one of the few men of your station I know who doesn't. You don't even have a concubine, which many do. Are you normal, Chief?"

The question was asked in jest, but it strained the proper limits of their relationship. Bei answered quickly, to save Yuan embarrassment. "Normal enough, Yuan. Just poor. Women are expensive, you know."

"True enough, Chief. The square inch that drives men mad always costs. Money, or something else."

"We'd best get started. Be discreet in your reconnoitering."

"I will. Enjoy the Flower Houses."

"Permit me, Commander Lin, to suggest that in General Fu's opinion any transition of government in the city would be accomplished more smoothly if command were turned over initially to a Joint Adminis—"

"What are you babbling about?" snapped Lin Piao. "You are here to ratify a surrender, not construct the best of all possible worlds for your warlord turtle." He quivered with indignation. Captain Li, sitting beside him at the table, stared coolly at Zhou.

"We are offering this war criminal a pardon for his thirty years of crimes against the people," said the frail figure. "What more dare he ask? For thirty years he has wasted the peoples' lives and crops to support his luxurious living, his warfare against other warlords, his dainty foods and lascivious concubines. We will pardon all this, overlook it. Dependent, of course, upon his making public a full confession of all his crimes and a sincere and humble apology for them."

"General Fu is willing to publicly support the Communist side, assuming that various conditions are met," Zhou patiently offered.

"Conditions?" shrieked Lin Piao, jumping up from the table. "He requires me to grant conditions?" His thin face was livid as he paced up and down the study. "He has no concept of honor, yet he wishes me to enter into an honorable agreement with him? We had an honorable agreement, worked out with Wei Lihuang at the Mountain-Sea Pass. He broke that agreement, stalled and stalled waiting for his six trainloads of filthy foreign arms to use against me."

"Commander Lin, I have explained that the delay was due to problems in maneuvering Chiang Kaishek out of office, that you could not expect him to refuse the arms, that they would have been used only to strengthen his own forces in Inner Mongolia, not against you, that—"

"I have heard more than enough of your 'explanations,' Colonel," said Lin in a shrill tone, heading for the door. "Captain Li will accept your surrender when you are ready." He left the room.

A long sigh from Zhou filled the room, then silence. He could not understand what was happening. All yesterday afternoon it had been like this morning: Lin Piao demanding unconditional surrender, refusing to even listen to Fu's proposals. And now to storm out altogether. Zhou sat there, fighting back the anger and fatigue produced by a long afternoon and morning of patiently enduring verbal abuse. He glanced over at Captain Li, staring at him with a cold, impassive face. Perhaps he was the key. What if Lin refused to entertain anything less than unconditional surrender, for face, but left it to Captain Li to discuss conditions, which he would then make a show of being persuaded to accept reluctantly? Perhaps that was it. Zhou summoned up more energy and composure, from very deep.

"Captain Li, your commander is a strong and willfull man." Zhou purposefully used the term "commander," which had a less grandiose connotation than "general," and was used by the Communist army to stress the egalitarian nature of the force and to set them apart from the Nationalists. He recalled the tales of the Communist leader Chu Teh removing his cap every time he addressed his troops, but could not picture Lin Piao making that humble gesture.

Li did not stir or change his expression. "My general is the same," continued Zhou. "It is sometimes difficult for him to picture reality, to admit the small necessities which run counter to his view of things." This was nonsense when applied to Fu, of course, but served Zhou's purposes at present. "So it is my job, as perhaps it is yours, to apply my general's view to the actual situation and permit it to have its full effect. We are translators, are we not, Captain Li, translating our commanders' minds into a tongue that others can understand."

Still the expressionless stare, as from afar, but at least he had not yet been shouted down. Zhou plunged ahead.

"Your Lin Piao has every reason to view his position as formidable. He surrounds the city, has reduced the flow of goods into it to a trickle, and outnumbers the city's defenders. He is experienced in siege warfare, having recently been successful at Mukden and Changchun. So, of course, he cannot himself tolerate the discussion of compromises, as a matter of face."

"My General Fu, on the other hand, has his own reasons for presenting the same face as your Lin Piao. He is surrounded by the most formidable walls in our civilization. He has two hundred thousand troops with ample artillery. His prowess in withstanding sieges has been marveled at for three decades. And he knows, Captain Li"—here Zhou leaned farther forward and jabbed at the table with his index finger, trying to jolt Li out of his impassive manner—"he knows that you want Peking intact." Zhou spoke in a theatrical whisper now. "He knows you want Peking as your own capital, want it unscathed, a magnificent ancient setting to dramatize your New China."

Zhou leaned back and spread his hands, in a gesture of sympathy and understood positions.

"So they both view their own position as strong. And in fact they are, are they not? Each is right, to a certain degree. And our job, Captain Li, is to mesh the views of these two strong men, and accomplish the vital aims of each without forcing them to publicly disavow their views, eh?" Still no comment or change of expression from Li. Zhou went on, hope building. "Your Lin Piao wants Peking. He shall have it. My Fu Tsoyi wants some minor face-saving measures to assist his giving Lin the city. What harm is there in granting him those, so long as Lin gets the city? The city is yours, intact, if the government is transferred first to a Joint Administrative Office, with our people and yours in equal numbers. Duration of its tenure? We can talk about that. Six months? Perhaps less. What does it matter, with your troops in actual control of the city? Then the Joint Administrative Office is in turn superseded by your own government. Troops: Permit us to march them out of the city in our present regimental organization, to sites you select. Then you can reorganize them as you wish. Pardons: General Fu has many loyal officers, both in Peking and in Suiyuan and Chahar in Inner Mongolia, who would willingly lay down their arms to your forces if assured that—"

"Colonel Zhou," interrupted Li crisply. His eyes burned with controlled anger. "Do not equate my Lin Piao with your Fu Tsoyi." He leaned forward in his chair slightly. "Commander Lin was thrust into the world on his own at age ten, because the landlords and warlords deprived his father of an adequate living. In nine years the boy had scratched his own way to Whampoa to study war, and in another two years, while only twenty-one years old, he was leading one of Chu Teh's five columns under fire out of Nanchang. He fought his way to Mao Tsetung's mountain base the next year. He commanded one hundred thousand troops by the time he was twenty-five years old. On the Long March he was the vanguard, fighting an opening

184

through Kuomintang and warlord armies the entire six thousand miles so Mao could follow. He lost half his men in that struggle. This is the man who defeated and scattered Japan's crack Itagaki Division in 1937. The man who recently conquered Manchuria. This is the man your warlord is dealing with, Colonel Zhou."

Li leaned forward, shaking now with suppressed anger, and hissed at Zhou across the table, eyes glowing. "You are not bandying terms with another warlord, Zhou. Your opponent this time is thin steel, not flabby flesh. He cuts, not wheedles. Steel does not bend, Zhou. I could not make it bend if I wished."

He sat upright, suddenly stiff and cold again. "Nor do I wish to do so. Because you are as mistaken about you and I as you are about Lin and Fu. I am not a translator of fire into honey, like you."

Zhou sat perfectly still and composed. For an instant he had been frightened by the man, and fright composed him absolutely, as it does all good soldiers. He was wrong. There was no ploy, no stratagem anywhere. It was unconditional surrender or annihilation, after all. He would try once more that afternoon. One always persevered at least once beyond the end in any negotiation, to insure that it was indeed the end. But he knew it would do no good. Then he would return tomorrow morning.

"When is lunch?" The least damn thing he could extract from them was food.

"It will be served to you when you wish."

"I wish it in twenty minutes. Professor Chang and I will take it together, in his room."

"Very well." Still cold, but now Zhou knew that Li's coldness was born of scorn and hatred. Li and Lin alike. Cold steel. Unbending. And lethally sharp-edged.

Dufeng sat in the meditation grove in the shadows cast by the ginkgo in the late morning sun, wearing no jacket. Few meditated outdoors in the depth of the winter. He relished the cold. When he was deepest, as now, only the cold existed, fresh and clean and pure. *It had been cold then, in Nanking.* His mother and brother had been cold, very cold, when he finally left them after the long night. Their cold was all he had left of them, and he cherished it. He sought it, and when it surrounded and penetrated him, as now, he felt close to them, and to his past. At one with everything, for is it not the fate of everyone and everything to be cold, finally? Cold, at the end, as cold as his mother and brother had been, as cold as he was now. Cold as the water of a high mountain lake, stretching perfectly calm and smooth as far as one could see, and clear, clear to its icy depths, as clear as the sheen of a blade.

Indeed, only one other person meditated outdoors upon occasion these days. A ripple broke the absolute, calm surface of his meditation as Meiling's image bubbled up. Meiling. The last person he would expect to meditate in the cold. She was warmth itself. He stirred a fraction, as her ripple undulated across the surface. *Oh, the warmth of her core in the Nourishing Essence Hall.* She made him forget the cold, nearly. Again he wondered. Was it wrong to appreciate her warmth? Of course not. Her yin essence brought him yang warmth. She balanced him. Cold turning into warm turning into cold. Like the seasons. Like his mother and brother, except cold was greater, cold more fundamental. *Like the heavens. The stars were warm, but the spaces were cold, the vast infinite stretches of nothingness between stars. That was where he belonged. Cold. Clean. Clear.*

It was late morning before Bei finished his rounds of the high-class Flower Houses and returned to his Chunghai Lake office. The job had taken much longer than he had anticipated. All yesterday afternoon and most of this morning. To begin, there were more Flower Houses than he had imagined, even fairly high-class ones. The city was a caldron of sexual activity. He had known that, of course. That was life. But he had not realized that the caldron bubbled quite so boisterously, to judge by the number of Flower Houses and girls employed by them.

He had received nearly a dozen invitations for free visits from the madams of the houses, and had turned down three offers for on-the-spot enjoyment of the facilities. As he put the teakettle on the stove and started a fire, he wondered why he had turned them down. He settled back into his chair, glad to be off his feet. Certainly not out of any feeling that sex was itself bad, or wrong, in any circumstance. Such notions were utterly alien to his civilization. Sex was a bodily function like eating. A need to be satisfied. Satisfaction could take many different forms. Cheap or expensive. Plain, merely to alleviate the craving; or elegant, turning the alleviation into an art. Again like eating. Sometimes a commercial transaction, from which both sides benefited; or an act of shared refinement and enjoyment, bringing two people together in an emotional bond.

So why did he decline the offers this morning? The craving was certainly there, and he had been sorely tempted. He was on duty, he had said, and it would not be proper. Yet he knew he wouldn't be back even after he was off duty. Too low-class? The places he had visited were elegant, and frequented by men more important and some just as cultured as he.

No. The "on duty" excuse he had used was the real reason. He realized it with resignation. He viewed himself as somehow different from the corrupt majority of people who held public posts in the Nationalist government. Accepting "squeeze" from various sources was common, even expected. Squeeze was nearly a way of life. His primary criticism of the Nationalists and the Kuomintang party members who comprised the government was their corruption. Their free and frequent trading of favors for squeeze, whether in the form of wealth, goods, or women. Or boys, for that matter. It was the corruption of it that had persuaded him to turn down the offers. He, after all, was different. He had his faults, to be sure, but he didn't stink of corruption. He held high ideals for his culture and his self. His personal ideals defined him, to a large degree. To betray them would mean betraying himself. And if he did that, what would be left? How could he enjoy what culture remained to him if he himself had no identity, no solid defining core?

He heaved a long sigh, pitying himself that so many pleasures were denied him. The Wind and the Flowers were forbidden if they were given to him, because of his position. And his position was such that he couldn't really afford to buy them, either. He laughed a pitying laugh as he got up to pour the boiling water into the ceramic pot. Too proud to accept squeeze from Flower Houses, and too poor to visit them as a customer. He brought the pot over to his desk and sat down, unwrapping the package of *chiaotse* he had brought from home. Too proud and too poor. It was the story of his life.

But then, there was Lufei. Eager to serve him Shansi food and other satisfactions for the cravings of the body. And Meiling. The thought of Meiling drove flower girls and Lufei out of his mind. Meiling. Such a strong and graceful body. A man could lose himself in such a body, exploring each firm curve with his hands and mouth. And accomplished in the yin-yang arts. Skilled in the various methods of trading pleasures with her partner, knowing well every joy that he could feel. Such a full mouth and expressive lips. He sat, lost in rapt contemplation of the woman and her undoubted skills.

She said his name twice, and finally had to tap his shoulder before she could get his attention. He jumped in his seat in fright at her touch. As he turned to her, she instantly recognized the glazed look in his eyes, and mistakenly concluded that he had been thinking of her.

"A plain lunch, Inspector, when Shansi food could be yours?"

"Oh. Lufei. Hello. Yes . . . a plain lunch. Please have a seat."

She sat down, smiling.

He suddenly remembered the tea, and hurriedly poured it into the insulated pot. "Have some tea. I'm afraid it has steeped too long. Far beyond four minutes."

She laughed at his flustered manner, thinking he was embarrassed to have been caught in sexual daydreaming about her.

He poured a cup out of the insulated pot, and handed it to her. "It will be far too astringent. I apologize. Although green tea doesn't get as astringent as red tea, nor so quickly."

She gazed alluringly at him over her cup as she sipped it, confident of her hold on him. It tasted fine to her. She continued to stare at him, knowing full well that a woman's hold on a man is not gained or enhanced by words.

He offered her a *chiaotse,* then picked one up and ate it when she declined. He sipped some tea with his second *chiaotse*. Not good, though not as bad as it could be. He finally regained his composure on the third *chiaotse*.

"So, how have you been? It's been, what, three days since I saw you?"

"Yes. I've missed you. And I needed you two days ago."

"Really? How so?"

"I received a terrible fright."

"Oh?" He was genuinely concerned. "What happened?"

She shuddered. "I saw—or thought I saw—my brother."

Fear and distress showed clearly in her face. Bei reached out and patted her shoulder.

"Your brother? Alive? But what would he be doing in Peking?" Then he quickly added, "And why would seeing your brother frighten you?"

Lufei clasped her hands tightly in her lap. "I don't know what he's doing here. I'm not even sure it was him. We didn't talk at all. It happened the fifth, the day after you and I discussed my cooking lunch for you." She blushed, but more from pleasure at his apparently sincere desire to accept her invitation.

"I was out, looking again for some cooking oil at a decent price. It was nearly dark. I had stopped to haggle with a vendor on Tachalan Street, just off Ch'ienmen Road. He wanted too much, and as I began to walk away I noticed a man across the street staring at me. I returned his gaze, and was astonished to be looking into my brother's eyes."

She shuddered again, sharply this time. Bei solicitously stood up and poured her another cup of tea.

"What made you so frightened about seeing your brother?"

"He . . . he was looking at me . . . not like a man looks at his sister," she stammered. She looked up at Bei beside her. "Like you would look at me, except with something hateful mixed in. Like he used to look at my sister!" She buried her head in her hands and began to sob as she said it.

Bei put his hand comfortingly on her shoulder. As she felt it, she wrapped her arms around his waist and raised her face to him, wanting and expecting an impassioned kiss upon her lips. Bei knew what she wanted, but his mind was still full of Meiling, and Lufei seemed frail compared to her. He had no desire for her. He gave her a fatherly pat on the head, and stood there, embarrassed.

She released her grip and sank back in her chair. Bei went back to his seat.

"Drink more of your tea, Lufei." She gulped it down. "Now tell me. What did you mean, he was looking at you like he looked at your sister?"

She glanced quickly at him. "Did I say that?"

"Yes, you did. And you said it scared you. Now what did you mean?"

She stared at her hands in her lap, sniffling. "He was a wonderful brother. But he . . . he had desire for my sister, I think."

"Did he ever . . . force her to do anything?"

"I don't know. But she, she might have let him sometimes. She was so full of life, she tried everything, especially with men. It was what got her involved with the landlord's son." She again began to cry, softly.

Bei walked over to a stand in the corner and dipped a cotton towel into a bowl of water. He wrung it out and gave it to her, returning to his seat as she rubbed her face into it and blew her nose.

"There. I'm being a bother to you. I apologize. I won't talk about it anymore."

"No. You need to tell someone about it. And I'm curious, frankly. Go on."

"There's nothing more to tell. She got involved with a landlord's son. The son persuaded the landlord to buy her. Father had to, to pay off his debts. It is common, as you know, to sell daughters."

"But your brother never harmed her?"

"No. But after my sister went to live with the landlord's son, he became . . . I guess you could say jealous. I don't know for sure whether she and my brother had been lovers, but he felt as if the landlord's son had stolen her from him."

"But why a look of hate from him?"

"Oh." She blushed again. "I think he felt . . . felt she had betrayed him. She was quite friendly to the landlord's son, actually. And she was quite happy to go with him and live in the landlord's compound."

Bei thought he understood. "So he desired his sister, and yet hated her because she had other men. And you thought you saw him looking at you the same way." He went over and patted her head again. "I can understand how it must have been frightening to you."

She sighed, mainly because Bei was treating her more like a daughter than a lover. Bei misinterpreted the sigh, of course, and hastily added, "But there's no need for you to worry. He never harmed your sister, did he?"

"No."

"So there's really no threat to you, regardless of how he looked."

"I suppose not."

"And you're not even sure it was him?"

"No. I was in a crowd, and just got a quick look at him. He was gone in a second."

"So. I think you're just nervous about things, Lufei. You need someone to talk to. Do you talk to Yuan much?"

"Some. He wants to marry me."

"Oh, really? You should consider it. He is a fine, dependable person. His job here is secure—well, I mean as secure as anything is, what with the war and the siege."

She pouted. "I would prefer to talk to someone more my own age."

"Oh, but so few men as young as you have steady jobs like Yuan. I think you should seriously consider him."

"Well, perhaps I will," she said coldly. "Although, of course, I wouldn't have as much time for other pursuits as a new wife."

"Well, being a wife has compensations," said Bei cheerfully, vaguely aware of her seething anger at his unselfish concern for her welfare, but his mind already on other things. "If you see this person who resembles your brother following you again, come straight to me and we'll arrest him. I don't want you frightened, little one."

"Of course. Well, I'd best be going. Good-bye, Inspector."

"Good-bye, Lufei. Keep in touch."

She was not yet to the door when his thoughts turned to Meiling. Would she find anything from the Buddhists? And Yuan. He would be seeing the fourteenth and fifteenth Te Wu men today. And the last ones tomorrow. Would the Baleful Star be one of them?

January 8

Captain Li walked Zhou and Chang across the courtyard to the waiting Citroën, its engine warming up in the morning cold. Guards opened the doors for them.

"Commander Lin will require an answer from General Fu by the eleventh," Li reminded Zhou, putting a sneering emphasis on the term "general." "If it is not satisfactory, he begins artillery bombardment the twelfth."

Zhou fought to retain his composure. "As I mentioned, I feel sure General Fu will have an answer tomorrow afternoon. You may call upon the Winter Palace then. I presume you still have our pass?"

"I have no need of a pass from your general to enter Peking."

"Fine. Until tomorrow afternoon, then."

"Remember: Artillery begins the twelfth."

The car pulled out of the courtyard and began the return journey to Peking. Chang's great relief at being allowed out of his room evaporated when he heard Li's words.

"Artillery? Do they really mean to shell Peking the twelfth?" he asked anxiously.

"Who knows what they mean to do?" Zhou answered.

"But are their terms acceptable?"

Zhou was too tired and angry to be as discreet as he should be. "Their terms are unconditional surrender," he snapped.

Chang stared at him, mouth agape. "But, but," he stammered, at a loss for words for one of the few times in his long life. "General Fu can't accept those terms. Yu Chenling won't allow it, for one."

Zhou regretted telling Chang what had occurred. "Professor, may I remind you that you are sworn to absolute secrecy in these negotiations," he said sharply. "And that it is not for you to speculate what General Fu may or may not do, or what others may wish him to do. And that this is merely the first round of the negotiations and not the final word." Zhou didn't believe this last statement, but saw it as a necessary lie.

Chang sank back in the seat, his mind racing. He felt no threat to his personal safety from any artillery bombardment of Peking, since he lived in Yenching. But he had many friends who did live in the city. And beyond that, the mere thought of Peking being shelled sent a distinct shudder through him. What if the Forbidden City were struck? Or the Temple of Heaven? Or the Temple of Confucius? Just shelling the Ch'uanchuteh roast-duck restaurant would be a calamity. No. It was unthinkable. Shell Peking?

.   .   .

Fu had been unable to concentrate all morning. His calligraphy lesson from Meilu had been wasted. He had met with Mayor Liu to coordinate final measures to airdrop food into the city from Nanking. But he had been unable to completely hide his excitement from the mayor. It was not good to let city officials know that something was afoot. He gave up trying to make sense of the grain inventories from the military units in the city, and began pacing in front of the window. Even his view of the garden held no delight for him. A knock arrested his pacing.

"Yes?"

"Colonel Zhou, General."

"Come in," he boomed. As he took his seat he was instantly composed and focused. Zhou entered the room.

"Have a seat, Zhou."

"Thank you, General." He sat down in front of Fu's desk.

"Tea?"

"No, thanks."

A brief silence.

"How did it go?"

Zhou hesitated only a second. "Not good, sir. He demands unconditional surrender. Pardon for only you and two others. Troop surrender of arms inside the city. And he would not listen to any counterproposals. Or talk about anything else."

Fu blinked several times as he absorbed the words. He waited several moments.

"He wouldn't listen, or talk?"

"No, sir. His manner verged on abusive, sir."

"Did he provoke you to anger, Zhou?"

"Never, sir. Although in retrospect perhaps I should have. But no."

"Did you attempt to lay our proposals on the table?"

"Many times, sir. Commander Lin shouted me down each time."

"Perhaps he wished to negotiate only through an underling. This young aide of his."

"That occurred to me, sir. Once, after Commander Lin had stalked out of the room in anger at my wishing to state your position, Captain Li and I were alone. I succeeded in laying out the main points of your position to him, sir. But he cut me off with a lecture on Lin Piao's life, and ignored everything I had said."

"How about using Chang to state our views? He was a neutral party."

"They kept Chang locked in his room the whole time."

Another silence. Fu felt neither disappointment nor fear. He in fact felt nothing. His mind catalogued the information and considered it dispassionately from several angles. Finally he permitted himself one emotion.

"I'm puzzled, Zhou."

"Yes, sir. I am too."

"Is it a negotiating ploy, comparable to a particularly rough first round, after which they'll come around?"

"That is possible, sir. My feeling is not, though. In fact, I am instructed to inform you they will begin shelling the city with artillery the twelfth if they have not received a satisfactory reply by then."

Fu glanced sharply at his aide. "Shelling Peking?"

"Yes, sir. The twelfth."

Fu pondered Zhou's information for over a minute. A deep silence hung over the room. Zhou noted the piles of unfinished paperwork on the desk, the half-finished cigarettes in the ashtray. He glanced at Fu's face. Impassive, but the eyes alert, dancing. Working on a puzzle. Perhaps the most important puzzle to which that lively intelligence would ever be directed.

He finally spoke. "I'm still puzzled, Zhou. Obviously our assumptions are incorrect. They do not particularly want Peking intact. They are treating it as they treated Mukden. And treating me as they treated Wei Lihuang."

A pause. "It will be easy enough to teach them that I'm considerably tougher than Wei. I have two hundred thousand troops and ample artillery."

He frowned, and became thoughtful again. "But is Peking indeed just another city? Is the commander of Peking indifferent to the destruction of his city?"

Zhou sat in silence, wondering what the answer to that question would be.

"A good question, eh, Zhou? They are gambling. Gambling that I will not allow myself to become the man who permitted Peking's destruction. Perhaps a good gamble. If they win, they win an intact city of two million, quickly and with no losses. It could dramatically and decisively tip the struggle in their favor. If they lose, though, they lose a good deal of time, assuming our grain holdings are what they are reported to be. They lose a considerable number of men, because their assaults on these walls will be costly. And if they lose an intact capital, they lose a great deal of goodwill from the intellectuals."

Fu weighed the sides.

"It's not a good gamble, Zhou. The possible losses are too great. I don't understand. Lin Piao is a military genius. He has been confounding the Nationalists and the Japanese for well over a decade. Yet this move makes no sense."

"If I may, General: This is a political more than a military move. Perhaps his political judgment is inferior to his military judgment."

Fu looked skeptical, and shook his head.

"Sir, merely because the two are joined in you does not mean they are joined in Lin Piao."

Fu laughed a dry laugh. "No flattery, old friend."

"It is no flattery, General," returned Zhou in earnest. "He repeatedly mentioned your 'betrayal' of the understanding Wei worked out. Kept harping on it."

"Betrayal!" Fu roared, glad of a chance to vent the anger that was rising in him. "Who was it that slaughtered a brigade of troops at Nank'ou Pass, troops who thought they had a truce in effect?" Fu stood up and began pacing. "Ling Jiaosun and Jie Fusan, two of my ablest officers, and hundreds of men, killed because Lin Piao violated our understanding." He stopped in front of the window. "Ling," he said softly. "He joined me as a raw recruit, not yet twenty. I nurtured him, rewarded his intelligence and bravery. I saw him grow, Zhou. Grow into a man of integrity and loyalty, tested by many battles. He was dear to me, Zhou."

"Good men die in war, sir. Regardless."

Fu sighed. "True." He sat down again. "Lin Piao harped on my 'betrayal,' eh?"

"Yes, sir. Perhaps his judgment has been impaired by his emotions."

"He rushed here after Manchuria very fast. He could be working under considerable strain, perhaps badly fatigued. Did he appear to tire easily, to be excitable?"

"He did. Our sessions were short. He constantly ate roasted beans, as if low on energy."

Fu considered it.

"So perhaps he has made a political mistake. What does it matter? Mistake or not, we must deal with it. He is our opponent; his armies surround us. It is his gamble, good or bad. The question remains: Will Peking's commander allow its destruction?" He stared out his window, seeing nothing.

After several moments Zhou coughed, and said quietly, "Sir?"

"Yes?"

"You have a staff meeting scheduled in an hour. Shall I cancel it?"

Fu turned around decisively. "By no means. We must gauge how ready and willing my officers are. Learn if their food reserves are indeed what they are claimed to be. Take inventory of our stockpiles of artillery shells and rifle ammunition. The question is important, Zhou, and the decision will be an informed one, whichever way it goes. Call each staff officer immediately and tell them we want their latest and most accurate figures on food, weapons, ammunition, and morale at today's meeting."

"Yes, sir. I'll get on that immediately." Zhou left the room, and Fu turned and gazed out the window, thinking of the dead Ling Jiaosun.

Bei looked up expectantly as Yuan entered their office in the late morning, his refugee disguise blending well with his air of discouragement.

"No luck?" inquired Bei, knowing at a glance that the Baleful Star had not been encountered by Yuan and the fat monk.

Yuan shook his head. "Not the two yesterday, and not the one this morning. That leaves one Te Wu on our list as a candidate for the Baleful Star." He stared accusingly at Bei, plainly fed up with the assignment and regarding it as a futile effort.

Bei bristled at the barely concealed hint of insubordination in Yuan's attitude. "The last address is in the safe," he said icily. "Get on it immediately. I have to report our results to General Fu this evening." He stared pointedly at Yuan until Yuan lowered his eyes, muttered "Yes, sir," then rose and crossed the room to the safe. He extracted the list, sighed deeply as he memorized the last address on it, then put the list back in the safe and left the room without another word.

Bei leaned back in his chair. It was, of course, highly unlikely that the last man on the list of Te Wu agents would turn out to be the fat monk's Baleful Star. If the Baleful Star was not a Te Wu agent, then who was he? A Buddhist or a rival Taoist? He would see Meiling tomorrow night to get her and her father's results on those possibilities. Somehow he doubted that the man who arranged the murder of Prior An did so out of some religious rivalry, though. That left only one obvious suspect behind the killing: General Fu himself. But why would the warlord holding Peking go to great lengths to assign his chief inspector to investigate a murder he had himself arranged? The reason for it would have to be some complicated, elaborate twist to Fu's situation that was beyond Bei's ken. He wished he knew more about Fu, his history and his personal traits. Bei's head began to swim as he tried to imagine plots and counterplots that might be emanating from the Winter Palace.

Perhaps he was making it more complex than it needed to be. Always start with the obvious and mundane, he reminded himself. Why are people murdered? Usually by jealous lovers or greedy business partners. The prior was not in business, unless you considered the Communist underground a business, which it surely was not. Jealous lovers? That could mean another girlfriend of the prior, angry at him for paying attention to Meiling. Or, on the other hand, it could be some other boyfriend of Meiling, angry at the prior for the same reason. He knew of one female other than Meiling who had been seen going into the prior's quarters: Hsiawen, General Fu's daughter. He sat bolt upright in his chair as his chain of thoughts looped back and made contact with an earlier phase. Fu's daughter, acting either as a jealous lover, or as the warlord's daughter. Or both. But then he shook his head. Why would she hire the Baleful Star to arrange a midnight burning of the prior, when she could simply slip a knife in him as he lay sleeping after a tryst with her? But he couldn't reject the idea outright.

What about another boyfriend of Meiling? That would make the Baleful Star himself the aggrieved party rather than someone hired or sent by some person or organization. His own attraction to Meiling made this possibility distasteful, but he should consider it. Who else might Meiling be seeing? Certainly any of the Purple Mountain males, in the Nourishing Essence Hall. Her odd comment at the Purple Mountain disparaging the chastity of Buddhist monks came to mind, also. Buddhists. Another link in the chain looping back upon itself. Bei smiled. Yes, this case was getting most deliciously complicated.

Fu went straight to his private quarters after the staff meeting, exhausted. He had drained his officers of information in the meeting, eliciting everything they could tell him, absorbing it all into his mind and etching it there with fierce concentration. The balancing would come later, the careful sifting and weighing of factors, the delicate journey toward a final decision. Later. Now he needed rest. He sprawled heavily on the bed.

A soft knock. He garnered the strength to say "Come in."

She entered softly, and read his exhaustion at a glance. Without a word she pulled his boots off, then perched astride his hips and began to massage his back through his jacket. He grunted and jerked his shoulders, signifying his desire to have his jacket removed. She did so, and resumed the massage, her strong hands working outward from his spinal column.

"A rough morning, my lord?"

He laughed softly. "Rough enough. Being a warlord is sometimes hard, little one."

She murmured assent as she worked her hands down his back, kneading the muscles in small circles, clockwise on the right, counterclockwise on the left.

"You are a great warrior, and great warriors have to make momentous decisions."

He raised his head to glance at her over his shoulder. "Sometimes I think you know more about my affairs than I do."

She laughed softly. "I know nothing. Except your muscles tell me that you are suddenly under a great strain that is mental in origin. You learned something this morning that requires intense thought and a decision of import."

"Do my muscles tell you what my decision should be?" he asked dryly.

"No. But I can give you some advice."

"By all means, do. I need all the advice I can get."

She continued to massage as she spoke.

"Disregard what is easy to do, because you are stronger even than you know. Disregard what others will think of your decision, because you are responsible only to the Tao, which is within you as well as the world. Abandon the hope for a perfect decision, because all important problems are complex, and their resolution cannot be fully satisfying. Listen carefully. Consider fully. Sketch out several decisions, and imagine what each of them would look like one year later, then a decade later, then a century. If your decision does not flow with the Tao, it will be reversed later, anyway. Balance the dictates of your mind with the feelings of your heart, then do what you think is best. And never, never look back."

Warmth and relaxation were spreading over his body, but his mind was focused keenly on her words. He committed them to memory, then asked, "Where did you learn such things, my precious jade?"

"You forget our pact, my lord. You must never ask from whence I came to you."

"Of course. Thank you for your advice, Meilu. It will help me."

She finished with his back and moved down to his feet, using the outer edge of her palm in a rolling motion up the soles.

"Did I ever tell you about Ling Jiaosun?" he suddenly asked.

"You mention him in one of your recent poems, I think. One of your officers surprised by Lin Piao's advance troops at Nank'ou Pass?"

"Yes. He was a boy when he joined the Twelfth Brigade. In 1938, maybe early 1939. Thin, nearly starved, but with a keen intelligence in his eyes. Jie Fusan, the Twelfth's commander, made him a messenger, and he soon was our best. That was back when we were fighting the Japanese, in the border region between Shansi and Shensi. Anyway, he was captured once by the Japanese, but escaped—by heaven, how he escaped!" Fu turned over and sat up in the bed, grabbing Meilu's forearm and staring intently into her eyes as he spoke.

"He killed his two guards with the handle of a metal serving spoon he had broken and sharpened on the rock walls of his cell. And then he crawled through the center of the camp—it was in the middle of the night—with one of the guard's bayonets between his teeth." Fu grinned as he pictured it. "Slithered past a drowsy sentry and into their brigade commander's tent—the brigade commander's own tent!" He dropped his hand from Meilu's forearm and sat staring into space, caught up in his tale, wonder on his face.

"And there, my love, there he cut out the heart of the sleeping commander. Cut out the heart, and crammed the bloody thing into a dispatch pouch full of intelligence reports on troop movements and such." Fu threw back his head and laughed, a full, throaty laugh. He shook his head for another moment. Meilu sat silent, absorbed. Fu took a deep breath.

"Then he crawled out of the camp, leaving the bayonet behind in the commander's chest—a theatrical touch, you see. Rejoined his brigade two days later. Jie sent the boy—and the dispatch pouch with its contents—straight to me. I made him a lieutenant on the spot, even though the blood from the heart made most of the papers unintelligible."

Fu leaned back against the wall, hands behind his head, and took up the story in a more matter-of-fact tone. "We soon realized that Ling had intelligence as well as nerve. Soon Jie and I relied heavily on his judgment. It was uncanny, absolutely uncanny, the way he seemed to know what the Japanese would do in any situation. Finally Jie learned his secret from him—with the help of a bottle of wine." Fu smiled wanly, then spoke quietly.

"Ling's family, it turns out, had been slaughtered by a Japanese patrol in early 1937. The usual thing—wife and daughters raped, father's testicles cut off and crammed down his throat until he choked to death. But the sergeant leading the patrol took a liking for Ling, and kept him as a sodomite. Ling was too dazed with horror to realize what was happening at first. And too malnourished and mistreated to do anything about it later.

"The sergeant kept him for seven months, then the brigade commander's aide saw him, and claimed him for the commander, who also was fond of boys. Ling spent another six months with the commander."

Meilu looked down, biting her lip. Fu pushed on with the story. "He developed two passions in his year and a month as a camp whore of the Japanese. Hatred of Japanese, which became the guiding force of his life. Such hatred. And an intimate feel for the Japanese psyche. A type of knowing that comes from intimacy with their genitals as well as their minds." Fu sighed. "He certainly knew what they would do, uncannily so, once he joined us."

Meilu breathed deeply, and shifted her position on the bed. "A horrible story. I suppose he . . . he never achieved anything like an inner peace with himself?"

Fu laughed bitterly as he sat up. "Inner peace? No, of course not. For one who is not inclined to sodomy, my dear, a year of it does irreparable damage, especially as a captive of soldiers. But happiness, now—yes, I assure you he was happy. He was supremely happy when he showed me the heart of his former lover in the dispatch pouch—yes, he had been captured by the brigade whose former whore he had been. Such . . . joy it gave him, to rip out that man's heart. And as an officer, directing our battles against the Japanese—yes, he was happy, to see how his insights let us anticipate the moves and reactions of the Japanese. His joy at seeing Japanese killed knew no bounds."

Fu stretched out on the bed, drew Meilu down beside him, and pulled the quilt over them. He simply held her, close, as he finished the story.

"After the Japanese surrendered, he stayed on—said we were the only family he had. Indeed, he and Jie and I were like family, after all our shared experiences in those years. I put Jie and him in charge of guarding Nank'ou Pass. They were the best I had, and the pass was my only connection with the bulk of my troops, who remained in Suiyuan and Chahar when I came here. I told them that Lin Piao and I had an understanding." His body tensed at the mention of Lin Piao. "I would not contest his entry from Manchuria onto the North China Plain—I could not contest it anyway—and he would not attack the positions we held. That was my mistake, Meilu, telling them of the agreement. A bad mistake. They assumed, as I did, that Lin Piao would act Chinese, not Japanese. That he would keep his word. They were lax. And Lin Piao took advantage of my mistake, and force-marched to the pass faster than any of us imagined he could from Manchuria, and fell upon them early in the morning. A well-executed attack. There were hardly any survivors. Jie and Ling were both killed."

Fu held Meilu tighter, and she felt a tear running down his cheek. "Both killed. I loved Jie as a brother, and Ling—Ling as my son. And now they're gone." His body shook softly with sadness. "For thirty years I've loved many Jies and many Lings as brothers and sons, and most of them are dead. Dead in my service." The tears flowed now, and he wept quietly, his body shaking gently against Meilu's. She snuggled closer against him, and clung to him. Soon he ceased to weep.

"Death, my lord, comes to all."

"Yes." He sighed a deep sigh, and cleared his throat. "But still it pains the heart."

"Yes. If you must assume responsibility for their deaths, though, assume responsibility also for their lives. For the comradeship you gave to Ling. For the opportunity to kill Japanese. For nurturing his growth from a shattered boy set on revenge to a man secure in the friendship of comrades. You are responsible for all that, for all your men, as well as for their deaths."

He sighed as he thought it over.

"And as for their deaths—you are not responsible for death itself. Death is part of the flow of the Tao—neither good nor bad, simply a given. You affect the timing and circumstance of death only, my lord. Do not take more than the proper burden upon your shoulders. You postpone death for many, by your courage and intelligence. You hasten death for some, by your mistakes. On balance, you have nothing to be ashamed of. You cannot be ashamed even of your sadness and your tears. They, like death, are part of the flow of the Tao."

He kissed her gently on the forehead, as a father would kiss his child, as he had wished he could kiss Ling.

"Do not ever leave me, Meilu. I do not know what I would do without your wisdom or your beauty."

She sighed, and shook her head. "My love. My love. Do you still not see how the Tao flows? Of course I will leave you. Perhaps soon, perhaps late. What you call my wisdom and beauty are but part of the Tao, and the Tao you have with you always if you open yourself to its flow."

"Nay, my precious jade. You tell me that the Tao is concrete and material, not an idea or abstraction. You are a concrete part of the Tao, and I want *this* particular material with me, *this* particular manifestation of the flow of the Tao." He pinched her buttocks hard with

202

each "this," and she screamed in pain and delight. They both laughed, and snuggled closer under the quilt.

The light faded outside the window and the garden disappeared. Fu settled back in the chair wearily, lit a cigarette, and opened the side window panel a bit more to clear the air in the room. He was exhausted. But it was good. He was active again. Not waiting, besieged—active, finally. He in fact lived for these days, when events and decisions crowded in. Never did he feel more alive than now. More full of the Tao, as Meilu would put it. He smiled as he thought of her, then repeated her advice to himself. It was good advice. Why had she given it to him? Because she cared for him? Possibly. But he could never forget how she had come to him, in Kalgan. It was October 9, 1946, the day before the battle in which he had finally captured the city from the Communists. Kalgan was the capital of Chahar province in Inner Mongolia, Fu's seat of power. When the Japanese left in 1945 he had swiftly reestablished his dominance over the entire region—except for Kalgan, which the Communists had seized and held before his troops could get there. So long as the Communists held Kalgan, his own military and political base was insecure. He and Jie and Ling had plotted for months, camouflaging their unfolding plan with feints and secret troop movements. Finally the net was fully cast, and in a swift series of moves the city found itself surrounded before it knew it was even in real danger.

Then the game began all over again, on a smaller scale. Where would Fu's armies penetrate the city? If the artillery concentrated here, did that presage the location where his troops would storm into the city? Or was it but a trick to lure the defenders away from the actual point of attack? Fu had assigned Jie and Ling to study Suntzu's *The Art of War* months before, in preparation for the attack. The two-thousand-year-old manual contained deft instructions for every stratagem, ruse, and subterfuge of war, flatly stating that "All warfare is based on deception." Mao Tsetung and Lin Piao were its most able practitioners, and Fu had turned to the manual initially to learn how his enemies thought. Soon he too was under its spell, and the attack on Kalgan was an intricate duel, replete with false reports planted by each side, sudden marches signifying nothing, deceitful lulls, swift concentrated probes, living agents, double agents, and expendable or death agents.

Every stratagem so brilliantly described by Sun-tzu and his commentators over the millennia was employed by each side, save one. Fu expected it, and when the beautiful figure materialized by his bed the night before the carefully veiled master attack, he knew who she was. "Give your enemy beautiful women to bewilder him." But because he knew who she was, and knew moreover that it was all a game, albeit a lethal one, he had thrown back his light covers and she had come into his bed. They had loved the entire night, with the unequaled passion of love between strangers.

The attack the next day was victorious. Fu was master of his domain once more. And the beautiful young woman never left him. She refused to divulge who she was, or where she had come from, or why she had come to him. In the two years they had been together he had come to know everything of her body, much of her mind, and something of her spirit. And realized that the same could be said by her regarding him. Ling Jiaosun had told him that she was far more dangerous than merely a beautiful woman sent to bewilder him. She was a living agent, one assigned to know him as only a bedmate can know another. Ling in fact had counseled him to kill her, and volunteered to be her executioner.

Fu had rejected his counsel, though, much to Ling's concern. It was not so much that he was caught in her web of passion, although he freely admitted that was a factor. It was a feeling he had that she gave him more than she took from him. That even if she was passing information to someone, she was strengthening him and sharpening his mind in return. Sometimes he thought she was not an agent at all. Sometimes he thought he had won her over and converted her from an agent to a double agent. But he knew she was too steady for that. And he knew that their relationship was too complex by now to be described. Disregard what is easy to do, because you are stronger even than you know. Disregard what others will think of your decision, because you are responsible only to the Tao. Listen carefully. Consider fully. Balance the dictates of your mind with the feelings of your heart, then do what you think is best. And never, never look back. That was not an agent's advice, nor even a double agent's. That was a *Laoshi* speaking, a teacher instructing a student. And for that role he was sure she had not been sent, if indeed sent she was.

A knock at the door.

"Yes?"

Zhou entered the room. "Inspector Bei, sir."

"Oh, yes. My last appointment, is it not, Zhou?"

"Yes, sir."

"Bring him in."

Bei entered the room and immediately sensed that something was different with Fu. To Bei he seemed, not more alert or penetrating, but larger and deeper. As if an extra dimension had been added to him, a mantle placed upon his person that conferred more substance to him.

"Have a seat, Inspector. Tea?"

"No, thank you, sir."

"So have you found the Baleful Star, Bei?"

Bei realized it was the first time Fu had addressed him by his name alone, rather than his title.

"No, sir. But I know now he isn't a Te Wu. Here is the list you gave me of their agents, with their descriptions and addresses."

"Zhou, burn it."

Zhou went over to the open window and held the sheet over a waste basket as he touched a flame to it. They all watched the list flare orange, then blacken. He broke the charred bits into the wastebasket.

"So, Bei. What do you think?"

"I have another possibility that is being investigated, General. There is the chance that An Shihlin was killed because he was a Taoist, not because he was a Communist agent. So I have . . . contacts that are looking into the possibility that a Buddhist sect or another Taoist sect had him killed in a religious rivalry." He declined to tell Fu about the Purple Mountain, just as he had not told Master T'ang about the Baleful Star. Nor would he reveal his conjectures of this morning about jealous lovers of Meiling or the prior. If Fu turned out to be somehow involved in all this himself, it would be best if he thought Bei had run into a blank wall.

"Religious rivalries very rarely result in death, Inspector, at least in a civilized culture," said Fu. "Although with the Buddhists, any-thing is possible. Once you create separate worlds full of demons and demigods, you have cast your moorings adrift."

"I agree it's unlikely, sir, but likely leads are few in this case. And, in fact, I'm contemplating an even more unlikely course. Desperate, even. I may simply station the monk who dealt with the Baleful Star at a busy intersection and have him look for the Baleful Star passing by."

Fu laughed. "Two million people in the city, and your monk is going to stand and look for the Baleful Star! You're right, it is des-perate. But do it."

"It will mean putting one of my men with him—I don't trust the monk not to disappear. And this at a time when all my men have loads twice or three times normal. But I'll go ahead and do it."

Fu gazed closely at Bei. "Some of my . . . associates are talking about a string of savage murders in the city's Flower Houses. They are quite concerned."

"Ah, yes. Yes. I have personally given a description of the killer and what we know of him to all the high-class Flower Houses—"

"Indeed?" commented Fu, with an amused look.

"Uh, yes. But there is little else we can do, other than warn them."

"At any rate, you presumably have more important things to work on."

"Yes, although everyone is working beyond their normal limits these days."

Fu offered his cigarette case to Bei and Zhou. "Cigarettes, gentle-men?"

Bei, flustered by the courtesy, took one, as did Zhou. Zhou struck a match and lit both the cigarettes.

"Bei, tell me about the city's mood."

"Its mood, sir?"

"Yes. What is the atmosphere on the streets? Are the people strained, irritable? Or blasé? How are food reserves holding out?"

"Ah. Well, it is not so . . . tense as it was the first several weeks of the siege. We are, what, three weeks into the siege—"

"Two days shy of four weeks, actually," interjected Fu.

"Yes. Nearly four weeks. At first, there was a good deal of tension and excitement. But now, people are used to it. It seems almost normal."

"Food supplies?"

"Food is expensive, as is everything. But there are very few people starving—at least publicly. I have seen one man, in the street, but no more."

"How do you judge the city would react to an intensification of the war here?"

"Intensification? What would that mean?"

"It could mean several things. Probes of the city's defenses by the Communists. Skirmishes at the walls. Shelling of the city."

"Is shelling to begin then?"

"Inspector, I do not know. It is my job to be prepared for anything. I am merely inquiring what you think the city's response would be."

Bei thought. "I don't know, sir. I doubt that there would be mass hysteria. People would not revolt against the Nationalist rule, certainly. Or pour out massive new support for the Nationalist rule, either. You are well-liked, General Fu, and truly respected. But there is not much . . . enthusiasm in the city anymore for the Nationalists. Or against them, for that matter."

"How much sympathy is there for the Communist underground?"

"Difficult to say, sir. No active support. As for sympathy—I don't know. It's more that the underground is, well, ignored. Not regarded as that important, in spite of the spate of propaganda sheets stuffed into newspapers and posted on walls here and there."

"So in your judgment it would be 'business as usual' if the war intensified here?"

"Exactly. We Peking people are, well, rather cynical, sir. And independent. We will carry on regardless of who is in or who is out."

"Yes. A maddening trait, although perhaps admirable. How is your wife, Bei?"

"I . . . have not heard from her, sir. I presume she is fine."

"Oh. Hangchow has got to be more pleasant these days than Peking."

"Doubtless."

Fu let a silence linger in the room, as all three men puffed on their cigarettes, Bei nervously. When he could stand it no longer Bei half-rose from his seat.

"I should be going, General Fu. Thank you for the cigarette."

"Not at all, Bei. Good luck with the investigation. Let me know if we can help you, or if anything comes up."

"Yes, sir. Good-bye."

Zhou escorted him to the door, motioned a guard to continue the escort, then returned to his chair. Fu took another cigarette, lit it, and shoved the case wordlessly at Zhou, who declined it.

"You're being quite courteous to the inspector, sir."

Fu puffed on the cigarette. "He is an intelligent man. And he may be of use to us in some capacity later." He leaned back to open the window further. "I wonder who his Buddhist connections are?"

"I have no idea. Shall I have him trailed?"

"No."

Zhou stared at Fu. He seemed so sure of himself always, even now.

"Will you have an answer for Lin Piao's aide tomorrow?"

Fu continued to puff away for a few moments. "I think so." A pause. "But I will not make a firm decision until late tomorrow morning. I am too tired now. You know I distrust decisions made when the mind and body are weary."

Zhou smiled. "I remember your imparting that lesson to a few. Ling, for one."

Fu sighed and put out the cigarette. "Yes. He learned all my lessons well. He would have been a strong asset to us now, and in the future. I neglected to teach him the most important lesson, though."

"What was that?"

"Never totally rely on your leader's judgment. Keep your guard up, even when he tells you that you can relax. Because he is fallible, like all men."

January 9

Fu sat erect before the window looking out on the garden, the early morning light falling feebly on the paper. In the corner the coal burner was sending faint threads of heat into the room. They had just finished warming their hands over it, made the ink, and sat down at the paper, taking up the brushes. He watched her hand intently as it rhythmically brushed the characters of the Kalgan poem onto the paper, pausing slightly between each character. Her deft turning of the axis of the brush in her hand to vary the thickness of the line was imperceptible to him. He shook his head.

"It is beyond me, my love."

"Nonsense. Do it slowly, as slowly as it takes," answered Meilu. "You already know how the characters should look, the placement of thick and thin, of blunt and of pointed. You know how it is produced, how to turn the brush in your hand, how to slant your hand to change the angle of your wrist. You know the posture and the position of your back and arms. All that is required now is putting all this together in such a way that the Tao can flow unimpeded through the brush."

"The Tao this, the Tao that! I tire of hearing about the flow of the Tao," he declared with a vehemence which surprised them both. "You speak as if it were the most natural thing in the world, yet I know it requires hundreds of hours of detailed, bone-wearying practice. What is natural about all this?"

She shook her head. "It takes millennia for water to work on a stone to produce a T'aihu. It takes centuries for an oak to grow to maturity. What is unnatural about the requirement of time?"

He put the brush down obstinately. She continued. "Then also we humans, alone of all the ten thousand things, resist the flow of the Tao. Do not ask why. It is given. We must unlearn our impatience, our resistance, and become as we were when young: pliant, accepting. We approach the Tao by stripping away, by becoming less. Yes, it takes time. And toil. But each step is its own reward. With each step rightly done, a little more of the Tao comes trickling through the bulwarks we have raised against it."

With a sigh he picked up the brush again and dipped it into the slurry of ink they had created. He stroked the first character, slowly.

"Good. Watch me now." She stroked the same character, also slowly, exaggerating the subtle movements of her hand.

He repeated the character, better this time. Again. Better again.

"Now a bit faster."

In several minutes his rendition of the character was acceptable to her, and they moved on to the second one.

Nearly an hour later she signaled the end of the lesson. Many sheaves of paper were filled around them, and his right hand and arm ached. He would not admit it to her, but he felt invigorated, relaxed.

"Tomorrow we will put all the characters together. And inscribe a copy of the entire poem the next day."

"That will be satisfying."

He rubbed his right hand with the left. She took his sore hand in her two and began to massage it, first the palm, then the thumb, the fingers last.

"Would you be frightened if the Communists began to shell the city with artillery?" he asked casually.

She continued the massage without a noticeable pause. "Frightened? No. Death comes to us all. I would take precautions, and continue living as fully as I could."

"Would destruction of the city sadden you?"

Again no perceptible pause. "Sadden me? Of course. There is much beauty in this old city. But the city has undergone destruction many times. The desire to freeze a structure—or a relationship, my lord— and prevent it from undergoing change is common to us humans, but thoroughly unnatural, against the—" Here she caught herself, and laughingly refrained from using the term which offended him. "—against the nature of things."

"So permitting destruction is no crime?"

"Not if it occurs as part of the process of creating a new order. Creating beauty and pattern always entails destruction. Although we humans often destroy without creating."

"You cannot create without destroying, but you can destroy without creating."

"Yes. And the touchstone is the Tao. Is it present in the movement? Is what you are doing part of the natural rhythm of things? Does it conform to the Tao's vitality, its thrust toward life and harmony and spontaneity? Is it part of the web of transformations of the elements into new patterns?"

He sat there, staring past her, fitting her words to his particular decision. She silently continued her massage of his hand. The poem, broken into groups of characters, lay scattered around them.

Bei had arrived at his Chunghai Lake office early and immediately began a wood and coal fire in the tin stove and set the teakettle atop it. He stood by the stove, warming his hands and letting his mind slowly focus on the courtesan murder case. The more violent and gruesome a case, the earlier in the day he generally thought about it, since his mind was freshest then and could escape getting mired in the depravity of the circumstances. Since Fu had specifically inquired about this case, he felt obliged to make further efforts in it.

The water began to rumble in the pot, and he reached into his jacket and pulled out a small packet of Jade Valley green tea. He smiled as he dropped the leaves into the porcelain pot, remembering Liao in his valley outside Hangchow. As the water in the kettle reached a boil, he poured most of it over the leaves, then added the last bit to an insulated pot to warm it up. He upended the four-minute timer absently, his mind shifting from Liao's valley outside Hangchow to the Shen family villa on the west shore of West Lake, and his wife there. It was strange how little he missed her. Perhaps that was a sign of how far they had drifted apart. He didn't even miss her physically, since their lovemaking had long been perfunctory and without warmth. Was he incapable of passion? Perhaps Yuan had been right to inquire if he was "normal."

He smiled ruefully, thinking that his feelings for Meiling were certainly normal enough, although the idea of a middle-aged Confucian such as himself yearning for a young Taoist priestess who regularly frequented such a thing as a "Nourishing Essence Hall" was—well, it was all very strange. Not the sort of thing he could readily understand or assent to. But then, everything these days was strange and difficult to assent to. China carved up by warlords, with Communist bandit armies sweeping down from the north. The Kuomintang, self-proclaimed bastion of traditional Chinese values, riddled with corruption and incompetence. His marriage as weak and directionless as his country. He felt a burning in his throat and angrily tightened the muscles and his emotions to prevent the tears that threatened to well up.

As the last grain of sand trickled out of the timer's upper chamber, he poured the small amount of hot water out of the insulated teapot, then poured the brewed tea into the prewarmed insulated pot. He stood there, holding the insulated pot of tea and staring out the window at Chunghai Lake's frozen surface, leaves and seed pods whipped across it by the wind. What was one to do in these turbulent times? The tea warmed his hands through the insulating cloth bag around the pot, and he smiled again, sadly. Hold on. That was all he could do. Hold on to those things that anchored him against the turbulence. His tea. His friends. His job. His absorption in the pleasure of unraveling the puzzles his job afforded him.

He nodded, pulled his wicker chair close to the tin stove, and poured a cup of tea as he turned his thoughts to the courtesan murderer. Respectable on the outside: youngish, well-dressed, sometimes in a uniform, polite, a strong and capable manner. A gentleman. With a Shansi or Honan accent. He shook his head. That description fit hundreds in the city. Every regiment had its young officers, many drawn from those North China provinces. But not all of them had the funds to frequent the city's best brothels several times a month. That narrowed it down some. The man would have to be relatively high-ranking in a well-funded organization. The Te Wu, for example. Or the military—including Fu's headquarters. Or one of the old businesses or temples of the city—including the White Cloud Temple. Either a high-ranking official in one of these organizations who had a large salary, or a low-ranking person who had the opportunity to embezzle the required funds. Lastly, the person could be independently wealthy, a member of the moneyed elite that Ho belonged to.

The courtesan murderer would be someone from one of those groups. A gentleman from Shansi or Honan on the outside. And inside, someone with a secret in his past, some event that had loosened his grip on sanity and sent some pocket of his mind spinning into a macabre dance mirroring the turbulence all around him.

Bei sipped his tea and stared out the window at the lake's frozen surface. He might well have met the murderer, or know of him. He knew many who fit the exterior description. But how to gain a look at the interior? What trick or technique pushes the outer mask aside to reveal that inner pocket of the mind, if only for a frightening instant? He sat and pondered the question.

. . .

The top Nationalist command in Peking sat stiffly around the large ebony table, now cleared for the special meeting. Wei Lihuang, Cheng Tingfeng, and Shih Chueh. Yu Chenling, Teng Wenchao, and Chi Ch'aoting. Li Wen and old Teng Paoshan. Most of them were generals, like Fu, although clearly Fu was the first among them, by virtue of his experience and strength, as well as the formal title and powers conferred upon him by Chiang Kaishek. Some of them had fled to Peking from the major cities of Manchuria as they had fallen to Lin Piao. Others had been assigned to the city for years, guarding the ancient capital. All were tough and cynical, and beginning to feel that their cause was slipping toward defeat. Which meant that desperation, delusion, and self-pity were liberally mixed with courage, hope, and new perceptions around the table.

"Gentlemen. We have all fervently pressed Chiang Kaishek's campaign for peace in the days since his New Year's proposal. Yet you no doubt heard of the January fifth radio message from Lin Piao and his political commissar, Lo Junghuan, the so-called 'open letter to Kuomintang officers in Peking.' They promised us all pardons and protection of our lives if we surrender."

He looked slowly around the table.

"I have called you together to reaffirm my absolute rejection of unconditional surrender." More than a few of those present were surprised to hear this. "We are the proud standard bearers of a proud tradition. Surrender does not become us, nor our tradition. Honorable men understand that peace does not mean surrender.

"My intelligence sources indicate that the enemy may be preparing to intensify his actions against us. An artillery barrage beginning three days hence is possible." A murmur of shocked voices arose from the table. "Nor can assaults on our walls be ruled out in the near future. Accordingly, I have decided to accelerate our defensive measures, effective immediately. I shall today assign duties to each of you, for the officers and men under your command to execute with the utmost speed."

He picked up a paper in front of him. "Wei, Cheng, and Shih— you are assigned to clear a ring fifty meters wide outside the entire perimeter of the wall surrounding the city. Destroy and remove everything. Houses. Homes. Factories. Give the adult residents of destroyed homes three hundred dollars in gold yuan, one hundred and fifty for children above twelve. Colonel Zhou will assist you in drawing those funds from our exchequer. I want the area to be absolutely clear and level. Provide your own guards for the work—I don't anticipate any Communist attacks upon you if you work quickly. Some initial clearing has been going on already for several weeks. I want you to complete the task within three days. You have no higher priority.

"Yu and Teng Wenchao—you are assigned to mount heavy machine guns and light artillery upon the wall, in such a pattern that cross-fire upon the cleared perimeter beyond the wall is maximized. You are authorized to confiscate one half the heavy machine guns from every unit in the city, and to assume tactical command of the light artillery units. This task must also be completed in three days.

"Li and Teng Paoshan—you are in charge of fortifications. Outside the walls, in the cleared area, I want a maze of trenches, in no decipherable pattern. Create also roadblocks and traps using felled trees and barbed wire. The objective is to preclude men or vehicles from advancing easily to the wall across the cleared area. Coordinate your activities with Wei, Cheng, and Shih so that you begin your work immediately after an area is cleared. You can begin tomorrow morning in the areas that are already cleared. The task should be completed within a week. Inside the walls, I want an abundance of pillboxes, foxholes, and barbed wire fortifications throughout the city, but concentrated in the area just within the walls. Again, within a week you should be finished."

He looked up from the paper. "These tasks have the highest priority, for all of you. Work should proceed through the nights as well as during the days. You are authorized to triple your requisitioned civilian labor, through the normal *Pao-Chia* channels you have previously utilized. We want labor, not money, gentlemen. I expect each of you to draw up detailed plans for your tasks this afternoon and evening, and to begin tomorrow morning. Forward copies of your completed plans to me. Any questions that arise should be directed to Colonel Zhou, who will give you further, written descriptions of your tasks as you leave this meeting. Questions?"

Yu Chenling cleared his throat, and glanced around the table. "I know I speak for all of us, General Fu, when I say we are proud to be associated with you and are fully supportive of this move. Some of us differ in certain aspects of policy, but we all join you enthusiastically in your abhorrence of the Communist bandit's crude demand for an abject surrender of this glorious ancient capital of our civilization."

Teng Paoshan, an old colleague of Fu, spoke up in a dry tone. "More important, General, it will give our troops something to keep them busy, and out of the whorehouses." Yu looked shocked, but the others at the table chuckled.

Fu glanced around the table. "I appreciate those comments—both of them. If there are no others to be added?" He paused, and no one spoke. "Then I leave you to your work, gentlemen."

They all rose, and congregated around Zhou to collect their detailed instructions. Yu Chenling walked up to Fu.

"I can't tell you how delighted I am by this move, General Fu."

Fu nodded.

In a lower tone, Yu added. "The Te Wu stands ready to be of service to you, General, if you require any . . . covert measures in this campaign."

Fu put his arm around the other's thin shoulder. "You are most kind and generous. Be assured that I shall let you know if we have need of the special talents of your men."

Yu Chenling beamed in a conspiratorial way, squeezed Fu's arm, and walked over to Zhou to collect the last packet of instructions. As he left the room, Zhou closed the door, and raised his eyebrows. "You have at least made the Te Wu happy."

Fu laughed dryly, and nodded. "They are happiest when they smell death."

"General, Lin Piao's aide is here to receive your initial response to the negotiations. He arrived during the staff meeting."

"Good. Bring him in."

Zhou left, and returned soon with Captain Li. The young man walked crisply into the room and stood before Fu's desk with a proud, nearly defiant air, his eyes glowing. Fu was seated, and did not rise or look up. After several seconds he slowly lifted his head and coolly appraised him.

Fu clearly read the hatred burning in Li's bright eyes. He hardened his voice to counter it, and added a tinge of malice.

"Captain Li. Please convey this message to Commander Lin Piao. We find his proposals totally unacceptable. We protest his abusive treatment of our envoys. We are particularly displeased with his arrogant refusal to listen to our own proposals. Commander Lin Piao seems eager to spill his men's blood upon our walls. We will oblige him in that if he insists. If he should decide to receive our envoys and our proposals in a civilized manner, however, we shall be happy at any time to reconvene the negotiations he so crudely aborted. You are dismissed, Captain Li."

The words had been delivered coldly, but with all the considerable force Fu possessed. Li stood there trembling by the end, as if he had received a whipping. He opened his mouth, but no sound came forth. He tried again, and managed to stammer hoarsely, "Commander Lin Piao has instructed me to inform you, in the event of a negative reply, that he will send me to give you one more chance to comply, the morning of the eleventh, the day before the shelling of the city is scheduled to begin."

Fu smiled sardonically. "Fine. Perhaps he will have something new for me then."

Li turned and stalked out of the room, glowering. Fu stared after him, with cold anger, wondering if Lin Piao had the same eyes as his young aide.

They sat on a bench at the northwest corner of the Forbidden City, facing the guardhouse with three layers of golden-tiled roofs across the moat. Their thick quilted coats and fur caps successfully hid the fact that they were twins, and among the two most beautiful women in Peking at that moment.

"How is Father?" asked Meilu.

"As ever," answered Meiling. "He has decided to relax the rule of secrecy."

"Oh? Well, it is not so important, these days, and hardly attainable at any rate."

"His reasons, exactly. You always thought more like him."

"I was sent away early, and so didn't have to rebel against him, as you did."

They laughed, and knew it was true.

"How is your life?" asked Meiling.

"Good, really. I dislike the seclusion, of course. But I have ample time for my meditation, T'ai Chi, and calligraphy. And he is so full of life himself. It is . . . it is very good to share his life."

"Truly?"

"Truly. I could not be happier with a man."

"It must be hard to have only one man."

"There are compensations. Especially with a man like him."

"What do you mean?"

"Well, if the man you're with is full of the Tao, full of life, then being with him is . . . is sharing that life in him. Having more life in you than if you were merely meeting men in the Nourishing Essence Hall."

"I wouldn't call the Nourishing Essence Hall 'merely meeting men'," Meiling bristled.

"No, I know it's good, and that much of the Tao flows through you there. I don't mean to devalue that. But . . . I don't know. I just feel very sure that I am fuller, more alive, now. That being with him, knowing him so well, sharing his life so deeply, is part of it. And that you have to be with one man, live with him, to achieve that."

Meiling was silent. As the thought of Bei crept into her mind, she angrily brushed it aside, and concentrated on Meilu and Fu.

"A warlord 'full of the Tao'?" she mocked her sister gently. "You cannot be full of the Tao doing war."

The other shrugged her shoulders. "So Father says. But now I am not so sure."

"We should take you back soon, before you are totally lost to us."

They laughed at the idea.

"I am not sure I would want to return."

"Your life is not your own. It belongs to the Tao."

"Yes. And that is fine. But it would make me very sad to leave him."

Meiling shrugged. "Sorrow is of the Tao." She paused. "Father wants me to ask if he ordered An Shihlin to be killed."

The other looked at her sister in shocked disbelief. "Meiling!"

"It is possible. He probably knew Shihlin was an agent of the underground. Through his own intelligence, or through his daughter, Hsiawen."

"He knew. But he did not have Shihlin killed. I am sure of it."

"How sure?"

"Very sure. In the first place, he knew long ago he would be surrounded and have to negotiate with the Communists. He is too smart to alienate those with whom he will be negotiating. In the second place, he does not order deaths wantonly. The underground is of no real importance, Meiling. The fate of the city will be decided by him and Lin Piao, regardless of the strength or weakness of the underground. He has killed, much, and had others killed, many others. This I know. But always for what he, at least, considers a compelling reason."

"You are sure?"

"Yes. It was not him. It probably was the Te Wu."

"Yes. The police inspector is investigating them."

It was the other's turn to scoff. "Investigating the Te Wu? That is like taunting a tiger."

"Perhaps."

"I must return."

"Very well. I must start for the temple, myself. Take care, Older Sister."

They laughed at the old joke. "I will, my one-minute Younger Sister. Take care yourself. Cleave to the Tao."

"And yourself."

They embraced each other, and parted for the last time.

Bei sat on the bench outside the White Cloud Temple in the twilight, waiting for the end of the evening devotional. This time he did not disguise his presence. The tall figure of Fu Hsiawen emerged through the temple gates and walked by. Shortly afterward Meiling came out within the main crowd of worshipers. Bei rose.

"Inspector," she said, nodding.

"Meiling. Shall we walk?"

"Certainly."

They headed down the alley towards Lishilu Street, in silence because of the crowd. At the end of the alley he said, "There are some benches not too far to the right."

"Fine."

They walked another several minutes in silence and arrived at the same place where the fat monk had met the Baleful Star. No one else was there, and they chose the bench farthest from the street. After an awkward silence, Bei began.

"So—have you or your father found out anything?"

"We have found no indications whatever that either the Buddhists or another Taoist sect was involved in it. The Buddhists were quite pleased that it had happened, but they apparently had nothing to do with it."

"And Fu?"

"There is no indication that he was involved. And several reasons to think that he would not be. We can, I believe, rule him out also." She paused, then looked at Bei questioningly. "And you, Inspector?"

Bei had been admiring her beauty and remembering her brief kiss, but with an effort he dispelled the diversion. "Yes. I mean, no. We have ruled out the Te Wu also, as a result of a thorough investigation. Although we doubted that it was them, all along, for other reasons."

"Have you considered any of the secret societies, or the underworld?"

"Briefly. They have absolutely no motive, so far as we can tell, and there are no clues at all pointing to them."

"What clues are there?"

He hesitated, and suppressed the impulse to confide in her about the Baleful Star. "A few," he answered evasively. He decided to plunge ahead. "Meiling. Most murders can be traced to simple causes, which should be examined along with more complicated possibilities. The hatred of a jealous lover is the root of many murders. Pardon me for bringing this up, but tell me: Did you or Prior An have other lovers who might be jealous of you two seeing each other?"

Meiling stared at him in bemused surprise. "Why, Inspector, I did not realize you were so curious about other people's love lives."

Bei responded in his cold, official voice. "Miss T'ang. It is not a matter of curiosity. I am merely investigating the possibility that the prior's death resulted from a more common root than we had earlier imagined. Since all our other suspects have been eliminated, this does not seem to me to be an utterly frivolous thing to look into."

She nodded. "You're right. But I'm afraid it won't be any more promising than our other ideas have turned out to be. Prior An had no other lovers—indeed, had not since his wife and son were killed."

"You are, uh, confident you would have known if he did?" asked Bei gently and diffidently, being cautious lest he give offense to her.

Meiling became angry in spite of Bei's precautions. "We had no secrets from each other, Inspector," she snapped. "None."

"All right, all right," Bei hastily said. He waited a moment. "And what about you? Would someone you met in the Nourishing Essence Hall become jealous, follow you into the city?"

She laughed at the notion, in spite of her anger. "Jealousy is non-existent in the Nourishing Essence Hall. And beyond that, no one could leave the Purple Mountain and come into the city regularly without being noticed."

"You are the only one who is ever sent?"

She thought. "Father sends Dufeng upon occasion, to contact me if something arises that cannot wait for my regularly scheduled return."

"Dufeng? Could it have been him?"

Meiling shook her head in exasperation. "Of course not."

"Why not?"

"Inspector. He visits the Nourishing Essence Hall. He can't do that and be consumed by jealousy, to begin with. Beyond that, he is a very shy person. He'd be incapable of masterminding a plan to murder someone. He just couldn't do it."

Bei reflected that the glimpse he had obtained of the Baleful Star at his meeting with the fat monk did not particularly remind him of Dufeng.

"What about other lovers, here in the city?"

"None, Inspector."

"Other than the prior, you mean."

She replied icily. "Yes, Inspector."

Bei stared up the street as he turned all this over in his mind. He noticed a figure a block away freeze, then melt back into the dim shadow of an alleyway. Slender. In a uniform. Somehow familiar. He leaped to his feet as it hit him: the Baleful Star.

With an exclamation he took off running toward the alley into which the figure had disappeared. Meiling remained sitting, astonished at his peculiar behavior. He reached the alleyway and turned in. Nothing. He dashed into it some thirty meters, passing several side alleys and courtyards. Nothing. It was almost completely dark within the maze of passageways. He stood still, but could hear only his own panting, the clang of cooking pans, and the vague murmur of families gathered around coal fires inside closed doors.

Damn! It was the Baleful Star, no doubt, thought Bei. The furtiveness, the place, the escape when I came for him. Damn! So close. He exhaled strongly, in disgust. Meiling appeared behind him.

"What was it, Inspector?"

He shook his head. No use for concealment, now.

"It was my last clue."

"Your last clue?"

"The man who met with the fat monk and gave him money to have An killed."

"You know who he is?"

"No. The monk knows him only by sight. I have glimpsed him, once before. And now. Both here."

"What was he doing back here?"

"I don't know. Listen, Meiling." He turned to her and took hold of her shoulders. "You may be in danger. From him, I mean. He had An killed, and he may well know that you worked with An. He was probably following you tonight. He is dangerous. The fat monk called him a Baleful Star."

Her eyes grew wide.

"That is just what the monk called him," he added quickly. "We know that is all superstition."

"Men are not stars," she answered, "but men can be as evil as we imagine stars to be."

"Yes. That's just it. You must be very careful." He cupped his hand around the back of her neck. "You now apparently have two groups after you: the Te Wu and the Baleful Star. Stay out of the city. Do you understand? Stay at the Purple Mountain."

She shrugged out of his grip. "Inspector," she said proudly, "I appreciate your concern. But I can take care of myself."

He became angry. "Yes, just like An Shihlin could take care of himself. How are you against a dozen attackers, woman? Or how well do you dodge bullets?"

Her eyes flared up. "Please don't concern yourself about me."

"Meiling! You have no magic powers! Don't delude yourself. They could kill you as easily as they killed Shihlin."

"And don't keep mentioning Shihlin," she burst out, nearly in tears.

Bei sighed, and nodded his head. "All right. I'm sorry. I just don't want anything to happen to you. You are too valuable."

She was staring up the alley, fighting back tears still.

"It's just that I need you. I need you to help find . . . his killer." A pause. "And I, I don't want anything to happen to you. It would make me too sad."

"Well," she said finally, facing him. "We can't have the inspector sad."

He flared at her words. "You know what I mean."

"Yes," she retorted. "I know what you mean."

He stomped out of the alley and turned left.

"Where are you going?" she demanded, hurrying to catch up with him.

"Walking you to the Hsipienmen Gate, you ungrateful wench. No, no," he added as she began to protest. "I'm not doing it to protect you. You are poison enough that you need no protection. I just cannot tear myself away from your gracious company and your sweet words."

They stalked up the street, both seething. In a block they both began to regret their words to the other, and by the time the wall and its gate loomed in the distance, the anger was completely gone.

Bei stopped and turned to her, his hands thrust deep in his pockets. "So. Now you must sweet-talk your own way through, or whatever you do. Meiling: Be careful."

"I will." She looked him full in the face. "And thank you."

He nodded and walked away, looking for a ricksha.

So many forms. She takes so many forms. I can hardly keep up with her. One form sent back to her restless grave, then she comes in another. But all so beautiful, so white and slender, pulsing inside with red life. The red of her blood. *The red of her Flower, pulsing, throbbing, hungry for my yang. I must liberate her redness, let it flow and flower and spread, dripping with life. She wants it that way, tires of her wantonness, desires the peace of her vixen coffin just as she desires the hardness of my Positive Peak.*

But her twin. Is it her, or her twin? Or are they both the same? No, not the same. Not then, at least. The twin was other, didn't go wild with the flowers, didn't meet me under the bush with the flowers and pulse with life, bloom, oh, bloom with red life, her softness around my Positive Peak, caressing it oh so warmly.

Now, though? Has she now taken over the other from her fox grave? Does she beckon to me from the other? I can hear her calling me, softly, from the other. They are both one, now. Both bending before me, embracing each other, thighs entwined, as their Red Flowers bloom together before me, thirsting for my hardness. First one then the other, my Jade Stalk mixing their moisture. They both bloom and bleed under my yang, their juices running down their thighs and flowing together, both flowing down my Positive Peak into a pool, a red pool of both their lives, red and warm and moist, running down their slender white necks, their mouths joined in a kiss of ecstasy, as the life surges out of them, puddling red and warm oh vixen and vixen you both want it so you squirm and caress me even as you kiss each other pulsing so slender and white and red and warm. . . .

January 10

The gray, cold morning seemed noisier than usual to Bei as he rode to work. Leaning out of the pedicab on Tung'anmen Street, he noticed groups of soldiers bent under heavy machine guns heading south at a fast shuffle. As he reached Ch'ang'an Boulevard, long lines of civilians carrying picks and shovels came into view, heading south towards Ch'ienmen Gate. They were mostly boys and old men, the poorest of the poor to judge by their appearance. Thousands of them trudged along the street, hurried on by soldiers alongside the line.

Civilian work crews had been common enough in the city since the siege began, but never so many, and never with the curious bustling atmosphere of this morning.

Arriving at the Chunghai Lake compound, he paused on the path to his office to gaze at the old pavilion in the lake, and tried to remember again the inscription on it. The pavilion's curved roof and slender columns glinted feebly off the surrounding ice, as light filtered through the trees of the nearby east shore of the imperial lake. A wind. Something about a wind. That was all he could remember. Those Taoist inscriptions, though. Impossible to understand, much less remember. Shaking his head, he walked into his office building.

"Not so fast, Chief," warned Yuan as Bei entered their office and headed for the stove, teakettle already in hand.

Bei groaned. "What is it now?"

"You won't like it."

"The fat monk positively identified the Baleful Star at the corner of Ch'ang'an and Wangfuching, and he was a crippled sweet potato vendor who hasn't left the corner in twenty years," Bei improvised.

Yuan laughed. "Honestly, Chief," he finally said, "sometimes you surprise me."

"It's this siege. It is reducing me to whimsy."

"You'll be hard-pressed to make a joke out of this, I'm afraid. Another courtesan murder."

"Damn. And Fu just mentioned them to me two days ago."

"Something unusual about this one, though."

"What is it?"

"I don't know. The warden for the district just said it was really bizarre. He called it in just a few minutes ago."

"Ch'ienmen district again?"

"Yes. And still very high-class: the Ch'inhuai."

"Ah. I was there several days ago, when I made the rounds. A rather peculiar place."

"It has a river theme, I've heard?"

"Yes. It's named for the center of social life in Nanking during the Ming Dynasty—an array of floating brothels, called "painted boats.""

"Our Ch'inhuai can't be floating," commented Yuan.

"True enough. But the interior is decorated as the interior of a boat. You'll see. Let's go."

Half an hour later they were met at the entrance off Ch'ienmen

Street by the district warden. Bei instructed him to guard the door, where a crowd of curious onlookers had gathered from the street. Bei shook his head: too much publicity. News of the series of courtesan murders was slowly spreading through the city, and demands for a solution from the upper-class patrons of the brothels would mount accordingly. Just what he needed: two major unsolved cases. Everything was indeed unraveling, if most of his time had to be occupied with courtesans and Taoist priests.

The madam was grim-faced and angry. Bei was feeling rather out of sorts himself, and said accusingly to her, "I thought I told you to be on the watch for this man."

She glared at him. "You said to be on the watch for a man asking for a Shansi girl. Not this, Inspector."

"What do you mean?"

"You don't know?" She exhaled with a snort, in disgust. "Come along." She led the way upstairs and along a corridor lined with boat furnishings to a door opening onto a large room. A spacious four-poster bed with lace netting stood in the middle of the room, with compasses and steering wheels on the walls. Through the lace Bei could make out a confused mass of red-stained arms and legs. He slowly advanced to the bed and lifted the lace aside.

Two young women lay naked on the bed, blood splattered over their white flesh, their heads at the odd angles that Bei had come to know so well. One was on her back, with her thighs spread. The other lay on top of her, straddling her hips, crushing the other's breasts with her own. Above the shoulders the congealed blood was so thickly splattered and the heads so oddly positioned that it was not obvious which head belonged to which woman.

"Tie this lace back, Yuan. Madam, have you removed anything?"

"Not a thing."

"Good."

The women lay with their heads to the left side of the bed, as before. Looking down at the two heads, Bei saw what he was looking for: The cuts had both begun on the right, severing the flesh there completely, and finished on the left, again as before. He got his pen from his coat pocket, and grasped it with his left hand so that one side faced down as he held it backhand in front of his chest. He slowly drew it across his body, from right to left. The first kill. Then, without changing his hold on the pen, he repositioned the hand to the backhand position and twisted his forearm clockwise. The "cutting edge" of the pen twisted easily around and now faced straight up. He drew it across his body, from right to left again. The second kill. He repeated the two movements quickly. Drawing the knife, right to left, blade down; rotating the forearm as the arm is brought back to the right side; and drawing the knife right to left again, blade up this time. It could be done in two seconds, maybe less. Assuming the blade cut cleanly through the flesh. But it could be done quite quickly. Before either girl knew what had happened, especially if they were in sexual passion.

Bei addressed the madam.

"How many clients ask for two girls?"

"It's not unusual, Inspector. But to be able to supply a client with twins—that's not very common, truly."

"Twins?"

"Yes. You didn't notice?" She glanced at the bloody heads. "Oh, but then . . . you wouldn't, would you?"

"No. Did he ask specifically for twins?"

"Yes. Insisted on it. They are always very busy. Being twins, and extremely talented too. So many new possibilities open up with three people involved, you know."

"I can only imagine, Madam."

"Well. They were already reserved for the evening, of course, but he insisted on obtaining them after the regular client, and was able to pay very well for this irregularity—in silver, yet."

"He paid in silver?"

"Yes. He had . . . a good deal of silver on him. That is what persuaded me. One doesn't often get a chance to obtain that much silver. A silver dollar is actually worth more than an American dollar these days, you know."

"So I hear." Bei turned to the scene on the bed. "So he obtained the two girls, the twins, late in the evening. I presume this . . . configuration is, uh, a common one?"

"Oh, yes. It is the Two Dancing Female Phoenix Birds. Nothing fancy, actually."

"If I may inquire, how does the male position himself?"

226

"Inspector, you did not seem so keen on the arts of The Wind and the Flowers when you visited us several days ago."

"A man had not murdered your celebrated twins then, Madam."

She sighed deeply. "They will not be replaceable. Certainly not in these times. It is an economic catastrophe."

"Madam, the male's position?" Bei reminded her.

"Oh, yes. He simply kneels in front of their paired Jade Doors. You will note that the Golden Cleft of each is presented openly to him, adjacent to the other, in this position."

Bei peered at the two inert figures. Their vulva were indeed quite close. He could not imagine that anything in the scene could be erotic, but then, the girls were now dead. He decided against examining the thighs or vulva for semen, with a twinge of revulsion at the prospect.

"He normally kneels upright, I presume?"

"Yes. He, of course, must move back a bit when his Lively Head goes from one girl's Shady Valley to the other's, but after a while he can do it without looking."

"So while he is penetrating one of the girls, he can lean forward, on the back of the upper girl?"

"Yes. He often enjoys watching the girls kiss and caress each other. It really is a most satisfying position."

"Doubtless. Could you please wait for us outside, while I finish my examination of the room."

He turned and surveyed the scene after she had left. "A left-handed cut. Positioned on the bed so that the left hand is free." He leaned over and shook the outspread leg of the girl on the bottom. "This is most peculiar, Yuan. Note the position that the leg has stiffened in. That is not the position that the leg would normally assume: thighs spread, knees up."

"Meaning?"

Bei shuddered slightly. "Meaning he remained mounted atop the girls for a considerable time after he slashed their throats. It was late at night, and"— he looked around the room—"there's no coal burner, so it was quite cold and rigor mortis could set in relatively quickly. But still—" He shook the outstretched leg, and the two bodies rocked back and forth in their ghostly embrace. "It had to be at least an hour. Perhaps more."

Yuan let out a cry of disgust. "What would he do for an hour atop two dead bodies?"

Bei thought it over. "He might continue to penetrate them for a while. I don't know much about the muscles of the Shady Valley, how they react after death." He looked at the bloodstained heads and torsos of the women. "And he also might have ladled blood over their bodies, with his cupped hands. Yes. He smeared blood over them. Played in their blood."

Yuan grimaced.

"And he may have simply fallen asleep atop them."

"That is difficult to imagine, Chief."

Bei pursed his lips. "Anymore, my friend, nothing about this man is difficult for me to imagine." He walked around the room, peering closely into the clothes closet and under the bed. The basin which had been on the table when they entered the room was filled with brownish water, and the towel had bloodstains on it. He smelled deeply, but the odor of congealed blood was all he could detect.

"Notes, Yuan. Four things different than in previous cases. One, two victims rather than one. Two, no ceremonial wrapping of bodies. Three, no discernible fragrance of flowers, although blood smell may have overpowered it. Four, murderer tarried after the deed and splattered blood on the bodies. Perhaps for an hour. Similarities: Victims were young courtesans. Details of wounds are exactly identical. Placement on bed is the same—" He suddenly examined the sheet to the left of the bodies at knee level. "Same blood stain to left where knife was wiped clean."

He looked over the room again, slowly. "Anything else, Yuan?"

"No, sir. Let's go. This makes me nervous. Like a baleful spirit is here." Yuan edged toward the door.

Bei stood staring at the two bodies, frozen in the bizarre imitation of passion. "Strange, isn't it," he said, speaking more to himself than to Yuan. "How fine the line between life and death, between warm, moving persons and cold, stiff flesh. And how different it is on either side of that line. So easily crossed, yet so vast a difference."

Chang and Ho were waiting for him in a banquet room when Bei arrived at the Ench'engchu restaurant on Hsitan Street. He was vastly relieved to have the pleasant company of his friends to dispel the memory of the morning's activities.

"Tan cuisine this week, old friend," boomed Chang as Bei entered the room. Bei always marveled that such a large voice could issue from such a small person. "To penalize you for being late, we've already ordered, and somehow managed without your expert advice."

"Although it remains to be seen how well we managed," added Ho smoothly. "Have a seat, Inspector Bei. I hope you have a good excuse for depriving us of your company."

"I'd rather talk about the food," Bei said as he sat down. "What did you order?"

Chang and Ho glanced at each other. "Don't be angry, but since you weren't here to insist on something exotic, we've stuck to very common Tan cuisine," began Chang. "Steamed chicken with mushrooms, which avoids gourmet powders and emphasizes the natural flavors of the ingredients. See how much we know, even without you. Then duck with crab meat, to exemplify the balance of sweet and salt characteristic of Tan cuisine. We wanted pork and bamboo shoots for the third dish, but they are out of pork, as is everyone else."

"Nearly everyone else," corrected Bei.

"Oh, really? Then let us meet there next week and gorge ourselves on pork. Where is it still available?"

"The P'ing K'angli brothel."

Chang and Ho glanced at each other in surprise, then back at Bei in consternation, before breaking into laughter.

"Now, friends," said Bei, attempting to quiet their laughter and not succeeding. "Friends. I can assure you—"

"Please, Inspector, spare us the details lest envy rise up and destroy our friendship," said Ho between laughs.

"All in official duty, I assure you," continued Bei.

The laughter finally subsided, and Ho said, more or less seriously, "Actually, I believe you. Wasn't it at the P'ing K'angli that one of the courtesans was murdered?"

"Yes. But I insist on sticking to important matters. What is the third dish and what teas did you order?"

"Fish with shallots," finished Chang. "And a green from Szechuan—Emei Shan, I believe it was—for the meal, and a red from Fukien for afterward."

"Not bad. Actually, very commendable. Old Tan Tsungchun and his son Tan Chuanch'ing would have been proud, had they lived long beyond the fall of the Ch'ing to see their composite cuisine ordered so well by two of the capital's leading citizens."

"What have we done to earn such flattery?" asked Ho as the three dishes were brought in and they began to help themselves from the communal bowls.

"Well, one of us at least has had some negotiating experience lately," suggested Bei after the waiter had left.

"There you are wrong," commented Chang bitterly. "I was kept well away from the negotiating table all three days. Luckily I had brought a good book along."

"You are too modest," offered Ho.

Chang laughed. "That is one virtue my peppery tongue cannot earn for me. Although perhaps these well-cooked, soft Tan dishes will mellow my tongue." He took a bite of chicken. "No. It is true. I was superfluous."

"Judging from the activity in the street, they missed your powers of mediation and compromise," said Bei thoughtfully.

"Yes. It certainly looks like some assaults are imminent, to judge from all the activity," added Ho. "Why, I saw foxholes and pillboxes being constructed all along Hsitan Street."

"And the destruction and removal of houses on the perimeter out-side the wall has increased in tempo," Chang commented, "at least around the Hsichihmen Gate through which I entered this morning."

"Surely it is all show," said Ho with a worried look. "You don't think the Communists seriously mean to assault the city, do you, Professor?"

Chang leaned back and sipped the tea. "I heard a most depressing story from a colleague at Tsinghua University. It seems that Lin Piao himself called up Liang Hsuch'eng, the eminent archaeologist and art historian there. The Communists had selected a site to breach the wall, using heavy artillery, in the west wall of the south city. Lin Piao wanted to know whether the destruction of that site would be objectionable on historical or aesthetic grounds."

Bei laughed disbelievingly. "That doesn't sound like the Communists to me."

Chang shrugged. "The story goes that Professor Liang informed Lin Piao that the site was indeed one of the few surviving pieces of unrestored Ming military architecture. Liang suggested another place or two, of no particular historical moment. And according to the story, Lin Piao accepted the suggestions!"

Ho and Bei shook their heads. "Who knows what to believe about the Communists. You hear stories of brutality in one breath, and tales of honesty and devotion in the next," said Ho.

"My wife tells me she had a very smelly visitor last week," said Chang with a straight face, looking at Bei.

"Oh, really?"

"Yes. Did you reach your destination?"

Bei glanced around conspiratorially. "Among friends—yes, I did. And spent the night there."

"Very impressive," commented Ho, resting his chopsticks across his empty plate. "And will you deprecate the success of your mission, like Chang?"

Bei tugged a piece of fish off a bone. "I learned a lot," he said after a pause. "But it didn't solve the case, by any means."

"Too bad," said Chang. "Well, Mayor, we've both reported. How about you?"

Ho smiled. "Very good news: Bright Jade's violin continues to improve. In fact, she will be delighted to entertain you after dinner at my home the night of the sixteenth—next Sunday evening. I hope you both can come."

"I'd be delighted," said Bei.

"And I also," added Chang.

"Professor—bring Madame Chang, of course. And Inspector." Ho turned to Bei with a twinkle in his eye. "Bring any one of your new acquaintances from the P'ing K'angli!"

Chang and Ho exploded in laughter as the waiter brought in the pot of red tea. Bei ignored them and checked the pot to see how far along the infusion was.

"Your talented youngest daughter, Mayor, shall be sufficient entertainment for me that evening," he commented archly.

"Good. I look forward to seeing you all then. Around six o'clock."

"Is Bright Jade still usurping your place in your bed, Mayor?" asked Chang with a smile.

Ho sighed. "Yes. I am getting rather used to the sofa in my study, actually."

They all laughed, and then sat pensively sipping the tea.

"Judging from all the stories, and the activity outside, we may be badly in need of entertainment by next Sunday," Bei glumly commented.

Ho nodded his head sadly. "True enough. It is impossible for me to imagine my city being shelled, or troops battling in the streets. Peking should be immune to all that sort of thing."

"Should. We should all be immune to that sort of thing. But we aren't," mused Chang. "Some of us are just luckier than others. And some cities luckier than others."

"Well, if worse comes to worst, let us hope that the three of us and our families are among the lucky ones," concluded Ho, as a presentiment of danger descended over the three friends.

Bei sat in his back courtyard, wrapped in his thickest quilt coat, with a blanket over his legs. His mind was full of the image of An Shihlin bursting into flames in the courtyard before Founder Ch'iu's Shrine Hall at the White Cloud Temple. Two insulated pots full of Liao's Jade Valley green tea perched atop the ledge before the iced pond. He sipped from the cupful in his mittened hand. The night was cold, but clear, and the stars shone brightly above him. He resorted to Two Pots in the Garden Late at Night only rarely, when a case had him completely baffled. Sometimes the marathon review of facts unlocked a fresh line of investigation, or even occasionally a solution. If it revealed nothing new, he invariably dropped the case.

He had the distinct feeling, though, that a solution lay hidden somewhere in the tangle of data stretching from An Shihlin's burning body to his meeting last night with Meiling. Perhaps it was just a feeling that he had collected all the data there was to collect. If the solution wasn't there, then it didn't exist for him.

He methodically reviewed the case, sipping tea as he went. His questioning of the guest prefect and search of the prior's room. The fat monk's rendezvous with the Baleful Star. The Yellow Dragon Monastery in Hangchow, and his sunset meeting with the tea server. An Shihlin, working with Chou Enlai in Shanghai in 1927. Then ten years at the Yellow Dragon Monastery. His mysterious summons by the Purple Mountain to set up the Communist underground in Peking. Bei's own call on the Purple Mountain. His initial meeting of Master T'ang in the Great Hall. The enormous jade pieces in the hall. A full two meters wide, the yin-yang disk above the fireplace. Dinner with Meiling and her father in the study. The Purple Mountain's history, intertwined with that of the White Cloud Temple. Dufeng's tale. Walking to his room with Meiling, and her fleeting kiss. The moonlight falling on the nape of her neck. Easy, Bei. The case, remember.

It all came back to the Baleful Star. Who sent him to have Prior An killed? The initial suspects: Fu, and the Te Wu, who would be killing An Shihlin the Communist agent. Other Taoists, and the Buddhists, who would be killing An Shihlin the Purple Mountain Taoist. Jealous lovers, who would be killing the An Shihlin who had betrayed their love for him or for Meiling. An unlikely, bewildering combination of suspects. All presumably ruled out. But was he overhasty to eliminate them? Could he believe Abbot T'ang's unnamed "source" that Fu had nothing to do with it, for example? Could he believe Meiling that there were no jealous lovers?

He moved an empty pot to one side and poured the first cup from the remaining pot. There were questions still, but the facts were in. Or at least all the facts that he was able to get. Now he would let it all simmer in his mind, and see what bubbled up, if anything. The Baleful Star, sent by whom? Fu and the Te Wu. Taoists and Buddhists. The jade disk, green and white swirling together in it. Yin flowing into yang flowing into yin. Communists and Nationalists. Male and female. The Jade Stalk and the Golden Cleft. Himself and Meiling. The sheen of her hair and the jade hairpins at dinner in the study. The jade disk. Yin and yang.

He poured another cup and reflected on how his thoughts kept returning to that jade disk in the Great Hall at Purple Mountain. The facets of the case and its setting fit so neatly into the yin-yang model. Communists versus Nationalists. Confucians versus Taoists. Within each, subdivisions still. Nationalists into Fu and Yu Chenling's Te

Wu. Taoists into the White Cloud Temple and the Purple Mountain. Ch'iu Changchun and T'ang Weilong. The White Cloud Temple into the guest prefect and the fat monk. An Shihlin himself into Communist agent and Taoist. Groups swirling within groups. But not totally neatly. Something was missing, some balancing data yet to be fit into the picture. The Baleful Star himself. Where did he fit? And if he fit, who would be the yin to his yang?

Bei sat up suddenly. The yin to his yang. Somewhere the answer dangled, within the maze of facts in his mind. Easy now. Don't push it over the edge into nothingness by thinking too fast or too hard. Easy. Let the mind wander lazily in this new direction. The yin to his yang. Where was it? He had heard someone say something. Somewhere. Master T'ang. In the Great Hall, with the jade yin-yang disk looming up. The Purple Mountain and the Communists in 1947. Chou Enlai giving the Purple Mountain the mission of infiltrating Peking. Lin Piao's armies sweeping down from the north later. "There is no point in quibbling whether your contact is Chou Enlai or Lin Piao surely— " What had T'ang answered? An empty space hung there, tantalizingly void. He let it hang, knowing it would have to fill itself or not be filled at all. Empty. Clear, like the night. Cold. Then a hint of movement, an intangible leaning of something in that direction, a barely perceptible rustle of air towards the vacuum. He could hear T'ang's words whishing into the space. "They are quite different men, actually." Yes. Of course. An Shihlin was killed after all because he was Chou Enlai's Communist agent. And thus the Baleful Star provides the last balancing yin-yang complement.

A shudder of realization jolted Bei's body and he leaped to his feet, the heavy blanket pushing the second pot over the ledge onto the ice. The tea spilled over the ice, gathering darkly in little crevices here and there. Bei stared at it, reminded of something else. Pools of blood. No. One case at a time. He rushed into his study and looked up Fu Tsoyi's private number. Without hesitation he dialed it, oblivious of the late hour. After several rings the groggy voice of Zhou Peifeng answered.

"What?"

"I've got it."

"What? Who are you? And what have you got?"

"Bei. I've got the Baleful Star."

234

"You've got the Baleful Star? Fine. Bring him by tomorrow."

"No. I mean, I know who he is."

"Fine. Who is he?"

"No. I don't know his name. But I know what he is, who he represents."

"Inspector. Why exactly are you calling me at . . . at 2330 at night?"

"Listen, Zhou. I need to see some of Lin Piao's officers. And have the fat monk see them too, if possible. We need to be with the next negotiations, or whenever you meet with some of Lin Piao's people."

A long pause.

"How important is this, Inspector?"

"I am . . . nearly positive it will help us know who the Baleful Star is. Who had the Taoist prior killed. And why. The general seems to be very interested in the case."

Another pause as Zhou shook his head at the other end of the line. He wasn't at all sure why Fu was so interested in this case. But he knew Fu well enough to know it would not be idle curiosity. And that Fu would be furious if Zhou let slip a chance to solve it, no matter how farfetched. And it could be arranged easily enough, actually.

"Inspector?"

"Yes."

"As a matter of fact, the general is seeing Lin Piao's top aide tomorrow morning. It's just one person, but it would be a start. I have no idea when we might be . . . meeting with them again."

"Only one? But—who knows. When shall we be there?"

"The appointment is for early. He'll probably arrive around 0800. We'll arrange for the general to see him at 0815. The general will have the final decision, but I imagine that we won't want the Taoist monk to be in the room."

"But the monk will have to make the firm identification."

"No problem. There is a peephole into the room through both of the doors. We'll put the monk behind one. You will be in the room, assuming the general agrees. Be at my office, with the monk, before 0800."

"Good. Until then."

Bei hung up the phone, and slumped into the nearby chair in a daze. What had he done? What if he was wrong? But no. It fit too well. And it was the only answer that made sense.

January 11

At 8:15 Bei sat in Fu's office. The fat monk was sequestered in the hallway leading to the private quarters, with a view of the room through the peephole in that door. Bei himself was wracked by nervousness. What if he were wrong? What a fool he would be to the general. It still fit, and was the only solution that came close to fitting. But he had encountered perfect fits before that were simply wrong. A case may have several perfect fits, only one of which was true. He had jumped at this one because it was the only solution he had been able to envision. But what—

Fu entered the room from the hallway door, frowning at having to walk by the smelly monk. Bei jumped to his feet.

"Good morning, Inspector. Zhou tells me you have a hint to the White Cloud Temple puzzle."

"Yes, sir. Only a hint. But it may turn out."

"I hope so. You want to see as many of Lin Piao's people as possible, I understand. We'll give you one this morning, and let you come along in any future contacts—if any more occur. Is there any strong need for you to speak when the aide is here?"

"No, sir. Just look at him. And have the fat monk see him, also, through the peephole."

"All right. I will refer to you, then, but not invite you to say anything. Do not speak, under any circumstances."

Zhou knocked and entered through the door leading to the ante-room.

"Captain Li is here, sir."

"Fine. Show him in."

Bei gripped the arms of his chair nervously.

Zhou returned, leading the aide. Captain Li strode arrogantly into the room. He noticed Bei as he was halfway to Fu's desk, and froze in mid-stride, a look of surprise and, Fu thought, alarm flashing briefly over his face. Bei sat white-faced in his chair.

"Captain Li," said Fu smoothly. "Thank you for returning. Allow me to introduce Bei Menjin, a high-ranking member of our municipal government. He will be assisting Colonel Zhou in any future negotiations with Commander Lin Piao."

Li ignored Bei and addressed Fu. "Commander Lin Piao wishes to know your final answer to his proposals, General."

"I had hoped you would bring to me a new set of proposals from him, or at least assurances of a new attitude toward negotiations."

"He sees no reason to change his position."

"Then please convey to him the same response I gave to you two days ago, Captain. You are dismissed."

Li stared briefly at Fu, executed a crisp about-face, and walked out of the room.

As the door shut behind him, Fu looked over to Bei. Bei's face was aflame with excitement. He hurried across the room and opened the door to the hallway. The fat monk was huddled against the guard, a look of abject terror on his face. Bei shut the door and turned to Fu.

"The Baleful Star, sir," he announced triumphantly.

Fu stared at him for several seconds. "I'm afraid I don't understand, Bei."

Bei walked to the front of Fu's desk. "Don't you see, sir? It's all a question of factions. Take the Nationalist government here in Peking. It's not a uniform entity. There's you, but there's also Yu Chenling and his Te Wu, who are quite different from you, but you're both Nationalists. The same with the Taoists. There's the White Cloud Temple, and there's the Purple Mountain. Both Taoists, yet very different entities."

Fu leaned back in his chair, his eyes narrowing, and Bei leaned forward over the desk.

"And it's the same with the Communists, sir. Mao Tsetung directed the Purple Mountain people to set up a Communist underground in Peking, with Chou Enlai as his contact with them. Chou had already called his old colleague An Shihlin up from Hangchow to become established at the White Cloud Temple, so he could coordinate the underground movement. Chou Enlai's structure is set up and functioning, as Mao has directed. Then Lin Piao and his armies come swooping down from Manchuria. Suddenly Lin Piao is involved with taking over the city, but he has to deal with the people Mao and Chou have had here for years. There's friction between them. There has to be, just as there has to be friction between you and the Te Wu. It's the natural order of things, the yin and the yang."

He began to pace back and forth. "That's what struck me last night. We all look at the Communists as a single, uniform movement. We know the Nationalists have factions that hate each other. We know the Taoists do. Why shouldn't the Communists? They must. Lin Piao the commander has got to feel friction with Chou Enlai the diplomat. 'They are actually quite different men,' I had been told. So Lin Piao, in an attempt to weaken Chou Enlai and strengthen his own hand in negotiating for the city, has his aide, this Captain Li, arrange for the death of Chou Enlai's top man in the Peking underground."

"Heaven above!" exclaimed Fu, a look of sudden understanding and fierce hope on his face. "Heaven above! Such a wild card!" He stood abruptly and rushed to Bei. "You are another Duke of Chou, another Confucius, Inspector," he said excitedly, grabbing Bei's arm in a firm grip. "Do you realize what you have done? You have given me a wild card such as I have never held! We now know the Communists are in fact divided. Chou Enlai will be furious when he learns who had his old friend killed. And we can exploit that division, that fury! We can bypass negotiating with that mud-splattered turtle's spawn, Lin Piao, and go straight to Chou Enlai and through him to Mao Tsetung." He stared into space, eyes shining, mind racing. "It could save the city, eliminate the shelling and the assaults on the walls. I can negotiate with Mao Tsetung or his representatives—I know I can!"

Bei and Zhou stood there, glowing with excitement, as Fu envisioned the future.

"But think, think," Fu said, beginning to pace up and down in front of the desk. "How do we contact Mao? Time is short—the shelling begins tomorrow." His pacing quickened.

"I can do it," Bei announced in the tense silence.

Fu stopped in mid-stride. "How?" he demanded.

"The Purple Mountain, General. The abbot there knows Mao Tsetung and Chou Enlai, works with them. I am certain he can contact Mao, and quickly."

Fu stared at Bei severely. "And how do you know so much about the Purple Mountain, which is in the Western Hills, my Duke of Chou?"

A clear look of discovery and guilt flashed upon Bei's face, and stayed there. "Oh," was all he could say.

"You actually got out of Peking, and made it to the Western Hills? And back?" asked Fu incredulously.

"Uh, yes. Yes." An awkward pause. "It was essential to the case."

"Don't tell me anything about it," commanded Fu, his arm stretched out in a gesture for silence. "I don't want to know. Only tell me this: Can you get there again? Today?"

Bei considered it. No way would he pull a manure cart again. "Get me a pass through the gates. And a bicycle."

Fu looked disbelievingly at Bei, at Zhou, then back to Bei. "A pass and a bicycle?"

"Yes. A good bicycle. Not a heavy one."

Fu gestured to Zhou, still in disbelief. "Zhou. Get a, a bicycle for the inspector. For Bei. Now." Zhou left, wondering how to obtain a bicycle on the spot.

"You realize, Bei, that I can't help you beyond the city's walls. If Lin Piao's men get you . . ." He considered it. "Does Captain Li know who you are, and that you know his role in the death of the Taoist prior?"

"He may well. He saw me meeting at the White Cloud Temple the day before yesterday with Meiling, An Shihlin's former mistress. And he ran off when I tried to apprehend him—lost me in a maze of alleys by the temple. In fact, I'm sure he knows I've figured out his role in An's murder. It was written on his face when he saw me just now."

"You're right there. All right. So Captain Li and soon Lin Piao know that their secret is known by you, and that if you spread it, Mao will learn how they have turned against him and murdered his chief agent in Peking. That means you're marked for death, Bei. If Lin Piao's men notice you outside the walls, you're dead."

Bei felt his bowels contract, and everything became sharp and clear around him.

"Are you sure you want to go?"

Bei wasn't so sure. He had not considered this before. Marked for death.

"Listen, Bei." Fu grabbed his arm again, and spoke fiercely, whispering in his ear. "Consider this also. You are marked for death anyway, wherever you are. This Captain Li comes and goes in the city at will, evidently, even without my pass. He may be after you, regardless. You may well be safer outside the city than in it. It is the last place he will look for you. And consider this: You will not be safe, finally, until and unless Mao Tsetung discovers Lin Piao's murder of the Taoist prior, and forbids Lin Piao and Captain Li from any more activity of that sort. With Lin Piao's armies around us, you are doomed, sooner or later. Only Mao Tsetung can overrule Lin Piao and save you."

Bei realized that Fu was using him for his own purposes. But he also realized, with absolute clarity, that Fu was right. In an instant, when Li had seen him and realized that his own identity was revealed, Bei's life was forfeit. There was only one man in China with the power to counter Lin Piao: Mao Tsetung. And only one man near Peking other than Lin Piao with access to Mao: Master T'ang of the Purple Mountain. It was inexorable. He had to return to the Purple Mountain. Quickly. Through the heart of Lin Piao's armies. To save his own life, as well as set up new negotiations.

"I'll need to change clothes. And I may be gone for a day or two."

"All right. Anything else?"

Bei thought. "Mao will want to know something about your negotiating stance, to gauge whether it is worth his while to meet you. An outline of your points would both provide that and prove your sincerity."

Fu resumed his pacing. After only a moment he stopped. "You're right. How are you feeling? Can you remember what I tell you?"

"Yes. Everything is . . . very clear and focused for me."

"I understand. It happens to me when I'm in danger. Which is why it is happening to you now. Sit down."

Fu took the seat in front of the desk, next to Bei. "Listen carefully. What I am about to tell you is strictly confidential. It is to be communicated to no one other than Mao Tsetung or the messenger to Mao. Do you understand?"

"Perfectly."

"Good. Tell them of Lin Piao's murder of Chou Enlai's man. Then tell them I am willing to negotiate a transfer of power to the Communists in Peking. I am willing to negotiate with any representatives Mao Tsetung may designate, *except* Lin Piao. I unconditionally refuse to negotiate with Lin Piao. Is that clear?"

"Yes."

"I insist that power be given initially to a Joint Administrative Office, comprised of Communist and Nationalist representatives. The balance of representatives in this body is negotiable. After a period of time, also negotiable but no less than four months, power can be transferred finally to a Communist military commission. Do you understand?"

"Yes."

"I am willing to surrender all troops in Peking. But I insist that they be allowed to depart the city in their Nationalist troop designations, armed. They will march to any selected location outside the city and be reorganized or incorporated into Communist units there. Is that clear?"

"Yes."

"Finally, I insist on full and unconditional pardons for myself and all of my officers who wish to remain in Communist territory. This must include my officers in Suiyuan and Chahar in Inner Mongolia. I insist also on respect for my personal property. Is that clear?"

"Yes."

"Good. What four areas have I given you instructions in?"

"One: who you will and will not negotiate with. Two: the mechanism of transfer of power. Three: troop dispositions. Four: pardons."

"Excellent. You are indeed my Duke of Chou. Emphasize that I am willing to negotiate these and all other points in a straightforward and reasonable manner."

He rose, walked behind the desk, and scribbled on an official document. A knock on the door.

"Come in."

Zhou entered, breathing hard. "I've got it, sir. Nearly new. Looks as light as any of the other bicycles I saw."

"Good. Here is your pass, Bei. Zhou: Assign one of our men to escort Bei to his home for a change of clothes, and to within sight of a gate." He looked up at Bei. "No sense taking a chance on Captain Li getting to you before you even start."

Bei swallowed hard. His bowels felt very peculiar. "Well. I'm off," he said hoarsely.

Fu rose, and walked around the desk. He bowed formally before Bei.

"Good luck, my friend."

Bei bowed back. "Thank you. Good-bye."

Fu watched them leave. When the door closed, he began pacing back and forth in front of the window, reviewing the developments, analyzing the possibilities. Truly an awesome wild card. Assuming it was not destroyed before it could be played.

Bei pedaled up Hsitan Street toward the Hsichihmen Gate, his guard following discreetly behind in a limousine. Foxholes and pillboxes lined the street, with barbed wire around many of the buildings. As he neared the gate, long lines of soldiers and civilians marched in either direction, those who had worked through the night covered with dust and sweat, trudging along wearily. Men swarmed over the top of the wall, mounting artillery and machine guns. He showed his pass to the guard at the gate, who read it suspiciously and checked with his superior officer before allowing Bei through.

The scene as he walked his bicycle through the walls shocked him. Where last week there had been buildings and houses, today there was only the bare yellow earth. Fifty meters of nothing. He looked more closely. No. Fifty meters of ditches and roadblocks of trees and barbed wire. He looked back at the massive wall. Twenty meters up, at its top, he could barely make out the thick barrels of machine guns trained on the area. He shivered. If the Communists took Peking by force, it would be costly.

He mounted the bicycle and slowly weaved past the ditches and roadblocks impinging on the road, feeling vulnerable and hoping no one would choose him for target practice. To either side, far in the distance, he could hear explosions and see clouds of dust where the demolition crews were at work. As he neared the end of the cleared strip, he suddenly realized how he must stand out to anyone watching him from the Communist side. His heart beat wildly as he pedaled into the row of buildings beyond the strip. But he soon found himself in a crowd, much like a street crowd inside the walls. The area was busier than it had been last week, by far. Then he realized that these were refugees, those whose homes had been destroyed outside the walls and who had, for the most part, been denied entrance into the city. He felt more comfortable as he slipped into the crowd. Soon he was merely one of many.

With each kilometer his anxiety diminished. By the time he passed Yenching University and turned onto Summer Palace Road he felt confident he would make it. The road began to climb beyond the Summer Palace, but the hills seemed easier this time. Not having pulled a manure cart to Yenching helped. The steep ascents west of Fragrant Hills Park didn't faze him. He knew he was literally pedaling for his life. The danger lent strength to his legs, and as he coasted down the hill into the little village where he had seen Meiling, he felt jubilant. It was early afternoon. A right turn, and he pedaled until the trail was too rough for the bicycle. A few minutes' walk brought him to the massive doors of the Purple Mountain. As he was wondering what to say, and to whom, the doors opened and Meiling stood before him. He saw with pleasure a welcome on her face, in addition to the puzzlement.

"Inspector. What brings you here again?"

"Hello, Meiling. It's good to see you again. I have a message for your father from General Fu."

She raised her eyebrows in surprise. "Come with me."

The gateman took his bicycle, and Meiling led him along the path and across the stream. They turned right onto a side path, and approached the area where Bei had heard the sound of bows before. This time there were only sharp yells and soft thuds. They came to an open area some thirty meters in diameter, with a hard-packed sand floor. Some twenty pairs of figures, male and female, were involved in sparring matches. Meiling led him around the perimeter to the far side. There Master T'ang was boxing with a young man. Bei recognized his partner as Dufeng. The young man was executing a spinning series of kicks, each of which T'ang deftly blocked as he retreated step by step. Then T'ang began a series of punches alternating with kicks. The old man crouched rather low throughout the sequence, scuttling back and forth like a crab, and after a particularly vicious kick suddenly swooped down nearly to the ground and came rushing up quite close to Dufeng's front surface. As Dufeng blocked his genital region, the old man's fist whished past it and caught Dufeng's neck in a jab that was pulled back only at the last moment. Even so it staggered the younger man backward.

"*Aiyee!* Old man, your specialty, and I still fell for it," Dufeng croaked, laughing.

T'ang was laughing also. "That's why it is my specialty, Dufeng. There is no real defense to The Wind Rushing up the Cliff. You can only choose between your genitals and your throat."

"Some choice," the younger man admitted, massaging his neck.

"Here, let me do that," said T'ang, as he began an intricate finger massage of Dufeng's throat.

An exclamation of surprise issued from Dufeng as he saw Meiling and Bei approaching. He signaled a silent message to the old man with his hands. T'ang turned around, and joined in the surprise.

"Inspector Bei. Do you ever show up anywhere invited?"

"I promise I will never sneak up on you, Master T'ang. I value my genitals far too much."

Dufeng did not join in the general laughter, as he noted the quick glance Meiling gave to Bei as he said this.

"I presume you are not on a social visit, Inspector?" said the abbot.

"No, sir. I've discovered who had An Shihlin killed, and I have an important message for Mao Tsetung from General Fu, who hopes you will be able to convey it."

"Indeed," said the old man. "You are full of surprises, Inspector. Dufeng, could you please have tea served to us in the Great Hall. Meiling, please escort the inspector there while I wash and change into fresh clothes."

Meiling and Bei walked back to the main path and turned right, toward the Great Hall.

"You know who had Shihlin murdered?"

"I do."

She remained silent as they walked to the Great Hall. Dufeng brought tea in shortly after their arrival, and the abbot glided into the room a few moments later. He took a sip of tea, then turned to Bei.

244

"I am eager to hear what you have to tell us, Inspector."

Bei put his cup down. "I shall spare you the thought process by which I came to the solution, except to note that your yin-yang disk here figured centrally in it." He paused. "Lin Piao had An Shihlin killed."

Both T'ang and Meiling gasped in surprise.

"His aide-de-camp, a Captain Li, has been positively identified as the person who paid the dissident monks in the White Cloud Temple to burn An Shihlin."

After a pause, Bei continued. "I surmise that Lin Piao is in a power struggle with Chou Enlai, and perhaps with Mao himself. Taking over Peking is at least one area in which they have clashed. Lin Piao evidently felt that eliminating Chou's chief agent in the city would permit him to assume the dominant rule in the city's takeover."

The abbot nodded his head. "I can easily believe it. I know for a fact that Chou Enlai, at least, has frequently and vehemently clashed over policy in the past with Lin Piao. While I cannot say Chou hates Lin—or anyone for that matter—I have much evidence that Lin certainly hates Chou. As I believe I mentioned to you earlier, they are very different men."

"It was that statement that provided the key for me."

"I am glad it assisted you in some small way. Knowing that it was Lin's aide who spurred on the dissident monks is conclusive, of course. This is indeed very serious."

"And that is where General Fu Tsoyi comes in."

"Fu Tsoyi knows of this?"

"Yes. It was in his office that the identification of Captain Li took place."

"I see."

"General Fu is willing to negotiate for the peaceful surrender of Peking. But not with Lin Piao. He has asked me to request you to expeditiously relay this message to Mao Tsetung, along with the main points of the terms under which he would transfer the city to the Communists, to demonstrate his sincerity."

"Speed is important?"

"Lin Piao has promised to begin shelling the city tomorrow."

The abbot considered it. "One does not disturb Mao lightly, even though he is not so far away, at Hsipaipo in southern Hopei. But we have two compelling reasons. To inform him of Lin Piao's turning his hatred of Chou Enlai into murder of one of Chou's colleagues. And to inform him that Peking can be taken peacefully, in spite of Lin's apparent determination to destroy it rather than bend his position."

He looked at Meiling. "Either one, alone, would suffice. Daughter, give me ten minutes to draft a telegram. Then escort the inspector with the telegram to Yeh Chienying's headquarters at Lianghsiang. He will have a direct telegraph line to Hsipaipo. The inspector can add Fu's detailed position on transfer of power to my summary of what he has told us."

He turned to Bei. "You know of Yeh Chienying?"

"No."

"You should. He will rule Peking once the city comes under Communist control, one way or another. Yeh taught at Whampoa with Chou Enlai and Nieh Jungchen in the mid-1920's when Lin Piao was a student there. He has been Chief of Staff of the entire Red Army since the Long March. He has in addition assisted Chou Enlai in several delicate negotiations, including the release of Chiang Kaishek when the Young Marshall kidnapped him in Sian in 1936. Yeh ranks behind only Mao and Chou in power. He is now several kilometers south of us here, at Lianghsiang, setting up the government which will assume control of Peking when the city is liberated. He himself will be very interested in your story, Inspector, although I do not believe he has the power to unilaterally curb Lin Piao. He will be glad, though, to promptly relay the story to Mao. Be courteous to him, Inspector: He will soon be your boss."

Bei shifted uncomfortably in his chair.

"Ten minutes, Meiling. Instruct Dufeng to secure a bicycle for you. I presume you are capable of another several hours bicycling, Inspector?"

Bei indicated he was, although without enthusiasm.

Dusk was well-advanced when Meiling and Bei turned off the village's street and began the return climb to the Purple Mountain. Bei was exhausted. Once the telegraph had been transmitted, the nervous energy which had impelled him all day dissipated completely. At

Lianghsiang he had learned that most of the troops in the vicinity of the Purple Mountain and the Summer Palace were under the command of Nieh Jungchen, an experienced commander who was of equal rank with Lin Piao, and had worked with Chou Enlai at Whampoa and in Shanghai. He was, in fact, safer in the Western Hills than in Peking.

His mission accomplished and his safety secure for the present, the aura of danger which had burned around him all day subsided to a faint glow. By the time they reached the gates of the Purple Mountain the stars were out, and he was nearly stumbling with exhaustion.

"You are very tired, Inspector," commented Meiling as they walked the bicycles through the gates and turned them over to the gatekeeper.

"I suppose so. It has been a long and busy day."

"There will be a hot bath awaiting you in the guest house and a fresh change of clothes. Dufeng will serve us a late meal in the study after your bath. I will meet you there."

"Fine."

The bath rejuvenated him considerably, a process which Meiling's glowing presence at dinner completed. She was wearing the same red robe embroidered with blue peonies and white cranes as at their previous dinner together, but now her necklace and hairpins were of ivory. Bei was staring at her with unabashed admiration when Dufeng walked into the room with a tray of food, his quick eyes taking in Meiling's glow and Bei's look. He set the tray down between them. On the tray were a bowl of pickled vegetables, two bowls of millet, and a small broiled chicken.

With a slight bow to Meiling, Dufeng picked up chopsticks in one hand and a thin knife in the other, and proceeded to carve the chicken with an alacrity and dexterity that was difficult to credit. The legs and wings seemed to fall effortlessly from the bird's body, and the body itself was separated into parts with scarcely a sound other than the whisper of the knife.

Bei found himself staring at the performance, mesmerized.

"Dufeng is showing off again. He loves to play Wen Hui's cook for guests," said Meiling.

"Wen Hui's cook?"

Meiling glanced up at Dufeng, who was standing, knife still in hand, with a slight smile on his face.

247

"In the *Chuang-Tse,* Inspector," he said quietly. "There is the story of Prince Wen Hui watching in admiration as his cook carves an entire ox with neither pause nor discernible exertion. When the prince asks him how he does it, the cook explains that he carves by following the Tao. 'I follow the natural grain, letting the knife find its way through the many hidden openings, hardly touching a ligament or tendon, much less a main joint. A good cook changes his knife only once a year because he cuts, while a mediocre cook has to change his every month because he hacks. I've had this knife of mine for nineteen years and have cut up thousands of oxen with it, yet the edge is as if it were fresh from the grindstone.' "

Meiling finished the story. "At which point, Prince Wen Hui exclaims 'Well done,' and marvels that 'From the words of my cook I have learned the secret of growth!' "

Bei politely inclined his head to acknowledge Dufeng's proficiency. The young man transferred the chicken pieces to a bowl, then glided from the room. Bei and Meiling ate in silence.

"I trust you have no desire to return to Peking tonight, Inspector?" Meiling asked when they were finished.

He laughed weakly. "No. If you will have me, I should like to stay."

"We would be honored to have you tonight," she answered.

"Will I see your father again before I leave?"

"Yes, but not tonight. Tomorrow morning."

An awkward silence ensued. Meiling broke it.

"It now appears that you are the one in danger in Peking. Neither the Purple Mountain nor Yeh Chienying nor Nieh Jungchen can protect you there. And Lin Piao's aide seems able to enter the city easily."

He breathed deeply. "True."

"My father wishes me to tell you that you are welcome to stay here for days, or weeks, until the matter is resolved."

Bei shook his head. "Your offer is generous, and I appreciate it. But my place is in Peking. It is now in danger, and I must be there, with my friends and my job."

She looked down. "It is your decision. But please be careful."

He reached over and brushed her cheek with his hand. "I will."

She spoke quietly. "You must be tired. Can you find your way to the guest room?"

He paused, and said hesitantly, "I might get lost in the dark."

Still staring down, she smiled faintly. "Then perhaps I had better escort you there."

She rose without looking at him and left the room, with him following. The night was dark outside, so that he could barely see her. The rustle of her gown and her fragrance guided him, though. At the door to the guest house she turned and stood in the doorway.

"We are here," she whispered.

He stepped forward, and in the next instant they were kissing eagerly and holding each other. His lips moved from her mouth to her cheek and soon he was kissing her neck as she arched her body backwards and pressed her hips against his. She opened the door behind her and they stepped into the room and fell upon the bed. As they lay side by side, still kissing eagerly, he reached down and placed his hand under her robe. Her thighs were like warm ivory as he slid his hand up them, and soon his fingers were enveloped in the wetness of her Golden Valley. She moaned aloud and spread her thighs to give him freer movement there. With a trembling hand he explored her Precious Door, glorying in the warmth and moisture. He felt the Red Pearl of her Jeweled Terrace swell and grow firm and he took it between two fingers and rubbed it back and forth. She arched her back high as she peaked, her tongue darting in and out of his mouth.

As she collapsed back to the bed she undid her sash and opened up her robe, revealing creamy breasts whose tips were taut with desire. He fell upon them with his mouth, sucking long and full while his hand massaged between her thighs. She undid his sash and opened his robe. Her hands told her that his manhood was ready, so she pulled him atop her and guided his Jade Stalk into her Precious Door. He groaned as he slid into her and felt her undulations begin. He joined his rhythm to hers and soon they were dancing in another sphere. Their entire beings were focused on the warmth and pleasure radiating from their groins. A mantle of radiant well-being slowly suffused throughout their bodies. Nothing existed except the joy of it all. No Communists, no responsibilities, no time, no death. This was all there was, a fullness and total immersion in the Tao. The yin and yang swirling together, locked in a passionate dance of life. This was what lay at the root of things, and was obscured or blocked by everyday concerns that they could neither remember nor imagine now. Only the now was, as they rocked up and down in an ecstatic clinging to each other.

He felt it rising from deep, and regretted that it would come and end the trance in which they writhed. But come it did, gathering force quickly and surely. She felt it coming for him also, and angled her own Jeweled Terrace down so that her longer and deeper explosions of pleasure quickened their pace. Together they cried aloud as his yang essence shuddered forth into the deepest recess of her Shady Valley. The undulations slowed, and came to a halt. She ran her fingers lightly up and down his back as he gently placed kisses around her face. She hooked her ankles around his as he snuggled atop her. They lay quietly, the mantle of warmth and pleasure still enveloping them. Their loving had been simple and she had called up none of her arts. But she knew that the Tao had coursed strongly through them, and that it was good.

He stirred and felt for her warmth. When his hand encountered only the quilt, he woke, and looked about the dark room. She was sitting wrapped in her robe next to the window, staring at the stars, her figure barely visible.

"Aren't you cold?"

She glanced back in his direction. "Cold? I suppose so." She returned her gaze to the stars.

He stared at the darkness in the middle of which she sat. "You miss him still, don't you?"

She didn't turn away from the stars, since they couldn't really see each other anyway, but spoke into the darkness. "An Shihlin? I wasn't thinking of him specifically."

"What then?"

She sighed. "These past few weeks, I have lived for learning who had him killed, so I could kill them. Now I know. And . . . it's not as simple as I had thought."

"You don't know whether it's Lin Piao's fault or his aide's?"

"No, not that. But to kill either of them would . . . would affect so many other things. We need Lin Piao. He's our best field commander. And to cold-bloodedly kill anyone—even a murderer—it seems so far from the Tao."

She smiled wanly, although Bei couldn't see it. "Some things are so clearly right. Making love. Meditating. Doing T'ai Chi. Fighting against the foreigners and the Kuomintang. But other things—it's not at all clear what's right."

"Like avenging An Shihlin."

"Yes. And other things too. I . . . I never expected to find as many situations as I have where the flow of the Tao is so difficult to follow."

"Do you doubt the Tao?"

She glanced toward his voice. "Doubt the Tao? No more than you could doubt a rock you hold in your hand. It is so clear, so present, in so many ways. It cannot be doubted by one who experiences it, anymore than you can doubt the stream beside this house. But discerning its flow, in a very complicated situation—sometimes it's difficult."

"So what do you do?"

She got up and groped for the bed, sliding under the covers when she found it and snuggling up against his warm body.

"Nothing. Cleave to the Tao, where you see it clearly. And let it work its own way, where you can't see it. Wait for its course to become clear to you, before you act. It's just sometimes hard to wait patiently for the clarity to come."

"And meanwhile?"

"Meanwhile, I'm sleepy. Sorry about my cold body."

He smiled, and rested his hand on her cold hip. As he closed his eyes, he marveled at how whole he felt with her, how at peace. He drifted toward sleep as he softly caressed her hip to warm it, but then an image floated into his mind. Another hip, then yet another, both pressed stiffly against each other, cold also, but utterly unable to be warmed ever again. The Ch'inhuai twins. He had discovered the murderer of An Shihlin. But the courtesan murderer was still unknown, and so long as he was, Bei's sleep would be haunted by these scenes.

Meiling slipped from under the warm quilt before dawn, put on her quilted robe, and silently left the guest house. The stars were just beginning to fade in the sky. She walked around the Great Hall and past the T'ai Chi courtyard across the path from it.

In the T'ai Chi courtyard a dozen indistinct figures were already stretching, their blue coats and trousers nearly invisible, only their mittens glowing faintly white in the predawn softening of the darkness. She hurried past them to a crude bridge over the creek and soon was on the western side of the compound and to the female living quarters, where she changed into the same clothing as the others and retraced her steps to join them. She had time only for a few warmup stretches before the group, now numbering some four dozen, began to arrange itself in informal lines. Master T'ang was at the left end of the first line, and the others followed his lead as he stood quietly for a few seconds facing north, then raised his arms in the beginning sequence. From a distance the stone-paved courtyard seemed alive with throngs of white birds swooping and banking, as the white-mittened hands traced the ancient movements in the darkness. The abbot led them first in "the square," a sequence in which precise movements of the trunk and limbs create in effect a series of stretching exercises, which systematically invigorate every muscle and joint in the body. "The square" was executed quite slowly and deliberately, exact placement and angles being the key element. By the end of the forty-minute sequence the winter dawn's early light had suffused through the surrounding ring of trees, and the figures in the courtyard were clearly visible, the moisture and warmth of their breaths creating little clouds in front of each face. With barely a pause the abbot went from "the square" into "the round." The movements were smoothed and transformed in "the round" into a style similar to that which most other schools called T'ai Chi: a graceful, flowing pattern of rotating trunks and swirling limbs. In "the round," rhythmic movement replaced precise position as the key element. Halfway through the sequence the sun's rays crested the small hill to the east and shone into the courtyard, their warmth and brightness paralleling the vigor and well-being which was now pulsing through the courtyard's dancers. Soon they approached the last, especially difficult sequence of movements, and all minds and bodies were focused especially keenly on the ritual. A final series of kicks and swirls and they each arrived back at the exact spot from which they had begun "the square" an hour ago. They stood silently for nearly a minute, permitting the final absorption into their bodies of the energy and warmth created by the ritual, then casually walked out of the courtyard in small groups, talking and bantering. All were headed for their favorite meditation spots, most of them indoors in the winter. Meiling went to the meditation room of the Great Hall and sat on the mat. She closed her eyes and let her mind slowly relax and empty itself. The hour's T'ai Chi had left her mind and body focused, integrated, and invigorated. Now she emptied her nervous system of most content, stripped herself down to elemental existence free from sensory input. As she slid down into her meditation, she marveled again at how similar the sensory vacuum of meditation was to the sensory richness of The Rain and the Clouds. There were many roads to the Tao. Or perhaps the Tao was everywhere, and many ways to experience it. She thought of Bei and smiled, then let her thoughts quiet down and slip away.

Thirty minutes later, she began to rise to the surface again. In a few moments she was back. Utterly refreshed, quiet, relaxed, immense reserves of strength and energy at her call, which would be available the remainder of the day, replenished by the afternoon meditation. She arose and walked back to the female quarters across the creek. While all the others were at the martial arts courtyard, she bathed in warm water, put on a fresh robe, and returned to the guest house.

As she was lighting the coal burner in the room, Bei awoke. He smiled at the sight of her, bent over the burner, the smooth contours of her back and hips outlined by the robe.

"Good morning. You are up before me."

"Yes. I've been up for a while."

"The fire feels good."

"Good." She bounced back onto the bed, almost playfully.

"You look as fresh and lovely this morning as you did last night. How do you do it?"

She shrugged, and laughed.

He bent over and tentatively rubbed her cheek, the quilt falling away and revealing his naked torso. When she did not move away, he cupped his hand behind her neck and pulled her to him, enveloping her with both arms and kissing her. She returned the kiss, then pushed him down and began to run her lips down his neck and chest. She removed the quilt and approached his Jade Stalk, now resting comfortably against his thigh. She blew air gently on it at first, from several directions, then shook her rich mane of black hair over it and tossed her head back and forth, her hair slithering across the organ. It began to pulse with life, and she blew air upon it again. As it began to swell, she lapped it with long, strong licks of her tongue, from the base to the tip. Soon the Positive Peak was thrusting proudly into the air, and she enveloped it in her mouth and sucked lightly. Bei groaned with satisfaction.

She glanced up at him mischievously. "But I am being selfish. It is your turn, my love." With that she lay back with her feet next to his head and undid her robe, revealing her long legs and full breasts. Bei stared enraptured as she lifted one leg and spread her thighs. In ten years of marriage he had never seen a woman's sex, but now her fresh young bloom was revealed to him. Her odor wafted to him, musky yet clean, enticing.

He got on his knees and imitated her practice, kissing her calves, then her thighs. As he approached her Cinnabar Cleft, the smell became exquisite, and he realized she had scented herself with some flowery fragrance. She spread her legs wide, and he blew over the entire Golden Gully, directing his breath now at the Strings of the Lyre, now at the Red Pearl which was beginning to bulge atop the Jeweled Terrace. The Cinnabar Cleft itself began to moisten, and he ran his tongue along the Strings of the Lyre up to the Red Pearl and back, feeling his own excitement rise.

"Very good," she groaned. "Very good. Now refresh your *ch'i* with my essence from the Cinnabar Cleft."

He directed his tongue to the Cinnabar Cleft, and soon it was wet with moisture. He lapped it up passionately, as she began to undulate her hips and moan louder. His tongue tired after a minute, and as he paused to rest it she laughingly sat up and pushed him onto his back, then kneeled over him and inserted his Positive Peak deep into her Cinnabar Cleft. She began to rock up and down on her flexed legs, her hands resting beside his shoulders, her breasts dangling before his eyes. He reached up and cupped and caressed them as she continued her rocking motion. She raised herself slightly so that his Lively Head passed in and out of her Cinnabar Cleft with each rocking motion. After a few moments of this he felt his peak rising within him. She bent forward more so that her pulsing Red Pearl rubbed more strongly against the base of his Jade Stalk, and began a vigorous series of rotating movements of her hips as she moaned aloud. He arched his back and thrust and she rocked at a frantic pace and they both let out a long, inarticulate cry of pleasure which finally ended in a broken series of whimpers. She slowly let herself down on him and stretched out full length on his body, both of them exhausted. He cried out in surprise as he felt her massaging his retreating Jade Stalk with the muscles of the Shady Valley, then relaxed and enjoyed the exquisite sensation.

He rubbed his hand gently over her buttocks. "So this is Nourishing the Essence, eh?"

She laughed. "So we call it."

"I think the description is apt."

"Good. But you are surely no stranger to it."

"No. But somehow, somehow it has not been so playful, or invigorating as this."

She snuggled down into him.

"I'm hungry."

She laughed again. "The first meal will be soon. And your water behind the burner will be warm now. I will join you in the study, in twenty minutes or so." She got up.

"Must you go?" he asked, his hands trailing along her thigh.

She glanced down at him, smiling. "I go, but my *ch'i* stays behind, in you." With that, she turned and vanished.

He lay there, basking in the warm air within the room and the warm glow within his body. My *ch'i* stays behind, in you. He liked the thought. And the corollary, that part of him was now in her.

. . .

The abbot joined them in the study for the breakfast of millet gruel, hard-boiled eggs, and wheat biscuits.

"When might I expect a reply for General Fu?" inquired Bei, hungrily lapping up the gruel.

"Probably soon. Mao and Chou work long into the night. I would imagine they would have come to some sort of decision late last night and relayed it back to Yeh Chienying."

"So I might know this morning?"

"Possibly. Are you sure you wish to return to Peking? If Lin Piao and his aide suspect you of interfering with them, you won't be safe there, regardless of what Mao says."

"I've already told Meiling that my place is in Peking. But thank you for your concern."

"It is, of course, your decision. More gruel?"

"Thank you, yes."

"Father, should I go to Lianghsiang this morning?"

"If we haven't heard from Yeh within a couple of hours, perhaps you should. But I rather imagine that in something this important—"

He stopped as Dufeng entered the room, glancing at his fluttering hands.

"From Yeh Chienying?" asked T'ang.

More silent signals from Dufeng.

"Ah. Yeh Chienying himself. Bring him here, Dufeng, in the Great Hall."

The young man left silently. The three of them quickly finished the meal and walked across the hallway to the Great Hall. A short time later Dufeng arrived, leading a tall, simply dressed man with a vigorous round face and decisive air about him. The face was not handsome, but a rugged vitality and openness rendered it appealing.

"Commander Yeh. You honor our Purple Mountain."

"Not at all, Abbot T'ang. The honor is mine, to be permitted to visit your community and see for myself what Mao and Chou Enlai have told me about." His voice was deep and gruff.

"I believe you have met my daughter, T'ang Meiling, and Inspector Bei Menjin of the Peking Municipal Police Force."

"Yes. Last night, when I relayed Inspector Bei's message from General Fu to Mao Tsetung. I have just received a response from Mao. Regarding the information you gave us about the murder of An Shihlin, Mao and Chou Enlai plan to come here sometime next week and personally meet with Lin Piao to rectify the misunderstandings which led to that unfortunate incident. We will inform you of a specific date for that meeting, Abbot. Mao requests that Miss T'ang and Inspector Bei be on hand for the meeting, to present their evidence, and that it be held here at the Purple Mountain."

"Of course," said T'ang.

"Will there be any punishment, Commander Yeh?" Bei asked bluntly.

Yeh smiled ruefully. "Punishment? I don't know. You must understand, Inspector. We have been fighting for over twenty years. Fighting the warlords, the Kuomintang, and among ourselves. Often fighting for our very lives." He shook his head at the memories of twenty years. "We have all made mistakes in those years, I assure you. In warfare, when you make mistakes, men are killed." He said it simply, flatly, and shrugged his shoulders. "We have all been responsible for men being killed, by various sorts of mistakes—mistakes in strategy, in judgment, and policy."

He looked Bei full in the face. "It is beyond the wisdom of heaven, Inspector, to decide and implement justice for each and every death in warfare. And certainly beyond the wisdom of men."

"You will do nothing?" asked Meiling incredulously.

"I did not say that," retorted Yeh. "At the meeting, some resolution will be provided. Now. As regards the negotiations with General Fu Tsoyi, Inspector. Commander Lin Piao's presence is required to successfully terminate the battle for Tientsin. He will relocate his headquarters there immediately and direct that campaign. The negotiations with General Fu will be continued by myself and Nieh Jungchen. Commander Lin Piao will have an observer at the negotiations, but will not participate. We request that General Fu send representatives to meet with us at the village of Tungchow tomorrow morning, prepared and empowered to discuss all aspects of a transfer of power in Peking."

"I will relay the message, Commander Yeh. May I assume that the artillery shelling of Peking is cancelled?"

"You may not," Yeh said severely. "Peking is under siege. It may expect acts of war against it until an accommodation with us is reached. However, you may inform General Fu that so long as he is actively exploring an agreement with us, the shelling will be restrained."

"I'll relay those messages. And I feel confident that the general will send representatives to Tungchow to meet with you and Nieh Jungchen tomorrow morning."

"Good. I will instruct our forces that your representatives will have safe conduct outside the city walls. Now, if you will excuse me, I must return to my headquarters. Good-bye."

Bows were exchanged all around, and Yeh turned and strode out of the room.

"I must be going also," declared Bei. "Thank you for your hospitality again, Master T'ang."

"We are honored to have you with us. Good luck, Inspector. Meiling will walk you to the gate."

They walked in silence to the gate. "When will I see you again?" he asked as the gateman left to get his bicycle.

"When I bring you word of the date of the meeting here between Mao and Lin Piao. Less than a week, probably."

"I will miss you."

She reached up and lightly touched his lips. "Be careful," she said softly. "Until the meeting here, you are not safe from Lin Piao or Captain Li."

Bei nodded, the thought sobering him considerably. He turned and walked his bicycle through the gates, not looking forward to the ride back to Peking.

From a meditation spot in a grove of trees, a pair of shining eyes observed Meiling and Bei part. Dufeng watched Bei walking down the path for a moment, then his dark eyes turned to Meiling and glowed even brighter as he drank in her languid movements and the silhouette of her body against the sun's rays.

Fu heaved an immense sigh of relief, and sank back wearily in his chair. "Thank the heavens. It has succeeded. We negotiate with Yeh Chienying and Nieh Jungchen instead of that treacherous dog, Lin Piao." He glanced up at Bei. "They are reasonable men, even though they are Communists. Perhaps we can avert the destruction of the city and come to reasonable terms for ourselves. Perhaps." He sat musing for some moments, then turned to Zhou, who was sitting in the other chair in front of his desk. "I'll send you, of course, Zhou. And who else?"

"Yeh is a high-ranking military man, sir, second only to Chu Teh. I would suggest General Teng Paoshan."

"Old Paoshan. Yes. He will be perfect. He has even had experience in negotiating with the Communists, in north Shensi during the war with the Japanese. I think you can look forward to a more rewarding negotiating session tomorrow morning, Zhou, than you had with Lin Piao last week."

Zhou grinned with relish. "Nothing would please me more."

"Bei, you have been an inestimable help in arranging these new negotiations. My gratitude to you and respect for your talents are great. May I utilize your skills again when the need arises?"

"I am happiest when I am helping my city, General."

"Good. Now let me also tell you this. You know of the curious relationship between the Te Wu and myself. So long as neither of us is actively threatening the other, we are courteous to each other and coexist fine. But you realize that our interests at times may diverge radically. If they should learn of these negotiations with Commander Yeh, they would rightly deduce that some sort of accommodation was being discussed. They would literally stop at nothing to prevent that. In a word, the lives of all those involved would be under dire threat. Zhou and I are used to this—it is a soldier's lot, especially a soldier in command of a city. I want you to be aware of it also, both to silence your tongue and to warn you, because you are now involved also."

"I understand."

"Be sure that you do. If your tongue or your actions betray what you know, it could well mean your life."

"I seem to be threatened from all sides," commented Bei wryly.

"You'll get used to it," Fu responded.

A muffled explosion sounded to the southeast. Bei glanced questioningly at Fu.

"Since early this morning. It caused considerable consternation at first. But so far they've only hit the airfields—Tungtan and Temple of Heaven. Still, I imagine the city is more tense."

259

"Hopefully, the situation will be resolved soon," offered Bei.

Fu shrugged. "We shall see. My wild card worked well when I played it. I must thank you again, Bei, for providing me with that wild card. Who would have dreamed, indeed, that the Communist high command would be so seriously split that Lin Piao's own aide would actually arrange the murder of the top Communist underground agent in the city." Fu shook his head at the notion. "Or that your discovery of Captain Li's complicity in Prior An's death would permit me to exploit that split. Exploit it to bypass that dog Lin Piao and negotiate the city's fate with more reasonable Communists."

He leaned back and laughed heartily, the laugh of a man fully engaged in a serious game, playing it with zest. But then he became serious, focused on his next moves.

"The game, however, is far from over, my friends. And the deck contains numerous other wild cards." He stared pensively at the ceiling. "Many of which are deadly."

Bei shifted in his chair, then rose. "I'd best check in at my office, General. I've neglected my routine paperwork for many days."

"Thank you again, Bei. By the way, I've had more inquiries from some of my associates regarding the series of courtesan murders. I understand another and particularly shocking one occurred several days ago. May I give my associates any assurances that these insane killings will not continue?"

Bei sighed in discouragement. "I've given the Flower Houses descriptions of the man and his preferences. They have all been instructed to contact my office immediately should anyone matching that description enter their establishments. Beyond that, I'm not sure what else we can do, although I share your dislike of merely waiting for him to strike again."

"A man of your talents should be able to find this crazed murderer. Please redouble your efforts, Inspector. I have the utmost confidence in your abilities."

"I shall do what I can," said Bei, wondering what that might be. "Good-bye, General. Zhou." A guard escorted him to the Eternal Peace Bridge. Bei paused and smiled at the Imperial View Pavilion, then crossed the bridge and onto the south shore of Beihai Park.

As he walked out of the park and turned east onto Wenchin Street, the driver of a limousine parked down the street turned and looked at the occupants of the back seat. Yu Chenling's eyes were fixed on Bei. Yu's aide Chan sat beside him.

"The inspector again," muttered Yu. "He comes, he goes. Too frequently, too frequently by far." Yu turned to Chan. "You were right to call Fu's increased consultations with the inspector to my attention, Chan. Something is up. I think it would be prudent if we monitored whom Fu receives and sends forth for several days. I have seen better men than him lose their resolve under pressure from the insidious blandishments of the Communist dogs. It's that Taoist whore of his, I know it."

Chan suppressed a smirk as Yu settled back into the seat, knowing that the old man was about to savor imagined scenes of himself with the "Taoist whore" he had just denounced. But Chan stared stonily ahead, resisting the scenes of his father's death which came insistently into his own mind at times of boredom such as these stakeouts. What was the warlord up to?

January 13

The black Citroën's exhaust billowed up in the cold dawn air as Zhou Peifeng and General Teng Paoshan crossed Eternal Peace Bridge and walked up to the car that would take them to the new negotiations with Yeh Chienying that morning. Across the street and up the block the driver of a newly arrived limousine tapped on his window, and Yu Chenling and Chan glanced up from the backseat. Yu uttered a soft exclamation as he recognized the two men disappearing into the Citroën, and urgently tapped the driver on the shoulder. The car shuddered to life, and slid out onto Wenchin street as the Citroën slowed to turn right onto Beich'ang Street.

The two cars traveled down Beich'ang Street, then east on Ch'ang'an Boulevard, past the Forbidden City, past Wangfuching Street. As they neared the Chiang'kuomen Gate at the east wall of the city, Yu motioned his driver to slow down, and they eased to a stop a block away from the gate. From there they observed the Citroën pass through a crowd of people at the gate, show the pass, then drive through the opened gate. Yu watched it with narrowed eyes, then told the driver to return to their Te Wu compound quickly.

"Chan, pull the files on Communist positions around Peking," Yu commanded as he and Chan entered the Te Wu office behind Yu's villa. He took off his heavy overcoat and sat down at his desk. Chan put the file in front of him.

"So, what is east? Tungchow, of course. Sanhe further on, and Hsianghe below that. Aha. Here it is. Nieh Jungchen. His head-quarters are in Tungchow. Originally in Sanhe, moved closer, into Tungchow, a month ago." He closed the file. "Nieh Jungchen. Lin Piao is north of the city, in Chihsien. Yeh Chienying is west, in Lianghsiang. So our 'moderate' General Fu is talking with Nieh Jungchen. And whoever else might drive there to meet with them also." He sat back and studied the ceiling.

"Nieh became a Communist in France, sir. He's considered a moderate," offered Chan.

"Yes, I know that, stupid," Yu retorted with annoyance. "But what does it mean?" He continued to ignore the other. "A so-called moderate talking to a so-called moderate." Chan began to speak, but checked himself.

"It probably means an agreement is in the offing," Yu concluded. "Each man is soft, and willing to compromise. Whether Nieh's compromises will be accepted by the Communists is their business." He sat up with an air of decision. "But I know what our answer must be. Chan. Get Jing in here, and Wen. We have some fast planning to do."

They took seats in a spacious room, Zhou and General Teng on a sofa on one side, Yeh Chienying, Nieh Jungchen, and Captain Li in three chairs on the other side. An aide served tea to all.

"Permit me to make introductions," said Nieh, who had met Zhou and Teng as their limousine pulled up before his headquarters. Although he was as plainly dressed as his comrades, the cut of his clothes had a smart St. Cyr look to them, and he spoke and carried his thin body with a refined air. Zhou found it hard to imagine him a Communist. "This is Commander Yeh Chienying, Chief of Staff of the Red Army. Commander Yeh: General Teng Paoshan of the Eighteenth Field Division, and Colonel Zhou Peifeng, aide to General Fu Tsoyi."

Yeh nodded formally as did Zhou and Teng.

"And this is Captain Li Sungji, aide to Commander Lin Piao, who unfortunately could not come here to be with us, due to pressing concerns at Tientsin. Captain Li: General Teng and Colonel Zhou. I believe you already know Colonel Zhou."

Li coldly acknowledged the others.

"Captain Li is here not as a participant, but as Commander Lin Piao's observer," Nieh said, more to remind Li than the others.

"General Teng," Yeh began in a voice suggesting discussion among equals, "I have long admired your tactical skill, as well as that of your colleague, General Fu. Your handling of the Japanese Sixth Division was superb."

Teng shook his head, but returned in a pleased tone, "You are too kind to me. I did not so much 'handle' them as manage to prevent my division from being mauled by them, while I stung them here and there."

Yeh smiled. "Nonetheless, I have long regarded that duel with the Japanese the best illustration I know of Sun-tzu's words: 'Lay on many deceptive operations. Be seen in the west and march out of the east; lure him in the north and strike in the south. Drive him crazy and bewilder him, so that he disperses his forces in confusion.' "

Teng smiled. "You flatter me, when it is you who are the master of Sun-tzu's skills. Nonetheless, I may quote you Fu Tsoyi's favorite verse from Sun-tzu's manual on war: 'A city, although isolated and susceptible to attack, is not to be attacked if there is the probability that it is well stocked with provisions, defended by crack troops under command of a wise general, and counseled by loyal ministers whose plans are unfathomable.' "

They all laughed, except Li.

"Touché," commented Nieh, showing off a small part of his fluent French.

263

"Actually," began Zhou, addressing Nieh, "General Fu regards his duel with you for Kalgan the most outstanding illustration of Sun-tzu's stratagems in modern times. On both sides."

Nieh's plain, unprepossessing face became serious. "It was exhilarating, even though I lost that particular duel. Now Kalgan is ours again. Too many men have lost their lives over that city, Colonel Zhou. On both sides."

Yeh put down his teacup, and signaled the beginning of the business. "We can all agree to that. Our job these next several days is to explore whether more men need be killed over Peking. I have heard the bare outlines of General Fu's proposals from the sagacious Inspector Bei already. Would you gentlemen care to state them in detail for us now?"

Li grimaced perceptibly at the mention of Bei's name.

"Very gladly, Commander Yeh," answered Zhou with a satisfied glance at Li. "We will gladly tell you General Fu's position."

Bei peered up at the office clock from the final report to the magistrate concerning the White Cloud Temple case. Nearly noon. Final reports were hard enough to draft, but this one was especially sensitive, and more had to be left unsaid than said. He dropped his pen wearily and slumped back into his seat. So much for the White Cloud Temple. The Baleful Star was still free, of course. And the Baleful Star doubtless realized that Bei had revealed him, and thus was directing his enmity at Bei now, in all probability. But at least Bei knew who he was, and could be on his guard. The courtesan murderer was another story. Bei had no idea who he might be. The crimes were so irrational, so shocking, so twisted that it was difficult to fruitfully apply logic to them. A young man with a forceful yet gentlemanly manner, left-handed, with a knife in his boot, who carries with him dried gardenias and an irresistible craving for sexual relations with Shansi girls and twins, capped by slitting their throats and smearing blood on their bodies. Then reverently enshrouding the dead bodies in silk sheets. Bei shook his head. What kind of man is that? One who had seen something beyond his powers to endure, probably something having to do with a woman. But where do you look for such a man? He had people who could identify the man, the mothers of the Flower

Houses he had visited so lethally. But where to post them? On busy street corners? He laughed aloud, then for some reason thought of the gatehouse overlooking Yu Chenling's compound. Equally ludicrous, yet . . . put one of the mothers in it for a day, to observe Yu's men? Why did the idea appeal to him so much? He was toying with it when Lufei walked into the office.

"Hello, Inspector," she ventured timidly.

"Oh, Lufei. Good to see you again. I'm afraid Yuan has already left for lunch."

"I, I didn't come to see him."

"Oh? Is anything wrong?"

"Well . . . I won't bother you. You are obviously leaving for lunch."

"Come along. I'm going home for lunch and could use some company." As he said this, he remembered her previous proposal to him, and hastily added, "Of course, my servant will be there, and serve the lunch. It, uh, won't be Shansi food. But come along. You look like you need to talk."

"That is true enough."

They got a ricksha and took off for the east side of the city.

"There seems to be a lot of activity in the city today," said Bei to make conversation. "I mean, other than the soldiers and the civilian work crews."

"Haven't you heard? They're issuing passes for refugees from surrounding areas to be allowed out of the city, to return to their homes in the countryside."

"Returning to the countryside?"

"Yes. As I've heard, the Communists aren't the brutal bandits people were told. Things are quite good in the countryside, actually. Especially compared with the shortages and tensions here in the city. The shelling yesterday clinched it. People would rather be out there than in here."

"So Fu is allowing them to leave?"

"If they have passes, which he controls. I suppose he wants to relieve the crowdedness."

An explosion shook the ground nearby as they turned north off of Ch'ang'an Boulevard into Tung'anmen Street. Lufei grabbed Bei and began to whimper as she buried her head in his thick coat.

"There, there. It's just the airfield at Tungtan. I understand they're not hitting anything else."

"It's not that," she cried, snuggling deeper into his coat.

"There, there," he said again in what he hoped was a comforting voice. He patted her head paternally, regretting now that he had invited her along. They pulled up to the gate of his home, though, so he helped her out of the ricksha and across the entrance.

The servant girl appeared in the courtyard to the right.

"Hsiaoyu. It will be two for lunch. In my study, in ten minutes."

Hsiaoyu smiled slyly. She knew that his bedroom led off his study. Bei was too flustered with the still-whimpering Lufei to notice. He led her down the covered corridor past the formal dining hall and into the study. He sat her down next to the small table where he often took his meals.

"There. Now you can relax. Whatever is the problem? Are you and Yuan having troubles?"

She sniffled. "Oh, no. He is a fine man. Fine old man. I suppose we'll marry. No, it's not him." She shuddered, and began to cry.

"Whatever is it, then?" exclaimed Bei, tiring of it all.

"It's my brother. I saw him again, the day before yesterday."

"Your brother? It was really him?" asked Bei, suddenly somewhat more interested.

"No doubt of it," Lufei said, between tears. "He talked to me. Just a few sentences, but it was him."

"Was he looking at you . . . that way again?"

"Yes!" she wailed, breaking into sobs.

Bei groaned. This was really too much. But he was intrigued. The day before yesterday. That would be the day he had gone to the Purple Mountain for Fu. "There, there. So what did he say?"

She stifled her sobs. "He . . . he said something very peculiar. About you."

Bei's mouth fell open. "About me?"

"Yes."

"How ever does he know anything about me?"

"I don't know. I think he's been following me a long time, and has seen us together."

Bei frowned. It made no sense. "What did he say?"

She shuddered again. "He said . . . he said you were dangerous.

Said you were dangerous to me. That if I didn't stop seeing you . . . ohhh." She began to wail again, louder now and buried her face in her hands.

"Heaven above, stop that. Please. Tell me—what if you didn't stop seeing me?"

She blurted it out, terrified. "That if I didn't stop seeing you, a throat would soon be slit!"

Bei sat back, dumbfounded. A throat slit? The image of the twin courtesans flashed into his mind, but he drove it out. One case at a time.

"Whose throat? Yours or mine?"

Lufei sat there, finally quiet, too exhausted to cry anymore. "I don't know. That was how he said it: 'a throat will be slit.'" She trembled, but did not cry again. "His eyes scared me. Like a demon possessed him."

Hsiaoyu brought in a tray of food and tea and placed it on the table, smirking. The master has chosen a weepy one, that's for sure, she thought. She glanced across the study to the bedroom door, and smirked again. Bei noticed nothing.

"Here. Have some food. It will help," he said, still perplexed by the whole thing. He began to eat also, realized how hungry he was, and devoted himself to the food and the tea. He was too preoccupied, though, to even notice the tea's taste. It was the siege. The whole city was being transformed into madmen. A great time to be chief inspector. Perhaps she was making it all up. A ploy to get attention and sympathy from him. She heard about the courtesans, and adopted the slit throat bit. He looked at her again. She certainly looked genuinely frightened though, and frazzled by some terrible experience. Who could tell?

"Look, Lufei. Don't go out on the streets again. Your brother sounds dangerous to me. I simply cannot assign a guard to you, unfortunately. My men already are working beyond their capacities. Yuan is good. You'll be in no danger when you're with him. And when he's gone, just bar the door and don't open it for anyone. You'll be safe."

She began to cry again.

He finished his bowl and the tea. "Finish up. I'll take you home, myself. And send Yuan home early today. Finish up."

She put the bowl down, and stared dumbly ahead. With her sauciness drained, she was merely a frail country girl, no longer attractive. He helped her to her feet, and walked her down the corridor to the ricksha.

The garden outside the office window had long since succumbed to darkness, but Fu worked at his desk still. If a critical juncture was approaching, as it seemed to be, he wanted the city's affairs to be strictly in order. He looked up in surprise when he heard the knock. Before responding, he pulled a drawer open, revealing a 9mm pistol, its safety off.

"Come in."

The door opened, and Zhou walked in, trudged across the room, and flopped down in one of the chairs.

Fu's face openly showed his shocked concern. "Zhou! What's wrong at Tungchow? Why have you returned?"

Zhou glanced up wearily. "Nothing's wrong. I've returned because everything is right. The negotiations have advanced so far that I need more detailed instructions already."

Fu let out a long sigh of relief, as Zhou grinned. Then Fu also grinned, broadly, and soon both men were chuckling with satisfaction.

"Good, eh?" asked Fu.

"Very good," answered Zhou. "Yeh and Nieh are—well, they are eminently reasonable men. Stubborn. Demanding. But reasonable. It is a pleasure to work with them. And do you know what the best part is?"

"What?"

"Lin Piao's observer is none other than Captain Li. So he sits there glowering while the rest of us pull and tug but get somewhere, finally."

"The Baleful Star. Shall we warn Bei that Li didn't go with Lin Piao to Tientsin?"

Zhou shrugged. "We probably should. Although since he's tied to the negotiations, I don't imagine he would be able to come into the city and exact any revenge on the inspector."

"I'll tell Bei, nonetheless. What points do we need to clarify for Commander Yeh?"

Zhou sat up and cleared his mind. "Mainly three areas, although they are complicated and will require some thought. First, the length and mechanics of the period between when we sign the agreement and the Communist forces actually march into the city. Which amounts to how do we manage the logistics of marching our troops out before the Communists are established here, especially the ones whose commanders disapprove of the agreement. Yu Chenling, for example, and General Shih Chueh. Secondly, they refuse to agree to the unlimited evacuation to Nanking of whichever of our officers and officials wish to leave, after the signing of the agreement but prior to their actual assumption of control in the city. They argue that once the agreement is signed, they in effect control the city, even if their troops are not yet here. Thirdly, they insist on the immediate disarming of the police force, before their troops march into the city, to prevent any sniping at them by diehards."

Fu leaned back in his chair and thought. "All right. We know we're going to have trouble with Yu Chenling's men, and Shih Chueh's. Let's figure out how we can diffuse that, to the Communists' satisfaction. Then, assuming we can come up with something that is realistic, we can go back and apply it to each of those three points."

Several hours later, while Fu and Zhou still talked, two men dropped onto the ice of Beihai Lake from the eastern shore of the park, just opposite the northeast corner of Jade Island. Here the distance to the island was relatively short, merely several hundred meters, and the surface was frozen solid clear to the island. They quickly wrapped themselves in flowing crystal-blue capes and hoods, and began to slowly crawl over the ice toward the tip of the island. Only the sharpest of eyes could have detected their slowly moving presence on the ice in the dark night. Straw sandals attached to their hands and knees acted as insulation and countered the ice's slipperiness. They inched along, stopping every five minutes and remaining stationary for a minute before moving on. In a little over an hour they reached the island, directly under one of the guards placed every thirty meters along the shore. The guard stared straight ahead, over the ice. They left their capes and sandals at the shore as they slithered onto the island. The guard stared resolutely past them as they crept next to him, stopping to get their bearings. Chan glanced up at him and smirked. Then he slowly crept away, toward the Winter Palace, the other following close behind.

"Anything else you can think of?" Fu asked.

Zhou thought. "No. We've covered everything they'll bring up tomorrow, plus several items more that may or may not come up."

"Good." A long pause. Fu looked closely at his aide, then spoke in a soft voice. "Do you feel good about this, Zhou?"

Zhou glanced up at Fu in surprise. "Why do you ask?"

"Well—we function so smoothly as a general and his aide. Sometimes I wonder what the aide really feels about the general's orders."

Zhou smiled. "I've always spoken my mind to you, sir. Even when not invited to, sometimes."

"Yes. So?"

"So. I feel good about it. Talking with Yeh and Nieh, especially. They are . . . so confident, so full of their mission. So open and— well, you can't tell about a man just speaking with him, but they appear honorable. Capable of being trusted." He paused. "Quite different in every respect from Yu Chenling, Chiang Kaishek, and so many of our Kuomintang allies."

Fu laughed. "Don't forget they have their Lin Piaos and Captain Lis also. Just as we have our Li Tsungjens we can be proud of."

"Yes. You're right. But nonetheless, I suppose what I'm saying is that they're no worse than we are, and perhaps better."

"I'm glad you feel that way. Of course, it is of some importance also that we're surrounded by several million enemy soldiers, well-equipped and well-led, with at the most another month or two of food in the city, and no prospect whatsoever of any military or political help from the south."

Zhou laughed bitterly. "Yes. That is of some importance."

Fu lowered his voice. "News from Nanking, from Li Tsungjen, today."

"Yes?"

"Chiang Kaishek is considering resignation."

Zhou snorted in derision. "I've heard that before."

"As have I. But he's under pressure from all sides this time. The word is that if Mao rejects his grandiose 'New Year's peace offensive,' he may well do it, this time. Perhaps only for show, retaining his real power. But resign, nonetheless."

"I will believe it when I see it."

Fu sighed. "You're right. It certainly can't be depended upon. The turtle has hung on for decades. How can a man with so many delusions retain power so long?"

Zhou shrugged.

"You're tired. Don't go back to Tungchow tonight. Get some sleep here, then leave early in the morning."

"All right. Shall I check with you in the morning?"

"Not unless you think of something else."

Zhou wearily stood up and trudged to the anteroom, off which his austere quarters were located.

Fu remained at his desk for a few minutes, then got up and walked down the hall to his private quarters. As he was about to enter his own room, his hand on the doorknob, he heard Meilu call him from her room next door. He walked back up the hallway and knocked softly on her door.

"Come in."

He entered the room. The lamp was lit on the calligraphy table near the window, a poem lying beside it, and Meilu was curled up on her bed with a book, the light glinting on the large jade hairpins holding up her mass of hair.

"Why are you up so late, my precious jade?"

She motioned him over to the bed. "I wanted to see you and hear your voice before I slept."

He took her hand as he sat on the bed, back to the window. They had been especially gentle and tender with each other the last few days. Although neither knew what the immediate future held, they both realized that significant change was about to occur. The sense that something was birthing and something was dying pressed in on them. And because they were not sure of the shape of the birth or of the death, they clung tighter to what was most precious to them—each other. He handled the centerpiece of the necklace she wore, a thin but heavy jade disk with fine sharp teeth along the edge, and small beads of gold sunk into the jade at the base of each tooth, which accounted for its weight.

"You have developed a real liking for this necklace. I don't believe you've taken it off for a week or more."

She smiled. "It was a gift from my father."

He laughed. "So! You have a father! Careful. Don't let any other clues to your past slip from those cinnabar lips, my love."

As she laughed also, she caught a reflection in the window over his shoulder. It was the private door leading to his bedroom, slowly opening. Her right hand went to the disk on her breast, grabbing it out of Fu's hand, as the door swung fully open and a man slid out from behind it, a pistol in his hand. In one motion, Meilu shoved Fu flat onto the bed with her left hand as she jerked the jade piece down off the necklace and with a fierce backhand motion of her forearm sent it spinning across the room. It sawed its way deep into the man's abdomen as he squeezed the trigger. The bullet dug into the wall beyond where Fu had sat just as the first of the gunman's intestines began to spill out onto the floor. As he crumpled forward, a second man—Chan—appeared behind him, pistol leveled directly at Fu. Meilu's right hand had gone straight to her hair as she released the jade disk and now held one of the large jade hairpins. Still holding Fu down, she threw the hairpin like a knife at Chan, her forward motion sending her over Fu's shoulder just as the shot rang out. Her body jolted atop Fu's as the bullet hit her. Fu rolled off the bed and caught her as she crumpled to the floor. He knelt down with her in his arms, oblivious to the second gunman with the jade hairpin sticking out of his arm struggling to raise the pistol for a second shot. He saw only the rapidly widening red stain on Meilu's nightgown over her heart. As she reached up feebly and touched his cheek he jerked his gaze from the blood to her eyes. They glowed unnaturally bright for a second as she looked into his face, then lost their focus and began to fade, the glow soon replaced by a dull, sightless stare.

Zhou burst into the room from the hallway in a crouch, pistol extended by both hands. The gun exploded and Chan was blown back against the window just as he had gathered the strength for a second shot at the kneeling Fu. Fu heard neither the shot nor the shatter of glass as the body crashed through the window. As the last

272

glow of life sputtered out of Meilu's eyes it had struck him with absolute clarity why she had been sent to him. Not to bewilder him, nor to spy on him. But rather to protect him. She had been sent to protect his life. And now she was gone.

"No," he wailed, a long, low protest that began deep in his throat and echoed in the room, to be cut off by a shudder and a sob equally long. This one was too much. Losing Jie was bad, Ling was worse. But this one was too much. No! He clutched her limp body to him tightly and shook his head, rocking back and forth on his knees, her long black hair swishing against the floor. "No, No, No." Her blood smeared his jacket, and began to drip onto the floor beside his knee.

Zhou remained frozen in his crouch, pistol extended before him, waiting for another gunman to burst into the room through the open door. For a full minute he crouched motionless, only vaguely aware of Fu's wailing. He then raised up slightly and advanced toward the door slowly, his finger still tight on the trigger. He kicked the door shut just as the first two guards ran into the room.

"Search the general's room," he yelled. "Another one may be there." He backed slowly into the center of the room, stepping over the first gunman's body. Two more guards rushed in. "Captain Wang: Light the grounds. Organize a thorough search of the entire island. Order the perimeter guards to remain at their stations, with no exceptions. Have your best man search the ice around the island for some sign of where they entered." The men dashed out.

Finally he lowered the pistol and relaxed his grip on the trigger. He turned around and saw Fu still kneeling in front of the bed with her body in his arms, sobbing but no longer wailing. He kicked Chan's feet off the window ledge and pulled the curtain across the window, then walked over and shut the door leading to the hallway. A great general must not be seen sobbing by his men. He rolled the body of the first gunman over, grimacing at the pile of intestines and blood which slopped through the gash in his abdomen. No life left there. What, or who, could have caused that wound? He rolled the body back on top of the intestines and left the room, closing the door behind him. He walked to Fu's office, found a match, and lit a cigarette, his hand trembling. After a minute Captain Wang rushed up to him.

"We found their gear, sir. On the northeast tip of the island, where it's closest to the east shore."

"How far from a guard?"

"Strange, sir. Very close to where Ruwen should have been. He swears he saw nothing, though."

"Bring him here. In front of the pavilion. And have a dozen men here, too."

The captain stared at him for a second. "Yes, sir," he said, and hurried off. Zhou lit another cigarette, puffed deeply on it for a minute, then put it out in the ashtray on Fu's desk. He checked his pistol, and walked through the anteroom to the courtyard in front of the pavilion. A group of soldiers there snapped to attention as he walked out. Soon Captain Wang appeared, dragging an obviously terrified guard. The man was shoved in front of Zhou.

"The assassins came ashore right past you. Why did you not see them?"

The man trembled violently. "I don't know. I didn't see them. I swear I didn't see them!"

"Silence!" Zhou commanded. "Stand at attention." The guard tried to stand straight, but continued to shake badly. Zhou stepped back two paces, raised the pistol to eye level and shot the man in the forehead. The man's head jerked violently back and dragged the body with it. The body lay still on the stones of the courtyard, a bloody mass where its head had been.

Zhou addressed the men in the courtyard. "General Fu is unhurt. Two assassins are dead, as well as their accomplice here. I want everyone stationed on the island tonight to know this. And no one else. Anyone who says so much as a word of tonight's events to anyone, wife or friend or whore, will receive the same punishment as this dog. I will personally deliver it. Captain Wang, see that everyone on the island understands this clearly. If anyone in the morning asks about the gunfire, inform them that a stray dog made some guards jittery, and they killed it." He turned and walked back into the pavilion and through Fu's office.

He knocked softly on Meilu's door.

"Zhou?" inquired an empty voice.

"Yes, sir."

He opened the door. Fu was sitting at the calligraphy table, facing the bed, his coat soaked with blood. Her body was laid on the bed. Fu had little more life in his eyes than she had in hers. He stared at her dumbly.

"General?"

A pause. "Yes, Zhou."

"May I move the body of the man out of here?"

A pause. "Yes."

"And her body?"

"No!" Fu shouted. He sunk deeper into the chair, drained by the effort of his answer. He breathed deeply. "It won't be long until dawn," he whispered in a cracked voice. "I'll sit with her until then. Then I'll have my calligraphy lesson. Then you can take her away." With this his shoulders began to shake, and he began to weep.

Zhou quietly turned the dead man over, stuffed his intestines back into his abdomen, and dragged him feet first into the hallway. He got a sheet from his own bed and swabbed up as much of the blood and tissue off the floor as he could. Then he left the room and closed the door.

Fu sat in the room, still weeping, but quietly now. The cold air coming through the broken window rustled the curtain. He looked at the blowing curtain, then slowly got up and walked to her clothes closet. He picked out the quilted blue silk robe embroidered with gold chrysanthemums and laid it over her body, then walked back to the table. He picked up a piece of paper from the table. It was his latest poem, the characters written by her that evening.

> "Twenty years of battling over the land,
> Hills and valleys darkened with the blood of colleagues.
> For what end? What does it mean?
> Crops are greenest at the site of major battles.
> Men are most alive when they fight desperately.
> But a precious jade has strengthened my eyes.
> I see life coursing strong on other battlefields now,
> And feel new leaves uncoiling in my own heart."

After staring at the paper for a few moments, he wearily leaned over and extinguished the lamp, then sank back into the chair in the dark, facing her.

D awn had not yet extinguished the stars in the western sky when Bei's phone rang. It was a moment before his mind surfaced, and several more by the time he pulled himself out of bed and stumbled through the dark to the desk in his study.

"What?"

"Bei?"

"Yes. Who's this?"

"Zhou Peifeng. We need you over here. Now."

"What's happened?"

"I'll let you know when you get here. And one other thing. Captain Li didn't go to Tientsin with Lin Piao. He's at Tungchow, observing the negotiations."

Bei's guts got that peculiar feeling again. "I'll be right there."

He put down the phone, switched on the light, and stared at the desk top, seeing nothing. The Baleful Star was sixteen kilometers east of the city. Perhaps in the city tonight. Perhaps—

He looked down at the bottom right drawer of his desk. Its brass lock gleamed in the light. An image of Li came to him—the hard hateful eyes—and made up his mind. He swiftly pushed the spring block to the hidden compartment, extracted the key, and unlocked the drawer. The pistol lay shiny in its shoulder holster. He picked it up, then reached deep in the drawer for the clip. Ten bullets. He extracted one of the bullets and threw it back in the drawer. Nine was the lucky number. He eased the pistol out of the holster and inserted the clip with a loud but clean snap. Should he put a bullet in the chamber? He decided against it, but did switch the safety off. Putting the weapon back in the holster, he carried them to his bedroom to dress.

Bei arrived at the Winter Palace just as the growing light was bringing the world into full view. Jade Flower Isle seemed quiet and peaceful in the cold morning. The guard took him to General Fu's pavilion, where Captain Wang met him and ushered him into Fu's office. Zhou was sitting in one of the chairs in front of the desk. Fu was nowhere in sight. The ashtrays on the desk were overflowing with cigarette butts.

"Bei. Thank you for coming so quickly."

"What's up, Zhou?"

"It is highly confidential, of course. There was an assassination attempt on Fu last night."

Bei drew in his breath sharply. "Attempt?"

"Yes. Fu was unhurt. His concubine was killed."

"And the assassins?"

"Both dead. They had an accomplice among the guards, who has also been killed."

"Who were they?"

"That is one reason you are here. Could you please view the bodies, and let us know if you recognize them?"

He led Bei down the hallway to the end of the pavilion, and out of the door. There, in a heap, were three bodies. One was uniformed, the guard. Zhou turned the other two bodies over.

Bei nodded. "That one is Chan, Yu Chenling's top man. The other is Te Wu also. I don't know his name. What's that sticking out of Chan's arm?"

"A jade hairpin, evidently hurled across the room by the concubine. She must have killed the other one also, but I don't know how."

Bei looked at Zhou disbelievingly.

"She was a woman of many skills," observed Zhou.

"You say she is dead also?"

"Yes."

"Where's the general?"

Zhou turned his head toward the back of the pavilion. "Atop the hill, in the upper reaches of the garden. He is in mourning. The concubine meant much to him."

"What will you do with the bodies?"

"Dump them in the lake. Except for the concubine. He told me to have you contact the Purple Mountain. Said he thought they might know of her."

"Ah." A woman of many skills. "May I see her body?"

Zhou shrugged. "Sure." He led Bei back into the hallway and into her room.

Bei walked toward the bed and suddenly jerked to a stop. It was the image of Meiling lying cold and unmoving underneath the blue silk robe. He looked closer. No, not Meiling. But so near her as to be her sister. Twin sister. No. Do not let it be her sister. It would be too much for her. And her father. Do not let it be her sister.

"What was her name?"

"Meilu."

He groaned. "Surname T'ang?"

"We never knew her surname."

Bei breathed in deeply, and let it out slowly.

"You think they would know of her at the Purple Mountain?" asked Zhou.

"Yes," Bei answered with resignation. "I am sure of it."

"Do you have someone you could send? We can provide a car."

"It would be best if I went."

"No. You must be here today."

"Why?"

"General Fu is . . . not functioning well this morning. And I must leave soon for Tungchow to resume the negotiations. We discussed it briefly this morning. You are the one to be here, to handle things. You already know as much as he and I do about the events taking place now. Are you armed?"

Bei reached into his coat and produced the 9mm pistol from the shoulder holster.

"Good. Do you know how to use it?"

"Yes." He replaced it in the holster.

"It will have to do. He doesn't have his deadly concubine to protect him anymore," said Zhou, glancing at the still form on the bed. "You are his last line of defense."

Bei flushed. "Do you expect another attack, then?"

"We do not. And we have taken, uh, measures to keep the perimeter guards on their utmost alert. But—" He shrugged. "Now listen. I imagine he will be down from the hilltop around noon, and if I know him, he will be fully functional then. In my absence, I am depending on you to be his confidential aide. Are you up to it?"

278

"Yes," Bei said, and immediately regretted it.

"Good. You could render no higher service to your city, Inspector. I must leave now. Come to his office with me."

Bei cast another look at Meiling's image on the bed, then followed Zhou down the hallway and into Fu's office.

"Set yourself up here. Captain Wang is in charge of things, under you, until Fu returns. You met him just now, on your way in."

Zhou reached into a desk drawer. "Here is a general pass, signed by Yeh Chienying. It is for the Tungchow negotiations, but give it to whomever you send through the countryside to the Purple Mountain." Zhou grinned as he handed it to Bei. "Presumably they won't be riding a bicycle and wearing the rags of a night-soil collector to permit them to blend into the populace in Communist territory." He took another piece of paper out of the desk. "And here is Fu's pass for getting in and out of the city itself. Wang will provide them with a limousine."

Bei shook his head. The one time a car was going to the Purple Mountain, and he would not be in it. His legs still ached from his last bicycle ride.

"Any questions?"

"Plenty. But I won't bother you with them."

Zhou laughed. "That's the spirit, Inspector. Good luck. I probably won't be back tonight. But send for me if anything . . . if anything major happens with the general."

Bei nodded. "The negotiations are going well?"

Zhou hesitated, then looked Bei full in the face. "They are going well. Very well."

"Good. Good-bye."

Zhou hurried out of the room.

Bei sat down in front of Fu's desk and reached for the phone. As he did so he glanced out the window. The garden. The T'aihu stone. Somewhere above there was Fu. What was he thinking? Or was he thinking at all? In mourning, Zhou had said, using the formal, Confucian term.

Bei dialed Yuan's number. Lufei answered.

"What?"

"Good morning, Lufei. This is Inspector Bei. Is Yuan still there?"

"Yes. Just a moment." A pause. "Oh, Inspector?"

"Yes?"

"I apologize for my weak behavior yesterday. I . . . I was feeling very bad."

"It's not important, Lufei. These are peculiar times. Are you keeping your door bolted?"

"Yes."

"Then no need to worry. And you are one of the few homes in Peking to have a telephone, thanks to Yuan's position. So you can call us if anything is bothering you."

"Yes. You're right. Here is Yuan."

A pause. "What?"

"Hello, Yuan. This is Bei. I want you to come straight to the Winter Palace this morning. I have a job for you."

"The Winter Palace?" Fright overwhelmed his voice. "But, Chief, listen, I have ten thousand things to do at the office," he began in a nervous, high-pitched voice.

"Forget the office," Bei snapped. "Be here in fifteen minutes. I'm in General Fu's office. The guards will be expecting you at Eternal Peace Bridge, coming onto the island." He slammed down the phone. "Wang," he yelled into the anteroom.

Captain Wang strode crisply into the room. "Yes, sir?"

"My aide, Yuan Jinli, will be appearing at the Eternal Peace Bridge soon. Please have him escorted here."

"Yes, sir."

Bei reached over for a piece of paper and began to draw a map to the Purple Mountain. After a minute he hesitated, then crumpled the paper. No. The Purple Mountain's location shouldn't be put on a piece of paper. He tossed the paper into the wastebasket, then thought better of it, as he noticed the blackened bits of burned paper in the bottom of the basket. He retrieved the paper, lit a match to it, and let the charred bits drop into the wastebasket. What a way to live—burning half the things you throw away. After the last ash had dropped, he took up a pen and piece of paper to write the note to Meiling and Master T'ang which Yuan would deliver. He paused, then dropped the pen, and slumped back in his chair. How to say it? After a minute he took up the pen again.

Abbot T'ang and Meiling: Meilu died last night, protecting her man. Her body is at his quarters.

It was strangely quiet and peaceful in Fu's office that morning. Bei had dispatched the quaking Yuan with directions to the Purple Mountain and the note for Meiling and her father. He had next phoned instructions for Chang and several of his other men at the Chunghai Lake offices, and made decisions on various minor matters that Captain Wang brought to him throughout the morning, usually asking and taking Wang's advice.

He was seated to the side of Fu's desk, feeling the first serious pangs of early afternoon hunger, when a shadow fell across the desk and he detected a movement outside the window. Before he realized it, he had drawn the pistol, chambered a round, and found himself in a crouch pointing the pistol out the window—straight at the staring figure of Fu Tsoyi. Fu looked impassively at him for several seconds, revealing not the slightest fear, then continued walking by the window. Bei sheepishly ejected the clip, then the round, put the round in his pocket, reinserted the clip, and holstered the pistol. In twenty minutes Fu emerged from the hallway and strode to his desk.

"You're very much on your guard today, Bei," he said in a flat voice. His face was devoid of all emotion or animation, and looked utterly weary, but he spoke and moved crisply.

Bei made no comment.

"You have contacted the Purple Mountain?"

"Yes. At least, I sent my aide there early this morning."

The phone rang in the anteroom. Captain Wang spoke a few words, then knocked on the door.

"Yes?" asked Fu.

"Inspector Bei's aide, sir, calling from the inspector's Chunghai Lake office."

Fu nodded at the phone on his desk. "Take it here, Bei."

Bei picked up the phone. "What?"

"Yuan, sir. I delivered the message."

"Meiling and Abbot T'ang are in Peking, then?"

"No. They refused to ride in the limousine. They hooked two

bicycles up to a cart, and took off immediately. Can they ever pedal! I imagine they aren't too far from the city by now."

"You gave them the pass from the general?"

"Yes."

"Thanks, Yuan. Anything else?"

"Just a lot of paperwork here at our office, Chief. Will you be in today?"

"I don't know. Good-bye."

He hung up the phone. "The Purple Mountain people should be here soon, General. They have bicycled in, and brought a cart."

"Didn't Zhou send a car?" Fu asked crossly.

"They, uh, they didn't care to use it, my aide says."

Fu sighed, and sat blankly for a few moments. Finally he roused himself. "Anything happening this morning?"

"Nothing important." Bei paused. "How did you know she was from the Purple Mountain, General?"

Fu didn't answer for a while. "I realized why she had been sent to me, very soon . . . very soon after she had died. As she died, in fact." Another silence, although he displayed no emotion outwardly. "She was obviously as skilled in the martial arts as in the arts of calligraphy and . . . other arts." Another silence, but briefer this time. "She had been sent to protect me. Which she did, fully, to the last. She saved my life. At the cost of her own.

"I knew that much, immediately. The only question was—who had this interest in saving my life? As I thought about her this morning, it struck me how similar she seemed to the murdered prior's concubine, according to what you'd told me about her. Taoist. Beautiful. Skilled. And deadly. It was too much of a coincidence. And the other is a Communist agent from the Purple Mountain. Therefore the possibility seemed quite strong that she too is—was—a Communist agent. From the Purple Mountain."

He paused. "She first came to me the night before the final battle for Kalgan. Nieh Jungchen and I had dueled for months. I immediately suspected that he, or his colleagues, had sent her. Over the years, as she benefited me more and more, in so many ways—" Here he nearly broke down, but mastered himself soon, and continued. "It seemed unlikely that the Communists would have sent her. But this morning, I finally figured the puzzle out."

He took a deep breath. "She was sent, after all, by the Communists. To protect me. The Communists saw, two years ago, that I would be their chief obstacle to the conquest of North China. And thus, to the conquest of China as a whole. They knew that I would be persuaded, by military reality and political necessity, to enter negotiations with them. And they also knew, two years ago, that when I began to talk reasonably and honestly with them, I would on that day be marked for death. Marked by the Te Wu."

He shook his head in wonder. "Two years ago, they knew who my deadliest enemies were. Knew my deadliest enemies were in my own camp, sat at my own conference table. Te Wu.

"That, Bei, reveals a firm grasp of history, and its lessons. They know how history works, my friend.

"So. They sent their best agent. To be with me at the times when I am most vulnerable to attack. To save me from the Te Wu, for the role they saw me playing, two years ago, at this point in history.

He stopped, shook his head, and turned in his seat to stare out the window.

"You think they will successfully sweep south?" Bei inquired.

"They have leashed themselves to history, Bei," Fu replied, still staring out the window. "I don't like their ideology. It is alien to my understanding of our tradition. All that is of no importance, however. History is theirs. They will rule China. And soon. Regardless of what I do here. I am but a ripple in history. The river will flow more smoothly if I act one way, but it will continue to flow, no matter what I do."

Bei reflected how tired Fu looked and sounded, outlined against the window. Not the vigorous leader Bei had come to know, but a man with nothing to live for.

"What will you do, sir, if they take over the country?"

Fu slowly swung back around to face Bei.

"Do?"

"With your life, General. Your career."

"My career?" Fu repeated hollowly. He stared emptily at Bei. "Why, I'll fly to Nanking when they take over the city, in the last plane leaving. Then . . . to Hong Kong. Probably to America, finally. I'll have a considerable fortune. I could be very . . . comfortable in

America. Li Tsungjen will go there, too. We've talked about it. New York, probably, or New Jersey."

Bei shook his head. "No."

"What?"

"No. You don't belong in New York or in New Jersey. You'd die there, inwardly. You belong to China. To North China. Using your brains and your energy to rebuild China."

Fu laughed hollowly. "You forget, my friend, that the Communists will rule North China very soon, and all of China not long after that, if I've guessed correctly."

"So what?" Bei retorted. "You're not a die-hard Kuomintang, not in Chiang's Whampoa clique. Not even in Li Tsungjen's Kwanghsi clique. You're an independent, really." As Bei spoke, he caught a glimpse of Fu in a role no one had imagined before. "Join the Communists' national government, General, when they unite the country. Be part of rebuilding China."

Fu stared fiercely at Bei, the words sinking in slowly. "Join them?"

"Yes. In fact, make it part of your price for peacefully relinquishing Peking to them. A post in their national government. A cabinet post."

Fu caught his breath, stared at Bei incredulously for a few moments, then leaped to his feet and began pacing the room in agitation. He stopped in the middle of the room, lost in thought, then slowly walked to the hallway and entered Meilu's room. He stared at her body for several minutes, then strode briskly back to his office and addressed Bei.

"You're right, my friend. It is clear to me. You're right. I owe my life to her. Therefore I owe it to those who sent her. I will give my life, my mind and energy, ransomed at so dear a price, to those who provided the ransom. I will help rebuild my China, for her. And for myself. For what was between us. What else could I ever have imagined doing?"

He spoke now in his most formal voice, with a hint of the strength and richness which Bei had come to know. "Bei Menjin, I want you to go to Tungchow for me tomorrow morning. Tell Yeh Chienying and Nieh Jungchen that I have added one demand to my position and will brook no compromise here: a cabinet post in the Communist government which will soon rule a united China. Will you convey that message for me, Bei?"

"Mc, sir?"

"Of course. It is your idea. Zhou is already there at the negotiations. I know of no one else other than you sufficiently competent to convey the demand. Tell me you'll go."

"Why, of course I will. Tomorrow morning?"

"Yes. Good. Very good." Fu pushed a button on his desk, and Captain Wang entered the room. "Yes, sir?"

"Lunch for two, Wang, Inspector Bei and myself. Here. As soon as possible. No—make it lunch for three." He looked at Bei, his eyes still flat, but with nearly a smile on his face. "My appetite is returning."

The lunch dishes had just been removed when Wang appeared. "The people from the Purple Mountain are here, sir."

Fu stood up, and Bei followed suit. "You have the pallet here?" asked Fu.

"Yes, sir," said Wang.

"Good. Show them in, then get the pallet." He turned to Bei. "Please make the introductions."

Wang returned, leading T'ang and Meiling. Their faces were impassive. Fu quickly glanced away when he saw Meiling, and took a deep breath to steady himself.

Bei spoke. "Master T'ang, Meiling. May I present General Fu Tsoyi. General Fu, this is Abbot T'ang and his daughter, T'ang Meiling."

Fu bowed, deeply and formally. T'ang and Meiling returned it.

"This way, please," Fu said, and walked to the hallway. They entered Meilu's room and looked at her lying on the bed. Fu had washed and arranged the body, dressing it in a white robe with golden carp flowing over it.

Tears began to stream down Meiling's face as she saw her sister, but she made no sound.

"May I ask how she died?" said T'ang quietly.

"I was sitting on the edge of her bed late last night, with my back to that door," began Fu, gesturing to the private door by the window. "She saw two assassins enter by the door. She killed one with the toothed jade piece on her necklace, and disabled the

285

other with her hairpin just as he fired the shot, meant for me, that killed her.''

T'ang nodded.

Fu sought for words in the silence that followed. ''It was an honor for me to have known your daughter, Abbot T'ang. The Tao coursed strongly through her.''

T'ang stared at Fu for a moment, then nodded proudly. ''What more could one say of a life?''

''Indeed,'' agreed Fu.

Wang and another guard entered carrying a pallet.

''We will carry the pallet, General,'' said T'ang. ''Will you place her body on it?''

Fu nodded, and walked up to the bed. He stared at her face for a moment, then lifted her body, turned around with it, and placed it tenderly on the pallet held at each end by T'ang and Meiling. Meiling was crying openly now.

''Thank you, General Fu. Good-bye,'' said T'ang.

''Good-bye,'' Fu said softly, looking at Meilu, with a catch in his voice. Wang covered the body with a heavy sheet, and they all walked out to the front of the pavilion.

''Wang,'' commanded Fu as the pallet headed down the path.

''Yes, sir?''

''Take your best three men, and escort the old man and the girl to the city gate. Be circumspect, but allow no one to approach them or speak to them. Leave now.''

''Yes, sir,'' Wang responded, and ran down a side path. Fu stood there, staring sadly at the path down which Meilu's body had disappeared.

January 15

As the limousine approached Chiang'kuomen Gate, Bei saw the mass of refugees waiting to be processed through. They had been there for hours, even though it was barely past dawn, possessions strewn about in bundles. The soldiers at the gate had attempted to maintain an open corridor for vehicles and the ubiquitous manure carts, but the refugees crowded into the space, making it impossibly narrow. His driver guided the limousine to the corridor, right behind one of the few manure carts pulled by a donkey rather than a man. The manure collector cursed and shoved the people ahead to widen the corridor as he tugged vigorously on the donkey, which was frightened and confused by the mass of people.

Bei's driver applied the brakes and slowed nearly to a halt. After a brief hesitation, he put his hand on the horn. The blast of sudden noise terrified all, including the donkey, which bolted not down the corridor, but straight into the crowd of refugees to the right, the contents of its full barrel sloshing out onto everyone. An uproar ensued, with cursing and shrieking all about as the man attempted to bring his frantic donkey under control. Bei's driver paid no attention to it, but guided the car past the cart and to the gate. Bei handed the pass to one of the guards, who briefly looked at it then waved them through. Looking back, Bei could see another guard in the process of beating the manure collector and his donkey as well as anyone else within reach, creating more disorder than he was quelling.

Although Tungchow was only sixteen kilometers away, the ride took nearly an hour, between the blinding glare of the sun straight in their eyes and the refugees and their possessions clogging the road. One of Nieh Jungchen's aides met Bei at the headquarters and escorted him to a waiting room. Several moments later Zhou hurried into the room.

"What is it?" he asked, a look of keen apprehension on his face.

"Nothing amiss. General Fu sent me with an addition to his proposals. A non-negotiable demand, in fact."

"A non-negotiable demand?" said Zhou, a hint of disbelief in his voice the only change in his customary composure.

"He wants a cabinet post in the Communist government."

Zhou stared at Bei, blinking several times. He sat down heavily, nearly missing the chair. "A cabinet post?" he repeated dully.

"Yes."

Zhou shook his head. "That is the most amazing man. He wants to not just turn the city over to the Communists. He wants to join the Communist side, to become a leading figure in their government?"

"Evidently," Bei answered. "He is convinced the Communists will soon rule all of China. A united China, a China without warlords or foreigners. United under one government that is actually governing, for the first time in nearly a hundred years. He wants to be part of that."

Zhou sat back. "Well, it is certainly possible, even likely, that the Communists will soon rule the whole country. Especially if they can assume control of Peking peacefully. But this is the first I've heard any inkling of Fu's wanting to be part of a Communist government, much less their national government. And I'm his closest confidant."

"It has much to do with his concubine," offered Bei. "To his mind, he owes his life to her, because of last night. He's convinced she was a Communist agent. Thus he owes his life to the Communists."

Zhou shook his head. "He is a strange man, in many ways. You are sure this is not just a, a passing thing?"

"I don't know. He seemed supremely sure of it yesterday, and this morning, when I talked to him briefly. The idea, in fact, seemed to breathe life into him, with his concubine dead."

Zhou shook his head. "Ling was right. She should have been dispatched long ago." He thought it all out, for over a minute. Then he slapped his knees and sat upright.

"Well. He is the commander of Peking, after all. He is Fu Tsoyi. We are not his equals, we are only his aides. One reason I have devoted my career to the man is that he is a man of vision. This particular vision eludes my understanding, and it certainly will complicate the negotiations. But he commands it, so we will execute it, and see what happens. You understand, of course, that it will not be possible for me to convey and argue for this point. I am too entrenched in various positions and compromises in the eyes of Yeh and Nieh for me to suddenly spring this on them. It's yours to announce and to argue for, Inspector."

"Mine? But I don't know a thing about the negotiations, or Fu's positions. It's . . . it's impossible."

"You won't have to handle everything, Inspector. I will still be there, after all, and General Teng. But as for this 'non-negotiable demand' from Fu—you've got to be the man to handle it. It would hopelessly compromise Teng or myself to do it. Now have a seat while I instruct you."

Fighting to control the panic that threatened to seize him, Bei sat down woodenly and directed his dazed attention at Zhou.

"You'll need to do two things. First, present the demand as if it were Fu doing a favor for the Communists, deigning to join them. Second, come up with a list of reasons why it is to their advantage to grant the demand."

"How long, uh, how long do I have to work on it?" asked Bei nervously.

"Approximately thirty seconds. That's how long it will take us to walk from here to the negotiation quarters. Come on."

They walked through two rooms and into a third. A long table ran the length of the room, covered with drafts and redrafts of proposals. Yeh and Nieh sat on one side, with Captain Li in a chair behind the table, against the wall. General Teng sat on the other side of the table, with Zhou's chair beside him.

"Gentlemen. I have new instructions from General Fu. May I introduce his envoy, Inspector Bei of the Peking Municipal Police. Commander Yeh Chienying, Commander Nieh Jungchen."

Yeh and Nieh stood and bowed.

"I have had the pleasure of working with Inspector Bei already," commented Yeh.

Nieh spoke up. "Inspector Bei, this is Captain Li, who is Lin Piao's observer to the talks."

Li did not stand, but glared at Bei.

"I am acquainted with Captain Li, in circumstances that do not bring credit to him," Bei said icily, anger now edging the fear that had gripped him.

Li sprang to his feet and stood trembling, evidently trying to decide whether to leap over the table or walk around it prior to throttling Bei.

"Gentlemen!" Yeh interrupted. "We are involved in negotiations. I must insist you maintain a civil atmosphere. Let us all be seated, while Inspector Bei conveys his tidings from General Fu."

"We were under the impression that all of General Fu's conditions had been made known to us," said Nieh, resuming his seat.

Zhou motioned Bei to a chair beside his and Teng's. As he sat, Bei realized that Zhou and Teng expected him to reply to Nieh's barb.

"Commander Nieh," Bei began, his confrontation with Li giving his voice a sharp edge suggesting more confidence and vigor than he inwardly felt. "You must appreciate that the situation changes by the hour both locally and nationally. And moreover, I assure you that this is no mere technicality to be added to the others. This, in fact, represents a major concession on General Fu's part, a significant strengthening of your side's national stature, for which we, of course, expect to be recompensed in other aspects of any agreement which results."

"Yes, yes," interrupted Yeh dryly. "Just what is this momentous development, Inspector Bei?"

"General Fu Tsoyi requests, indeed he insists, that he be given a cabinet post in your national government once you have united the country."

The reaction of Yeh and Nieh was a replay of Zhou's. Shocked silence, then rapid blinking as the mind struggled to cope with the idea.

At last Yeh spoke. "Indeed that is a major and unexpected development, Inspector. Although it sounds to me more like a plum you should pay us for, rather than our paying you. Do you realize there will likely be only a dozen or so cabinet posts in our national government? Why should we overlook our colleagues who have fought alongside us for decades and put a Nationalist in one of them?"

Bei spoke forcefully, with an appearance of absolute control, even though he was improvising as he went. "Because firstly, that is the price you must pay for the peaceful assumption of command in your capital city. Because secondly, it will significantly enhance your image as a government of all of China if you place a former Nationalist leader in your government." He jabbed his index finger on the table, a gesture he seemed to remember Zhou or Fu displaying. "Because thirdly, such a move will persuade many other Nationalist leaders that they may expect decent and honorable treatment from you, and thus greatly facilitate your conquest of the rest of the country. And because fourthly, Fu Tsoyi is inferior to none of you or your colleagues in intelligence, experience, and dedication to China's interests, and will make one of the best cabinet ministers in your government."

He sat back. "That is why we expect generosity from you regarding other points in the agreement."

Zhou marveled at Bei's impromptu *tour de force*. Yeh and Nieh remained silent for a moment. Bei concentrated on not trembling uncontrollably.

"Inspector Bei," began Yeh. "We do not deny that our granting General Fu one of our few cabinet seats will accrue to our advantage in certain ways. Yet the fact nonetheless remains: It is a prestigious appointment, which is ours to grant or withhold."

"And may I remind you, Commander Yeh, that General Fu does not request this; he has made the rest of the agreement contingent upon it," Bei promptly stated.

"Certainly the agreement as a whole then must reflect that we are granting this favor to General Fu—if indeed we grant it. Quite frankly, for such a proposal, we must have the opinion of Mao and Chou Enlai."

Zhou spoke up. "We understand that, of course. Might we not work out, today, an agreement which incorporates this new feature, for their consideration?"

"Of course," answered Nieh. "But I also feel we must reconsider the concessions we made to you this morning regarding the composition of the Joint Administrative Office and the evacuation south of Kuomintang officials after the signing of an agreement, if we are to provide General Fu a cabinet seat. Moreover, we will need further assurances that General Fu can guarantee the surrender of Tientsin in conjunction with the transition of power in Peking. How much control does he actually have over the Tientsin garrison commander?"

"Commander Nieh," answered General Teng. "General Fu's authority extends over the military establishment of both Tientsin and Peking. Just because he is located in Peking does not mean that Tientsin's officers are independent of any higher command authority."

The negotiations began again in earnest, each point being reworked in the light of Bei's presentation of Fu's new demand. Lunch was served in the conference room, and the discussion continued through it. Bei participated as an adjunct to Zhou, on a par with General Teng, admiring Zhou's performance, how he could back a position forcefully one moment, then suggest a compromise in it half an hour later that permitted the resolution of some other impasse. Soon Bei began to anticipate the compromises that Zhou would countenance, and suggest them himself, permitting Zhou to feign more reluctance to accept them and thus demand more in the next point to compensate. By turns gracious and yielding, then blunt and stubborn, Zhou slowly extracted more than Bei would have thought possible, although Yeh and Nieh were bargaining hard as well, and yielding concessions only after much show of reluctance themselves.

By midafternoon they were working on drafts of an agreement, arguing over this word or that. By late afternoon an overall draft was nearing completion, when a guard brought a sealed note in for Captain Li. Bei saw Li take the note in his left hand, transfer it to his right, absently reach down with his left hand and smoothly extract a large gleaming knife from his boot which he used to slit open the note. He returned the knife to his boot as he read the note.

"Gentlemen," Li announced. "I have news which will affect your work further." The other four joined Bei in looking at Li, although none with the peculiar look Bei had fixed upon him.

"Commander Lin Piao informs me that Tientsin fell to the Red Army late this morning. He himself will return to Chihsien tomorrow."

Yeh and Nieh smiled. "Another triumph for our intrepid Commander Lin," Yeh said with relish. "At this rate, we'll be in Nanking before we're finished here." He and Nieh chuckled.

"Gentlemen," said Zhou dryly. "May I remind you that the small matter of Peking is still far from resolved."

"Yes, yes," admitted Yeh. "Where is that draft about Tientsin? We shall now be able to omit it altogether." They resumed their work in earnest, hoping to finish before dinner.

Bei had only vaguely heard Li's announcement and the negotiators' comments upon it. He remained staring at Li's left boot, a thoughtful look on his face.

Zhou and General Teng were quietly exultant during the limousine ride back to Peking. They had worked hard for three days, and carried with them a draft agreement which might, with luck, mean the end of the war for them and Peking. Bei was subdued, though, and sat deep in thought the whole trip. It was dark when they passed through the huge walls of the city. Soon the car glided to a stop in front of the Eternal Peace Bridge in Beihai Park.

"Zhou, I'm bushed," said General Teng. "I'll leave it to you and the inspector to brief General Fu, if you don't mind."

"Your service has been outstanding, General," said Zhou. "You've done plenty already. I'll have the limousine take you to your quarters. Bei, you will, of course, report to General Fu with me."

"If you insist."

"I do." Zhou and Bei walked across the bridge and around the island to Fu's quarters, the guards along the way saluting them smartly.

Fu was sitting in his office, in the dark, when they arrived, his figure outlined against the window behind him. Captain Wang sat in the anteroom, with a lamp.

"Is he all right?" Zhou asked Wang softly.

"I think so. He just never bothered to turn on the light when it got dark, and I didn't feel I should disturb him."

Zhou nodded. "We'll be in conference for several hours or so. Have someone relieve you out here for the night."

"Right. I've got double guards posted throughout the island."

"Good. Thank you, Wang."

Zhou knocked and entered the office, Bei beside him.

"Good evening, General," he said in a cheerful voice. "Mind if I put a light on?"

Fu leaned over and switched on a lamp. "Don't bother. I was just resting."

Bei looked carefully at his face. The eyes still flat, but otherwise not too bad.

"So, gentlemen. How did it go?" inquired Fu.

Zhou put the draft agreement down on the desk. "Not every detail is tied down firm, sir. But the main points are there, the best we could get. Inspector Bei presented your new condition quite competently, and proved to be valuable in the ensuing negotiations as well."

"I am not surprised. But the draft: Is it acceptable?"

Zhou shrugged. "I think it is. You won't like some of it. They still want General Shih Chueh and General Li Wen turned over to them, for example."

"How about my cabinet post?"

"They have to check with Mao and Chou Enlai about that, sir. But the draft is predicated on that being acceptable. If it's not, we're back to the table again."

Fu picked up the draft and flipped its pages. "It just may be in here, gentlemen. The end of the war for us, Zhou. And for your city, Bei. And perhaps for the country. It's close, my friends."

Zhou grinned. "Hard to believe, General."

"Yes." Fu sighed deeply. "It's been a long time." Then he sat up, and turned on another lamp. "And because it's been a long time, we have to make sure it's right, and that we've squeezed all we can squeeze out of them," he said with determination, almost with enthusiasm.

Bei sighed with relief.

"I'll read this tonight, gentlemen. While you two are here, though, we need to review some things. Please be seated. One. The Te Wu."

Zhou and Bei sat down and struggled to shed their weariness and focus their minds. "Any sign from them today?" Zhou inquired.

"No. But since their agents haven't returned, and things are functioning here in the Winter Palace, they will have concluded that the assassination failed."

"And they'll also assume you know the identity of the men," said Bei.

"Yes."

"Captain Wang has put a double guard on the island, sir," Zhou reported.

"There may be rumors around the city about the assassination attempt," mused Bei thoughtfully. "You might consider arranging for several civic leaders to meet with you tomorrow, to demonstrate you're still alive and in control."

"Yes. Good idea, Inspector. Who should it be?"

"Perhaps we could make use of ex-mayor Ho Szuyuan's North China Peace Promotion Committee," answered Bei. "Yeh suggested they might visit him the day after tomorrow at Fragrant Hills Park, in fact, to lead into any transfer of power that may finally occur."

"Good. Please give Ho a ring tonight, then, Bei. Ask him to be here at nine o'clock tomorrow morning."

"Fine."

"Arrange also for someone from one of the workers' organizations to see me along with Ho. One of Ho's committee. The railway union, or postal workers."

"Yes, sir," Bei replied.

"That will persuade the city that you're well," interjected Zhou. "Do we want to persuade the Te Wu that you're strong?"

A silence fell over the room. Fu lit a cigarette and offered the case to the others. Zhou declined, but Bei took one and lit it.

"I've thought of that a lot today," Fu said softly. He leaned back and puffed on the cigarette. "They are doubtless expecting retaliation, and heaven knows a part of me wants to give it to them." He sat up.

"On the other hand, there are several disadvantages to retaliation. One, it may galvanize the right-wing commanders into an alliance around Yu Chenling, just when we are about to attempt to persuade them to acquiesce in a transition of power to the Communists. Two, to justify it we would have to reveal their attempt on my life, which inevitably reduces my aura of power. Three, it makes us look like a quarreling, divided command, just when it is important we present a strong, united front to the Communists for the final phase of negotiations. Lastly, if this had been an attempt on someone else's life, I could move to punish Yu with impunity, my cause being disinterested justice. But since the attempt was on my life, any punitive action by me is bound to be tainted with the appearance of selfish revenge, reducing the action to a sordid power struggle, regardless of who started it."

He looked at Zhou and Bei. "Disagreements?"

"If we weren't in the midst of negotiations with the Communists, I would think you should do it, to reassert your authority over the Te Wu," Zhou offered. "But, in fact, we are in negotiations, and at the final, delicate stages. Things are looking reasonably hopeful. Retaliation could only complicate the picture, at best, and might lead to a drastic reduction in their perception of the strength of our position. So, I agree with you. Best to sit tight, but be alert."

"Bei?"

"I suppose I agree."

"Good. Did you gentlemen hear of Mao Tsetung's radio broadcast today?"

"No."

"He rejected Chiang's New Year's peace offensive. Flatly. Laid down uncompromising conditions of his own. Far more strict than we have in here." He ran his thumb over the pages of the draft.

"So what does that mean?" asked Bei.

Fu shrugged. "Good and bad. I was frankly hoping, against reason, that the peace offensive would lead to something. I dislike the idea of making a separate peace with the Communists." He got up and began to pace the room.

"Part of me knows it is inevitable. They are strong, and getting stronger daily. We are weak, even in the south, and getting weaker daily. Like it or not, they have the popular will on their side, especially in the countryside. Even the intellectuals are sick of the Kuomintang's incompetence and corruption." He stood still. "It's a lost cause, gentlemen. The whole thing will collapse soon, just deflate. I know this."

He resumed his pacing. "On the other hand, another part of me rebels at the thought of deserting the Nationalist cause. Deserting, gentlemen. Making a separate peace while others are holding firm."

"They are corrupt men holding firm in a lost cause, General," Bei offered.

"Yes. But they are holding firm. I just don't like making a separate peace while others hold firm, regardless. In the first place. In the second place, this draft will be a lot easier to sell to the right-wing generals Shih Chueh and Li Wen—and Yu Chenling—if it is part of an overall peace movement that Nanking is involved in also."

Zhou nodded.

"So I was hoping that Mao would accept Chiang's New Year's peace offensive—at least start some talks on the national level. It would make a transition government here in Peking a lot more palatable, to me and to the right-wingers we have to contend with here."

"But didn't you tell me Chiang might resign?" asked Zhou.

"Yes. That is our second—and last—hope now to ease this draft through. If Chiang resigns, my duty to him is released. Li Tsungjen becomes acting president, and Li will approve our separate peace. No problems. It would be enough to persuade Shih Chueh and Li Wen, I think. And if they are persuaded, Yu Chenling won't be able to block it by himself."

"And if Chiang doesn't resign, and soon?"

Fu shook his head. "We'll have a difficult time getting Shih Chueh and Li Wen to accept it. Not to mention Yu Chenling. Which means, at best, we will have to make separate deals with them to sweeten it. At worst, they'll not be mollified, and we may have to persuade them by force of arms—fighting in the streets." He paused. "I don't know if I would want to do that, gentlemen."

Fu resumed his seat. "So we've got to make the agreement as generous to us as possible," he said decisively. "To make it as palatable as possible to Shih Chueh and Li Wen. If we convince them to acquiesce, we needn't worry about Yu Chenling."

"Much could still happen," commented Bei.

"Yes. Much can always happen, Inspector. I am in close communication with Li Tsungjen in Nanking. If Chiang resigns soon, our course is relatively easy. If he does not—our course may be difficult, or it may be bloody. Or impossible."

Zhou sat glumly. "Did you hear about Tientsin?"

"Yes. By telegraph, just as it fell. It is nothing, compared to what we've been discussing. It may even help, if it persuades Shih Chueh and Li Wen that an accommodation is inevitable."

He picked up the draft and began to read it.

Bei said quietly, "And you? How are you, Fu Tsoyi?"

Fu looked up, surprised, and stared at Bei. He looked far older, and sadder. The T'aihu in the garden loomed darkly beyond the window. He answered in a soft voice. "I shall never again be as happy as I was with her. But the Tao flows on, Bei."

Zhou and Bei nodded, rose, and wearily trudged out of the office.

Bei sat in his easy chair, a cold pot of tea on the side table. Under his heavy coat he felt the weight of the pistol in its shoulder holster. Sleep was impossible. Every time Bei closed his eyes the image of the Baleful Star reaching his left hand to the knife in his boot flashed before him. So he sat armed and bundled in the study in the dark, dozing fitfully. Images stumbled through his agitated mind. Spilled tea forming dark pools in the ice crevices. Heads attached to shapely bodies at odd angles. The fat monk cringing in the hallway. The knife slipping easily out of the boot. He jerked up in the chair, and found himself staring at the three war axes on the wall. Their sharp edges gleamed dully in the dark. Why hadn't he heard from his wife? He had written twice. Perhaps the few planes coming into the mortared airfields weren't bringing mail anymore. He drifted off again. *The Baleful Star. Two dancing female Phoenix birds. Dark pools. Like his eyes were far away, looking through his body at you.*

January 16

Bei ignored the pile of paperwork he had shoved to one corner of his desk in the Chunghai Lake office. His attention was fixed on a piece of paper before him. Down the left margin he had written the dates and sites of the four courtesan murders. The right part of the sheet was blank. He picked up a pen and made a note to the right of the first murder, indicating he had seen the Baleful Star in Peking on that date. He made another such note opposite the fourth murder.

Two dates unaccounted for. The second and third murders. He dialed Fu's private number.

"What?"

"Zhou? Bei here."

"What's up?"

"I need to know the dates that Captain Li has been in Peking to see you or Fu."

"Whatever for?"

"Too complicated. Can you get them for me?"

"Sure. Hold on while I check the general's appointment calendar." Several minutes passed.

"All right. This is highly confidential, you understand. I saw him to arrange an early negotiating session on January third. Then he was here January ninth to get Fu's reaction to those negotiations. And, of course, you saw him here January eleventh with the fat monk."

"Right. Thanks, Zhou."

He hung up the phone and looked at the paper. Next to the date of the second murder he wrote a note indicating Captain Li had been in Peking on that day. Next to the date of the fourth murder he added a similar note, under the existing entry regarding the Baleful Star.

Then he added the date January 11 at the left margin, and wrote a note beside it also.

He sat back and stared at the paper. One murder still unaccounted for, the third one. From his desk drawer he took his daily log and leafed through it, looking for the dates of his meetings with Lufei when she had told him about meeting her brother on the streets of Peking. He found what he was looking for, nodded solemnly, and wrote beside the third murder that Lufei's brother was seen by her in Peking that day. He did the same under the January 11 entry. At the very bottom of the paper he wrote "January 15," and after it a comment.

He sighed and leaned back again, his eyes fixed on the paper before him, not wanting to believe what he saw.

December 27, LAO SOOCHOW MURDER	*Baleful Star* seen by Bei, White Cloud Temple, meeting fat monk.
January 3, P'ING K'ANGLI MURDER	*Captain Li* meets Zhou in Peking.
January 5, HUAMEI MURDER	*Lufei's brother* seen by her on Peking street.
January 9, CH'INHUAI MURDER	*Baleful Star* seen by Bei, again White Cloud Temple, observing him. *Captain Li* meets Fu in Winter Palace.
January 11	*Captain Li* in Fu's office. *Lufei's brother* speaks with Lufei. Threatens to slit a throat.
January 15	At Tungchow, Bei observes *Captain Li* extract knife left-handed from boot.

All circumstantial. But too coincidental to be ignored. Too much interlocking of identities. Too much tangling of names and horrors to be happenstance. He picked up the pen and wrote in large characters across the middle of the sheet. "Baleful Star = Captain Li = " He paused, then completed the line with his hunch, muttering "Heaven help us if it is true," as he did so: "= Lufei's brother? = courtesan murderer?"

He stared at the incredible equation for a minute, a distinct chill rising along his spine. Then he picked up the phone and dialed.

"What?" answered a timid voice.

"This is Bei, Lufei. I need to talk to you, now. Can you meet me at your skating place, south shore of Beihai Park?"

A pause. "Yes. Now?"

"In ten minutes. See you there."

He hung up the phone, put on his heavy coat, and walked outside, glancing at the small pavilion standing in Chunghai Lake. Something about a wind. Spring wind? No. Autumn wind? Maybe. He hurried out the gate fronting on Beich'ang Street and walked north up the street. Walking in the cold air helped, seemed to dispel the mists of horror that pushed in on him, the images of the dead twins that had been seeping into his mind at unguarded moments recently. He noticed the sweet potato vendor and stopped to buy a hot one for Lufei. In another ten minutes he had reached Wenchin Street and soon walked into Beihai Park. He saw her frail figure huddled on a bench, looking out onto the water and beyond that the Jade Flower Isle.

"Hello."

She jumped in fright, in spite of his saying it gently.

"Have a sweet potato."

She stared at it in surprise, then managed a small smile as she remembered the last time he had bought her one. Or had she bought it for him?

"How are you feeling?"

She shrugged, then began to munch on the sweet potato.

"I have some questions to ask you, Lufei. They won't make you feel any better. Just a few, though. About your brother."

She stopped eating. "You believe me, then?"

He rubbed her hair. "Of course I do. And I think you are being very brave about it."

She resumed her gnawing of the food. "What do you want to know?"

"Little things. Like, was he fond of flowers?"

She looked at him, puzzled. "Fond of flowers? Of course not. Now, my sister was fond of flowers." She laughed, a small weak laugh, but one, nonetheless. "She used to meet her boyfriends behind a huge flowering bush not far from our home. My, what went on under that bush!" She smiled enviously at the thought. "Said she loved to meet men there because of the smell. It was a gardenia bush."

Bei nodded.

She finished the sweet potato and licked her fingers. Bei stared at them, so slender and quick. He wished he had desire for her, that he might bring some pleasure into her life.

"You were close to your sister, weren't you?"

"Oh, not as close as most people assumed we would be."

"Since you were twins, you mean," said Bei.

"Yes," she answered, still licking her fingers. "Oh. How did you know we were twins?"

Bei shrugged. "Just a guess. One more thing. You mentioned earlier that there were rumors that someone, perhaps your brother, was seen around the landlord's compound the night your sister died. Perhaps he could have seen it happen. Do you know anything about how she died?"

Lufei looked at him, puzzlement mixed with fright. "Why do you want to know all this?"

"No matter. I do."

She looked out over the ice. A few skaters sailed by. Jade Flower Isle loomed across the water, the bare branches of the willows along its shore drooping nearly to the ice.

"We don't know anything for sure. But the story was that the landlord's son invited a few of his friends over for a party, mainly soldiers. Kuomintang soldiers, of course. He invited them to enjoy my sister. They . . . they were taking turns with her, and playing awful games. Soldiers are coarse. My sister tired of the game—although such games were nothing new for her. One of the soldiers had brought along his bayonet, and threatened her with it to make her continue. She struggled. And . . ." Here she closed her eyes tight and began to cry.

Bei finished for her. "And the bayonet accidentally . . . slit her throat?"

She nodded silently, eyes still shut tight.

Bei sighed and leaned back on the bench. Behind the branches of a willow he could see the roofline of the Imperial View Pavilion curving elegantly upward on Jade Flower Isle. The delight he took in that curve and in the slender columns upon which the roof rested seemed pale and insubstantial next to Lufei's pitiful tale of her sister. And what he now knew it had done to her brother.

Lufei was quietly weeping next to him, and he put his arm around her and pulled her against him. She sighed and nestled into him. He ran his fingers through her hair as a father would a child's. She misinterpreted his caress, and snuggled closer with a groan.

"Oh, Bei. I need you, too. I dream of running my fingers over you, also."

Bei removed his hand and tried to sit upright, but she didn't notice. "I'll come to you tonight," she declared.

"No," he protested, but his heart melted when she lifted her tear-stained face to him. "I mean, I won't be there. I have a dinner engagement with Ho Szuyuan. I'll be out late."

"Tomorrow night, then."

"Uh, Lufei, why don't you take comfort with Yuan. He's a fine man."

She pouted. "A fine old man. I have. But . . . there's no joy in it between Yuan and me. It's an obligation for him. It . . . it has to be urgent. Like between you and me."

Bei squirmed uncomfortably on the bench.

"I know!" she said in a happy voice. "Yuan plays Mah-Jongg on Tuesday nights with friends. Day after tomorrow. I'll come then. He stays out late and won't even know I've been out."

"But, Lufei," Bei began.

"You surely don't have another dinner party on Tuesday night."

"No, I . . . I suppose not. But my schedule is so full these days. I'm, uh, I'm doing a great deal of work for General Fu. He calls me all hours. I have to keep my schedule flexible. Let's, let's make it tentative, all right? I'll let you know."

She pouted again. Bei mistook it for acquiescence.

"In fact, I have to get back to the office. All this work for the general has left me no time for my own work. I have huge piles of reports and correspondence to catch up with. Really. You should see my desk."

He stood up. "Can you get back home by yourself?"

She glumly nodded her head.

"Lufei. Keep the bar on your door. I'm convinced your brother is . . . in the vicinity. And he's not well, he's unbalanced. He's dangerous. So keep inside, and the door barred."

She nodded resentfully. "But I'll be coming out. I can't stay in a cage like an animal."

"Well, no more than you have to. Good-bye."

He turned and walked away. Soon Lufei's brother had pushed her out of his mind. The dried gardenias, the twins, the slit throats. His cold, distant eyes. A Baleful Star, sent to do us harm. The aide of Lin Piao, whose armies surround the city. He shivered, and walked faster.

The afternoon was a disaster. Bei had desultorily dipped into the stack of papers, unable to concentrate. He had no real proof that Li was the courtesan murderer, only a series of coincidental dates and details. It wasn't enough to bring before Fu or the magistrate. What could they do, anyway? He was the right hand of Lin Piao, who commanded most of the armies strangling the city. And he certainly couldn't pay a special visit to Yeh Chienying to babble about his fears of Baleful Stars and deranged brothers.

No. All he could do was wait for the meeting between Mao, Chou Enlai, and Lin Piao promised by Yeh Chienying at the Purple Mountain. That was his only hope. Assuming he could protect himself from the Baleful Star until then. He hated the cold weight of the pistol under his shoulder. But he kept it there constantly.

He sent Yuan home early, and soon shoved his stack of paperwork aside and left the office himself. The glint of the afternoon sun's last feeble rays on the roof tiles of the old pavilion in Chunghai Lake caught his eye. He paused and drank in the sight of the pavilion, rising above the icy surface of the lake some six meters beyond the shore and the willows there. The pavilion's twelve columns rose gracefully from its broad circular base, and both layers of the curved roof seemed to float atop the columns rather than rest upon them. The structure's grace and elegance calmed his agitated mind as he pondered it, and he wondered again what the Taoist inscription was on its tablet, looming darkly under the roof. The tablet seemed to pull him, and before he was consciously aware of it Bei had moved to a nearby point where the bank sloped gently to the surface of the lake, and gingerly stepped onto the ice. Shuffling slowly, he covered the six meters, tested one of the columns and found it solid, and pulled himself onto the platform.

Bei hesitantly walked up to the tablet and rubbed his sleeve up and down it several times to better read the four characters inscribed there many centuries before. They gleamed dully in the dusk before him, and he caught his breath and staggered back in shock as he read their message. The balustrade seat ringing the pavilion stopped his surprised retreat, and he sat heavily onto it, eyes still held by the old inscription. A wind rushed over the ice, lifting up small drifts of snow, dead leaves, and seeds from the willows surrounding the lake. Bei sat small and alone in the circular pavilion, wondering, strangely exhilarated, feeling as if he were looking down at his beloved city from a far distance.

Bei was the first to arrive at Ho's mansion for the dinner party that evening. He walked from his own home, since Ho lived on the northwestern edge of the Wangfuching district, not far from Bei. Professor Chang and his wife arrived soon after Bei.

The meal prepared by Madame Ho was sumptuous, although it lacked pork, and merry. Ho had received General Fu's request that day to convene his North China People's Peace Promotion Committee to confer with Yeh Chienying and his Communist high command the next day in Fragrant Hills Park. He was on this account ebullient at the prospect of peace for the city, and his own role in the process. Ho chattered happily throughout the meal, jumping up frequently to heap spoonfuls of the various dishes onto his guests' plates, over their mild remonstrances that they were truly stuffed. He served a white wine from France with the meal, which he had been saving for a decade for the right occasion. Even Madame Ho and Madame Chang were aglow with the wine and the festivity of the occasion.

Finally all had truly had their fill of wine and food, and Ho clapped his hands for attention. "So. Now for the entertainment." He turned to a servant. "Tell the children they may come." He turned back to the party. "Let us all retire to the study for the entertainment."

A strong red tea was served in the study. Ho's children came rushing in, delighted to be part of the party, and to see the Changs and Bei again. Finally the oldest children staged an original play depicting a scene from *The Three Kingdoms,* an historical romance set in the third century A.D. The scene was perhaps overly long, but roundly applauded by the guests. Then it was Bright Jade's turn. She stepped shyly to the front of the study, a lovely picture in her pigtails and bangs. Although not yet six, she seemed to have grown quite a bit in the six months since Bei had last seen her. He could readily understand why Ho doted on her. Her shyness disappeared as she lifted the little violin to her shoulder, and she bowed a respectable étude, with a delicate melody. The applause was especially warm, and she ran onto her father's lap and permitted a decorous hug from him.

"Well done, Bright Jade! Well done, all of you. Now. It's already late. Off to bed," commanded Ho. He pointed a finger severely at Bright Jade. "Your *own* bed, little one." She grinned back mischievously. The children, of course, ignored Ho's command as long as they could, but soon the guests were left alone again in the study. Madame Ho and Madame Chang withdrew to another room for their own conversation, leaving the three friends in the study.

"Mayor, it's been a remarkable evening," said Bei. "I've enjoyed it immensely."

Ho smiled. "You have seemed a bit more . . . outgoing than usual tonight, Bei. Things must be going well at work for you."

Bei smiled. "Quite the opposite, actually. That's why I've been so determined to enjoy myself here, which has been easy to do, thanks to our excellent host and the sparkling entertainment he arranged."

Ho poured himself another cup of tea, and refilled his guests' cups as well. "It is easy to be hopeful and happy tonight. The prospects for peace have not looked better for our city for years."

"I devoutly hope you are right," said Chang.

"And I," added Bei. "We could all use happier and easier days ahead."

Chang shook his head. "Indeed it has not been an easy time to live. The warlords fighting amongst themselves the first several decades of the century, even before the Ch'ing Dynasty fell. Then the Nationalists fighting the warlords in the twenties, the Communists and Nationalists fighting in the thirties. We thought it could not get worse, then the war with the Japanese in the late thirties and forties. And now the Communists and Nationalists again." He shook his head sadly at the dreary recital. "We have not known peace, nor a united country in our lifetimes, my friends. It seems almost unreal, too much to hope for."

"I know," agreed Ho. "And yet, we have survived. You especially, Chang, have made full use of your talents. How long ago was it that you leaped into prominence in the science-philosophy debates?"

Several hours later, the three were still discussing Chang's varied life as a newspaper and journal editor, proponent of the study of Western philosophy, and active advocate of constitutional government. There was hardly a prominent figure in China's intellectual life of the last five decades about which the peppery old man could not tell an amusing, or at times, salty story.

It was nearly midnight when Chang finally ran out of steam. There had been much laughter among them. "That's it, Mayor, Inspector," he sighed, slumped back in his chair. "I'm out of stories. Time to get myself to bed."

"You're staying the night with Professor Chou Pinglin at Peking University?" inquired Ho.

"Yes. Since Madame Chang does not bore Madame Ho with lengthy tales as I do you, she is doubtless already there, and I must join her."

"You've had a fascinating career, Professor," said Bei thoughtfully.

"Yes," admitted Chang. "And tomorrow Ho goes to talk to Yeh Chienying, and what that son of a Hakka merchant thinks will count for more than everything I've ever thought."

They laughed. "You're tired, Chang. Here, let me help you out."

"I'll get a ricksha for you," said Bei.

"No, no. Peking University is not five or six blocks away. I'll walk."

"Very well." Ho escorted Bei and Chang to the front gate and bade them a good night. The cold night air woke both of them up, and Chang briskly headed north while Bei headed south. As Bei turned the corner of Ho's compound, he noticed a man leaning against the wall across the street, who promptly looked down and pulled his hat over his eyes. The man looked vaguely familiar, but Bei could not place him, and he hurried on to his house, some fifteen minutes away.

Bei's sleep was fitful. He sat again in the study, his pistol under his shoulder. His awareness of his personal danger from the Baleful Star was diminished somewhat by his exhaustion and the stimulating evening, yet faces still floated across his mind. Something was bothering him, something to be remembered, but he couldn't pinpoint it. He set the feeling aside as merely another aspect of his anxiety about the Baleful Star. The Baleful Star. The fat monk, consuming bowl after bowl of noodles as he and Yuan watched the Te Wu. The gateman in the gatehouse across from Yu Chenling's compound.

Bei jerked straight upright in the chair. That was where he had seen the man on the street corner at Ho's house. One of the Te Wu agents who had left Yu Chenling's compound while Bei had arranged for Yuan and the fat monk to use the gatehouse. A Te Wu agent at Ho Szuyuan's house, past midnight? The night before Ho was to lead a peace committee to talk with Yeh Chienying. Bei stood up unsteadily and looked at the clock. Nearly three o'clock. Heaven above, let him be wrong. Call Zhou Peifeng? What if it was nothing? He stood irresolutely for a second, then bolted for the door, ran down the corridor, and opened the front gate. He took off up the street towards Ho's house at a dead run. It was bitterly cold, yet he was sweating profusely after only three blocks, and slowed his pace somewhat. He turned a corner; over halfway there. The walls on one side of the street cast black chunks of shadows into the streets illuminated by the soft light of the full moon.

Ahead, where Ho's home was, a quick flash of light lit the street, followed soon by a deafening roar. Bei stopped, cried aloud in anguish, and took off again, faster than before. A second explosion shook the street just before Bei arrived at the house. The windows in the back of the house were blown out, and wailing noises could be heard from inside. Bei pounded on the front door frantically, but no one came. Somehow he scaled the side wall of the compound, dropped heavily into the courtyard, and made his way into the bedroom area. Smoke filled the rooms, and servants were dashing around in every direction. Bei made his way to where he thought Ho's bedroom was. A loud wailing issued from the room. He dashed in and jerked suddenly to a halt.

The bomb had destroyed the room, ripping out large chunks of wall as well as the window. Through the smoke he could see Madame Ho sitting on the floor in a corner, bleeding from her head and legs. The wailing came from her, as she looked with horror at the opposite corner of the room. Ho was there, kneeling before a small crumpled shape in the corner. Bei rushed up to him.

"Are you all right, Mayor?"

Ho didn't answer, didn't hear him. Bei noted with relief that he had only several small wounds on his face, bleeding but not heavily. Then he noted Ho's fixed stare into the corner. The crumpled shape resolved itself before his eyes. Slender arms, dainty fingers, many missing. Two small legs, bent at horrible angles. A lovely head, the back half flattened. Bright Jade, lying like a limp doll in the corner. Perfectly still. Perfectly still.

Ho leaned forward and picked his daughter up gently. He stood, staring down at her in his arms, his eyes blank, refusing to comprehend.

Bei staggered back, then walked over to Madame Chang. Many cuts, some bad bruises, and in shock. But no life-threatening wounds. He turned and stared at Ho's still figure holding Bright Jade, then strode quickly out of the room. He walked to the hallway and dialed Fu's private number on the phone.

"What?"

"Zhou. It's Bei. Listen carefully. The Te Wu just bombed Mayor Ho's home. Get a couple of ambulances here, from the Peking Union Medical School Hospital—they're the best."

"Is Ho all right?"

"Yes. But his daughter's dead, and his wife is badly hurt."

"You'll be there until the ambulances arrive?"

"No. I'm leaving."

"Where to?"

Bei hung up the phone without answering, unbolted the front door, and walked into the street. He turned left, and began to walk quickly and purposefully. After a block he pulled the pistol from its shoulder holster as he walked, took out the clip, and found the bullet in his pocket he had chambered then ejected in Fu's office when Fu had surprised him at the window. He pushed it into the clip. A full nine now. He snapped the clip into the handle, chambered a round, and checked to make sure the safety was off. Gun in hand, he strode down the street.

In ten minutes he was just a block from Yu Chenling's compound. Turning a corner, he saw the six heavily armed guards at the entrance. He stepped back and turned up an alley. The location of the back entrance, which he had found when reconnoitering an observation spot for Yuan and the fat monk, was clear in his mind. Everything was clear and focused. The night. The sharp air. The smells of the alleyway. The image of Ho standing in the corner, Bright Jade's limp body in his arms. Her standing erect and determined with the violin under her chin. Meilu's body on the bed, and the white robe with orange carp. Fu staring at him impassively through the window, utterly beyond caring that a pistol was aimed at his head.

The door from the alley into Yu's compound was locked, as he had expected it to be. And unguarded, which he had also expected. He quietly pulled a crate over against the wall, put his pistol in its holster with the safety on, and climbed atop the crate. He could barely reach the top of the wall. He jumped, grabbed the top, and clumsily pulled himself up. He lay still on the black tiles. No guard below. Just a pile of debris, some shrubs, and beyond that another wall with an open moon gate. He dropped to the ground, landing in a crouch. Creeping to the next wall, he took the pistol out and slipped the safety off again. Cautiously he peeked around the edge of the moon gate. A large enclosure, walled on all sides. Another gate on the far side, with six or so more soldiers at it, but outside the enclosure. To his left, against the wall behind which he stood, was a small building, brightly lit. That would be it. He glanced around the enclosure. Another gate, small and closed, beyond the building. As he looked, a man walked out of the building and toward this gate. Bei peered desperately through the night. No. Not Yu, thank heaven. When the man had passed through the gate and closed it behind him, Bei took one final look around the enclosure, breathed in deeply, and silently dashed through the moon gate and to the building. He peered in through a window. Yu Chenling sat alone at a desk, studying a piece of paper. Bei looked around the enclosure again, then walked in front of the building and through the open door. As he closed it behind him, Yu glanced up.

"What? Inspector! What in the world—" He saw Bei raise the pistol at him.

"Good morning, General Yu. You've had a busy night." Yu looked frantically out the window, and began to rise.

"Don't move," Bei commanded, extending the pistol at arm's length. "Or even think of calling for help."

Yu sat down, staring at the pistol. He opened his mouth and spoke with authority. "What right do you have to enter my office, unannounced, Inspector? And point a pistol at me. I will have you severely punished for the outrageous breach of law, Inspector."

Bei laughed. "Dead men have difficulty dealing out punishment, Yu."

A hint of alarm began to creep back into Yu's eyes, and he glanced anxiously out the window.

"What in the world do you mean?"

"I mean you are going to die, General. Now. For the murders of T'ang Meilu and Mayor Ho's daughter Bright Jade."

"You are insane. You don't know what you are talking about."

"I am talking about the Te Wu's two latest victims, General. Their last two under your direction."

Bei was surprised at how calm he was, and how absolutely clear and right what he was about to do seemed to him. He had not the slightest thought of risk or consequences. He took a step forward, to make sure he hit the man, and began to squeeze the trigger. As he did so, a loud rattle of automatic weapons' fire crackled outside, and Bei involuntarily looked toward the window. Yu stood up and fumbled at a drawer.

"Don't move!" yelled Bei, and then he retreated against the wall as the bursts of gunfire continued outside. He extended his pistol full length in front of him again and trained it straight upon the standing Yu's frightened eyes, as he leaned back against the wall.

The firing outside was louder now, and there was more of it. A spray of machine-gun fire shattered the window, the rounds hitting the wall to Yu's left with a violent thud. Yu jumped, and began to tremble. Bei himself was trembling. He had absolutely no idea what was happening. Several rounds hit the outside of the wall against which he leaned, their distinct thuds jarring his body. Sudden silence. Then the sound of several men running toward the building. Bei looked down the barrel of his pistol at Yu's eyes. If it was Yu's men, he would kill Yu first, then take as many of them as he could.

The door shattered open and three men burst into the room in a crouch, pistols extended. Fu. Zhou. Wang. They froze as they saw Yu cowering unarmed against the wall, then followed Yu's eyes to Bei, bracing himself against the opposite wall with his own pistol trained on Yu.

No one spoke for several seconds. Fu glanced swiftly around the rest of the room. Empty.

"Wang. Check the cubicle there, then post yourself outside the door. Watch that small gate against the wall, especially. Send the rest of our men through there when they've completely secured the outer courtyard and this one."

Wang left, and Fu shut what was left of the door.

"Inspector Bei. You are indeed full of surprises."

Bei lowered his pistol with trembling hands. He was unable to speak.

Yu slowly moved back toward the desk and reached for the drawer again.

"Sorry, General Yu," said Fu, raising his pistol. "Zhou, get the pistol out of that drawer."

Zhou moved forward, and tossed the pistol into a far corner.

"Now have a seat, General Yu, while we decide your fate. I seem to have interrupted your execution."

Yu fell into the chair and pointed at Bei with a jerky motion. "You did indeed," he said in a hoarse voice, stumbling over the words. "Have this man arrested."

Fu laughed, and stared coldly at Yu. "Yu Chenling, you are a dead man. You have killed your last innocent person tonight."

Yu's eyes bulged, and he tried to protest, but no sound came forth.

Fu continued. "Indeed, your methods are so coarse, and your men so incompetent, that you seem to specialize in the killing of bystanders. And women. Young women and little girls." For a second an intense hatred flared up in Fu's eyes, but was just as quickly replaced with the professionalism of a soldier.

Yu regained his voice. "In war, General, many are killed. And this is war, between the forces of civilization and those of chaos."

"It is not clear to me which side you are on, General Yu," interjected Bei in a strange voice.

As Yu began to argue, Fu cut him off with a roar. "Silence! We are not here to bandy words with you. You are dead, Yu Chenling. All that is left to decide is your manner of death."

Fu turned to Bei. "I regret that I arrived when I did. I would have preferred that you killed him, for my own selfish purposes. But here we are, and I think that a simple execution is no longer tenable. There are too many of us here now.

"Actually, Yu, I would not be here if it were not for your clumsy attempt on Mayor Ho's life," Fu continued. "So long as you only attempted my own assassination, my hands were tied. But now—now I can charge you with a crime against a third party, and a very respected one at that. Ho is well thought of in Nanking, and has many influential friends there. And here, even Generals Shih Chueh and Li Wen think highly of Ho. They will not come to your rescue. Indeed, they will probably be as appalled as we all are."

"Fu," Bei interrupted, surprising them all with the blunt address. "I want no trial, no possibility of bribed judges or interminable delays in justice."

Fu stared at Bei. He finally spoke. "You are right. But may I suggest that justice not be administered by your hand or mine. Although sweet at the moment, personal revenge sometimes has a bitter after-taste. And my Meilu, at least, would not approve. It distresses me to avenge her in a way that would be repugnant to her."

Bei stared hard at Fu, fighting the exhaustion that was rising like a tide within him.

"Then who?"

Fu shrugged, and looked at Zhou.

"No," Bei said with vehemence, and shivered as an idea sent surges of pleasure through his body. "I have it. Let me deliver him to—" he turned to Yu, "to the Communists. Let Yeh Chienying have him, to do as he pleases with the head of the Te Wu in Peking."

Yu half rose, a moan of abject fear and deep anguish on his lips, his face contorted by a look mixing alarm and supplication.

Fu laughed. "A splendid idea, Bei. Look at his fear and anguish. We are already rewarded. They will abuse you, Yu, then they will execute you, in a horrible manner. Think on it, in the short time left to you. Wang!"

Wang appeared at the door.

"Everything quiet out there?"

"Yes, sir. All his men here are either dead or have surrendered."

"Splendid. Take General Yu here to the municipal jail, under heavy guard. See that he communicates with absolutely no one. And that no one is aware of his presence there. Guard him yourself, do not leave him. We will transport him to Yeh Chienying tomorrow."

"Yes, sir." Wang walked to the desk, jerked Yu roughly to his feet, and dragged him out of the room.

Fu and Zhou and Bei finally sank down into chairs around the room. No one spoke. Fu lit a cigarette, then passed his case to Zhou and Bei, who each took one and lit it. They sat puffing deeply for some minutes.

"This room is oppressive," declared Bei. "Let's move the chairs outside."

They picked up the chairs and carried them to the courtyard outside. Fu's men were dragging off the last of the bodies. There remained in the courtyard the acrid smell of gunpowder and the sweetish smell of blood, but all three men were accustomed to violence, so the smells did not strike them as unpleasant. In a minute the activity of the soldiers died down, the last jeep but one roared off, and they were alone.

Fu passed his cigarette case around again, and they all sat there, smoking. The courtyard was bathed in moonlight, the scattered pools of blood on the ground gleaming black against the gray stones.

"Ho has other children?" asked Zhou quietly.

"Yes," Bei answered. "But she was the youngest, his favorite."

Zhou nodded.

Fu pulled out his pistol and put the safety on. Zhou did the same. Bei ejected his clip and the round in the chamber.

"You were really about to shoot him, weren't you?" commented Fu in a soft voice.

Bei nodded. He closed his eyes, and after a moment opened them, and spoke while staring up at the moon. "I actually don't have a distinct memory of what I did or thought between the moment I saw

Ho holding his daughter's body until you burst through the door here. Something sort of snapped in me, I suppose."

"I know the feeling," said Fu. "It is not rational, but it is usually right. At any rate, it cannot be denied, once that something snaps in you."

Fu passed the case around again, and they all began another cigarette in silence, loath to end the moment of peace and tranquillity which seemed to have descended onto the bloody moonlit courtyard.

> *"To refresh our sorrow-laden souls,*
> *We drank wine far into the night,*
> *Its moonlit charm far too precious for sleep."*

Fu began a poem over a thousand years old. This night too struck him as too precious for sleep. As Fu paused and stared upward, savoring the last line, Bei completed the poem.

> *"But at last the wine overtook us,*
> *And we lay ourselves down on the innocent mountain,*
> *The earth for pillow, the heavens for cover."*

"It seems strange," said Zhou after a pause, "to be sitting here in this of all courtyards, enjoying the night."

Fu smiled sadly. "My Meilu would say that the Tao flows in all places."

It reminded Bei of something her sister Meiling would say.

"I don't know about the Tao," Zhou commented. "But I'd say we exorcised some demons from our ranks tonight."

They all nodded, and enjoyed the thought. Fu flipped the last of his cigarette into the center of the courtyard, and they watched it, glowing bright on the gray stones.

"I wish we could exorcise demons from the Communists' ranks, for your sake, Bei," said Fu finally.

Bei remained silent.

"Would it help if I approached Yeh Chienying, and told him that we're worried about Captain Li trying to take revenge on you for exposing him?"

Bei shook his head. "Yeh knows all about it already. Besides, he has no jurisdiction within the city—yet. And I don't think he could tell Lin Piao to keep Li in rein if he wanted to. Lin Piao is very powerful, especially now." He sighed a deep sigh. "No. Only a formal session with Mao, Chou Enlai, and Lin Piao can clear the air and address what has happened, and what will happen. I expect such a session within days."

"Really?" drawled Fu. "Where?"

"At Purple Mountain."

"Do you want guards around your home until then? I'll be happy to provide them."

Bei thought about it, then shook his head. "I don't mean to question your guards' abilities, Fu. But if I could sneak by guards tonight and get Yu Chenling alone, I have no doubt that, if he wanted to, Captain Li could get me alone sometime, somewhere. And I'm not about to have a personal bodyguard in my bedroom all night."

"We could arrange it. You could have Wang."

"No. Thank you, but no. I'm overreacting, anyway. It's just an irrational fear." He decided not to tell them about Lufei's brother and the courtesan murderer. Too long a story, too flimsy the evidence. And too insane and frightening a conclusion.

"Let me know if you change your mind," said Fu. His cigarette flickered out on the stones. "Come on, Zhou. May we at least give you a ride, Bei?"

"All right. It's been a long day, and I've done plenty of walking tonight."

The three stood, took a last long look at the moon, and walked to the waiting jeep.

January 17

Bei allowed himself only three hours of sleep, but these were in his bed for the first time in two nights. He awoke after dawn and was heading groggily out the door of his study when the telephone rang.

"What?"

"Zhou here, Bei. Will you see Mayor Ho this morning?"

"I'm headed there now."

"General Fu wants to know if Ho is up to leading the peace committee to the Fragrant Hills Park. If he isn't, we could reschedule it for tomorrow. Ho is important, the former mayor and elder statesman of the city. We'll postpone the meeting if he can't make it."

"I'll call you from his house."

"Fine. And convey Fu's condolences to the Ho family, if you would. Good-bye."

Bei marveled on the walk to Ho's home how normal everyone on the street looked. Bei himself has incurred the enmity of a deranged killer, the ex-mayor's home has been bombed and his daughter killed, the Te Wu headquarters has been wiped out in an early-morning raid, the warlord who holds the city is balanced delicately between war and surrender. And in spite of all this, the people go about their business as usual, either ignorant or unconcerned with all that bubbles about them. It struck Bei forcefully that the city indeed has its own inertia, the sum of its two million inhabitants' preoccupations with their own private pursuits of buying and selling, eating, copulating. And dying.

A municipal official met Bei at the door to Ho's home, and showed him into the formal dining room, now full of other officials and friends arrived to offer their condolences. Bei had barely sat down when word came that the family would see him.

They were gathered in the study, Ho and Madame Ho and their remaining children, seated very close to each other, somber. Ho's wife was bandaged on her head and arms, and appeared badly bruised and uncomfortable. Ho himself had cuts on his forehead.

Bei bowed deeply and formally to the group. "I'm very sorry for your loss. We will all miss her."

They nodded.

Madame Ho spoke. "We are so happy you were able to see her last night."

Bei nodded.

"My wife tells me you were here just after the explosions," Ho said in a hollow voice.

"Yes. I was . . . walking, enjoying the evening, and happened to be close."

"It must have been you that called the ambulances."

"Yes."

"Thank you for that."

Bei nodded again.

"Mayor, General Fu has asked me to convey his deepest sympathy."

"Please thank him for us," said Madame Ho.

"And, Mayor, he has asked me to talk to you regarding rescheduling the committee's visit to Fragrant Hills, if you wish it."

Ho rose stiffly. "Let us walk in the garden, friend." He shuffled for the door, moving like an old man. Suddenly he stopped, whirled around, and hobbled swiftly back to his family and gave them a collective embrace, as if uncertain that they too might not be lost to him without a moment's notice. He then walked out of the room and led Bei to a small courtyard.

"How dear they all become, once you lose one, without warning," he said in a weak voice.

Bei stared wordlessly into his friend's eyes.

Ho mustered strength to talk. "As regards the committee's visit to Fragrant Hills Park—I simply cannot do it today. I have too much to do to honor Bright Jade properly. And beyond that, I simply do not have the strength or concentration for political affairs today. It all seems . . . less important now than honoring Bright Jade."

"General Fu understands perfectly."

"The committee could go without me."

"He thinks you are essential to the committee. Would you be able to do it tomorrow?"

Ho stared into space. "Tomorrow?" He sighed deeply. "All right. It was Bright Jade's city, too. I shall consider it an errand of mercy for her city, and that will carry me."

"I will tell General Fu."

"Thank you." A silence. "All the visitors are assuming it was a wayward artillery shell from the Communists that happened to miss the Tungtan airfield and land on our house," Ho continued. He looked at Bei. "But if you were here moments after the explosions, I suspect that it was something else."

Bei stared at the pebble design on the pathway. "Do you want to talk about it?" he asked.

"Not talk about it. Just know."

Bei nodded. "It was the Te Wu."

Ho sighed wearily. "I thought as much."

"I can assure you that we have already made firm arrangements for them to pay the highest price for the crime."

"We?"

Bei did not volunteer any more explanation.

"You are deeply involved in all this, old friend, aren't you?" asked Ho.

Bei looked up at him. "It is my duty to one of my dearest friends."

They stared into each other's eyes for some moments. Then Ho said simply, "Thank you." He stared past Bei, at one of the ornate windows in the courtyard wall. "I feel very old without her, Bei." He shuffled to a bench and sat down heavily.

"She gave me so much of her energy. I enjoyed life more because she enjoyed it so fully."

"You have other children still. Fine children."

"Yes. But they do not give me what Bright Jade gave me. No one in the world gives me the joy she gave me. And now she is quite gone. She was already gone when I picked her up out of the corner last night." He spoke softly, but with no visible sign of emotion at all, just an unbounded weariness in his voice and face.

Bei groped for words. "I have a friend, a Taoist, who would say that Bright Jade was special because she was full of the flow of the Tao. That you can best honor Bright Jade by honoring the Tao that so freely flowed through her. That this Tao is everywhere, and in you, if you open yourself to it. She can be with you still, in the Tao, if you permit it."

Ho stared ahead. "With me still, in the Tao, if I permit it?" He pondered it. "That would be good. But it would not be the same, not truly her."

Bei nodded. "I know. The Tao takes many forms. But it is still the Tao, the same Tao that took her particular form while flowing through her."

Ho sighed. "Perhaps that will help. I don't know. I am so tired, so old suddenly. Help me up."

Bei steadied his forearm as he got up from the bench.

"Ho." Bei's voice was firm. "I know your sorrow is deep. But you cannot grow old so soon. Your city has great need of your strength. Your family has great need of your strength. Bright Jade's Tao is here, my friend. Draw on it. Honor her by letting the Tao that was in her course through you. Honor her."

Ho stared severely at Bei, offended at first. But a thoughtful look slowly replaced the offense. Then a look mixing puzzlement and hope. He nodded imperceptibly, jerked his forearm out of Bei's grasp, and walked back to the study.

"Good." Fu nodded decisively. "Tomorrow will be all right for the committee. Now I have another duty for you, Bei."

Bei groaned. "General Fu, I am happy to help you. But I also have duties as chief inspector."

"I understand that. My duties are more important, and you are uniquely suited to them. Indeed, I'm wondering how I ever got along without you. I want you to inform Yeh Chienying of the delay in the meeting with the committee."

Bei looked up in protest. "All the way to Fragrant Hills? Really, General, I can't."

"Nonsense. I'm not asking you to pull a manure cart there, Inspector. You'll go in my limousine. Think of how pleasant the ride will be. If you wish, you can take a bicycle along and ride it back just for old times' sake." He leaned back in his chair and laughed, the first laugh he had uttered since Meilu's death.

He sat upright again. "On second thought, you can't take a bicycle. The trunk of the limousine will already be occupied, by the little present you suggested we give Yeh Chienying."

A vicious pleasure flashed in Bei's eyes.

"Wang will go with you, as the driver," continued Fu. "Now please listen carefully, Bei. I can't put any of this in writing."

Bei leaned forward in the chair, concentrating.

"Tell Commander Yeh that we are delivering General Yu Chenling to him for the peoples' justice. Nothing more. He will know what we mean, and will accept Yu with alacrity, no questions asked."

"All right."

"As regards Ho's peace committee: They wish to meet tomorrow at the same place, due to Ho's tragedy this morning. Again, I don't think he will raise any difficulties."

Bei nodded.

"Fine." He pushed a button on his desk, and Wang entered from the anteroom.

"Can you be ready to leave in ten minutes, Captain Wang, with Inspector Bei's special baggage?"

"Yes, sir."

"Good. The inspector will meet you in front of the park then. Let Zhou know you're leaving."

He turned back to Bei. "By the way, have you heard of Lin Piao's ultimatum yesterday afternoon?"

"No. What kind of ultimatum?"

"If we do not surrender by 1400 hours on January twenty-second, he will storm the city, regardless of cost."

A chill seized Bei. The twenty-second. This was Monday the seventeenth. Saturday, then.

"But doesn't he know we are negotiating with Yeh and Nieh, that we have a rough draft of an agreement?"

"Oh, he knows that, through Captain Li's presence at the negotiations. This is just his way of telling Yeh and Nieh that he has as much power as they do, and he's not going to wait long for them to try to reach a political agreement. Their command is split, Bei. But Lin Piao is doubtless fully in charge of military matters. If we haven't come to terms with Yeh by Saturday, I don't doubt Lin Piao will indeed attack us with all he's got. And he's got plenty."

"Can you reach an accommodation with Yeh by Saturday?"

"I don't know. Plus I've got to persuade the other generals here to accept it before then. That will be a problem only for Shih Chueh and Li Wen, but it may be a major problem."

"What about the draft that Zhou and General Teng and I brought back from Tungchow?"

Fu shook his head. "It will never get past Shih Chueh and Li Wen. It's close, but we clearly need to wring a few more concessions from Yeh and Nieh. Ho will meet with them tomorrow, if Yeh agrees to the postponement. That leaves three days after Ho's meeting, before

Lin Piao's Saturday deadline. Do you know yet when Mao and Chou Enlai are coming here to confront Lin Piao?"

"No. I'll ask Yeh. I imagine the meeting will be later this week."

"We've got to present our changes in the draft before then. They'll take advantage of Mao's presence to come to some sort of a decision on how far they'll go with us. I'll have our changes ready by tonight. Zhou will carry them to Yeh tomorrow morning."

Bei shook his head. "So much could go wrong, still."

Fu stared at him somberly. "Yes."

"Well," said Bei, standing, "I'll join Captain Wang in the limousine now. I'm eager to deliver our present in the trunk to Yeh."

Fu smiled, looking nearly like his former self.

They pulled out of the Hsichihmen Gate, across the cleared strip and into the bustling refugee area. Wang skillfully maneuvered the car through the crowded streets, with liberal use of the horn, and soon they were in the countryside, traveling north on Paishihch'iao Road. They passed an old man pulling a manure cart, his calf muscles bulging as he tugged against the harness and the cart handles. Bei stared at the sight, snuggled deeper into the limousine's cushions, then began to chuckle. In a minute he was laughing aloud, and it was another minute before the laughter died away.

Wang glanced back in the mirror. "You all right, sir?"

It triggered another laughing spell, but Bei assured Wang that everything was fine.

"How long have you been with the general, Wang?"

"Not long. Four years."

Fields sped past them on the left, brown and barren. They were on Haitian Road now.

"Really? And before that?"

"Yen Hsishan, sir, in Shansi. Or rather, one of Yen's generals."

"Why did you switch to General Fu?"

"He's a better man."

"Pardon?"

"He's a better man."

Bei knit his brows. "What do you mean? Smarter?"

"That. But also . . . he's honorable. Decent. A gentleman."

"That matters to a soldier?"

Wang glanced back in the mirror. "Of course it does. To the better soldiers, at least."

"Why? You're paid the same, aren't you?"

"Usually, I suppose. But it's not that. You just feel better, and safer, with a commander you respect."

Bei shook his head. "But a soldier just follows orders. Regardless of his commander's character."

"That's just it, sir. It's because we follow orders, without needing to understand them. That's why you want to be serving under the best commander you can find. You have to trust him, even if you don't understand what he's doing."

It didn't square with what Bei had always thought about soldiers. He leaned forward in the seat.

"Does it feel strange to be driving to a meeting with Commander Yeh Chienying?"

A pause. "I don't understand," said Wang. "Why should it?"

"Why, Yeh being a Communist, and Fu being a Nationalist."

Wang shrugged his shoulders, and executed a left turn onto Summer Palace Road. "I don't know much about ideologies, sir. Or care."

Bei frowned. Now he was puzzled. "But you just told me you joined up with Fu because of what he was fighting for."

Wang glanced back in the mirror. "Beg your pardon, sir, but I didn't say that at all. I joined Fu because of the kind of man he is. It has nothing to do with Communist or Nationalist or just plain warlord, if you'll pardon the term, sir."

"But surely what cause he believes in is part of the kind of man he is?"

"Possibly. But it's not as important as many other things. How he handles himself. Whether he cares for his men. Does he keep his word. Does he choose his battles carefully. Whether he is a man of honor. Do the soldiers feel proud to be fighting under him. That's the key. Do the soldiers feel proud to be fighting under him."

Bei slowly sat back. Incredible. He thought of Yeh Chienying and Nieh Jungchen. And compared them with Yu Chenling, Chiang Kaishek, and other top Kuomintang generals. Better men. Men you could be proud to fight for. And now Fu Tsoyi; perhaps Fu Tsoyi might go over to the Communist side.

Why was the tide switching to the Communists? Because they had more soldiers, who fought better. But maybe they had more soldiers who fought better, because they had—what? Better men as officers? Maybe the Communists attracted the best men as officers, and those men attracted the most soldiers. And the best soldiers. Soldiers who would fight, unquestioningly and tirelessly, for a commander they were proud of.

He thought of the corruption of the vast majority of Kuomintang generals and high officers. Then he thought of Fu, and Zhou, and Yeh Chienying, and Nieh Jungchen. With a genuine shock he realized he was growing to like these men. And Wang. Actually like them, and respect them.

What was happening to him? Mo-tzu's "Good iron is not made into nails, nor good men into soldiers" used to be unquestioned by him. Now he was not so sure. Indeed, Mo-tzu was wrong. What was coming over him? In the company of soldiers, and rather enjoying it. Suggesting to Fu that he demand a cabinet post, and then arguing with the Communist high command that they grant it. Copulating lustily with a Taoist priestess. On the point of shooting a man between the eyes last night, with no compunction. Spouting advice about the flow of the Tao to a bereaved friend. None of that was him, or at least the Bei Menjin he had carefully put together over the years. Was he turning against everything he had formerly believed in? And if he betrayed all that he used to define himself, what was left? There should be nothing left. Yet, strangely, he had never felt more full, more alive. What was filling him up?

Wang turned into Fragrant Hills Park, and followed the road up and around to the Jade Flower Villa in the middle of the park. As they pulled up, Yeh Chienying himself stepped down the stairs fronting the villa. Bei emerged from the back seat.

"Inspector Bei! I did not expect to see you, although of course it is a pleasure."

"Thank you, Commander Yeh. I have a message from General Fu."

"Of course. Come inside to my office."

323

Bei followed Yeh, who vigorously strode up the steps into the villa and turned into a modest office.

"Please be seated, Inspector."

"Thank you, sir. May I be brief?"

"Please."

"Mayor Ho's home was bombed last night. By the Te Wu. Mayor Ho was unhurt, but one of his children was killed. He wishes to postpone the meeting until tomorrow, and Fu assents. We apologize for the delay, and hope you will agree."

"Of course," Yeh answered immediately, a pained look on his face. "Please convey to Mayor Ho my deepest sympathy for the death of his child. I trust he has other children?"

"Yes."

"Good. Although it does not lessen his pain, I am sure."

"There is something else, sir."

"Yes?"

"We have, bound in the trunk of the limousine in which I arrived, General Yu Chenling."

Yeh's open face registered his astonishment.

"General Fu has instructed me to tell you that we are delivering Yu Chenling to you for the peoples' justice."

Yeh stared at him for several seconds, blinked his eyes several times, and arose, expressionless. He stepped into the hall.

"Sanwu," he said quietly.

A guard quickly walked up to him. "Yes, sir?"

"Assist Inspector Bei's driver in transferring a prisoner from the trunk of his car to our keeping. Place him under heavy guard in the Pavilion of Varied Scenery."

"Yes, sir." The guard hurried off.

Yeh returned, and sat down again. "Please inform General Fu that he may depend absolutely on our dispensing justice to the Te Wu's chief officer in North China. Today."

"I will inform him."

In the silence, Bei heard the trunk being opened, then shut a moment later. He stared down at the table top. "I have no other business for you, Commander Yeh."

Yeh did not speak. Bei looked up to find him staring at him, again with no expression.

"Inspector Bei," he said, in a casual tone. "Are you concerned that Captain Li might . . . wish to harm you for your discovery of his role in the Taoist prior's death?"

Bei looked up sharply, then returned his gaze to the table top. He paused, wondering what he should say, and why Yeh had asked.

"Yes."

"Good," said Yeh in a vigorous tone. "You should be on your guard. I do not know whether you are in danger, but you should be on your guard." He paused. "I wish I could help you, Inspector. Much to my regret in this matter, however, I cannot police Lin Piao's every action, much less place his chief aide under house arrest. I am doing my best, however, to keep them both extremely busy. That is the best I can do. It is extremely delicate."

"Thank you for that."

Yeh nodded. "The meeting at the Purple Mountain with Mao and Chou should bring everything out, and provide some form of resolution. You will be perfectly safe after that, I can assure you."

"When will that meeting be held?"

"Within several days, depending on Mao's schedule. I expect to hear from him this afternoon, and will send Meiling this evening to inform you of the date."

"Thank you. I will admit that I am . . . eager for the meeting."

"I can appreciate that." He rose, and Bei followed suit. They walked back to the car outside.

"Thank you for coming, Inspector."

"You're welcome, sir."

Bei started down the stairs.

"Oh, Inspector."

"Yes?" Bei paused halfway down and looked back up at Yeh.

"Take care of yourself, Inspector. I will have much work for you soon, when I am Mayor of Peking."

Bei stood there a moment, then nodded, and walked to the car, where Wang held his door open for him.

Bei was silent during the drive back to the city. His mind, though, was full of Yeh's warning to be on his guard. And full of the Baleful Star, haunting the city now on two counts. The instigator of the burning of An Shihlin, and the sadistic murderer of courtesans in the city's Wind and Flower quarters. A Baleful Star, come to do us harm.

A Baleful Star, his hatred and attention now doubtless focused on Bei. Would Captain Li passively wait until the meeting with Mao? Or would he, despite Yeh Chienying's precautionary efforts to keep him busy, find the time and opportunity to strike at Bei before the meeting? I must expect that, thought Bei. Expect that and be ready for it. He steeled himself against the shiver that threatened to run through his body.

It was well past noon when Wang guided the car through the refugee city, and they entered the barren strip outside the wall. Barbed wire and trenches and logs crisscrossed the strip to either side of the road. Ahead of them loomed the wall, glowing bloodred in the waning rays of the sun behind them.

Bei stared at the wall, stretching as far as the eye could see to either side. It rose nearly twenty meters high, massive at its base, wide enough for vehicular traffic at its top, where machine guns and light artillery bristled. If the Communists had an air force with bombers, the wall would be obsolete. But they had no military planes at all, none. So the wall was just as imposing, its massive dimensions just as formidable as a century ago, before airplanes. Just as formidable as it had been for over five hundred years since Kublai Khan built its first version.

Bei knew that when Peking had been taken in those past five hundred years, it had resulted from internal decay more than successful assault. He knew that Fu Tsoyi was strong inside the city. Yet Lin Piao had modern artillery, lots of it. And if Fu failed to reach an acceptable agreement with Yeh and Nieh within three days, Lin Piao would use that heavy artillery. Could he find a weak spot in the wall, batter it with his big guns, and breach it? It would be costly. The breach site would be apparent long before the final rush of men into it. They would have to cross fifty meters of open space with the defenders knowing full well by that stage where they would be coming to, with extra machine guns on the walls by then, and their own artillery trained on the spot now. He shook his head. It would be carnage. Absolute carnage. Yet if Lin Piao were willing to sacrifice enough waves of soldiers to build a bridge of dying humanity across the barbed wire and trenches and into the breach, it could probably be done. The defender's artillery could only be loaded and fired so fast. Machine gun ammunition could only be carried and loaded so fast.

326

It could probably be done, if they could persuade thousands upon thousands of young peasant boys to charge across the cleared strip to their death. He knew they could. And would. Pay a price of unimaginable horror to capture the city.

The limousine glided to a halt outside the gate. Wang presented their pass, and soon the gate opened and swallowed the car into the city. Several minutes later Bei arrived at the Winter Palace, and despite being very hungry reported to Fu directly.

"No problems?" Fu asked from behind his desk.

"None. Tomorrow is fine for the meeting with Ho's committee. Commander Yeh said to inform you that you could absolutely rely on the peoples' justice being applied to Yu. Today."

Fu leaned back and stared at the ceiling. "Good. It doesn't bring them back, and they wouldn't approve of revenge. But I'm glad that deadly dog is out of the way."

He shifted his gaze down to Bei. "You look tired, Bei."

"I am. And hungry. And scared. Other than that I'm feeling super."

Fu grinned. "Sure you don't want a guard until the meeting with Mao?"

"Sure. What I need most is food, followed by sleep. If you'll excuse me, sir."

"Certainly. And thanks."

His villa was very dark when he stepped through the gate. He vaguely remembered having given the servant the day off, and closed the gate behind him but forgot to lock it, a task she usually performed each night. He carried the bag of *chiaotse* he had purchased on the way home up the corridor and into the study, placing it on the side table before turning on the lamp. He eased himself into the chair, wondering when Meiling would come with a firm date for the meeting at the Purple Mountain. A movement to his right caught his eye, and he turned toward it with a smile, expecting to see Meiling. The smile froze horribly as he saw instead the cold eyes of the Baleful Star rise from behind the chair beyond the table. Bei reached for his pistol and had it out and the round chambered by the time Li leaped to him and grabbed his pistol hand in a grip of steel. Vainly Bei tried to turn the pistol onto Li as the men grappled. The struggling pair lurched

327

across the room and slammed into the wall, where Li banged Bei's pistol hand hard into the wall until the pistol dropped out of the numb hand. As Li stooped to reach for it, Bei jammed his knee hard against the side of Li's head and watched him roll dazed against the large armchair. Bei frantically searched for the pistol on the dark floor, but had no success as Li collected his wits and rushed at Bei's midsection, pinning him against the wall again amid dull crunching sounds from Bei's ribs. Bei struggled, but couldn't free himself, then realized that the pressure in his back came from the trio of war axes on the wall against which he was pinned. With an effort he twisted his torso, gasping at the pain in his ribs, then jerked one of the heavy axes off the wall, and swung it clumsily down at Li with both arms. Li looked up just as the blow was coming, and the broad side of the ax glanced off his cheek, raising an ugly bloody mass. Bei's body was pulled down by the course of the ax as Li twisted away clutching the bloody side of his face, and before Bei could right himself, Li's foot shot out in a desperate, barely aimed kick which somehow caught Bei square on the chin, throwing him back against the wall as he lost his grip on the ax. Bei leaned dazed against the wall, his arms and legs trembling. The younger Li leaped up and drove his bloody hand into Bei's open midsection. Bei doubled over, feeling he would never be able to draw a breath again, and waited helplessly for the next blow. It came, on the back of his neck, and toppled Bei unconscious to the floor at Li's feet.

Li ignored Bei's twitching body. His eyes were fixed, fascinated, on the war ax on the floor. He picked it up, looked closely at the razor-sharp edge, and smiled. He lifted the heavy ax easily above the table where the bag of *chiaotse* sat, and relaxing his grip let it fall of its own weight. It passed right through the table, splitting it cleanly into two halves. Li laughed and gazed down at Bei, then back at the ax. With a thoughtful look on his face he sat down in the chair next to the shattered table and stared at the ax, breathing heavily. Absently he brushed at the blood on his cheek with his sleeve. In a moment he got up, lay the ax flat on the floor with the end of the two-meter-long handle just under the desk, and lifted the axhead a meter up off the floor. He twisted the handle ninety degrees so the edge of the axhead faced down. Then he let go of the ax. It pivoted down and bit cleanly into the hardwood floor, embedding itself with a sharp crunch some three centimeters deep. He tugged it out of the wood and lifted it up again, the other end of the handle still jammed under the desk. He let loose of the axhead, and it again fell true and cut deep into the floor.

With another delighted laugh he jerked the axhead out of the floor and pivoted it up again. He held it there, thinking. Directly above him was a simple chandelier; he looked up at it, then at the door some two meters away. Next he glanced at the remaining two war axes on the wall, and noted the long strands of leather attaching the handles to the heads and wrapping the lengths of the handles. He absently let loose of the axhead, and it fell and bit deeply into the wood a third time. Extracting his knife from his boot, he stepped over Bei's unconscious body doubled up on the floor and strode to the two remaining axes on the wall. He lifted them off and cut the leather knot next to the axhead, then quickly unwound the leather wrappings. A full three meters of leather rope from each ax. With a look of wonderment on his bloodied face, he began to work.

Bei slowly regained consciousness. His mind floated toward the surface lazily, tentatively. When all it found there was pain, it shied away and dove down again. But it floated up again, and again, and each downward dive was shallower, until finally he was forced to break the surface. He found himself staring up at the massive head of a war ax, its sharp edge poised a meter above his throat. He shut his eyes quickly, knowing it was a bad dream. When he opened them again, it was still there, strangely. He glanced toward a movement to the side, and saw Li sitting in his chair beside his shattered table. He quickly shut his eyes again—a very bad dream, this one. Then he remembered. He struggled to react to Li's presence, to get away, but nothing happened. His body simply wouldn't respond.

"So you're back, dog."

What was happening?

"Oh, yes, it's real, Inspector," Li said, spitting the title out derisively. "Not a dream. But I can sympathize. I sometimes have trouble myself, keeping my dreams apart from the real world. My dreams often take over, yes, swell up until they're as large as this world. It actually feels good, having two worlds to live in. The mixing of the two is the best, though, by far the best." His voice, normal as he began, veered sharply toward a sibilant tone, so that by the end he was hissing out the words.

Bei stared at him, uncomprehending. The eyes still glowed darkly with hate on the surface, but below that lay something shattered and sharp and alien. It was as if . . . as if the eyes were far away, looking through the body at you.

"We've never really talked, have we?" he resumed, in a normal voice now. "Our conversation will be one-sided, though, since I've gagged you as well as trussed you up with leather to one of those admirable ax handles running up your back side."

That was it, the full feeling in his mouth and throat. The inability to move in any direction. Don't watch the eyes; look at the mouth instead.

"How I hate you," he suddenly hissed. "Your smug Confucian air of superiority, your easy acceptance of wealth and luxury while all around you others toil and struggle desperately to just barely survive." His voice had raised until these last words were shrieked. "It's a dream world, you turtle. You live in a dream world farther removed from reality than the total of all my dreams."

He leaped from the chair and put his face next to Bei's, whispering fiercely now. "I'm strong, dog. I make my dreams happen. I know they're dreams, but I take them and get them out of my head and onto a bed in front of me, real and firm and red, flowering with the juice of life, squirming with delight in me, then I turn them back into my dream, pulsing and gurgling and covered with blood, just exactly like my sister in my dream, just exactly alike, and the two worlds are one, one real dream, warm and sweet-smelling and flowing all over my hands, gurgling . . . no . . . puddling warm and red . . . no, no, no."

He staggered backward into the chair again, breathing heavily, and shook his head violently.

"No! No!" His shrieks echoed from the walls.

Soon his breathing was back to normal. He laughed. Then he spoke normally again, quietly. "That's the one danger, Inspector. The one danger. You can't mix the two worlds just anytime or anywhere. Only certain times, certain places." He took a deep breath, and wiped his bloody cheek again with his sleeve.

"But you'll mix up my two worlds, in your death, Inspector."
Another laugh, this one a bit too long. "You'll get your throat slit,
slit real good by your own war ax, as it beheads you, Inspector. And
just who will slit your throat and behead you?" He sat up excitedly.
"Follow the leather strands, dog. They hold the ax above you, see?
See how they pass up through the base of the chandelier then back
down and over to the door latch? Now watch this, Inspector. Watch
close!" he shouted, "so you'll have something vivid to dream about
in your last hours of life."

He rose, jerked Bei's bound and trussed body to one side, then
strode over to the door. He stopped to pluck the leather rope, stretched
tight from the door latch at one end to the poised axhead at the other.

"You can see how the axhead and the door are connected by the
leather rope which passes through the base of the chandelier, right?
When the door opens inward, it lets the ax drop down. In fact, because
the axhead is so heavy, it is pulling on the door very hard even now,
and as soon as the latch is turned and the door is free, it's jerked open
quickly and forcefully by the rapid fall of the axhead." He thrust his
head back and laughed delightedly. "But here—a demonstration is
what you need."

He turned the latch slowly, and as the latch became free of the
restraint of the doorjamb, the door flew open and the ax dropped,
biting deeply into the floor inches away from Bei's face with a re-
sounding crunch. Bei winced. As he opened his eyes and saw the
massive axhead embedded in the wood, he realized what was going
to happen to him.

Li was laughing again. "Scared, Inspector?" He suddenly turned
serious, pointed a shaking finger at Bei, and hissed his next words.
"Before you die, you'll know what it's like to be scared, to know
for a fact that you're going to die horribly, to know that it can happen
at any moment. That's how most of China lives, yes! From moment
to moment, you disgusting turtle, never knowing when the soldiers
or the landlord's thugs will take a liking to your land or your house
or your daughter. You'll get to know a little of what life is really
like outside of your dream world in this obscene city, in the moments
before you die."

Trembling with anger, he wrenched the axhead out of the floor,
then walked back to the door and shut it, the axhead rising back up

to its former position in the air as the door closed and latched into place.

"There's only one question, Inspector," said Li as he returned and moved Bei's body back under the axhead, positioning his neck directly over the latest gash in the floor.

"Which whore will kill you, dog? I know they visit you every night, that you take pleasure in their flesh and their Red Flower every night. Which one will turn the latch, have the weight of the axhead jerk the latch out of her weak and unsuspecting hand, and hear the ax slice through your throat? Which one will hear the blood spurt from your neck and flow over the floor? My sister? Or the Taoist whore who coupled with the prior before I had him burned? Or your servant girl?"

He stood, towering above Bei. "But it doesn't matter, does it?" Bei watched him walk over to the wall and grab the two remaining axheads and walk back.

"I trussed you up with the extra leather, Inspector, so tight from your shoulders to your feet that you can't move, especially with the long ax handle running up your backside." His voice was now grim, and efficient. "But just in case you're thinking of rolling over or wrenching yourself to one side and away from the ax, I'll put an end to that last hope for you now."

So saying, he drove one axhead deep into the wood beside Bei's right shoulder, then jammed him up against it and drove the other axhead deep into the wood next to Bei's left shoulder. Bei cried out through the gag as a sharp pain seared through his shoulder.

"How clumsy of me," Li said with mock sympathy. "I've sliced off part of your shoulder trying to wedge you in tightly. I hope you don't bleed to death before your whore comes."

Bei was indeed immobile, the massive axheads precluding movement to either side, the ax handle running up his backside precluding his sitting up or inching his body up or down.

Li stood up and grimly surveyed his handiwork. "You don't have a chance, Inspector. You are doomed, just as surely as any Shansi peasant is doomed. Just as surely as that big-headed Hunan braggart is doomed. I am your doom, and his doom, and no one will escape me." Li's eyes burned bright with pleasure as he switched off the light, then stepped to the door and held it with both hands as he turned the latch. He put his foot in front of the door, and leaned into it, managing to permit it to swing open only slowly as the latch cleared the doorjamb. With a laugh he saw the ax descending slowly to Bei's neck, and cut the skin slightly. Thin beads of blood formed along the cut. Li then slipped through the half-open door and closed it behind him, the axhead rising again as the door closed.

Bei lay in the dark, heard Li laughing down the corridor, then the front gate open and close. He was a mass of pain. His battered wrist and ribs throbbed with a dull pain that sent long, deep waves through his entire body. The ax wound on his shoulder produced a searing pain acutely centered there. And he could distinctly feel the beads of blood along his throat as they swelled to a large enough pool to suddenly dribble down the side of his neck—or was that merely a tingling anticipation of the bite of the ax?

He knew it was hopeless, but he made an effort to wrench his body out from under the ax. He could scarcely move. The ax handle along his spine and legs and the tight leather trusses kept him from even inching up or down. He quickly exhausted his ebbing strength. He tried to yell through the gag stuffed in his mouth, but only a soft muffled groan came out.

Hopeless. So it would end like this. At least it would be quick. Should he think about his life, total it up? What had Li meant about a big-headed Hunan braggart? He couldn't think, much less reflect philosophically. There was only the dull throbbing pain, the acute piercing pain, the blood dribbling down his neck, and the blade of the ax gleaming dully in the dark above his head. Nothing else existed. Only the pain, the blood, and the ax. And the dark. Soon, only the dark would exist, swallowing him up mercifully. The Baleful Star, come to do us harm.

A sound riveted his attention. The gate from the street, opening. Then closing. Don't. Don't come in. Stay away. Soft footsteps up the corridor, hesitant, searching. Go back. Relentlessly they came, and stopped in front of the door to the study. No. Then they walked around, to the courtyard, and stopped in front of the large window. He turned his face stiffly, and saw Lufei's face peering in. Here I am! Down on the floor! She gazed blankly about the dark room, then returned to the door. He heard her place her hand on the latch. Then freeze. They both heard it, the distinct clank of the street door again.

Open. Close. Steps up the corridor. All the way, to within two meters of the study door.

"Who . . . who are you?" Lufei asked.

A pause. "A colleague of the inspector's," answered Meiling's voice. "What are you doing here, miss?" she inquired politely.

Another pause, then in a brash tone Lufei answered. "I'm here for a rendezvous with him. We are lovers."

He could hear Meiling chuckle. "Then forgive me for disturbing your tryst. I have a very short message for the inspector. If you could permit me to say just a word to him, I will then depart and leave you two to your dalliance with The Wind and the Flowers."

Another pause. "All right. But don't be long," answered Lufei. She stepped back, giving Meiling access to the door. Smiling, Meiling walked up to it, grabbed the latch, and began to turn it. She paused.

"What's the matter?"

No answer.

"What is it?" Lufei insisted.

Meiling stood there, her hand on the half-opened latch, staring at the door.

"I . . . I don't know. Something is . . . wrong."

"What do you mean, wrong? This is just a trick to get me to leave!"

"Quiet!" Meiling commanded. She stood there still, senses alert, vibrating.

"Whatever is it?" Lufei whispered after a full minute.

No answer. Meiling was perfectly still, not a thought in her mind, her nervous system totally passive, every sense exquisitely receptive, fully open and revealed, a pure yin posture.

"This is ridiculous. I'm going in if you're not," declared Lufei.

Meiling brushed her back. "Don't move. Something is wrong."

"Don't you dare hit me! And what do you mean by wrong?"

"The smell is wrong. Perhaps blood, I'm not sure. And there's a low sound from inside. Perhaps . . . I don't know. And the door feels strange, too heavy on the latch. And . . . beyond that, there's a bad sense to the place. Just a bad feel. Like the *ch'i* has been twisted, distorted."

Lufei snorted in derision. "The *ch'i?*" Now I know who you are. You're the Taoist woman. Yuan has told me about you. Look, I can't stand here listening to you babble of *ch'i* all night. I have a rendezvous with Bei."

"Fine. But let me look around a bit. Don't touch the door." She walked around to the courtyard window and peered in. It was too dark to see anything.

"I'm going in through the window," she said.

"But the door isn't locked. We can go in through it."

"There's a bad feel to the door. Stay away from it." So saying, she picked up a stone and broke the window, then quickly chipped away the jagged edges along the bottom of the pane. She pulled herself through the window and into the room. Immediately she noticed a dull gleam in the middle of the room.

"I don't believe you broke that window!" cried Lufei.

She opened the door, and screamed as it jerked away from her.

Meiling saw nothing but the movement of the dull gleam, and without thought dove for it. Her outstretched fingers caught only the very top edge of the descending axhead, pushing it hard away from her. The axhead swiveled in midair and landed on Bei's chest with a heavy crunch.

"What's going on?" wailed Lufei.

"Turn a light on," Meiling commanded. "On the desk there."

Lufei found the lamp and switched it on. Bei lay unconscious, surrounded by axheads, bleeding heavily.

Lufei screamed again at the sight of him.

January 18

He awoke quite suddenly, with the realization that if he could feel pain, he could not be dead. But he refused to open his eyes. He could not bear to look again at the blade of the war ax dangling over him. After a minute he noticed that the pain was all dull now. And it seemed to be light in the room. In the background he could hear the murmur of voices, normal voices saying normal things.

Puzzled, he cautiously fluttered one eye half open. Light. A strange ceiling. No war ax. Someone standing over him, a lady. He opened the other eye. Fu Hsiawen, with an anxious look on her face. In a hospital uniform.

"Captain Wang," she called, turning around.

Wang stuck his head in the door.

"Call General Fu. Tell him the patient is awake."

She turned back to Bei. "How do you feel, Inspector?"

He gazed blankly at her.

She leaned closer to him. "How do you feel, Inspector?"

He realized she was talking to him, and expected an answer. He opened his mouth, but nothing came out. He tried again.

"I . . . I'm not dead."

She laughed, but gently. "No. You're alive. Barely, but alive."

"I'm alive?" It had a good ring to it. "I'm alive," he repeated, liking the sound of it immensely.

She laughed again. "Is that so hard to believe?"

He looked at her completely seriously. "Yes. Yes, it is hard to believe."

"Well, whatever, you are indeed alive and out of any serious danger, other than an infection. Luckily, the blades that cut you were quite clean."

"My throat is . . . all right?"

She became professional. "A slight superficial wound on your throat—it will heal completely. You have a very nasty wound on your chest, where that large blade—whatever it was—sliced into you at a shallow angle. It took quite a lot of skin off, and bit into your sternum and several ribs. Most of the pain you feel is from that wound, and it will hurt for a long time. But there were no arteries or nerves severed, luckily. It will leave a bad scar, I'm afraid."

"My shoulder hurts."

"Yes. The other bad wound. But again, relatively superficial. A large chunk of skin is gone, and a bit of muscle, but no damage to arteries or nerves."

He reflected. Amazing. What had happened? He remembered Lufei and Meiling talking. Then Lufei had opened the door and screamed. He had blacked out as the door opened. What had happened? But Hsiawen was talking again.

". . . be aware that you have other injuries as well. Your right wrist is badly sprained. And several ribs appear to be broken."

He shook his head slightly.

She laughed again. "You kept me very busy for a good deal of the night. You would be a severe challenge to the best of wound dressers."

He laughed, only slightly, then winced at the pain in his ribs and chest.

She put a hand on his arm. "You have a visitor, if you feel up to it."

"Who?"

"The young lady who checked you in last night."

He nodded.

She left, and soon Lufei came into the room timidly. He was disappointed, thinking it would be Meiling.

She haltingly approached the bed, face awash with guilt and shame.

"I . . . I'm so glad you're alive, Inspector."

"Me too."

"I . . . I'm so ashamed of myself. It is all my fault. If I hadn't opened that door . . ."

"Someone else would have. Don't worry about it. Tell me what happened. Why am I still alive?"

She stared wide-eyed at him. "You don't know?"

"I apparently blacked out."

"Oh. Well . . . the other woman, the tall, strong one—"

"Meiling."

"Yes. She had broken the window, and climbed into the room, and as that horrible ax fell on you she hit it, and tilted the edge away from you. Although it still got you."

Ah. So that was it. The oblique entry on the chest, rather than the vertical entry on—through—the throat.

At the mere thought of it she buried her face in her hands and began to sob.

"There, there. It's over. No sense in that anymore." He had never seen a woman who cried so much.

"Who . . . who did this to you?"

A pause. No need for her to know. "No one you know of. Some criminal I caught a long time ago, trying for revenge."

She stood there, awkward. What to say?

Wang walked in the room. "General Fu to see you, sir."

Lufei jumped. "Oh! I must leave. Good-bye!" She hurried out of the room, Wang behind her, then popped in again. "I almost forgot. The strong woman—she wanted me to give you a message."

"Yes?" he said eagerly.

"It's a note—here," she said, handing him a folded piece of paper.

Bei opened it. In firm characters, Meiling had written "Wednesday, four o'clock, Purple Mountain." And underneath her signature, in the flowing, intimate grass script characters, "To nearly lose a treasure is to suddenly realize how precious it is to you."

Lufei disappeared. As Bei savored the message, Fu strode briskly into the room.

"By heaven, you do look awful!"

Bei laughed, then moaned at the sharp pain, which prompted a loud laugh from Fu.

"Does it hurt to talk as well as laugh?"

He took a breath. "No. Not as bad, at least."

"Good. First, I want to apologize, Bei. I should have insisted on giving you Wang as a guard."

Bei attempted to shrug his shoulders, bringing an explosion of pain in his left shoulder. He winced and exhaled slowly.

Fu shook his head. "You are lucky to be alive, it appears. Well, Wang will be with you until your Purple Mountain meeting. Do you know yet when it is?"

Bei nodded. "Wednesday. I presume this is Tuesday?"

"Yes. Nearly noon Tuesday."

"Good. Tomorrow late afternoon."

"Will you be able to go?"

"Yes," Bei answered emphatically. "With Wang's help."

"You have it."

A pause.

"Did you send Zhou this morning with the revised drafts to Yeh?"

Fu nodded.

"So what do you think? Will it be acceptable to them?"

Fu shrugged. "Who knows? I asked for more than I think we need, of course. Our problems are not with the Communists now, Bei. Our problems are with General Shih Chueh and General Li Wen.

And Chiang Kaishek. And Lin Piao and his deadline on Saturday."
He shook his head. "Many problems. Always."

Bei stared straight at him. "There's only one place you'll have no
problems, Fu. It's very dark there."

Fu stared back, then nodded. "Yes."

"Well," he said after a pause. "I have to be off. I'll visit you tomorrow. Wang will stay with you until then, and also escort you to
the Purple Mountain in the limousine tomorrow. Unless you'd rather
ride your bicycle?"

Bei closed his eyes tight to prevent the impending chuckle from
erupting.

Laughing, Fu left. In the hallway he saw Hsiawen, and called to
her. "Nurse?"

She walked up, past his three bodyguards. "Yes, sir?"

He took her aside and walked to the vacant end of the hallway.
"How are you, little one?"

She nodded with a smile. "Good, Father."

"Can you keep a secret?" he whispered.

"It's my job," she whispered back.

He leaned over and whispered in her ear. "I've asked for a cabinet
post in your Communist national government."

Her eyes grew wide, and she gave him a hug, which made the
bodyguards jump in alarm. "Oh, Father. I'm so glad." She stood
back decorously, but still beaming.

He looked at her warmly, happy to have given her a surprise which
made her proud. "They haven't formally agreed. But I'm sure they'll
find a useful job for me somewhere."

"You are a strange man," she declared.

He answered with full seriousness. "I couldn't stand not to be a
part of China's future."

She nodded. "I must go, Father."

"Yes. Sorry to have kept you from your work. Take good care of
Inspector Bei. He's important in all this—very important."

They walked back up the hall, and his bodyguards closed around
him. As she turned up the hall, Hsiawen put her hand in her pocket,
encountered a paper there, and turned back to Bei's room.

"Inspector. I nearly forgot. A note arrived for you late this morning. From your office, the young man said."

Bei groaned. The last thing he wanted to think about was his office and its never-ending details. He opened the note, then flushed and sat very still as he read its contents: "I understand your Taoist whore saved you last night. She will not save you next time. Remember, I am your doom."

"Anything wrong, Inspector?" inquired Hsiawen as she saw him flush.

Bei looked up. "Wrong? Why, no . . . Did General Fu say that Captain Wang would be on guard here today and tomorrow?"

"Yes. In fact, he's just outside the door now. Shall I ask him to step in?"

Bei shook his head. "I was just wondering."

He relaxed somewhat as Hsiawen left the room. So he was safe here, now. But he would not have Wang with him always. And Wang would not be allowed in the Purple Mountain for the meeting with Mao, at which Captain Li would doubtless be present. At some point, at some time, Bei would have to confront the Baleful Star and best him. But how? He steeled himself and banished the glowing eyes from his consciousness. How? The Baleful Star, come to do us harm. What did the note say? I am your doom. Li had said that last night also. "I am your doom, and his doom." Who had he meant by "his doom"? Oh, yes. "That big-headed Hunan braggart." But what did that mean? Bei willed himself to replay the frightening events of last night in his mind, searching for clues to a Hunan braggart or for an opening through which he could get at the Baleful Star and do him harm, reverse the flow of doom. Yes. He had to be strong, and somehow find a way to reverse the flow of doom emanating from the Baleful Star, turn his hatred and sickness in upon himself. Bei flushed and began to sweat as the images of the Baleful Star from last night grated across his mind, image after terrible image, until one lodged there and wouldn't pass on, and as he wondered why it refused to move on, Bei looked more closely at it, and saw. Saw the flow of doom weaken, then begin to trickle back upon itself, and finally reverse. Saw that Li's hatred and perversion could be turned in upon himself. Saw how he could master the Baleful Star and do him harm, finally do him harm as he had harmed so many others so horribly. Bei closed his eyes hard and began to cry for hope and for strength to do what he had to do.

Fu shoved the paperwork to the side of his desk. Meaningless details. Necessary, but meaningless. He turned his chair and stared out into the garden. The waiting was the hardest. Waiting for word from Li Tsungjen in Nanking. From Yeh Chienying in Lianghsiang.

He glanced at the door to the hallway. How he missed her. At moments like this, to be able to walk through that door and into her room, and be warmed and cheered by her laughter, her vitality, her youth. He ached for her still.

A lesson would do him good, get his mind off the work, invigorate him. He rose and walked through the door and into her room on the left. The calligraphy table was littered with sheaves of paper from yesterday afternoon. He could not rouse himself sufficiently to practice in the mornings without her cheerful prodding, so he had switched the lessons to the afternoons. He sat down at the table, added water to the ink bowl, and mixed a slurry of ink. As he did so, he reviewed what she would have been saying to him. The posture, holding the brush correctly, the slant of the wrist. The concentration, letting the Tao flow through the brush. Spontaneity through disciplined practice. The characters, a representation of the ebb and flow of the Tao, waxing and waning, yang and yin.

He sat there before the window, his mind full of her precepts, his body open to incarnating the flow of the force which had coursed through her so strongly. He brushed the characters of the poem he had composed two days ago, four days after her death. They flowed slowly, but smoothly. After twenty minutes he put down the brush and looked at them critically. The transitions from one stroke to the next within the characters were too rigid, too mechanical. But that would come with practice. He smiled feelingly as he sat gazing at the poem, looked up and stared out the window, then quietly arose and walked softly back to his office and his work. The poem lay on the table, sunlight glinting off the still wet characters.

> "From Heaven rain falls to earth, gathering in a pool.
> The water shimmers, mirroring the beauty around it.
> In time's course the water completes its journey,
> Flowing from pool to lustrous depths of the sea,

There to give life to yet another world of creatures.
So you fell into my life, shimmering and vital,
And are now gone, joined in the great transformation,
The autumn wind over the sea of life."

Bei had fallen into a deep sleep after the procession of the images of the Baleful Star through his mind, and lay unmoving for six hours. It was late afternoon when he opened his eyes again, remembered where he was, and became aware of a ravenous hunger. A figure was sitting across the room.

"Mayor Ho."

"Hello, Bei."

The two smiled at each other, the knowing smile of friends who have seen each other through difficult times.

" 'Disasters never come singly,' " quoted Ho.

Bei shook his head gingerly. "Do not class my accident with your great loss, old friend." A pause. "How did your peace committee meetings with General Fu and Commander Yeh this morning turn out?"

Ho smiled wanly. "Fine. Perhaps it will lead to something." He stared gently at Bei, and spoke softly. "I've been thinking a lot about what you said to me, in my courtyard yesterday morning."

"Yes?"

"I don't know that I understand the talk about the Tao. I'm a Confucian, of course. But what you said—Bright Jade's Tao is here. Draw on it. Honor her by letting the Tao that was in her course through you. That says something to me." He smiled wanly. "I'm not sure what it says. But it has comforted me. Considerably. And actually given me the energy to . . . to continue living. Perhaps even with enjoyment, someday."

Silence filled the darkening room. There was no need for many words between them.

"Good," Bei said simply.

Ho stood up. "I'll go now."

"No hurry," answered Bei. "I feel quite rested. How is Madame Ho?"

342

Ho breathed deeply. "Very sore. And clutching tight onto the other children. She hardly allows them out of her sight."

Bei nodded.

Ho stood there in the middle of the room, his figure spare and dark in the fading light. "I'm still sleeping in the study. Even though there's plenty of room in our bed now." He began to weep softly. Bei averted his eyes. The sight of him standing alone, shoulders shaking in the dim light, was too painful. His muffled sobs filled the room, then tapered off.

"Thank you for coming," said Bei after Ho had stopped weeping.

Ho nodded. "Can I do anything for you?" he asked in a broken voice.

"Yes. Tell the nurse I'm incredibly hungry."

They both laughed weakly.

January 19

Bei spent the morning drifting in and out of sleep, troubled as usual of late by images of dead bodies and hateful eyes. He surfaced, of course, for lunch. The ravenous appetite he had acquired since his brush with death was a surprise to him. He had always been rather a gourmet, inclined to indulge his appetite only in those dishes which piqued his interest. Now he consumed everything, indiscriminately, and actually enjoyed it. Imagine. Relishing tomato and beef. As outlandish as enjoying the company of soldiers. And Taoist priestesses. He had changed in the past few weeks. Not even the Baleful Star could alter that. In fact, he was already looking forward to his next meeting with Captain Li. For now he knew. Knew what it would take to master the Baleful Star, and how he might do it, if indeed it could be done. This afternoon.

The nurse who took his lunch tray away handed him two letters forwarded from his office. One was in his wife's hand, with a Hangchow postmark. The other was from his brother, a Nanking postmark. He

343

opened the letter from his wife and read it. The letter dropped to the sheets as Bei stared at the wall for several minutes, hurt, sad, but not surprised. He didn't bother to read his brother's letter. After several more minutes of staring at the wall he sighed, and thought of the Taoist inscription on the tablet in the Chunghai Lake pavilion.

Wang appeared at the door. "General Fu to see you, sir."

Bei nodded, and put away the letters as Fu strode into the room.

"You look better today, Inspector. Ready for the meeting at the Purple Mountain monastery this afternoon?"

"Not just ready. Eager for it."

Fu looked at him closely. "Yes. I imagine it will be a relief to confront the Baleful Star before his superiors, and . . . what?"

"I know how to master the Baleful Star, Fu," declared Bei calmly. "Or at least how it is to be done if it can be done at all."

"Indeed? And how is that?"

Bei shook his head. "No need for you to know. It would sound too incredible, too nightmarish to you. To anyone who wasn't there when . . . when it happened. But I'm sure I can rely on it. And use it to undo him, to bring some justice to bear on the perverted world in which he lives."

"And if this secret plan of yours doesn't work?"

Bei stared hard at Fu. "I don't know. I only know it is my only hope. So it must be done."

Fu stared back. "Yes," he finally said. "I understand. One can only play one's part to the full, and hope that somehow it contributes to the sweep of 'The Autumn Wind Over the Sea of Life'."

Bei looked up sharply at Fu. "What did you say?"

Fu stared back, puzzled. "I was just wandering. Philosophy."

"Where did you hear of 'The Autumn Wind Over the Sea of Life'?" Bei demanded.

Fu looked pained. "Why, it . . . it was a favorite saying of Meilu's. We discussed it often."

"Do you know where it is inscribed?"

"No. I don't."

"It's on the marble tablet in the old pavilion that sits in Chunghai Lake."

Fu smiled, and nodded. "That I can believe. I can see a Ming Emperor sitting there five hundred years ago, pondering the words."

"What do they mean to you?" Bei asked bluntly.

"To me? I only know what Meilu taught me about them. She said that life is a grand, onrushing drama. That some of us are fated to live in an autumn age when an act of that drama comes to terrible fruition. When the Sea of Life around us is shaken by that Autumn Wind." He paused, and added softly, "A time of death, and dying, autumn."

Bei nodded his head in the silence. "Yes. But a time of promised rebirth, also. A time when the seeds of the next act of the drama are formed, and secreted away deep within the fruits of the dying age."

Fu sighed deeply. "She said something like that also. That destruction is necessary for regeneration. But I . . . I seem to be caught up mainly in the deaths. The dying." He thought of the men at Chochow, of Jie, and Ling, and of Meilu, and fought back his tears angrily.

Bei spoke quickly, to pretend he didn't hear the catch in Fu's throat. "I know what you mean. The dying seems so much more apparent than the seeds hidden in the fruit. But it's also important, to me, to realize that the Autumn Wind is relentless. We can only watch it sweep over the Sea of Life. Play our parts as best we can, to be sure. Remember the seeds of promised rebirth secreted away within all the death, to be sure. But . . . it somehow comforts me. To step back in the midst of it all, all the dying and birthing, and realize that it is all . . . all a great, relentless drama. And wonder at the sheer drama and . . . terrible majesty of it all. The Autumn Wind Over the Sea of Life."

"Yes. You're right," admitted Fu. "I must remember all that. It helps me. Thank you for reminding me." He looked at Bei kindly. "And I suppose it helps you, as you go to the Purple Mountain to confront a man who has already tried to murder you once."

Bei drew in a deep breath. "Yes, it helps. But I'm still scared. Even knowing what I have to do, and how to do it, I'm still scared."

Fu nodded and resumed his brisk, business manner. "At the meeting, Bei, please remind Mao and Yeh Chienying for me that we must know before Saturday whether they will accept the final draft of the transfer of power document which Zhou delivered to them yesterday. Remind them that Lin Piao has threatened to assault the city Saturday if we have not come to an agreement."

"Of course. I will not leave the Purple Mountain without an answer from them."

"Thank you," Fu answered.

After Fu left the room, Bei called for Wang.

He appeared at the doorway. "Yes, sir."

"The limousine is here, ready to depart?"

"Yes, sir."

"Good."

Fu Hsiawen walked in. "What's this talk about a limousine?" she asked, as she checked Bei's dressings.

"I have a ride to take this afternoon to a meeting."

She glanced up in surprise. "A ride? To a meeting? Absolutely not."

Bei laughed, then winced.

"I'm perfectly serious," she persisted. "I forbid it. You have a good many stitches in you, and your numerous wounds are only half-healed, if that. A bouncy car ride and walking around would quite likely open some of them up again."

Bei shrugged gingerly. "Sorry. It can't be helped. I have to be there."

"I'm sorry too. But you'll have to tell them you can't make it."

Bei regarded her with amusement. "Lean over here, Hsiawen, and I'll whisper to you the people who are expecting me at the meeting."

She did so, and her eyes steadily widened as he listed the persons who would be there. Without a word she left the room, returning a minute later with a large syringe in her hand.

"What do you plan to do with that?" Bei asked in alarm.

"Stick it in you, Inspector," she answered. "It's penicillin. Straight from Nanking. About the only thing aboard the few planes braving the shelling is antibiotics—our courageous Kuomintang generals have a horror of infection, it seems."

"So?"

"So you will open some of your wounds today, and likely get an infection started if you aren't protected. This is your protection," she said, holding up the syringe. "Roll onto your side."

"Miss Fu, this is not decorous!" Bei protested sternly.

She smiled. "Many things will happen soon which will not seem

346

decorous to your Confucian mind, Inspector. Shall I pull up your gown, or will you?"

Bei sat uncomfortably in the back seat as the limousine bounced up the trail between the village and the Purple Mountain. She had been right. He hurt, and knew that some of the wounds were reopening. No matter. Soon it would be over, one way or another.

"Are you sure this is the right way, sir?" Wang asked for the third time, glancing back in the mirror.

Bei nodded. "Yes, Wang. Positive. But find a place to pull over soon. It gets nothing but worse from here on, and it's not too far for a walk."

"Gladly, sir. This is rough going, and General Fu wouldn't appreciate my ruining his Citroën."

Wang helped Bei out of the car, Bei wincing at the strain put on the wounded shoulder.

"Thank heaven my legs are all right," he remarked, glad to be out of the bouncy car. They walked in silence in the soft late-afternoon light. The only sounds were the occasional cawings of a faraway group of crows, and the continuous splash of water against rocks from the stream to their right. It was bitterly cold, even in the sunlight. Bei breathed the crisp air deeply. Living in Peking, one forgot what air was like without dust and coal in it, especially in the winter.

The gates to the Purple Mountain were open, and Abbot T'ang, Meiling, and Dufeng stood in the opening. Meiling came forward and appraised Bei's appearance with an anxious eye.

"Well. I'm alive, anyway," Bei said with embarrassment. "Thanks to you, I understand."

"It was nothing. Repayment of a debt I owed you for the same service."

He nodded.

"Welcome, Inspector Bei," said the abbot. "Meiling will escort you to the Great Hall. Only Mao and Chou have not arrived, and I will bring them myself."

He glanced at Wang. "I presume neither of you are armed?"

"No," said Bei and Wang in unison.

"We know the inspector, but we do not know this handsome young officer, so you will excuse us if we verify his word. Dufeng, search him."

Wang raised his arms and Dufeng deftly searched him, then stepped back.

"Thank you. Please make yourself comfortable in the gatehouse here, Officer."

Bei cast a glance at Wang, then proceeded up the walkway with Meiling.

"You appear to be in considerable pain, Bei," said Meiling.

He looked at her in surprise. "I didn't know it was so obvious. Although I was fine before I left the hospital."

"How is Hsiawen?"

Bei smiled. "Fine. She is a good nurse."

Meiling paused. "Yeh is here, and Lin Piao. And Captain Li." Bei stopped walking, looked at her, then resumed. "We have placed you at one end of the semicircle of chairs and him on the other end, so you are far apart, yet you can keep an eye on him."

Bei nodded.

"I will be next to you, and my father next to Captain Li. Two chairs will separate each of us from the middle four chairs in the top of the circle, at which Yeh and Lin and Mao and Chou will sit."

They arrived at the Great Hall and walked in. Turning right from the hallway, they entered the room. Bei's attention was captured by the enormous fire raging in the large fireplace of the opposite wall, above which the yin-yang jade disk floated upon the wall. The fire sent shadows flickering across the room as it took the chill off the air. All the chairs faced the fire in a semicircle, as before. Meiling led Bei to the last two chairs on the right. As they sat, Bei nodded to Yeh Chienying, who was seated on their side of the two empty capstone seats in the middle of the semicircle. On the other side of these empty seats sat a thin, severe figure whom Bei took to be Lin Piao. Bei's gaze swung past three empty chairs beyond him and rested upon the Baleful Star. Hatred and something akin to blood lust were written in Li's eyes, although he did not stir. Bei grimly noted the ugly bruise on Li's face, then looked away into the fire. Huge logs gave themselves eagerly to the flames, crackling and exploding as the fire transformed them into heat and gas and glowing red coals. Bei rehearsed what he would do, repeating the words in his mind, and wondered if his hunch about the braggart's doom was right.

A bustle in the hallway grabbed everyone's attention, and soon three figures strode in. One was T'ang, who quietly proceeded to the seat next to Li, opposite Meiling and Bei. Mao Tsetung took command of the room immediately, before a word was spoken. He appeared huge in his winter coat and hat, and surveyed the room quickly as he removed his gloves. Even after he had taken off his coat and hat and handed them to one of the three guards who followed him, it was apparent that he was the largest person in the room, an impression created by his height and bulk as well as the authority which emanated from him in nearly palpable waves.

Beside Mao, Chou Enlai appeared small, although this was not actually the case. Whereas Mao was bathed in an aura of raw power, Chou radiated a warm competence and suave self-composure. The two men complemented each other perfectly, and had worked in tandem for twenty years, with Mao by now the first among them by virtue of his uncanny ability to pull the right decision out of a tangle of conflicting men and motives. Or perhaps to galvanize that tangle of men and motives into directions which made his decision the right one.

Mao and Chou took the center seats, nodding warmly to Yeh and Lin Piao, and cursorily to the four gathered at the ends of the semicircle. The three guards stationed themselves inside the door.

Mao turned in his chair and spoke to the guards in a thick Hunanese accent. "Close the doors and station yourselves outside them." Bei caught his breath as he heard Mao speak.

When the doors had swung shut and they were alone in the room, Mao breathed deeply. His head was large, with a mass of jet black hair swept back to either side from the center. His face belied his fifty-five years, giving him the appearance of a young scholar. The expression on his face was beyond self-assurance. It was the expression of a man supremely convinced that he had fashioned history in his own image, bent it to his own vision by sheer force of intellect and sacrifice.

At last he spoke, warmly but with authority. "It has been a long battle, has it not?" He glanced at the three men seated next to him, Chou, Yeh, and Lin Piao. "Kwangchow, Whampoa and the Peasant

349

Institute. The Kiangsi Soviet, among the pines and mountains. The Long March, a day ahead of death for a year and six thousand miles. The Japanese War, honing our guerrilla techniques. And this last phase."

He smiled, and embraced the entire room in his pleasure. "Yet here we are, ready to establish the capital of a new China. Soon we shall put aside some of the things we know well, and be compelled to do things we don't know well. We shall put aside guns and killing and mountain hideouts, and take up brushes and committees and cities." His smile faded imperceptibly, leaving a warm glow behind. "A long road, to be sure, to here. A very long road."

He gazed inward, and all followed that gaze. "We've struggled so hard, for thirty years. Fought desperately for thirty years. Seen our friends, wives, lovers, children killed by our enemies. The price has indeed been great."

He sighed deeply. "And we have repaid our enemies in kind. We have fought, and killed. Revolutions are made no other way. For centuries the people have been destroyed like so much straw; justice, the tide of history, demands that their oppressors taste the same fate."

The firelight flickered on his large, impassive face. "So when we have made mistakes, the consequences have been serious. In thirty years, mistakes occur. Sometimes people die because of our mistakes. When you total up thirty years of death, a single death seems slight. But we can learn from mistakes, just as we learn from history. We can redirect our efforts and avoid the mistakes in the future."

"So." He glanced around the chairs. "Let me recount my understanding of the events which have brought us together. In conjunction with the Purple Mountain, Chou Enlai brought An Shihlin to the White Cloud Temple to direct our infiltration of Peking in 1937. For over a decade Comrade An worked hard and well to build our underground in the city. Last November Lin Piao completed our conquest of Manchuria, and moved his Liberation Army south to invest Peking on December thirteenth. On December twenty-fifth An Shihlin was killed by a group of monks in the White Cloud Temple."

He nodded his head decisively. "So much we know for sure. I understand there is some evidence that an associate of Comrade Lin was involved in Comrade An's death." He shifted his massive head to direct his gaze at Bei, who inwardly quailed at his attention. "I presume this gentleman to my right is the Peking police inspector who so capably investigated Comrade An's death. What did you learn?"

Bei gazed at the floor to organize his answer. "The leader of the monks who burned An Shihlin said that he had been paid and encouraged to cause trouble for him. I observed the monk receive money from Captain Li, Lin Piao's aide, shortly after An's death. The monk later positively identified Captain Li as the man who paid him to have An killed."

"How reliable is the word of this Taoist monk?"

Bei saw Abbot T'ang raise his eyebrows at Mao's inflection of the term "Taoist monk," but answered quickly.

"We applied no torture to him, nor did we pay him for the identification. In addition, I saw Captain Li with the monk. And finally, Captain Li rewarded me for my labors by trying to kill me the night before last."

The fire crackled in the silence that followed. Mao sighed. A phrase wafted softly into Bei's consciousness. As doomed as that big-headed Hunan braggart. He shifted uneasily in his seat.

"Comrade Lin, what do you say to all this?" Mao intoned.

Lin Piao sat stiffly upright and stared straight ahead. "You had ordered me to surround the city and accomplish its surrender, Comrade Mao. In my judgment the activities of An Shihlin and his motley underground were not merely superfluous to that task, but made it more difficult by virtue of their ineffective scheming and diversionary plots. So I took steps to eliminate this distracting nuisance from the picture."

Mao pursed his lips. "Did you order your aide here to have An Shihlin killed?"

At this question Chou Enlai leaned forward and directed a hard gaze at Lin Piao. Lin stared straight ahead still, but paused a moment before he spoke. "I instructed my aide to encourage the monk to disrupt An's activity. I did not specifically direct him to arrange for the death of the man, but neither did I specifically preclude that. I . . . I regard the man's death as unfortunate, but I accept full responsibility for it, since I have the utmost confidence in Captain Li."

Li, who had sat stiffly through the proceedings up to now, turned a face full of admiration and gratitude to Lin Piao.

Mao stood, picked up the cup of tea from the table beside him, and walked slowly to the fire. He stared into it for several minutes as he sipped the tea. No one moved or spoke. He turned, and walked deliberately back to his chair, and sat down, holding the teacup in his hand still.

"Comrade Lin," began Mao in a weary voice. "You have been one of us from the beginning. You commanded the vanguard in the Long March. You have conquered Manchuria for us faster than even I had anticipated. You are indispensable to our final, imminent victory, in which you will play the leading role in the field."

Li's eyes glowed as Mao spoke, and he directed an admiring look at Lin Piao.

"Yet your judgment in this instance was wretched."

Li jerked in his chair as if the lash of a whip had hit him.

Mao continued in a hard voice. "You were wrong in your assessment of the Peking underground, and wrong in your decision to harass its leader."

Li began to tremble at Mao's words, and looked desperately and furiously from Lin to Mao.

"Worst of all, you were terribly wrong to give an obviously unstable aide free rein in such a sensitive matter."

Li sat perfectly still at Mao's reference to him, which struck Bei as more ominous than his previous agitation. Soon he would know if his hunch were correct.

"You will henceforth stick strictly to—"

"No!" shrieked Li suddenly, the cry erupting from him violently as he jumped to his feet facing Mao. "You will not lecture Commander Lin, you will not!" With this he reached into his coat and jerked out a pistol which he pointed directly at Mao's massive head.

Everyone in the room gasped, except Bei and Mao. Mao sat there impassively, staring into the barrel of the pistol with not a trace of alarm or fear, his teacup steady in his hand.

"Commander Lin is your superior in strategy and revolutionary fervor—how dare you lecture him! I can end your pompous lecture for good, here and now!"

No one moved, for fear of frightening the agitated Li into a rash act. But only one person in the room knew that underneath Li's instability lay a premeditated decision to kill Mao, the big-headed braggart from Hunan. Bei stirred in his chair, and leaned over to whisper to Meiling.

"Signal your father to be ready. I'll draw his attention to me."

Meiling clutched Bei's arm and stared at him in alarm. No longer neutral, thought Bei with a surge of satisfaction, which was immediately displaced by a grim concentration on the scene before him. As he had suspected, it had come to this.

Li had stepped back from the semicircle of chairs when he rose, placing himself near the hearth of the fire, with a commanding view of the full array of seats before him as he stood with his eyes staring down the pistol barrel at Mao in the center. Yet if he were forced to turn towards Bei, then T'ang on his right would be out of his view.

"Li." Everyone in the room jumped at Bei's voice, again excepting Mao, whose teacup was still perfectly steady in his hand. Bei rose as he called Li's name, and heard with relief the muffled click of Meiling's fingers as she signaled T'ang the message from her fluttering hand.

"You're mixing your dreams, Li. You know what happens when you mix them. Put the pistol down," Bei said in a sharp voice.

Li calmed perceptibly, and backed a step closer to the fire, so he could catch a glimpse of Bei out of the corner of his eye without losing sight of Mao in front of his pistol. Bei grimaced, realizing that the backward step would make it harder for T'ang to make it to Li unobserved.

"You mean to kill Mao, don't you, Li?" Bei said in the quiet that had gripped the room. "You told me that on the night you tried to kill me, didn't you?"

Li's hands began to tremble now, shaking the tightly gripped pistol at the end of his outstretched arms, still aimed directly at Mao's massive head.

Li laughed, too loudly and too long. "You have a sharp ear, yes, you do. But he won't be the only dead man in the room, you turtle. You'll be next, for soiling my sister. How dare you soil her!" His hand began to jerk convulsively now, and with each jerk Bei and the others winced for fear the pistol would go off into Mao's head. Bei knew he would have to get to Li quickly now, but Li's last comment convinced him it could be done.

"Oh, she was perfect last night, your sister," said Bei. "Just like in your dreams, Li. Lying before me, quivering, her Red Flower blooming, Li, blooming. Can you picture what I'm saying, Li? Picture it."

Li shook his head and yelled, "No!" He moved a step closer to Mao. But then with a moan, two soft words escaped from his lips.

"Blooming . . . quivering."

"That's right, Li," said Bei. "Quivering in front of me." He noted T'ang sitting very still beyond Li, his body beginning to vibrate delicately as if gathering strands of energy.

"She was blooming, Li, and moaning," continued Bei. "She closed her eyes and moaned aloud, arching her neck, Li, so lovely and white."

"White . . . lovely, white neck," Li groaned, beginning to cast desperate short glances in Bei's direction away from Mao and the line of his pistol. The others in the room watched in horror as the vision began to grip Li. Yet the pistol was still trained on Mao. Meiling's right hand crept slowly to her neck, and she exhaled in anger as she realized she was not wearing the jade disk.

"Then I took my knife, Li, and put it beside your sister's slender neck, saw the edge of the knife gleaming in the candlelight, Li."

Li shook his head again, trying desperately to clear the dream from it, and took another step toward Mao, thrusting the pistol at full arm's length at Mao's head. He tensed, ready to pull the trigger. But again he groaned.

"Slender neck . . . gleaming. Oh, no, no," he wailed.

T'ang edged to the front of his seat, and positioned his feet.

"Look at me, Li," Bei commanded. "Look at me putting the knife blade on your sister's pulsing throat. I'm pulling it across her throat, Li, cutting into the white skin, and now—"

"No!" Li shrieked, and shaking violently turned his body to aim the pistol directly at Bei. As he did so, T'ang erupted unseen from his chair and scuttled low the few meters to Li. In a blur The Wind Rushing Up the Cliff whished past Li's groin and up through his outstretched arms. The pistol fired as T'ang's hand ripped into Li's throat with tremendous force. Meiling screamed. Li's head was thrown back by T'ang's blow, blood surging from the severed carotid arteries. The pistol dropped to the floor as Li fell backward in slow motion, the last two beats of his heart shooting forth long fountains of blood: the first arching gracefully up and splattering against the jade disk on

354

the wall, the second spluttering into the fire to sizzle and snarl as the blood vaporized. Li's body hit the floor, his head on the hearth of the roaring fire, still sizzling with his blood.

Bei swayed, his ears ringing from the roar of the bullet that had passed within an inch of his head. He became aware of Meiling clutching his chest, and realized she had thrown herself in front of him as Li had fired the pistol. She was sobbing convulsively, and both of them were thinking now of Meilu, and Meilu's death. Bei felt his throat constrict and tears well up as he put his arms gently around Meiling, felt her sobbing for her dead sister, and realized what she had done for him. Such a precious gift he held in his arms.

T'ang remained standing before the fire, his left hand bracing the right still, the right hand red with blood to the wrist, clutching parts of Li's larynx and esophagus. He held the position as if in a trance, which indeed he was. Blood dripped from his hand, splattering on the floor in counterpoint to the sizzling in the fire.

Mao's voice gently cut into Li's sizzling blood and Meiling's muffled sobs. "Miss T'ang. It would be filial of you to bring your father a bowl of water and a towel to clean his hand."

She detached herself unsteadily from Bei's embrace and left the room. The others sank back into their chairs, drained by the spectacle. Except Mao, who stood, poured himself another cup of tea, and walked between T'ang and Bei to Li's body.

T'ang awoke from his trance, and tossed the bits of Li's throat into the great fire, where they quickly disappeared.

Mao stared at the fire's consumption of Li's throat. "Wasn't An Shihlin burned to death, Inspector Bei?"

"Yes," answered Bei hoarsely.

Mao set his teacup aside, and stooped down to Li's body and searched through the coat and trousers, removing an extra clip of bullets.

"Lin. Come here."

Lin Piao walked up to the fire.

"Grab his feet and swing them up to the hearth."

Lin Piao stared at Mao, then did as he was told. Mao grabbed the body by the shoulders and lifted it up easily, Lin still holding the feet.

"For you, Lin, it will be a ceremonial honor to a comrade whose responsibilities were heavier than his sanity could bear. For Inspector Bei, it will be a fitting end for the man's crime."

They swung the body out, then into the fire with a grunt. It landed well back in the flames, and instantly ignited.

"And for the rest of us," concluded Mao as they watched the body flare and disappear in the intense flame, "it will be just another death."

The flesh evaporated as a sweetish smell wafted through the room, then the bones stood out stark and white against the orange of the flames. Soon the air was fresh again and the bones began to crumple into delicate chunks. A large knife slid off some coals where the feet had been and dropped silently to the floor of the hearth, glowing brightly like a star amidst the flames.

Mao turned and walked over to Bei. "Our friend T'ang and his ancestors have been saving lives crucial to China's destiny for decades, even centuries. They are beyond mere thanks. But you, Inspector—this was not your fight. Thank you for saving my life."

Bei nodded in response to Mao's thanks, as Meiling returned and cleaned her father's crimson hand in a bowl of water. Bei gazed at her, marveling.

Mao continued, Bei reluctantly returning his attention to him. "Tell your General Fu that the agreement Colonel Zhou brought to us yesterday is acceptable. Yeh Chienying here will sign it in General Fu's office the day after tomorrow."

"I will gladly relay that message," Bei said, restraining an indecorous grin of relief.

"It would be appropriate if you were there for the signing, Inspector," added Yeh from his seat.

"Yes," Mao said. "I understand from Yeh that you would be valuable to him as a personal assistant or perhaps chief of police when we liberate Peking. So please be there for the transfer of power."

"Certainly," Bei said softly, humbled by the honor.

"Meanwhile, we all have much work to do," Mao said briskly. He walked out of the Great Hall, the others in the command trailing behind him.

Meiling finished drying her father's hand and looked over to Bei. "You'll stay with us tonight?"

He stared into her eyes. So lovely. So dear to him. "If you want me to be here."

She returned his gaze, solemn, unblinking, then simply nodded her head.

Epilogue: January 22

Fu sat stiffly in his office at the ebony table, which had been cleared of papers and moved to the center of the room. To either side of him on one side of the table were Zhou and General Teng Paoshan. Bei and a representative from Nanking occupied the chairs at either end of the table. All were awaiting the arrival of Yeh Chien-ying and his party in order to commence the ceremony of signing the agreement.

Chiang Kaishek had resigned January 21, two days after Mao had informed Bei at the Purple Mountain of his acceptance of the final proposals for transfer of power in Peking from General Fu to the Communists. With that resignation and Li Tsungjen's ascension to the presidency of the Nationalist government, the right-wing opposition in Peking to Fu's agreement with the Communists had evaporated.

Fu was wearing his full-dress uniform for the signing, and the room was resplendent with formal touches: his army's banner in one corner; a large and elaborately carved jade bowl from the Forbidden City in another corner; a lapis lazuli landscape carving sitting in the middle of the ebony table, golden flecks suffused over its rich blue surface; and flanking it two steaming teapots of the finest white porcelain, with crimson and gold dragons winding around the pots. Matching cups were placed in front of each chair at the table.

Ordinarily Fu would have disdained to adorn his office with these touches. But it was clear that the occasion would be historic. The signing of the first peaceful transfer of power in a major city from a Nationalist government to a Communist-dominated "coalition" government, the forging of a pattern which could be copied in other cities and might permit the inevitable union of the nation to occur relatively smoothly and bloodlessly.

Captain Wang entered the room. "Commander Yeh Chienying and his party, sir."

"Please escort them in, Captain Wang," said Fu.

Yeh Chienying entered with two officers. Everyone rose from the table.

"Commander Yeh: We are honored to have you in the Winter Palace," said Fu, noting the simple uniforms without adornment the Communists wore even on this occasion.

"Thank you, General Fu. May I introduce two of my officers: Commander Ying Lubo and Commander Ju Taohsing."

Fu bowed. "And allow me to introduce my officers: General Teng Paoshan and Colonel Zhou Peifeng. From Nanking representing President Li Tsungjen, General Hsia Jiwen. And representing the city of Peking, Inspector Bei Menjin, whom most of us know well already."

Bows were exchanged all around.

"Captain Wang, please serve the tea. Shall we be seated?" Fu said, indicating to Yeh the seats on the opposite side of the table.

"Please do, gentlemen," said Yeh. "But may I have a word with you, General Fu, before we proceed?"

"Certainly," answered Fu, successfully hiding his surprise. "Please enjoy your tea, gentlemen." As Wang poured the tea, Fu and Yeh walked to the far side of the room, behind Fu's desk, and stood with their backs to the others, facing through the window toward the garden.

"A lovely garden," opened Yeh.

"Thank you," answered Fu. "I understand the T'aihu was brought from Lake T'ai Hu by the Yungle Emperor himself in 1422."

"It is indeed a treasure. Which all the people of China may be proud of."

"Quite so," said Fu, with a slight smile at Yeh's insertion of the Communist viewpoint.

Yeh paused for a calculated moment, then spoke in a low voice. "We want to have the Kuomintang Generals Shih Chueh and Li Wen."

Fu was not surprised. He answered quickly and firmly. "They are not mine to give."

"Of course they are, General. You could give them to us today."

"Only at considerable cost and risk, Commander. They command a full division each, both of which are currently on full alert."

"Nonetheless, you command in Peking. It could be done, even though at a cost."

"Perhaps. There is another consideration, though. I gave them my word they could leave for Nanking before your forces occupy the city. It was the price I had to pay for their agreement not to contest the transfer of power."

"I understand that. But circumstances change, and I have had to alter some few understandings myself, General Fu, in the course of thirty years."

"As have I, Commander Yeh. But like you, only rarely, reluctantly, and for very important considerations."

"They have caused the deaths of many of the Chinese people, General. Their crimes are legion. Justice demands their death."

"They are ghosts already, Commander. You will have their troops and their weapons. Without their troops they are nothing. They will fly south and disappear. They will do nothing to haunt you."

A trace of anger rose in Yeh's voice. "It is not fear of them that prompts us, General. We shall soon sweep them and their kind to the south before us as leaves are swept by the autumn wind. We want them because of their crimes, and because of the people's stolen wealth they will take with them."

Fu was silent, desperately calculating how far Yeh would go, balancing the stakes on either side. One last puzzle to grapple with. He came to a decision.

"I appreciate your concerns, Commander Yeh. I refuse your request, however, on the grounds that it would violate my word and, moreover, risk the successful implementation of the transfer of power."

Fu and Yeh stared out the window, neither willing to yield to the other, yet neither willing to sacrifice the historic agreement they had so painstakingly reached. Yeh finally broke the tense silence.

"Would you agree to a binding arbitrator on this last point, General Fu? A man in whom we both have absolute confidence?"

Fu stared straight ahead grimly. Finally he turned, and said in a smooth voice, "Inspector Bei. May we have the pleasure of your company?"

Bei rose and walked around the desk to the window.

"Sir?"

"It appears one last obstacle blocks our path, Inspector. Commander Yeh insists that I deliver to him Generals Shih Chueh and Li Wen, on the grounds that they have committed crimes against the people which demand retribution. I have refused, on the grounds that it would violate an understanding with them on my part that won their support of the agreement we are—or may be—about to sign. Your decision on the matter shall be binding."

Bei stared mutely at Fu, then at Yeh, for a long moment. Silence gripped the entire room.

"May I presume, Commander Yeh, that these generals would share the same fate as General Yu when I delivered him to you last week?"

"You may. And for the same reasons, I should add."

Bei reflected.

"And I presume, General Fu, that you gave your word to these generals that they would be able to leave the city unharmed?"

"That is correct."

Bei stared out the window. The T'aihu stone loomed on the hillside, its surface pitted and scarred by the centuries. It reminded him of the tablet in the pavilion in Chunghai Lake.

"Gentlemen. I do not contest that these two generals may deserve to die. Nor that death is a necessary part of the unification and rebirth of China. But I, for one, am tired of death. I wish to see no more of my fellow Chinese die. For whatever reason. That is why the agreement we are about to sign is so important. Let us get on with it, gentlemen."

After a long moment, Yeh sighed. "Very well. I suppose it should comfort me, General Fu, that you value your word so highly, since we will be working together in the cabinet soon. Let us sign the documents."

The three men returned to the table, Bei to the end seat, Fu and Yeh to the middle seats on either side. Zhou had placed an official copy of the agreement in front of the two leaders, along with pens. Each of them quickly perused the document before him.

"I have read the document and agree to its terms," announced Fu after a minute.

Yeh looked up, over the lapis lazuli at Fu.

"And I have read the document and find its terms acceptable."

360

They each picked up a pen and inscribed their name and the date January 22, 1949, at the bottom right margin of the last page of their copy. Then they exchanged copies across the table, quickly perused the other's copy, and signed and dated these as well. An audible sigh rose from around the table.

"Gentlemen, would you please witness the signatures," Fu requested. Each copy was then passed clockwise around the table, and the other six men inscribed their signatures to the left of Yeh's and Fu's.

In the silence, Yeh and Fu sat stiffly across from each other at the table, each tingling with emotion, similar thoughts in the mind of each. Thirty years of strife. Thirty years of death. Coming now to an end. No more would they see their colleagues fall, never to rise. After thirty years of destroying, they could turn now to constructing, building a new and united China. They felt very proud, and very humble. And suddenly very weary.

Bei was thinking not of the past, but of the future. His Peking, once again at peace, once again the capital of a united China ruled by Chinese. He and Meiling, together, serving his beloved city, nurturing its life and their common life in it. His eyes came to rest on the lapis lazuli piece in the center of the table, and the porcelain dragons of the teapots to either side of it. Lapis lazuli from the earth, and dragons from the heaven. Blue specked with gold, balanced against crimson laced with gold. The ancient conjunction of heaven and earth, sky and soil, crimson and blue, yang and yin. For millennia his civilization had grasped that these polar forces were not opposites but complements. For millennia the forces inherent in each had been valued, and the strength and power gained by balancing them had been perceived and practiced, lost and forgotten, then rediscovered. Each time they had lost the secret and had focused only on the dragon or only on the lapis lazuli, a foreign invader had conquered them. First the Mongols, then the Manchus, then the West. Perhaps this room was witnessing yet another moment of rediscovery of the secret. Perhaps the crimson and the blue were to be rejoined in the gold yet again, and the fused power of yang and yin would once again lift their civilization to another peak. Perhaps.

FACTUAL RÉSUMÉ OF ACTUAL HISTORICAL EVENTS AND FATE OF HISTORICAL CHARACTERS

(For documentation, see Sources, which follows)

ANCIENT TIMES

Mid-700's	T'ang Dynasty Emperor Hsuan Tsung donates statue of Lao-tzu to T'ian Chang Temple.
1202	T'ian Chang Temple burns.
1224	Genghis Khan invites Ch'iu Changchun to reside in rebuilt temple, renamed T'ai Chi Palace.
1227	Ch'iu dies, cremated, ashes buried under main Shrine Hall, temple renamed Changchun Palace.
1420's	Restoration of temple in early Ming Dynasty, renamed White Cloud Temple. (For purposes of the narrative, the exact location of the temple is moved somewhat east, to within the city walls.)

| 1644 | Wu Sankuei lets Manchu forces under Dorgon enter through Mountain-Sea Pass, conquer Peking. |

MODERN TIMES PRIOR TO THE NARRATIVE

Mid-1920's	At Whampoa Military Academy in Kwangchow: Chou Enlai, Yeh Chienying, Lin Piao, Nieh Jungchen.
1927	Fu Tsoyi gains national renown by lengthy and courageous endurance in siege of Chochow.
1927 April 12	Shanghai Chamber of Commerce, gangsters, and foreign community conspire in surprise attack on Communists and worker unions, massacring thousands; Chou Enlai captured, but escapes.
1934–37	Fu Tsoyi gains national renown by resisting Japanese advances into Suiyuan and Chahar provinces in Inner Mongolia.
1937	Sino-Japanese War begins; Japanese pillage Nanking in December.
1945 August	Japanese surrender; Communists under Nieh Jungchen occupy Kalgan.
1946 October 11	Fu Tsoyi retakes Kalgan from Communists.
1947 March 2	Kuomintang-Communist peace talks break down; Chou Enlai returns to Yenan, joining Mao Tsetung there.
August	Fu Tsoyi appointed Commander-in-Chief of North China Bandit-Suppression Headquarters, assumes command of Peking; daughter is secretly an agent of Communist underground in city.

THE PERIOD OF THE NARRATIVE

| 1948 Spring | Dissident monks in White Cloud Temple burn An Shihlin, prior of the temple, in courtyard fronting Founder Ch'iu's Hall. (The date of this historical event has been switched to later in the year for purposes of the narrative.) |

September 12	Lin Piao launches final stage of Manchurian Campaign.
October	Chiang Kaishek to Peking, directs his American-trained armor division in campaign to relieve Lin Piao's siege of Mukden; campaign fails; half a million troops surrender to Communists; Chiang Kaishek returns to Nanking.
November 1	Mukden falls to Lin Piao; General Wei Lihuang flees to Peking.
Late November	Wei Lihuang meets former Whampoa classmate, Lin Piao, at Mountain-Sea Pass with proposals from Fu Tsoyi.
December 10	Fu Tsoyi's division at Nank'ou Pass obliterated in surprise attack by advance elements of Lin Piao's army.
December 13	Peking and Tientsin surrounded by Lin Piao's armies, which intercept six trainloads of American arms in Fengtai railroad yards.
December 24	Kalgan recaptured by Communists.
1949 January 1	Chiang Kaishek proclaims "New Year's Peace Initiative."
January 6–8	Zhou Peifeng and Chang Tungsun sent to Chihsien by Fu Tsoyi for secret negotiations with Lin Piao.
January 13–15	Zhou Peifeng and General Teng Paoshan sent to Tungchow by Fu Tsoyi for secret negotiations with Yeh Chienying.
January 15	Tientsin falls to Lin Piao.
January 16	Ex-Mayor Ho Szuyuan's North China People's Peace Promotion Committee scheduled to meet with Yeh Chienying in Fragrant Hills on January 17.
January 17	In early morning, Te Wu bombs Ho Szuyuan's house, injuring Ho and Madame Ho, killing Ho's youngest daughter.
January 18	Ho leads his committee for peace talks with Fu Tsoyi in Peking and with Yeh Chienying in Fragrant Hills.

January 21	Chiang Kaishek resigns; Li Tsungjen assumes Acting Presidency.
January 22	Fu Tsoyi and Yeh Chienying sign peace agreement, after Fu refuses Yeh's last request for custody of General Shih Chueh and General Li Wen.
January 31	Communist garrison troops enter Peking, followed by Communist leaders over next several days. Yeh Chienying becomes Mayor of Peking. Nieh Jungchen becomes Garrison Commander of Peking.

IMMEDIATELY AFTER THE PERIOD OF THE NARRATIVE

1949 March 25	Mao Tsetung and Chou Enlai move from Hsipaipo to Peking, take up residence in Chunghai Lake compound, not far from old Taoist pavilion offshore of Chunghai Lake.
April 23	Nanking captured by Communists.
May 3	Hangchow captured by Communists.
May 25	Shanghai captured by Communists.
October 1	Mao Tsetung proclaims People's Republic of China from T'ian'anmen Gate.
Mid-October	Fu Tsoyi appointed Minister of Water Conservancy of People's Republic of China, holds post through the mid-1950's.
Late 1949	Yeh Chienying assumes command of Kwangchow area, his home region; succeeded as Mayor of Peking by Nieh Jungchen.
1952	Chang Tungsun relieved of all academic and political positions because of his consistently independent stance, which fails to conform to official Communist views.

TWO DECADES AFTER THE PERIOD
OF THE NARRATIVE

Late 1960's — White Cloud Temple closed down by Red Guards during early years of "Cultural Revolution."

Early 1971 — Lin Piao attempts murder of Chou Enlai as Chou returns by airplane from Hanoi.

1972 September — Lin Piao directs attempted murder of Mao Tsetung in Hangchow; Chou Enlai orders Lin's arrest in Peking; Lin Piao escapes by jet, which crashes mysteriously in Outer Mongolia; Lin Piao presumed dead in crash.

1974 April 19 — Fu Tsoyi dies in Peking.

1976 January 8 — Chou Enlai dies in Peking.

September 9 — Mao Tsetung dies in Peking.

Autumn — Yeh Chienying ends "Cultural Revolution" by personally directing arrest of "The Gang of Four."

1984 Spring — White Cloud Temple reopens, with contingent of Taoist priests; open to public for visits.

1986 October 22 — Yeh Chienying dies in Peking.

At this writing, Nieh Jungchen is still alive in Peking, although, of course, retired from active political life.

SOURCES

The events of 1948 and 1949 in China and specifically in Peking are recounted in A. Doak Barnett's *China on the Eve of Communist Takeover* (1963, Praeger), C. P. Fitzgerald's *The Birth of Communist China* (1964, Praeger), and Derk Bodde's *Peking Diary: A Year of Revolution* (1950, Schumann). All three authors were in Peking during the siege, and went on to become eminent Sinologists. In addition to the public events recounted, many of the "private" events in this novel are based on material from these sources (e.g., the unusually cold night of January 4–5, freezing water pipes throughout the city; the American lady's stuffing money into the jacket of a starving man on the street; the frightened donkey plunging its manure cart into a crowd by one of the gates through the wall; the robed foreigner wandering the grounds of Peking Union Medical School Hospital, etc.). It was A. Doak Barnett who commented on the citizens' remarkable adherence to the "normal business of buying, selling, eating, procreating, and dying" throughout the siege.

The material on Chinese sexual practices, including the erotic poetry, is drawn mainly from the late R. H. Van Gulik's remarkable *Sexual Life in Ancient China* (1974, Brill, Leiden). The best sources for serious study of Taoism are the Van Gulik book; the second volume of Joseph Needham's monumental *Science and Civilization in China* (1964, Cambridge University Press; a paperback abridgement of the first two volumes of this work was published in 1980 under the title, *The Shorter Science and Civilization in China;* I, with Colin A. Ronan as the co-author); and Holmes Welch and Anna Seidel's *Facets of Taoism* (1979, Yale University Press). The Welch and Seidel book contains, in addition, information specifically describing the White Cloud Temple and An Shihlin and his fiery death there (Introduction and Chapter 7). The early history of the White Cloud Temple was drawn from the Chinese Daoist Association's booklet "The White Cloud Daoist Temple" (1983).

Several popular introductions to Taoism exist in English, although all are marred by serious shortcomings of one sort or another. We still await an author who will accomplish for Taoism what D. T. Suzuki did for Zen Buddhism.

Finally, Peking. The material on the city itself was drawn from the Barnett and Bodde sources mentioned earlier, Liu Junwen's *Peking: China's Ancient and Modern Capital* (1982, Foreign Languages Press, Peking), and my own sojourns in the city and conversations with its inhabitants in 1982 and 1984.

ABOUT THE AUTHOR

RAYMOND BARNETT is professor of biological sciences at California State University, Chico. He received his B.A. in Chinese history from Yale University, graduating magna cum laude, and also studied the Chinese language intensively there. After a year studying the philosophy of religion at Union Theological Seminary in New York City, he joined the U.S. Army and served a tour of duty in Vietnam. He then obtained a Ph.D. in zoology from Duke University, and moved to Chico, California, where he has taught human anatomy and introductory biology for eleven years. Dr. Barnett has led tours and traveled independently in China, has studied T'ai Chi Ch'uan in California and Hong Kong, and has collected and enjoyed teas from many regions of China.